HUDSON'S LUCK

A FOREVER WILDE NOVEL

LUCY LENNOX

Cover Art by: AngstyG www.AngstyG.com

Cover Photo by: Wander Aguiar

Editing by: Sandra at www.OneLoveEditing.com

Beta Reading by: Leslie Copeland at www.LesCourtAuthorServices.com

ACKNOWLEDGMENTS

(IT SERIOUSLY TAKES A VILLAGE.)

So many people to thank for this one!

Sloane for amazing, invaluable feedback and general cheerleading. I am a better writer because of you.

Leslie as always, for putting up with me and making me laugh.

Hailey Turner for being a sprint sergeant and for cat pics. Duh.

Liv for adding the Irish touch. Cheers.

Wander for creating the gorgeous cover image.

AngstyG for making the image into a lovely cover as always.

Sandra for going above and beyond with another round of edits at the last minute.

Lori for being a thorough and kind pair of eyes at the end.

To my readers who had to be more patient than usual this time around. When I posted that Hudson was being stubborn, your outpouring of love and support floored me. Thank you from the bottom of my heart for everything.

And finally, to my family who had to hear “I can’t, I’m working on Hudson” every day for what felt like ten years. Guess what? I’m not working on Hudson anymore. But I still can’t. I’m working on Saint...

THE WILDE FAMILY

Grandpa (Weston) and **Doc** (William) Wilde

Their children:

Bill, Gina, Brenda, and Jaqueline

Bill married Shelby. Their children are:

Hudson (book #4)

West (book #1)

MJ

Saint

Otto (book #3)

King

Hallie

Winnie

Cal

Sassy

Gina married Carmen. Their children are:

Quinn

Max

Jason

Brenda married Hollis. Their children are:

Kathryn-Anne (Katie)

William-Weston (Web)

Jackson-Wyatt (Jack)

Jacqueline's child:

Felix (book #2)

1

HUDSON

Hudson's Words To Live By:

Don't ever, ever give a woman a present in a tiny box unless it's an engagement ring.

And sure as hell don't do it if the present is also a tiny metal hoop device that could be easily, horribly misconstrued as an engagement ring.

Oh, and maybe also don't give said present on your one-year dating anniversary.

I was doing that thing some people do where the coin flips through each of your fingers and back again, except instead of a coin, I was doing it with the small ring that had gotten me into this predicament in the first place. I'd named it the Wilde Ring, but it was technically a head constrictor. Which meant, of course, that my brothers had called it a cock ring.

It wasn't a cock ring.

I was fifteen hours into a thirteen-hour trip from Dallas to Cork, Ireland, when I realized sleeping was just not something I was going to be lucky enough to experience on this flight. At least my company was big enough to spring for a first-class seat to accommodate my long legs. My legs went on for days, according to my girlfriend.

Correction. My *ex*-girlfriend.

The sigh that came out of me was enough to unsettle the older lady next to me. Okay, so maybe it hadn't been my first put-upon sigh. I was annoyed as hell at how I'd let myself be lured by the promise of an executive position. I should never have mixed business with pleasure and gone to work for her dad's company.

I sighed again.

"Something on your mind, hot stuff?" the woman asked. "Might help to talk about it."

"Sorry. I didn't mean to disturb you," I said, shifting in my seat. Despite the nice wide space, I still couldn't get comfortable. Every time I touched anything, I couldn't help but think of all the bodies that had spent time in the same seat and touched the same surfaces. I wondered if my hand sanitizer was empty yet.

"You don't seem like a regular flyer," she began with narrowed eyes. "This your first time traveling overseas?"

"No, ma'am. My parents live in Singapore. I visited them there last year."

"Oh, I could have sworn you were experiencing jitters like a newb."

I gawped at her. *Newb?* She had to be ten thousand years old.

"Well, I guess it's a little true. I tend to stay close to home. I'm not one for adventuring, if you want to know the truth," I admitted. I didn't tell her the trip to Singapore had been a disaster that had resulted in me swearing off travel for the rest of my life.

"Shame. Some of my fondest memories are from travel adventures," she mused, snuggling under the navy-blue airline blanket and turning to face me. "You meet the most interesting characters."

I laughed. "Ma'am, I'm the oldest of ten siblings. My life is full to overflowing with interesting characters already."

She smiled at me. "So tell me what has your knickers in a twist if it's not the travel."

I took a deep breath before turning to face her and doing something very out of character—telling my personal story to a stranger.

"I dated this girl, Darci," I began.

"You dated a little girl?" she gasped. Her reaction seemed a bit melodramatic.

"No. God no. She's a grown woman," I stammered.

The lady narrowed her eyes at me. "Then refer to her as such. Continue."

An octogenarian teaching me about gender respect. Nice. I thought about escaping to the lavatory, but that would involve exposing myself to even more germs than I'd already come into contact with on this hellish trip. Even the thought had me putting the little metal ring in my lap and searching out the hand sanitizer in the seat pocket in front of me. I liberally doused my hands and, as expected, the bottle was nearly empty. Fortunately, I had a couple more stashed away in my checked bags. As I worked the gel into my skin, I began explaining the disastrous set of circumstances that had landed me in the seat next to the old bird.

"Ah... okay. So, I dated this grown woman named Darci." I looked at her and saw a slight nod. "Who was a very nice... *woman*. Anyway, several months ago she suggested I spend some time learning how to brew craft beer with her father. Her family loves microbrews, so her hope was that it would be a good way for me to bond with them, I guess."

"Mm, she was trying to get you in with Big Daddy. I see."

"Right. So I learned all about it, and because I'm a bit of a tinkerer on the side, I thought what better way to impress her father than to improve upon the process? I invented this little doohickey that goes on the tap nozzle to control the amount of head, or foam, that comes out when you dispense a beer into a glass."

"Woah, really? Impressive. Let me guess, Papa Bear felt threatened by the new cub's ingenuity?" Her face looked eager for confirmation.

"Ah... no. That's not exactly what happened," I said, holding up the little metal piece. "You see, I made the mistake of presenting it to

Darci as an anniversary gift... in a tiny little box. You know, like a ring box."

"Oh shit."

"Yep."

Her eyes were wide, and her mouth was open in a little round "o" shape. "No kidding? Really? You didn't. You're pulling my leg."

"No, ma'am," I said. "I wish I was."

Her laugh, when it came, was low-pitched and cackling. And absolutely *did not end*. I noticed two other little old ladies across the aisle craning their necks to see what was going on.

"Right," I said in an attempt to quiet her down. "So it was a disaster. Her mother was screaming with excitement. Her sister had begun videotaping the scene. And her father was already going for the bottle of champagne."

"What happened when she saw the doohickey?"

"Um, well... it looks like a ring so..." I felt the familiar heat of embarrassment crawl up my neck. "She put it on her finger and said yes."

At this point, I realized my audience had grown. Instead of just my seatmate and the ladies across the aisle, I also now had two flight attendants and four additional first-class passengers craning their necks to hear. My humiliation was going to make for some rip-roaring good stories when everyone got where they were going later.

"Liar," she laughed. "What happened next? Surely you went along with it and popped the question."

I felt my eyes bug out. "Me? Marriage? That soon? What? No. Heck no. *No*. We'd only been going out a *year*. It wasn't part of the plan yet."

Ten pairs of eyes seemed to bore holes into me.

"So, what then? What did you say?" one of the flight attendants asked into the anxious hush.

"I..." I gulped and looked around, unsure if they deserved the actual truth. Oh, what the hell. "I stammered something like, 'No, oh god no, you don't understand. This is just so I can give your dad a little head.'"

At least someone could benefit from the damned experience. Because it certainly wasn't me. The crowd around me went wild as I knew they would. I tried not to recall how my brothers had reacted.

"Go on, laugh it up," I muttered. "Glad my humiliation is good for something." I began twirling the ring in between my fingers to calm my jittery nerves as even more people began tuning into the humiliating conversation.

The young woman in the seat in front of me frowned from her spot facing backward toward me. "Och, sweetie. What happened after that?" Her Irish accent was lovely just like the rest of her, but it did absolutely nothing for me. I'd sworn off women and love.

Fuck 'em.

"It forced the big conversation about where the relationship was going. And that's when I learned that saying, 'It's going fine,' was not the right response."

More giggles from the peanut gallery.

I sank lower in my seat.

The old lady next to me sounded disgusted. "So, what? Now you're running away? Chickenshit?"

"No. Needless to say, she broke it off with me. And to make matters worse, before any of this happened, I'd let her father talk me into coming to work for him. Now I'm kind of stuck. He's sending me to Ireland to assess a company for acquisition. He's not happy with me."

I'd taken the job with Darci's father's investment company after he'd implied I'd be quick to make vice president there. Getting to that level would help my career tremendously. I'd worked my ass off for over a decade at one of the largest mergers-and-acquisitions firms in Dallas, but when it had come time for me to be considered for the higher-level positions, they'd come with mandatory relocation to other parts of the country.

I was ambitious, but nothing was worth me leaving my family. With Ames International, I'd be able to have the VP title and stay in Dallas. But first I needed to prove to Bruce Ames I was damned good at my job despite being not as great at relationships.

"You let that man make you his bitch?" asked the tiny grandma from across the aisle.

I immediately went on the defensive. "I feel like I owe it to Darci. I don't know... to prove I'm not a total loser. We finally worked things out as friends, and I care about her. I don't want to let her or her family down. If only I'd been able to prove my commitment this way before the ring fiasco, maybe she wouldn't have been so quick to dismiss me."

I looked around, expecting nods of support and encouragement, but only found looks of sympathy.

"What?" I asked.

"Lovie," the mother of the young lady in front of me said with a sigh. "The girl didn't want your business commitment. She wanted romance. She wanted you to tell her she was the only one for you. She wanted you to tell her you couldn't live without her. Sweep her off her feet and all that."

I shook my head. "See, that's where you're wrong. She's practical. I mean, she's a nurse for god's sake. So she'd have been way more interested in knowing I could provide financial security for her and a future family than some kind of big romantic gesture like flowers and a bunch of meaningless words."

More *tsk*s and head shakes.

"You don't know her," I said lamely. "It doesn't matter now anyway. It's over."

The older lady next to me poked me in the side with a pointy finger. "Did it ever occur to you to bring her with you to Ireland?"

I thought about it. "No. Why would I? It's a business trip. A quick in and out. Plus... she's ah... moved on. I heard she's already seeing someone else." I'd been in denial about that last part, but it was true. I assumed she was doing it deliberately to prove she never cared about me much in the first place. It was working.

More head shakes all around.

My seatmate sighed like I'd disappointed her with my stupidity. "Forget it. One day you'll meet someone you'll want to show the world to. In the meantime, go ahead and kick ass on the work thingie and get a big promotion. That way, when the time comes, you'll have enough money to live a big life with your true love." She turned to say something to the ladies across the aisle, and I felt dismissed.

Everyone wandered away, seemingly disappointed in me, and all I could think was, *Join the fucking club.*

Because no one was more disappointed in me than I was.

After a few minutes of silence, my seatmate spoke up again. "Have you considered maybe you're swimming in the wrong pond?"

I had no idea what she meant.

"Pardon?"

"Maybe you'd be more interested in sausage than tacos," she tried explaining.

One of the ladies from across the aisle spoke up. "Can it, Tilly. Not every man likes the D."

I almost choked on my tongue. My face ignited, and I sank lower in my seat.

"Shit," the lady next to me muttered as she eyed me and my reaction carefully. She'd clearly mistaken my embarrassment at the turn in conversation for something else because she added, "He's a homophobe. And now I'm stuck next to him for the rest of the flight. Switch seats with me, Irene."

"I'm not a homophobe," I argued, taking major offense. "Practically every guy in my family is gay."

"Practically?"

"Except me. Obviously," I clarified.

"Maybe that's your problem. Try batting for the other team and see if that doesn't solve it."

Clearly the woman had some fucked-up notions of sexuality. Did I dare correct her?

"Sexuality doesn't work like that, ma'am. You can't just 'choose' to be gay if being straight isn't working out for you," I said. I could feel the tension in my jaw. It was a familiar sensation I felt whenever I found myself defending my siblings from ignorant assholes.

"You think I don't know that?" She pointed a thumb over her shoulder to the two ladies across the aisle. "My two besties are lesbos, and I have about a million gay grandsons. I volunteer at an LGBTQ youth shelter in San Francisco and lost my brother thanks to my homophobic parents kicking him out years and years ago, so don't you go lecturing me on gay, young man."

She'd gathered up a full head of steam, and I could tell I was in for a wild ride.

"Sorry," I began, but she cut me off.

"No. You listen to me. If there's one thing I've learned in all these years of living, it's that love is love. What the hell does it matter what bits and pieces someone has on their body? If you can open yourself up to love, you might be surprised at the package it comes in. Ever thought of that?" Her finger poked me in the chest, punctuating each word as she spoke.

"But," I said, intending to explain that I had no hang-ups about being open to attractions from all kinds of people.

"But nothing. Maybe your destiny isn't some sweet 'daddy's girl'. Maybe your destiny is a motorcycle leather daddy in Ohio."

"God, I hope not," I blurted. "Motorcycles are dangerous. I'm always lecturing my brothers about them. Darci calls them donor—"

"Fuck Darci," the woman growled. "Clearly she's not the one. Stop going for the expected safe bet, and try something new, something adventurous. You need some passion in your life. I'm not sure the sweetie-pie nurse lit your fire. When was the last time you took a vacation?"

"Ah... you mean besides visiting my parents in Singapore?"

"Yes, besides that."

"Um... I went camping with a couple of my brothers about four years ago."

"More than two hours away from home?" she asked with narrowed eyes.

"No, ma'am."

"Have you ever gotten lost on purpose?"

"No, ma'am. Why would I?" Even the thought of not having a plan or schedule to go by each day made my neck feel hot and itchy.

"Have you ever said yes to something crazy? Something you would normally have said no to?"

"I'm not really the crazy type," I explained. "I'm more of a planner."

"Have you ever had sex with a stranger?" Her eyes were twinkling, and I noticed her two friends leering at me.

"Certainly not."

Since when did I sound like such a square?

"Maybe it's time for you to live a little," she said gently.

I thought about how settled my life had been this past year. How, with a steady girlfriend, I'd felt... good. Not perfect, of course, but steady. Like my life was following the path it was meant to. The high-level job, the modern high-rise apartment, the lovely and kind woman on my arm. It had been...

Nice.

"But Darci—"

"Fuck Darci. Do you hear what I'm saying? *Fuck* the ex-girlfriend. Tell her to take a long walk off a short pier. You deserve someone a hell of a lot better than a chick whose idea of fun is setting her boyfriend up with Big Daddy for macho male man shit."

I stared wide-eyed at the woman, both for her language and her forthright assessment of my situation. She didn't know me at all, so why the hell did she think she could make such bold proclamations about what I needed?

"She's a nice gir—*woman*. Encouraging me to get along with her family was just practical."

Her face softened as she reached across the space between us to squeeze my arm. "Life's too short to settle for 'practical' and 'safe.' Have a fling. Do something crazy. Get lost somewhere and fly by the seat of your pants for once. Let someone else be in charge, and stop being responsible for a little while."

I stared at her some more. "What makes you think I'm so boring and predictable?" Out of the corner of my eye, I spotted the tiny and now very empty bottle of hand sanitizer sticking out of the side pocket of my bag. I ignored it.

"You said you were the oldest of ten. That usually means you're reliable, structured, cautious… am I right so far?"

"Maybe," I admitted.

"And you've probably stayed fairly close to home in case someone needed you?"

I nodded, thinking of what it was like for the oldest of ten siblings when one of the parents was rarely around to help. I remembered nights of cooking boxed macaroni for everyone when I was seven, of helping clean up spills the babies made and doing the dishes when my mom was singing lullabies and bedtime stories to my younger siblings. I remembered changing disgusting diapers when I was as young as five and my brother Cal throwing up on me ten minutes before my high school graduation.

Even as recently as the previous year, I'd been called home to help my baby sister Sassy deal with a pregnancy scare. Had my mother not been half a world away, I was sure she would have been the one Sassy ran crying to. But the minute my parents had moved overseas, I'd become the default stand-in parent. I'd never known any different. And I loved my siblings with the ferocity of a thousand warriors. I couldn't imagine it any other way.

"Maybe it's time for you to figure out who you are without all that other stuff."

"What other stuff?" I asked, though deep down I knew what she meant. How many times had I wondered myself what things would be like if I'd been allowed to be more like my younger siblings… if I'd been allowed to just be a kid?

"Rules. Responsibilities. Expectations… Labels."

I closed my eyes and considered her words. *Was* I unhappy with my life the way it was? No. I had almost everything I'd ever imagined. A solid career as a financial analyst just like my father, a loyal and loving family in Texas, and a pretty, sweet girlfriend… well, until recently anyway.

"No. I think you're wrong," I told her. "My life is fine the way it is." I hated that my voice sounded just a little *too* insistent. Like maybe she wasn't the one I was trying to convince.

She studied me for a moment before shrugging. "Meh. Maybe it's not your time yet. But I'll bet fifty bucks you could use some spice in your life, and a powerful missile in your silo wouldn't go amiss if you know what I mean."

The tiny frail woman across from us snorted and reached a bony hand across the aisle to fist-bump my new friend.

"What are the three of you doing in Ireland?" I asked in an effort to get the focus off me.

"A tiny bit of family genealogy with a whole lotta whiskey drinking," my seatmate said before all three of them howled with laughter and then began talking about the bedroom talents of someone named Harold.

I kept pretty much to myself for the remainder of the flight and tried to think of whether or not I should try to rekindle things with Darci. Maybe if I just explained to her about the plan...

By the time the plane landed in Cork, I'd already started to formulate a strategy to talk to Darci about *the plan*. But as soon as I turned my phone on, a text from my brother came dinging through.

West: *Sorry to be the one to confirm it, but it's true Darci is with someone else. Couple days ago, I saw her sneak into the on-call room with one of the pharmacy reps. The next night Otto and Seth saw them holding hands at the Pinecone. Sorry, brother.*

I was surprised to feel something akin to relief, but I wondered what that would mean for my future at work. Would things be even more awkward between Bruce Ames and me or would it actually help the situation? Was he relieved his baby girl had gotten over me so quickly? And what did that mean for my love life? I was something of a serial monogamist. I'd always had a girlfriend.

What would my life be like now without someone to take care of? I'd always dreamed of the wife, the white picket fence, the two point five children. Was I really going to have to start all over? The thought had me absently reaching for the hand sanitizer again before I realized what I was doing. I glanced at the woman next to me and listened as she and her traveling companions talked excitedly about whiskey and Irish men. Their unabashed enthusiasm made something loosen in my chest just a little and I turned to stare out the window as I considered my seat mate's earlier words.

Maybe she and the other two old ladies were right. Maybe I *did* need to do something wild for once.

2

CHARLIE

Charlie's Words To Live By:

Never date the ones named Rory. Oh, or Simon or Pat either.

They're cheating bastards, every last one.

That was another one down. I'd run up to the pub in Doolin for a quick pint with my sister, Cait, and run right into Rory with his fucking tongue rammed in some bloke's face in the corridor to the jacks.

Classic case of my having assumed the relationship was more than it was.

"What the fuck, Rory?" I squawked.

He and the tosser he was with jumped apart and started in with some nonsense about it not being what it looked like. Whatever. I should have known better, to tell the truth. The first boyfriend I'd ever had warned me early on that one of the benefits of being gay was not having to deal with all that monogamy bullshit.

But stupid Charlie kept trying for it anyway.

Stupid dope Charlie.

I turned on my heel and made my way back out to where Cait sat.

"Shut your gob before flies get in," I spat. "Let's go." I tossed down a tenner before disappearing out the front door without another word.

Cait came running after me, but I ignored her. Heat ignited my face, and I was sure it was all splotchy. Fucking pale skin—couldn't hide feelings for shite.

"Charlie, wait. Fuck him, brother. Really. The guy's a royal jackass if you ask me," she said, jogging a bit to keep up with me. She was one of the only people I knew who was smaller than I was.

I spun to face her. "I *did* ask you! Jesusfuckingchrist, Cait. I did ask you. Two months ago when things seemed to be getting more serious, I said I fancied him for more than a fuck and what did you think of the guy. And you said, 'yeah, fine.'"

"*Yeah, fine* isn't the same thing as saying he's an amazing human being, Charlie. What did you expect me to say?"

I threw up my hands. "I expected you to say, 'Charlie, he looks like another user who's going to step out on you when you least expect it, in your very own local pub no less.'"

Cait winced. "Yeah, what was up with that? Couldn't he have gone to Dan Lowrey's instead if he was going to fuck around behind your back?"

I rolled my eyes and started walking again. "That's not the point."

"No, but seriously. Why would he have done that when he knows we share a pint here every Thursday after your dog meeting?"

"He thought I was scheduled to go out of town for that big delivery run for Uncle Dev. I got the dates wrong. It's actually day after tomorrow," I admitted. "Did you see that bloke he was with? I wouldn't have ridden him if he'd had pedals."

We arrived in front of my sister's flat and stood on the pavement. I couldn't wait to get back home to my cottage instead. I loved my solitude on the old family property. Just me and the sound of the sea over the cliffs. Thank fuck I hadn't asked Rory to move in with me yet. That would have been a disaster.

"Agreed. Did you even know he wasn't looking for something serious? I mean, had you ever talked about relationships?"

"Yes. I knew he didn't want to take anything at light speed, but he seemed really into me. I'm a decent catch."

That had sounded less pathetic in my head.

She rolled her eyes at me. "No shit, Sherlock. I wasn't suggesting otherwise. But maybe you need to take a break from looking for something serious and stick to sex in the clubs for a bit instead, hmm?"

I knew she was joking, but it still rankled. "Cait, I live in a cottage at the edge of the sea in nowhere, Ireland. You want to talk to me about hooking up in gay clubs? Christ."

"Another reason you should move to the city with me and Donny one day," she said with laser eyes burning holes in my face. "Cork is full of gorgeous men."

Now it was my turn to roll my eyes. "Gay men in Cork? Please. I've either already fucked them or deliberately not fucked them."

That got her attention. She knew I wasn't a casual-sex person. "Pardon?"

"Well, it seemed that way anyway. Before college, I mean," I muttered. "And anyway, Dublin is much better."

"You last lived in Dublin, what? Four years ago? You don't think things have changed since then? You dope."

I leaned in to give her a kiss on the cheek and a quick hug. "Doesn't matter. No more men for me. I'm on a break."

The last thing I heard before I walked back in the direction of the car park near the pub was the snide chuckle and my sister's bratty "Yeah, right. Famous last words. I'll prove you wrong. I'm going to find someone irresistible and send them to the pub during one of your shifts to tempt you into a casual fuck, no strings attached. Remind you of the freedom of walking away after."

It only took twenty-four hours for me to spot the man she must have found for me. He was hot as fuck, and I knew he was the one she'd sent because he certainly wasn't a local and he wasn't with anyone else the way the tourists were. But he didn't look like a player. He looked like a Forever Man.

I tracked the stranger from the doorway to the spot he selected at the bar. His soulful eyes were so fucking beautiful, I was sure I stared at him like an idiot until another customer down the bar asked for her party's bill. Sorting out the separate checks bullshit for the woman took longer than I expected, and when I was done, I heard the stranger call out from behind me.

"Excuse me... may I have a beer please?" he asked. *American.* And his voice was lovely.

I turned around and saw the usual moment of surprise when the stranger realized I wasn't a woman. It was over in a flash, but it was there. With my long hair and feminine features, it happened more often than not, but this time around it did make me wonder why Cait hadn't given the man my description ahead of time. Maybe he wasn't particularly picky?

He spoke again, only this time it was with noticeably rosier cheeks that had my own face warming as my lips tugged into an unbidden smile. The gorgeous man was blushing. "Ah... what do you have on tap? How about a lager?"

I stared at those lovely rosy cheeks until the man turned around to look behind him before looking back at me in confusion. "You okay? Do you need me to find someone else?"

A full-body shudder passed through me and woke me up out of my ridiculous stupor. "No, fine. I'm grand. Yeah. Lager, coming right up."

As I pulled his beer into the pint glass, I tried studying him out of the corner of my eye without being obvious. He had medium-brown hair clipped short on the sides and left longer and styled on top. His cheeks showed a couple of days' beard growth, which only enhanced his full rosy lips. Every single aspect of the man was beautiful. But nothing, *nothing*, compared to his bedroom eyes. They were a mix of green and blue I wanted to dive into and get lost in.

I couldn't help but also admire the cut of his crisp suit on his tall, wide-shouldered frame as the fine material hugged his body as he moved. I watched with a mix of amusement and curiosity as he patted his pockets almost frantically until he found a small bottle of what looked like hand sanitizer and began rubbing it into his palms. I almost called out to make a joke about my bartop being too dirty for him when I realized that his body noticeably relaxed the more he worked the gel between his hands. As soon as he was done, he began stacking a few nearby coasters neatly together. It hit me then that his behavior probably had nothing to do with the bartop's cleanliness at all. Before I could even consider what any of it meant, he turned to stare at me, and I realized the pint glass was overflowing all over my hand.

"Jesus, fuck," I muttered, closing the tap and grabbing a bar rag from the back pocket of my jeans. I cleaned up the glass and my hands as best I could before setting the pint in front of him, making sure to put it on the coaster he'd set out for the purpose. "Hungry? We have a great menu for dinner."

He smiled his thanks and took a deep draw from the beer before answering. His satisfied moan of appreciation went straight to my dick and seemed to also cause my eyes to pop out of my head. Was it possible to *over*stare at someone?

"God, this is good. What's it called?"

"Cliffs. It's one of the lagers brewed here. A bit less malty than Harp," I explained. "Very popular with Americans."

And then I *winked.*

It was like time stood still. The awkwardness I'd just brought upon myself was legendary. My face suddenly felt like an inferno. I would have said the tables had turned, but he blushed again as well.

We stared at each other. Oddly, I wanted to apologize. For daring to wink at the man? Why? He was there to hook up with me, right? What the hell was my problem?

"F-food," I stammered. "Let's get you some."

I reached down the bar for a laminated menu and slid it in front of him before busying myself with nonsense chores. I wiped up a clean area of the oak surface, cleaned some already clean pint glasses, and finally counted the coins in the till.

"Charlie?"

I whipped around to face him. How did he know my name? Oh right, Cait. God, the sound of my name on his tongue made me want to beg him for things. Many, many things.

"Yes? Found something you like?"

Me, perhaps? Maybe Cait was right. Maybe a one-nighter was just what I needed to kick the memory of shitty Rory once and for all.

"I'm embarrassed to admit I don't know what several of these things are. I've never been to Ireland before. What do you recommend?"

I wondered if he'd like my father's specialty coddle dish.

"Do you like sausage?"

The man's eyes widened until he looked like a deer caught in headlights.

What had I said?

3

HUDSON

Hudson's Note To Self:

Not everyone offering you sausage is referring to dick.

When I walked into the historic Fig and Bramble pub and guesthouse, the first thing I saw was a gorgeous woman behind the bar. She had long red hair full of thick waves and was wearing an oversized fisherman's sweater hanging off one pale, slender shoulder. Her skin looked so smooth and delicate, I suddenly imagined brushing the hair away from her neck and dropping an openmouthed kiss on the exposed surface to test how warm it was.

My heartbeat kicked into high gear. I'd never had such a visceral reaction to catching a glimpse of someone like that.

Before I could get a closer look at her, she turned her back to do something at the cash register. I took a spot at the bar and peeked over the wide wooden surface to see more of her. I noticed the ivory sweater hung down almost to her knees where a pair of snug-fitting blue jeans were rolled up to capri length the same way my sister Sassy did hers back home in Texas. My slow perusal continued down over slim, smooth ankles to a pair of well-loved gray Converse sneakers. What was it about her that was pushing my buttons?

I took advantage of the fact she was still facing away so I could check her out. As she shifted from foot to foot, I caught the barest hint of the curve of her compact ass under the bulky sweater. The stretched-out neckline fell farther down the exposed shoulder until I could see the rounded outline of small but well-defined deltoid muscle. It reminded me of a woman I'd dated several years before who did CrossFit. Heather had been insane about her workouts and sported biceps that made even my brothers envious. Imagining this delicate creature behind the bar in a skimpy sports bra and tiny workout shorts with damp tendrils of hair sticking to her neck made my pants noticeably tighter.

When I sensed the woman was finished with the register but still hadn't noticed me, I spoke up to get her attention. It took me a moment after she turned around to realize the bartender wasn't a woman at all. I'd been lusting after a man. I'd been *getting hard* for a man.

But he had such feminine features. He was downright gorgeous, regardless of his gender. It took me a minute to gather my wits and regroup. So what if she was a he? Did it matter? Of course not. I might have been straight, but I could still appreciate a beautiful human being of any gender or sex.

In addition to all of the things I'd noticed about him before, he also had stunningly bright green eyes the color of the clichéd four-leaf clover I'd happened upon just outside the door to the historic building. There were a few freckles scattered across his nose, and his dark eyelashes were made even darker by a thin smudge of eyeliner.

My confusion over lusting for a man had caused my nerves to kick in, and it'd been all I could do not to stare at the gorgeous creature behind the bar as he'd been getting the drink for me. Once I'd admitted I had no idea what any of the items on the menu were, he'd gone and asked me the loaded question about liking sausage. Since my brain was still subconsciously chanting *dick doesn't matter*, the question caught me off guard. Not to mention my traitorous mind had decided to remind me at that exact moment of the words of the little old lady on my flight. *Taco versus sausage.*

I'd never once been attracted to a man. And I'd had plenty of opportunities to know if I was. My brothers had dragged me to dance clubs many times and paraded good-looking men in front of me for years. Never once had I felt the telltale butterflies of attraction to a member of my sex until that moment in the bar.

The minute I'd locked eyes with him, I'd felt like we were the only two people in the room. I'd noticed his name tag and decided right away I wanted to feel his name on my tongue. Was that weird? That was probably weird.

He was noticeably smaller than I was, maybe five foot seven inches with his shoes on, and every bit of him was covered in the smoothest, creamiest skin I'd ever seen on a man. Scratch that... the smoothest, creamiest skin I'd ever seen on *anyone*. Except for the smattering of freckles. And, man, those freckles were killing me. They made him look... almost... god, was it possible I thought this guy was *adorable*? No. I was just having a moment of lusting after a redhead who looked like a woman who just happened to be a man. Plenty of people had a thing for redheads, even if I'd never particularly thought of myself as one of those people before.

I'd wondered at my reaction to him. There was a part of me that still thought he was the sexiest human being I'd ever seen.

Sexy.

A dude.

Jesus, Hudson, your brothers have brainwashed you into scoping out dudes. And if it was acceptable to maim little old ladies, I might have to look up the one from the plane.

I was going to kill my brothers. I should have known going to gay clubs with them would make me start seeing every man as a potential hookup. But why this time did it feel more like he'd be one for *me* rather than any of *them*?

I shook off the silly thoughts and shrugged. "Sausage is good. I mean... fine. That is... I'd be willing to try your sausage, yes. Well, not *your* sausage, I mean *the* sausage. In the dish. The sausage dish. What is it again? Just sausage? Anything else in it besides... sausage?" I gulped.

Shut up, Hudson. How many times are you going to say the word sausage?

The bartender blinked at me again, only this time he had a smirk to go with it.

"Dude, you don't have to have it. I can recommend something else for you, no problem."

I took a deep breath and met his eyes. "No. Someone suggested I try new things. Bring me whatever you like best."

There was a mischievous teasing in his eyes. "Well, I mean, if you want to know what *I* like best... it's definitely the *sausage*."

He was gay. Why did that make my stomach flip over and over even more? It wasn't like I wasn't used to being around gay men. I was. I totally was. Gay was fine. I was fine with gay.

Gay.

Was the word stuck on repeat in my brain or something?

I slammed the rest of my pint and pointed to the empty glass. "And another one of these too please," I croaked.

As the evening progressed, the bartender—Charlie...Charlie was his name and it fit him perfectly—got flirtier and flirtier while I got drunker and drunker in an effort to cover my discomfort. There was something about the way he moved that drew my eyes to him like a magnet. Whenever he spoke to me, I felt my face heat and my tongue tie in knots. I stammered and babbled like an idiot in a way I'd never done before, but through it all he was calm and kind, asking questions about where I was from and how my flight had been. I tried explaining the mix-up that had led me to fly into Cork rather than Shannon, the tiny rental car I'd barely fit in, my attempts to navigate roundabouts going the wrong way from the wrong side of the car. But I could barely get a word out without stammering.

Instead, I focused on lining up the salt and pepper shakers, my knife and fork, and the bottles of condiments near me on the bar. I squared the drink napkin and straightened the one left by the man who'd come for a quick pint and left already. After that, I snuck my hand sanitizer under the bar to do a once-over. The bar was hundreds of years old, after all. No telling what was baked into its surface after all this time.

Every now and then I'd sneak a glance at the sweet bartender. At some point, he'd shoved up the long sleeves of the sweater, revealing the slender muscles of his forearms. His skin was peppered with a few freckles there too, and I noticed his hands gripping the bar towel tight enough to turn his knuckles white.

There was a small window open behind the bar letting some fresh air in. The slight breeze ruffled the reddish waves around Charlie's ears and shirt collar, catching my attention and making my fingers itch. I'd never seen hair that color. It was like a mix of all the different shades I'd ever seen on another redhead. Strawberry-blond streaks mixed in with deeper auburn hues and even some carrot-orange bits. I wondered if it was so varied because he spent much of his time outside.

"See something you like?" Charlie asked with a raised eyebrow.

I felt a lump form in my throat at being caught out, and my mouth opened before I had a chance to stop it. "Your hair is really, uh, nice. Different."

Oh my god, I did not just compliment the man on his hair.

My face ignited with humiliation, and I worked desperately to keep from gasping at my own inappropriateness.

"Um, sorry," I stammered. "I only meant... that, ah... I've never met someone with... Oh, hey, do all Irish people really have red hair? Ha. Um, and I found a four-leaf clover. So, that's a thing that happened. Weird, right?"

Oh my god. Kill me now.

Charlie turned to stare at me. "Are you feeling okay?"

Shit. Fuck. Damn.

"Maybe I'm a little jet-lagged. I think it's going to be an early night for me. It's late my time, I think." I scrambled for any excuse.

His lips turned up. "Let's see... it's ten in the evening here, which means it's the afternoon in the States."

Oh. Well.

I looked down at my beer and took a few more sips. No justifiable reason for why I was being weird.

"I liked the coddle," I said out of the blue a few minutes later. Charlie was pulling a pint for another customer, but just as he looked up to answer me with a grin, I felt someone slide onto the seat next to mine. Charlie's grin quickly died.

"I like to cuddle too," the woman said with a chuckle. "Are we listing things we like in bed?"

I turned to her in confusion. We were at a historic inn in rural Ireland. It was about the least likely place for a random pickup as I could imagine outside of maybe a cathedral.

The woman was younger than I was by about ten years and had similar red hair and freckles to the bartender. I flicked my eyes back to Charlie to take another look.

For comparison purposes only.

Charlie narrowed his eyes at the woman before wrinkling his forehead in confusion. "Cait, what are you doing?"

"Can't a girl meet a nice man in a pub?" the woman asked.

"You're dating Donny. Plus, you already know this man," Charlie growled. Something about the tone of his voice made my stomach clench with nerves.

The woman, Cait, looked back at him. "No I don't. How would I know him?"

"Because you sent him here," Charlie said.

I realized I'd had three too many beers when I couldn't make out the hidden meaning in their exchange. And I sure as hell couldn't remember ever meeting the woman next to me.

I risked a glance back at Charlie and felt a low whimper in my throat. That's it. It was time for me to go to bed. I was there for work, not... whatever this was.

Instead of getting up, I took another long sip of beer from the never-ending pint.

Cait looked between Charlie and me before humming, as if she was trying to decide something. "Yes. Yes I did. You two have a great... night," she said before patting me on the back and leaning in to whisper in my ear. "Go for it. I hear the man sucks dick like a Hoover."

Beer shot out of my nose and all over the bar top. The young woman laughed as she walked out of the pub. I scrambled for some napkins and flashed an embarrassed apology at the bartender.

"So sorry," I stammered. "So, so sorry."

His grin was cute as hell. "What did my sister say to you?"

I choked again and squeaked. "Sister? Your sister? That woman was *your sister*?"

Charlie's laugh surrounded me like the warm air of a mild summer evening, familiar and comfortable, buzzing with possibility. I wanted to hear more.

"Yes, she's my sister. Judging from your response, I'd say whatever she whispered was extremely inappropriate." Another chuckle.

"You have a wonderful laugh," I said on a sigh.

Oh fuck.

"And I need to go to bed," I added quickly. "Check please."

He looked at me funny before turning to the register to prepare my tab. He seemed to pause for a moment, and then he returned to the spot across from me. "On the house. Don't worry about it."

I handed him my credit card. "No, I insist. I'm here on business anyway, so my company pays for it."

He glanced at the card before handing it back. "My treat. I enjoyed the company, Hudson."

"I don't want to get you in trouble with your boss," I tried again.

He laughed. "No worries, mate. I've got him wrapped around my little finger."

I stood up, a bit unsteady on my feet. "I can see why," I mumbled under my breath. There was something seriously weird about the guy that must affect everyone around him. Like voodoo magic or witchy spells. That was it. It wasn't just me. He was mesmerizing to everyone.

I smiled up at him. "Good night, Charlie. Thank you for the coddle."

In an effort to get out of there before saying more stupid shit, I spun around and ran right into a thick wooden beam holding up part of the room.

What happened next was a bit of a jumble. A few people gasped, someone cursed, and I was fairly certain I apologized more than a reasonable amount.

"I'm sorry. I'm fine. I just need to get to my room," I said. "I might need some help finding it. The lady said it was up the stairs and down the hall and down another hall and up another set of stairs and I can't remember where my room is, so I might need some help finding it."

Soft laughter and strong arms. I remembered those. The smell of beer mixed with honeysuckle and fresh air. I wanted more of that smell. It was warm and inviting... *different*.

"You smell good," I told the strong arms.

"Not me, him," said a gruffer voice I didn't recognize. "I smell like pork sausage and arse."

More laughter, only this time it was the familiar good laughter I knew was Charlie's.

"Was that your sausage I ate?" I asked as politely as I could. I opened my eyes to see who was helping me up the stairs, but all I could see was a large burly form in a wrinkled black chef's coat. "It was delicious. I'm glad I tried something new. The old ladies were right."

More easy chuckling.

"Well, I made the coddle. Dunno about any old ladies. Now up to bed with you."

There was the sound of a door being opened, and then I was on a bed in my small room at the inn above the pub. The soft quilt smelled like fresh laundry detergent, and the dim light from the bedside table lamp made Charlie's freckles fade.

"That's a shame," I murmured, closing my eyes. "I like your freckles."

I felt my shoes and socks being removed. Charlie's voice was gentle as he spoke. "For a Texas boy, you sure do have a low tolerance for beer."

"I took some medicine. Think maybe that's what happened," I said, remembering the antianxiety meds I'd taken on the plane. "Sorry. So sorry."

A cool hand smoothed over my forehead, and I leaned into the touch.

"No need to be sorry, gorgeous," he whispered. I could feel the cool slide of his silky hair falling against my cheek. "I'm the one who's sorry. I would have really liked to have taken you to bed tonight the proper way."

My heart pounded in my chest, and my lungs felt tight. I opened my eyes to see Charlie's face inches from mine. His lips were dark, shiny, pink, and full, and his eyes were the same vibrant green I'd been lost in all night. I was pretty sure this was all a dream.

"You're really beautiful," I told him, reaching out to tuck the fallen hair behind his ear. "My brothers would love you."

His eyes widened in surprise. "Your brothers?"

I nodded, which made my head spin. "But they can't have you."

Charlie's smile was slow and sexy as hell. "Why not, Hudson? Why can't they have me?"

"Because you're... you're mine," I admitted, closing my eyes to fully appreciate the dream. I brushed my thumb over my chest and felt my heart hammering along as if it had never been this excited before.

The feel of soft lips on my cheek, the gentle hands removing my belt, the careful tucking of a blanket over me... all of those things made me fall even harder into the dream. The rational part of my brain puzzled through which of my single brothers would make the best partner for Charlie while the complete lunatic side of my brain kept chanting *mine mine mine* all night long.

When I awoke the following morning and remembered all of it in a single flash of mortification, I chalked it all up to mixing prescriptions with alcohol. Yeah, that was it. That was the reason my dick filled out when I remembered Charlie's long hair and freckled nose. The medicine and alcohol thing.

Thank god I'd only interacted with the bartender and possibly the chef. Seeing as how I was there representing the firm I worked for, it would've been a disaster if I'd made that drunken scene in front of the manager, or god forbid, the family who'd owned the brewery for generations.

I showered and dressed in a button-down and suit pants before gathering my messenger bag and making my way downstairs to search out some food. I kept my head down and tried desperately to ignore the jitter of nerves in my stomach. The night in the bar had been so out of character for me. What the hell would I do if I had to face Charlie or the chef again? I would die of mortification. Hell, I was already dying of mortification.

And a hangover.

Thankfully, breakfast for the inn customers was served in a different room than the pub. It was a sunroom full of windows and various-sized round wooden tables and chairs. The food was set out along two sturdy sideboards on one wall, and an older woman in an apron wandered through the room offering coffee and tea.

"Take a seat anywhere, love," she called to me from across the room. I selected a small table and set my bag down before going to help myself at the small buffet. I was too hungry to allow myself to worry about whether or not the other guests had used sanitary methods to serve themselves from the communal trays.

When I was halfway through eating and most of the way through my first cup of coffee, a large older man rushed into the room and seemed to take over the entire space with his personality.

"Are you Hudson Wilde?" he asked with a big grin, as if he already knew the answer.

"Yes, sir," I said, standing up and holding out a hand for a shake. "And you are?"

"You don't remember me from last night?" There was a twinkle in his eye that said he sure as hell remembered last night.

Fuck.

"I'm afraid last night I made the mistake of mixing medicine and alcohol," I confessed. "Forgive me."

He had thick red hair and a ruddy complexion. By his girth, I assumed he'd been the chef who'd helped me up the stairs with Charlie the night before.

"Well, now. You're not the first young man we've had to cart up to his room after a few too many pints." His voice was so boisterous, I couldn't help but look around in hopes no one was sharing in my shame.

No such luck. Eyeballs were everywhere, and they were all focused on the stupid American.

"Devlin Murray. Owner of this fine establishment. Nice to meet you, Hudson."

Oh dear god.

Of course the man who'd seen me fucked up the night before was the owner of the company. That was just my luck.

Shitty, shitty luck.

He took the other seat at my table and waved to the server for a cup of tea. Once he took his first sip, he seemed to study me. I gulped down the bile rising up in my throat.

"What do you need from me to make your assessment?" he asked, losing the smirk and becoming all business.

I tried my best to act normal and swallowed another gulp of coffee in hopes it would quell the incessant desire my mouth had to begin spouting apologies like a lunatic again. I'd never felt so off balance before. So much for trying something wild... all it'd done was make me lust after a gorgeous guy, fall at said guy's feet, and ramble incessantly like the water that slid over the mossy rocks in Sugar Creek back home. "Well, I'd like to start with a tour of the place so I can see what's included in the real estate assets. Then I'd like to go over some questions I have about P&L statements and—"

"Whoa," he said, holding up a big paw. "I'm going to stop you right there. Tour. We'll begin with that. I'll pair you up with our best tour guide, and then I'll meet you in the brewery so you can show me this little tap invention I've heard about. Sound good?"

I nodded, grateful he'd dropped the embarrassing events of the previous night and focused on the job ahead. I was a bit surprised Bruce Ames had mentioned my tap ring, but I took it as a good sign I was on my way to returning to Bruce's good graces now that Darci was seeing other people. Maybe Bruce had thought it would make a good icebreaker.

"Good," Devlin said, looking around before settling his gaze back on me. "Listen, I'd like to keep the purpose of your visit quiet if you don't mind. No sense in worrying anyone about changes before it's even a done deal, yeah?"

I nodded. Despite rumors to the contrary, not everyone involved in corporate acquisitions was an unfeeling asshole. And confidentiality was a large part of our business.

"I understand," I assured him. "Let me just finish my breakfast and I'll be ready for the tour. From what I saw of the place when I came in last night, it's gorgeous."

A bittersweet expression stole over the man's face. "That it is, Hudson. That it is. This property has been in my family for nine generations. If the acquisition takes place, it will be the first time in over two hundred years the property hasn't been majority owned by someone in the family. Ever since my brother moved away last year, it's just been me in charge. It's not the same."

His words stayed with me long after he'd left to arrange my tour guide. As I finished the last bites of my food, I realized how important it was I keep the purpose of my visit to myself. If this historic brewery and inn had been in the Murray family for that long, there was no telling how upset the locals would be when they learned it could be majority owned by an American investment firm within weeks.

The woman in the apron asked if I needed anything else.

"No, thank you. I'm all set. I just need to know where to find my tour guide."

She smiled up at me. "Och, that'd be Charlie. You can find him in the bar across the way."

Charlie.

No.

No no no.

4

CHARLIE

Charlie's Revelation:

Everyone has daddy issues.

It was way too early in the morning when my uncle's text came: *Need you to do a tour. Be here by nine.*

Fuck. Here and I was enjoying a nice lie-in with thoughts of the tall American with the sexy eyes. So much for that. Dev probably wanted me to take a group of old ladies around. They were the only tourists who came to the pub that early in the morning.

I texted back: *Make Cait do it. I did the last one.*

His response wasn't wrong: *She sucks at it. You're way better. This is a financial analyst doing an assessment for me. Need it to be good.*

Fuckity-fuck.

I rolled out of bed and made it into the shower. A businessman. Even worse. I hated those types. And they usually had absolutely no interest in the history and details of the place. They mostly wanted to see the numbers or drink the beer. Or chase after my sister.

I wondered if I needed to shoot Cait a warning text that there were business blokes around this morning. Nah, maybe I'd wait and see who they were first.

After dressing and shoving down a quick bite, I made a tea to go and began the long walk along the footpath to the B&B. The sun was up, but the October air was fresh and cold. My dog trotted along the path ahead of me, up and back, up and back, until she settled down to the familiar distance.

By the time I arrived at the front desk, I'd decided to keep my eyes open in case I was lucky enough to catch a glance of the American again. There was something about Hudson Wilde that had captivated me the night before. He'd looked vulnerable in some kind of way I couldn't quite identify. I wondered if he was simply out of his comfort zone by being in rural Ireland. I'd heard many times how few Americans were interested in international travel. Maybe he was one of them. Maybe he wasn't comfortable in a strange place with strange customs. Either way, I was anxious to catch another glimpse of him and hopefully even more than that.

A quick fuck with the man would be pretty bloody amazing. But, in typical me fashion, I couldn't help but also wonder what caused his eyes to look so lost and why he'd mentioned his brothers when he'd been flirting with me the night before. While I would have pegged him as straight the minute he sat down, by the time I walked him up to his room, I'd realized how wrong my initial impression had been. He'd flirted and blushed at me all night. He'd called me beautiful.

He'd called me *his*.

And fuck if that hadn't made me a bit loopy inside.

Stupid.

"Ah, Charlie, there you are. Your man is here ready for you to take round."

I hadn't realized just how off in my head I'd wandered until I heard Liv's voice calling me from the reception counter in the lobby.

"Huh?" I asked before remembering the purpose of my early-morning arrival. "Oh, right. Yes. I'm ready. Who do you have for me?"

I should have known. Of course it was him.

Hudson stepped out from the far side of a postcard carousel and caught sight of me. His eyes widened comically, and a deep blush seeped up the sides of his neck.

"Oh," he said. "Oh, uhh... hi. I mean, ah, hi. Hello."

Oh my god, what a dote. The man was the cutest fucking thing on the planet.

"Hi," I replied with a grin. "How are you feeling this morning, Hudson?"

Was it possible for him to blush more? If so, he did.

"Oh, ah..." He seemed to realize he was repeating the same stammered response, so he gulped and glanced at Liv before looking back at me and starting again. "Fine."

I bit my lip to keep from laughing, especially when he began checking his pockets, probably for his beloved hand sanitizer. I doubted he was even aware he was doing it. He was just so fucking sweet and flustered.

"I doubt you're fine in the head, Hudson. Would you like some paracetamol?"

He blinked at me like I'd just spoken in Mandarin Chinese.

"I don't know what that is," he admitted, looking anywhere but at me. "But I took some headache medicine in my room."

He seemed overly nervous. I got the feeling I wasn't the tour guide he'd wanted, and that thought disappointed me. Maybe he was just embarrassed about the stuff he'd said to me the night before? I really hoped that was all it was because already I was feeling the sting of rejection.

I forced a smile and nodded. "Right then, we're off. Come with me, Mr. Wilde."

Hudson winced at the honorific but dutifully followed. I left my dog salivating at Liv's feet and led Hudson out the front door and partway down the front path before turning back around to face the front of the building. The rumble of one of our delivery vans was accompanied by the crunch of gravel, drawing my attention away for a moment.

"You're a money man, right?" I asked, remembering what my uncle had said about the reason for the tour.

"What? No. I'm a... yes. I mean, no. I'm a financial analyst. But I'm here for..." Hudson hesitated and swallowed. Maybe there was something wrong with him. Perhaps it wasn't nerves at all but a true affliction of some kind.

"I was under the impression you were here to help with the finances," I said. "You're here to assess the books, right?"

He let out a breath. "Yes. I'm here to assess the books. Exactly."

The man was odd. And he was a corporate type after all, which meant he was most likely a selfish prick under all that aw-shucks charm. I needed to remember that and not get distracted by his cute blushes or odd little quirks that seemed to worsen when he was tense.

"Right. Well, let's begin with a little history. This land has been in the Murray family for hundreds of years. Originally, there was a small cottage on the land, and the family kept sheep, as did most of the other people around these parts. That timber cottage burned down in the early 1800s, and the family built a larger house with brick made by a traveling brickmaker.

"As the area grew and populated a bit more, the original pub was built with local slate flagstones. I'll point out a spot where you can see eel fossils in the flagstone. Pretty cool," I added, raising my arm to point out which part of the large sprawling building in front of us was the original pub. "You can see the flagstone walls there to get an idea of the size of the original pub. As the place grew more popular and the area here with the cliffs became more of a tourist destination, the Murray family added on the guesthouse portion of the building above and to the right."

I pointed to the part of the building where his room was located. He seemed interested enough for me to continue.

"That window there with the curtain still drawn is your room. The reason it's difficult to find is because of the way the buildings were added on to over time. There was never any singular grand plan, just wings and additions added as the needs grew. Fig and Bramble is the only guesthouse located within easy walking distance to the Cliffs of Moher, which means it's always benefitted immensely from the tourists visiting the area. The rooms are almost always sold out.

"To the left you can see a different wing of rooms that were added on more recently. That section is the newest portion tacked on to the original building, and it was built in the 1960s to accommodate this tourism effect."

Hudson shifted to face me. "Why haven't more pubs and inns sprouted up nearby? The closest place is eight kilometers away."

I nodded. "That's what makes Fig and Bramble so special. Because the land was in the Murray family so long ago, when the tourism to the Cliffs became a thing, the trails and footpaths to the best views were through the Murray holdings. The family is the only one with rights and property this close. Hence, the success of the company and the continued pride of the Murray family."

For some reason, I refrained from mentioning I was a Murray. I wasn't sure why, but something held me back. Perhaps I didn't want to make it weird between us since he was there to assess the family business. I knew since Uncle Devlin had taken over for my father, money had been tight. I assumed Dev wasn't as good at the money side and was struggling. Cait and I had tried to help, but he wouldn't hear of it. If things were as bad as we imagined, maybe I didn't want Hudson to paint me with the same brush and assume I was bad at business too.

As we walked toward the far end of the main building, I pointed out the direction of the cliffs. "Be sure to visit the cliffs so you can tell your friends and family you've seen the real Cliffs of Insanity from *The Princess Bride*."

"Never seen it," Hudson responded.

I actually stopped in my tracks. "What? You've never seen *The Princess Bride*? How is that possible?"

"Don't know... too busy I guess."

"Doing what?" I asked, completely serious. But when I saw him shift uncomfortably, I quickly added with a grin, "I think that might actually be a crime in your country."

Hudson smiled and then that damn blush was back on his too-perfect cheeks. I began walking to keep from reaching out to see if his skin actually felt as warm as it looked.

"Is that cotton?" Hudson asked a moment later, pointing to a distant field. I followed his gesture and bit back a laugh when I saw what he was pointing to.

"No. Those are sheep. It's farther away than it looks. I helped train that man's dog and it takes me fifteen minutes by car to get there," I said.

"You trained his dog?"

"Sheep dog. I train them on the side. A bit of a hobby really," I said with a shrug. "You may have seen my Mama in the guesthouse earlier. She's my bitch."

Hudson stopped walking and turned to me with a confused expression. "What?"

"Mama. She's a good girl. Won mass loads of awards for trials. And she's damned good at breeding too."

"Please tell me we're talking about two different things?" His face seemed to have gone a bit ashen. "The receptionist is your mother?"

"Who, Liv? No. Why would you think she's my... oh... no! I only meant my bitch. My collie, Mama."

Hudson rubbed his face with his hands before glancing at me with a sheepish grin. "Mama, the *dog*. Sorry, you can imagine some of that was lost in translation. I thought... never mind."

"Do you like animals?" I inquired to get past the awkward moment.

He nodded and I noticed a soft look cross his face. "I've always loved to ride. My grandparents have a ranch and keep a horse for me. His name is Kojack."

We'd passed the end of the main building and headed toward the edge of the sea. It wasn't a normal part of the tour, but I didn't want to interrupt him by suggesting we head for the brewery where there would be more people to interrupt our conversation. Especially since he was finally starting to look more relaxed. He hadn't checked his pockets for the hand sanitizer in at least three minutes.

Hudson continued with a soft chuckle. "Actually, when I was younger, I had a pony named Charlie. He was so spoiled. I used to sneak him apples and carrots all the time. I still wonder how he didn't get too fat to carry a rider."

I imagined a young Hudson sneaking out to his grandparents' barn to give treats to his little pony. Had the boy worn little cowboy boots and a straw hat? Had he played with bows and arrows and pretended he was part of the American Wild West? The image of him as a child standing on a fence rung watching his rancher grandfather made me smile.

"I've never ridden," I admitted. "I'm definitely more of a dog person. Do you have a dog back home?"

Hudson looked down to where our shoes made crunching sounds on the tiny shell bits along the pathway. "No. I live in the city and work too many hours to have one. Plus, they wouldn't like living in a high-rise apartment. But my grandfathers have three dogs on the ranch. An old coonhound and two little yippy mutts. I have to admit to playing favorite. That coonhound stole my heart when they found him."

While he talked about home, about his love of animals and his family, Hudson's face changed completely. Gone was the stuttering and stumbling over words. Gone was the nervous blushing. I could see where his heart lived, and it was unexpectedly sweet.

He looked over at me. "How did you get into dog training?"

"One of our neighbors did sheep trials with his dog, Sweep. I was about ten the first time my father took me to a trial. It was in Dingle. They've an aquarium there, so I guess he'd wanted to take me to see the sea animals. It happened to coincide with the neighbor's trial, so we were able to do both. I don't remember the penguins and otters, but the dogs? I was hooked from the first run. The way the dog and trainer seemed to read each other's minds... it seemed special, that relationship. It wasn't until I got my first pup a few years later that I discovered the absolute joy in creating that bond. His name was Jacko. I loved that dog. Unfortunately, he passed before he was ten years old."

"Charlie, I'm so sorry." Hudson's sympathy was genuine and kind. He must have known what it was like to lose a beloved animal.

We talked a bit more about our respective childhoods, and I learned his parents lived abroad. "Were you raised by your grandparents?" I asked.

"Oh, no. Mom and Dad only moved to Singapore a few years ago. My youngest sister was almost done with high school before they felt Dad could take the promotion overseas. But even with them around... we spent much of our time with our grandfathers in the main house on the ranch. Our house was on the ranch property too, but Dad worked two hours away in Dallas and Mom was always busy with her charity projects and running the household. I don't know how she managed to raise ten kids with my dad in the city during the week. I guess because as West and I got older, we helped as much as we could."

"Is West the oldest?"

"No, I am. But he's next. After that came a set of twins. MJ and Saint were a handful. Mom had four kids under four for a few months, if you can believe it. Once I started school, I remember her calling me her godsend. All her friends called me her little helper. From then on, I think I just felt it was my job to help raise the others." He shrugged. "They're amazing. We're all pretty close. Everyone either lives in Dallas or Hobie now. Except my brother King. We're not really sure what he's up to most of the time. He sort of travels for work and flits through town whenever he's able. Sassy is the youngest at nineteen."

I pictured the tidy man taking on the responsibility of nine siblings to help his mother. It made me wonder if he'd taken to horse riding as a way of escaping, of getting away from the noise or the chaos of that many children around all the time.

"What made you decide to go into finance?" I asked, suddenly even more curious for some reason about what made him tick.

"My dad is in finance. He always told me I'd succeed at it and always have a solid, steady job."

Something about the way he said it caused me to perk up.

"Do you like what you do?"

He opened his mouth to answer, but then closed it again for a moment. When he spoke, it was hesitant.

"It's... yes. It's a good job. I enjoy the way numbers are organized and... everything works out into clean lines. I'm not saying this right... I think it's good to have a job where mistakes are easy to spot and you can double-check your work to make sure it's correct."

His face pinched and he shook his head a bit. "No, that's not quite right either. I wouldn't say I like it, really. It's more that I'm happy to make a good living and prove my worth by working hard."

Hudson's chin tilted down as if he was nodding to himself. "Yes. I like doing my share to help the company succeed."

It sounded bloody awful.

"I'm sure your father is proud of you," I mumbled, unsure of what else to say.

He glanced up at me, and I caught just a hint of vulnerability in his face. "I hope so."

We'd reached the edge of the cliffs, and I explained the history of the location a bit more before we turned to find our way back.

"What about you, Charlie? Are your parents still around?"

Well, shite. Whose idea was it to talk about people's parents?

5

HUDSON

Hudson's Words To Live By:

When in doubt, blame the alcohol.

I could sense Charlie's body stiffen beside me. Perhaps I shouldn't have asked after his parents.

"Nah. My mum took off when I was twelve. Decided to move to a big city for a corporate job. We never saw her again. My dad moved abroad almost a year ago," he said before clearing his throat. "Remarried."

His clipped answers confirmed this topic was not a good one for a stranger to pursue.

"I'm sorry. I didn't mean to pry," I said softly.

His hand came to rest on my arm, stopping me from taking another step down the shell path. I felt the warmth of his slight touch before he pulled it away. The varied shades of his hair caught the weak sunlight struggling through the clouds above. It looked both golden and auburn and so incredibly touchable. But his self-deprecating smile was what really set my heart tripping.

"It's okay. You didn't know. Not my favorite topic. I never really forgave my mum, but I've had loads of time to get past her leaving. My dad, on the other hand… well, let's just say if I saw him right now, I might be thankful we've no safety rails at the cliffs' edge."

I could tell he was joking about the cliffs, but clearly the subject wasn't a pleasant one. How had we even gone down the path of sharing personal stories in the first place? I almost never shared personal information about myself the way I had with Charlie and the woman on the plane before him. Had something happened to me? Had my breakup with Darci brought out all the feelings or unleashed some need to share my innermost thoughts with others? We needed to get away from these personal topics and back to the business at hand. I was there to do a job.

Despite how easy Charlie was to talk to, he was there to give me a tour of the place. I needed to understand the property in order to do good work for Bruce Ames and earn back some of the respect the man had lost for me after the fiasco with his daughter. "So, that's the brewery building up ahead?" I asked.

Charlie cleared his throat before responding. "Yes. That's where we make the beer. We currently distribute to four countries in Europe besides delivery to most of the UK."

"Seems a lot for such a small facility," I said without thinking.

"The building is much bigger than what you see there." With that, he continued the tour as if we hadn't just shared pieces of our past and revealed vulnerabilities we had in common in the form of our parents. As he spoke of the history of the facility and how the company had started brewing its own beer, I noticed a new comfort between us, as if we were no longer strangers but something a little more than that. When the natural silences came into our conversation, they were easy rather than awkward, and for the first time in a long time, I felt at ease like I usually only did with family and close friends. It made me wonder if my attraction to him, which hadn't waned in the least despite my brain now being alcohol free, was because of this ease between us, rather than his physical presence.

That was it.

He was a kind human. I was naturally drawn to him because of his gentle and interesting personality, not because he was sexy. I must have sensed his magnetic personality the night before when we'd first met. Charisma. That's what it was called when certain people drew others to them so effortlessly.

Charlie was charismatic. That was all.

It was a relief to finally understand I wasn't actually attracted to him physically... it was a different kind of attraction all together. I didn't have a problem with men being attracted to each other of course, but if I was feeling attraction to a man for the first time in my midthirties, it sure as hell would be confusing. I should have felt relief at the realization, but all I felt was my stomach rolling around like it did on the few occasions I got a calculation wrong in my reports at work.

I tried to ignore the sensation, but as we approached the brewery building, Charlie leaned over to pick up a cigarette butt off the ground. His shirt rode up to expose a strip of pale, creamy skin above a colorful, rainbow striped waistband peeking out from his jeans.

My dick went straight for it, filling and jutting out so quickly, it reminded me of the time one of the girls in my biology class in high school leaned over to pick up a dropped pencil and showed half the class her thong. The sudden blood rush left me dizzy with want.

Oh god.

It wasn't just his sweet personality after all. I was pretty sure I wanted to see him naked, to touch his bare skin and kiss his full lips. Could it really have taken me thirty-four years of life and thousands of miles from home to realize maybe I wasn't as straight as I'd thought? No. That couldn't be right.

Surely my confusion was simply a combination of jet lag and a hangover.

I hated traveling.

~

When we entered the brewery, Devlin Murray called out from across the reception area.

"Oy. Over here then. I was wondering if you wanted to test out that ring bit you was telling me about earlier."

I glanced at Charlie who clearly had no idea what his boss was referring to.

"I do have a sample of the, ah..." I took a deep breath and tried to get my shit together. "I brought several samples of the device I came up with in case you wanted to play around with it."

Devlin stood up from behind the reception desk. "Let's go put that little yoke to work, shall we?"

I wasn't sure what a yoke was, but I had to assume it was my head regulator.

The older man winked at me before leading us down the hallway through a doorway to a big open warehouse space where I immediately saw a long bar set-up with several different sets of taps.

I pulled out the constrictors sample I kept in my pocket. Bruce had suggested the doohickey might make for a good ice-breaker. I didn't expect the thing to actually interest anyone beyond the novelty of it, but I was happy to have a chance to let him play around with it and see what he thought.

Devlin went around behind the bar where he gestured toward a single tower tap. "Hudson, you're up. This one's Beamish unless you want something else?"

"I don't know what that is," I admitted. "But any lager is fine."

There was a beat of silence before he and Charlie plus four or five men working in the warehouse behind us began laughing. My face went hot, and I realized just how ridiculous of an idea this invention had been.

Devlin moved to another single tower. "Try this one then," he said through his laughter. "It's Harp. Just a suggestion, but you might want to learn the difference between a stout faucet and a regular one, aye?"

I looked closer and noticed the faucets. "Oh. Right. I knew that. I just hadn't looked closely," I mumbled. And that was true. But it was, admittedly, one of the very few things I knew. The truth was, I knew jack shit about beer. I'd learned just enough to try and impress my girlfriend's father at the time. It wasn't my job to know beer, though. I was a master of finance integration, forensic accounting, and market share assessment, not to mention financial risk reduction, human capital optimization, and negotiation strategy.

I stepped forward with the small metal ligature and began installing it, babbling the entire time about what I was doing when, in reality, I could have simply said, "Twist it on like this."

Once the tool was on the tap nozzle, I found a stack of pint glasses under the bar and poured one with the lowest amount of foam, explaining that adjusting the tool with a twist to the right lowered the amount of air and twisting it to the left, let all the air through.

Devlin watched me pull several pints with increasing amounts of foam before nodding and looking at me seriously. "You know how to pull a pint, don't you?"

I shrugged. "Lager anyway. Not as great at the stouts yet."

"Come here and let me show you a thing or two, Hudson," he said in a kind voice. I stepped down to a different tap and watched him pour a perfect pint of Guinness from a tap without my ring on it, all the while explaining what he was doing and why it mattered. "Now you try," he said, handing me a fresh glass.

When I began the first part of the two-part pour, he took a big swig of his pint, smacking his lips together afterward in satisfaction. I sat my glass on the bar as if I had a customer present and waited for the bubbles to do their thing before picking it back up for the rest of the pour.

"This is where I generally screw up," I admitted, trying to get the perfect dome without overflowing. This time, the beer gods were with me, and I ended up with a good pour.

"Ah, perfection. Just took being in Ireland to get it right," he boomed with a hearty slap to my back followed by a chuckle.

I grinned at him. "Maybe you're right. A little luck of the Irish?"

After following his lead and taking a sip, I noticed Charlie out of the corner of my eye. He was studying the row of Harp pints I'd left farther down the bar. His forehead was creased with concern as he seemed to be assessing the different amounts of head on each pint.

Once he seemed satisfied, he removed my head control device and poured a pint. His eyes were on the first pint I'd poured rather than the one he was currently pulling. Without even seeming to try hard, he duplicated my pour by hand.

Then he did it again. This time the pour matched my second one.

And again, the third.

And again.

Until he had a nearly identical row of pints lined up next to mine —all done by hand without the benefit of my special device.

He was showing me up, and I was mortified, despite having predicted this type of challenge if I'd ever decided to actually pitch the idea to pub owners.

Was his intention to humiliate me in front of his boss? And why did it sting more coming from him than it would have coming from Devlin himself?

I opened my mouth to make the argument I'd already thought through a million times, but he beat me to it. His voice was the kind of quiet, steady voice that hushed a room just so people could listen in.

"The Irish take their pint pulling very seriously, Hudson," he began. The sound of my name in his soft lilt made something strange happen in my gut. Maybe it was the Irish accent and the fact I wasn't used to it.

I tried to cut in, to tell him that times were changing and not all bartenders were properly trained or experienced in pulling pints anymore, especially in the States, but he continued before I could get a word in.

"The problem is time," he said. "Pulling the perfect pint takes time and attention, which is all well and good when it's halfway through a lazy Sunday and you're only serving auld Johnny who's been holding down his same stool for fifty-odd years. But when you're serving loads of university students or stacks of customers at a festival or game, there's no time for the perfect pour, is there? And chances are, you haven't hired the type of bartender who knows how to pull a pint the right way because he hasn't been tagging along with his dad for twenty years to every public house in Ireland watching how it's done."

Charlie turned to Devlin. "He needs to pitch to the city pubs, not ones like ours in the middle of nowhere," he said before turning and walking out.

I stared after him. He'd made my argument without me saying a single word.

6

CHARLIE

Charlie's Words To Live By:

Even when a tangled-up snake says he's straight, take him at his word.

I let Devlin natter on while I waited outside the door for Hudson.

He was a bit prim and uptight in a way. Buttoned-up and tidy with a noticeable desire for things in their place. I didn't usually go for blokes like that. I preferred messy and free, the sort of man who didn't mind a bit of fuss and spontaneity. But there was something inherently attractive about a man who loved his family and animals and someone who wasn't afraid to tinker around with things to learn how they work and improve upon a process.

Watching him muddle his way through the pouring demonstration had been painful. Clearly, he wasn't comfortable being the center of attention when he didn't have all the answers. It was refreshing to see a business man who didn't pretend to have all the answers, and I realized I wanted to learn more about him.

As the two of them made their way out of the building, Dev was still chuckling at the American for his tap device.

"You laugh now," I warned, "But that man's going to go home, apply for the patent, and be a millionaire this time next year. He's sitting on a gold mine with that little ring."

Hudson's eyes widened in surprise and his ears turned red. "It's just something I came up with to impress my boss. He's a beer lover."

I could tell he wasn't interested in talking about it any further, so we wrapped things up with Dev and headed back toward the main building. While we walked, I decided to ask him how he knew Cait.

He looked confused. "I don't know her. You were there when I met her last night. At the bar."

Now it was my turn to be confused. "Then how did she convince you to come see me while you were here on business?"

Hudson rubbed both hands over his face and squinted at me. "I think maybe you were right about my not being fine in the head. I really don't understand what we're talking about right now, Charlie."

"My sister sent you into the pub last night to hook up with me."

Hudson's eyes bugged. "What? No she didn't. No. No, she did not. I'm... I... I don't sleep with men."

That took me completely off guard. He wasn't gay? But the man was clearly attracted to me. In addition to the things he'd said the night before, he'd even gotten hard earlier on our walk; I was sure of it. I narrowed my eyes at him. "Bullshit."

"No, I swear. I never met your sister before last night."

"I mean bullshit you don't sleep with men," I clarified. "As for Cait, how did you know my name if she didn't send you?"

"You were wearing a name tag, *Charlie*," he replied. "Why in the world would your sister send someone to sleep with you? Is that an Irish custom or something?"

I heard a gasp from over my shoulder and turned to see a couple of locals wandering up the path.

"Mr. and Mrs. Driscoll, ta," I greeted lamely. The elderly couple scowled at me. They'd never been my biggest fans anyway.

Once they'd moved past us into the building, I turned back to Hudson and bit out, "Long story, but no, it's not an Irish custom."

He held up his hands in defense. "Fine. No need to hiss at me. What do I know about how things are done here?"

I let out a breath. "I wasn't hissing. But as the resident gay man around here, I'm already persona non grata with the older folk in town. No need to add my sister pimping me out to the list of Charlie's kinks, yeah?"

Hudson lifted an eyebrow, and... was that a smirk? "What else is on the list?"

I replayed my previous statement to figure out what list he was referring to. Once I realized what he was asking, I snorted. "Ask me again when you're naked, Hudson, and I'll be happy to clue you in. But considering you said you don't *sleep with men*, I'm guessing you're just asking to be polite anyway."

The flush returned to his neck and ears as he looked away. I couldn't help but reach out and take hold of his elbow. His skin was warm under the button-up shirt he wore, and it reminded me of how cool the morning air was.

"I'm sorry. I shouldn't have said that," I said softly. "That was inappropriate and sarcastic. You're here for work. Not only that, but your sexuality is none of my business."

He looked like he wanted to say something, to answer me, and I was desperate to hear it. But within a moment, he'd obviously changed his mind. He swallowed and looked off to the far right in the direction of my uncle's house.

"What's that building over there?"

I hesitated for a moment, trying to get back in the mindset of a tour guide.

Before I could answer him, he blurted, "Straight. I'm straight. *Straight*."

I stared at him, wondering if he truly thought that repeating a lie made it true. Regardless, the man was trouble, and I needed more man trouble like a hole in the head. Not to mention I was smarting from the realization that there was a good chance he didn't even remember the words he'd said to me the night before about me being his. I'd known he was drunk, of course, but a little part of me had believed there'd been some truth to them. His adamant insistence he was straight was a punch to the gut, and I wondered it it was time to find an excuse to just get the hell out of there for a while.

7

HUDSON

Hudson's Words To Live By:

If you repeat something enough times, maybe it will come true. Hell, it worked for Dorothy.

Straight.

Why had the word felt wrong on my tongue? And why, for the love of god, had I repeated it so many times? The man looked at me like I was insane.

"Sure thing, Hudson," he'd said before moving seamlessly back into tour guide mode. The rest of the tour had been straightforward, as if Charlie was gone and in his place stood an automaton. It had still been the best damned historical tour I'd ever been on. The facts and anecdotes of the pub and surrounding area he'd relayed were fascinating. Fig and Bramble was rich in family history, and I'd felt the pride coming off him in waves as if just by working there, he was a part of it.

But way too soon, the tour was over, and he'd disappeared in the blink of an eye, leaving me standing in the lobby again staring at the woman I'd heard him refer to as Liv.

"Where did he go?" I'd asked.

"Said he was off for a delivery. He'll be doing the Waterford run for Alan, I'd imagine. An overnighter, that one."

So as I'd been escorted into the narrow hallway of business offices and shown the files I'd needed, I'd felt a pang of... something. Loss, perhaps? Disappointment? Maybe I'd wanted to learn a little more about him or share another evening chatting across the bar. Not for any other reason than friendly companionship of course, but it still would have been better than dining alone.

But it turned out to be a moot point because that evening, I had company of another kind.

"Hiya, handsome," Cait said, sliding into the booth in front of me. "Join you for dinner?"

I looked around the half-full pub, wondering if she'd landed at the wrong table.

"Um, I'm fine," I said.

She flashed me a giant grin full of straight white teeth. "You sure are. So, what are you ordering? Do you need a suggestion? I'm Cait, by the way."

"Yes, I know. I'm Hudson." I glanced at the menu in my hands and back up at her. "I was just going to get the coddle again."

"Pfft. Now why in the world would you do that? Don't you want to try something new?"

I stopped myself from rolling my eyes. Why did everyone think trying new things was a good idea? Sometimes old favorites were better. Comfortable. Expected. Predictable. "I liked it. Why order something different when I know there's already something I like on the menu?"

"Spoken like a man who only dines at his local chip shop," she said with a chuckle. "Have the beef and Auld Best stew. I guarantee you'll like it as much as the coddle. Our recipe is the best stew around, and it's a cold enough night for it. Auld Best is the brewery's stout. Kind of like Guinness, yeah?"

When I'd been seated in this booth, I'd felt a shimmer of happiness that it was located next to the fireplace with its huge wood-burning fire. I'd gone for a short walk before dinner to see the ocean beyond the cliffs and had gotten cold enough to be grateful for the cozy warmth. Cait was right: a stew seemed just the thing for such a night.

"Sold," I said, laying down my menu. "But don't make me drink a pint of Auld Best with it. Not sure my head or stomach can handle any more of Fig and Bramble's special brews."

Cait threw her head back and let out a laugh. "My brother did you wrong last night, is that what you're saying?"

I couldn't help but smile. "Yes, it was all Charlie's fault." My gut did a mini pirouette at the feel of Charlie's name in my mouth, and I quickly told it to stand the hell down. No silly butterflies for the bartender when I was supposed to be here working to impress Bruce Ames.

I wanted the promotion he'd dangled in front of me when he'd hired me. If I could get the vice president title, I could check off one of my biggest goals. In order to do that, I had to stay focused on my job.

"Speaking of my brother..." Cait began in a teasing tone.

I just stared at her and kept my mouth shut. She tilted her head to study me. "Did something happen on your tour today?"

"Why do you ask that?" I asked, my voice going just a bit too high.

"Because he volunteered for the most dreadful delivery run we do."

Volunteered? I'd assumed it was part of his job.

"I have no idea what you're talking about. After our tour, the woman at the front desk said he was off on a delivery route, but as far as I knew, that was normal for him."

"He hates deliveries, especially to Waterford."

"Why Waterford?" I couldn't help but ask.

Her lips pursed. "Shitty ex-boyfriend lives there. Pat works for our largest customer in Waterford and always makes the delivery hell on Charlie."

Prickles of unease assaulted my skin. "Like how?"

She shrugged and took a sip of my soda without asking. "Sometimes it's little annoyances like saying he's too busy to take delivery during the afternoon, so he makes Charlie come back at midnight. Sometimes it's more personal than that. He touches him without asking, cries about wanting Charlie back. One time, Pat told Charlie to come into his office for some paperwork, and when they got to the office, Pat had some guy naked on the sofa where they'd clearly just been fucking. Drives Charlie bonkers."

I winced at her straightforward language and the image of Charlie being put in those uncomfortable situations. My nostrils flared and my fingernails bit into the skin of my palms as my hands fisted. The urge to rush out of there and find a ride to Waterford was like a living thing beneath my skin.

"Why does he do it, then? Why not get someone else to deliver to Waterford?" My voice was grumblier than normal, and I realized belatedly this was affecting me more than it should. I didn't really know any of these people.

"He did. That's what I'm saying. He came home from that one and said never again. So why the fuck would he volunteer to do it? Did he make a pass at you and get rejected or something?"

My heart thumped faster in my chest. "What? No."

Not exactly.

I felt like I owed her more than that. "I'm... I'm straight."

She snorted. "Yeah, right."

Now I was annoyed. "Why do you both think I'm gay? I'm not."

Cait held her hands up. "Calm down, Hudson. No need to get all bent out of shape. It's just clear to me, and most likely Charlie too, that you're attracted to him. If you're worried about him wanting more than a quick hookup, don't be. He's sworn off relationships. They always seem to bite him in the arse, Pat being just one of many."

That angered me even more. Charlie was a sweet and fun guy. He deserved to find someone to spend his life with instead of settling for a quick fuck. Dammit, just the thought of him fucking random guys made me want to kick something.

I looked around at the historic pub, realizing it couldn't be easy for a gay man to find true love in the middle of nowhere on the Irish coast. "Has he ever thought about moving to a bigger city?"

"He'd hate the city. Needs to be near sheep. He's a successful breeder and trainer for trial dogs. It's a side business we keep trying to get him to pursue full-time. But he can't leave the pub. The man's loyalty is as big as his heart. He's not just a bartender though. He's the fix-it man around here. Does what needs doing, regardless of what it is. Honestly, Dev would be lost without him, and Charlie knows that."

I wondered, not for the first time, if Charlie knew his boss was attempting to sell half the business. I tried reminding myself it was none of my concern. Why did I even care? Perhaps it was just the need to have a conversation with another human being rather than sitting and eating dinner in silence.

The rest of our shared dinner was spent in lighter conversation, though I had to admit it was hard to keep my thoughts from straying to Charlie. Cait told me about her time at college, her boyfriend, Donny, and his plans to move them to Cork, and her hope of finding a job there in corporate marketing. I told her the comedic version of Darci and the messed-up accidental proposal, and we laughed at the similarities and differences between our two cultures. It was a nice, comfortable dinner, and I enjoyed the easy company.

I spent the next couple of days trying my best to focus on the work I was there to do. What should have been comfortably endless hours of profit and loss statements, distribution analysis, market assessments, and other reports required in order for me to make my recommendations were actually a torturous chore as my thoughts kept going back to the one place… or person, rather, they shouldn't.

And the nights were even worse because they were full of dreams I'd never had before.

Warm skin covered in coarse hair, the scrape of prickly scruff against the sensitive skin of my neck, deep-voiced grunts and moans, and the absolute giving over of myself to hot, sweaty sex unlike anything I'd ever experienced before.

Sex with a man.

Sex with *Charlie*.

By the time he returned to the pub three days later, I was desperate to find out if the reality of sex with a man was anything at all the way it had seemed in my dreams. I'd spent hours debating whether or not I could bring myself to sleep with a man, but when the hottest dream of my life happened the night before Charlie came home, I awoke gasping and rock hard, realizing five seconds of sex with Charlie in my dream was better than any sex I'd ever had with anyone in real life.

I wondered if I could ever get up the nerve to try it. Just sex. Just to see once and for all what my brothers were always bragging about. Surely I wouldn't actually like it. I couldn't have possibly made it to the age of thirty-four not knowing I was attracted to men. Could I maybe... experiment? I'd never done anything crazy in college or any other time, really. But perhaps the lady on the plane was spot-on when she said I needed to live a little.

Everyone had at least one big insane sexual exploit they could look back on and reminisce about, right? Didn't I deserve to go wild for once and do something impulsive and crazy?

But I knew I wouldn't do it. After everything Cait had told me about Charlie being used by assholes in the past, the last thing in the world I wanted was to be another asshole added to his list. I never wanted to be the cause of pain for such a sweet man.

In addition to not wanting to use Charlie that way, I just wasn't a casual-sex guy. While I was Mr. Wilde, I wasn't Mr. Wild. I wasn't impulsive or crazy. I was a serial monogamist, always the dutiful boyfriend. I was the guy who opened doors for women and who knew how to buy tampons. I knew when to offer a woman Ben & Jerry's after a bad day and when to offer her my suit jacket against the cold.

And I liked that. I liked having a woman's softness and sweetness pressed up against me. I liked having someone to protect and take care of. I liked the idea of building a steady life with someone back home and settling down near my family.

No. I'd just go home and let my life get back to normal. Recommend the acquisition and move on with my life and career in Dallas.

It was fine.

I was *fine*.

8

CHARLIE

Charlie's Revelation:

For fuck's sake, absence really does make the heart grow fonder.

By the time I pulled the van into the brewery car park, my head was pounding and my jaw was sore from grinding my teeth. I kicked myself for the stupid fucking decision I'd made to flirt with Pat in Waterford.

He'd come on to me the way he always did, and I actually thought a quick fuck with the man would help erase a certain straight American from my daydreams. All I could think of was how grateful I'd been when a couple of drunk patrons had accidentally slammed into his office door, cutting short my delirium before I'd been able to take Pat up on his offer. But coming so close still made me feel like a complete arse.

And it made me feel desperate, which pissed me the hell off. I was mortified at myself—so much so that I'd put off coming home for an extra day until Cait had called and bitched me out.

I slammed the door behind me, slung my overnight bag on my

shoulder, and ducked into the warehouse office to turn in some paperwork and the van keys before making my way down the footpath to the pub for a pint.

Please don't let the beautiful Yank be there. Please don't let the—

"Oh, hi."

The familiar cadence of his voice wrapped around me, causing my eyes to slide closed and my chin to drop to my chest. A deep sigh blew out of me, expelling all of the shit that had happened in Waterford. If I was going to sleep with someone I shouldn't, it was this guy, not Pat.

"Hudson. How has your week been?" I opened my eyes and saw him. His arse was propped on a wooden barstool, and he was wearing blue jeans with a blue-and-green plaid shirt that made his eyes look like deep pools of *yes please*. Other than a sliver of insecurity in his expression, he looked like a walking wet dream.

Out of the blue, I realized I probably smelled like week-old cheese.

My uncle walked up and clapped me on the shoulder. "There he is. I need you to run Hudson here into Cork. His flight is tomorrow morning, and his hire car was smashed to bits by a lorry delivering kegs this morning. You can book a hotel and come back in the morning."

Without waiting for a word from me, Devlin gave Hudson a handshake and then ambled off.

I heaved out a breath. Despite my exhaustion from already driving all day to visit a couple of stud dogs I'd wanted to check out, I couldn't say it would be a hardship to spend a couple of hours alone with the American.

"I should probably shower first," I admitted. "Smell like week-old cheese. Sorry." I turned to go, but his strong hand reached out to grab my upper arm.

"Wait. Charlie, wait."

I turned to look at him, noticing the pink on his cheeks and the nervous fluttering of his eyelashes.

"You don't smell bad. You, ah... you smell really good."

I looked around the room before returning my gaze to Hudson. "Are you drunk again?"

His smile was like damned sunshine, and I basked in it. "No, but... are you sure it's okay for you to drive me? I know you just got back from a long trip."

"Yeah. It's fine. Give me twenty minutes to get cleaned up and sort out the dog, yeah?"

Once we were on the road, conversation came easy. I had to admit that surprised me. From how awkward and stumbling Hudson had been around me, I'd expected two and a half hours of uncomfortable silence.

But the time flew by. We talked about a little of everything. Hudson told me more about his grandfathers who lived on the ranch in a tiny town called Hobie, Texas. He told me more about his siblings and their quirky personalities. I told him more about my experiences dog training and trialing.

"You've never been outside of the UK?" he asked in surprise.

"No. I'm terrified of flying. Those giant heavy tubes shouldn't be able to stay in the air, and don't bother trying to explain it to me. It won't work. The fear isn't in my rational brain."

Hudson grinned his lovely shy smile. "They have medicine that can help, you know. I'm not a fan of flying either, but I've had to get used to it because of work."

"Do you travel a lot for your job?"

"Not really. But when I do... well, I take a little something. That's why I made a fool of myself the first time I met you."

I glanced at him. "You were adorable. All stammering and blushing. It's no wonder I thought you were gay."

The red creeped up from his collar. I wanted to brush my thumb across it.

Hudson faced away from me, out the left side window of my Rover. "I thought you were a woman."

The words were quiet, and I could tell he was unsure of how I'd take them.

"That's pretty common. I don't mind, in case you were wondering,

Hudson. I fought my looks for a very long time before going off to college and finally feeling like I could embrace my true self. Once I accepted my feminine side, I got so pissed off at all the years I'd wasted fighting it and all the men out there who will never be able to know the freedom of embracing both aspects of themselves."

He turned back to face me, now in full blush. "You're so fucking beautiful. You're the most beautiful person I've ever met. I can't seem to control my tongue around you. I'm not usually such a babbler."

I felt the inane flutter of excitement in my gut and tried to ignore it. The man had made it very clear he wasn't into me in that way.

"Thank you. I have to admit, I kind of like you as a babbler."

He snorted and looked away again. "I kind of like that you're a man instead of a woman."

I glanced over again, trying to read between the lines. He'd mentioned his gay brothers and grandfathers, so I knew he most likely wasn't a closed-minded homophobe. But then again, was I at all interested in being an experiment?

Not really. There would be way less complication in finding my release with a random bloke in a bar instead of this straight business man from America.

"We're almost to town. Where are you staying?"

"Cork International by the airport."

I made quick work of dropping him off. The farewell was plenty awkward in front of his hotel, but we shook hands and wished each other well with fake smiles plastered on both our faces.

It was after ten on a Friday night, and I most definitely had a second wind despite my heavy heart. After sitting that close to the sexy American for three hours, my cock was begging for a turn at one of the two gay bars in the city. Maybe Cait had been right. Maybe I needed to try a hookup with no strings.

I made my way to Chambers and got my drink on. By the time midnight rolled around, I was buzzed and happily chatting up a table of four cute men and wondering which one might be interested in taking me back to his place when I heard the telltale sound of the crowd's reaction to new blood walking through the door.

I turned to see who the newbie was, and fuck if it wasn't Hudson Wilde.

"Dibs," blurted the man to my left.

"Fuck no, ya langer," snapped the one on the other side of him. "That man was made for me, sugar."

"He looks American," the third said. "Bet a tenner he has a cut cock."

My heart was going to thunder out of my chest. Poor Hudson looked like a mouse at a snake festival.

The fourth man at my table stood up and smoothed down his shirt. "You boys are all talk. Time for some action."

Before he could take a step toward the front of the bar, I was out of my seat like I'd been shot from a cannon.

9

HUDSON

Hudson's Words To Live By:

Good things happen in Cork. Very *good things.*

It had taken me three shots of whiskey and as many pints of beer at a pub down the street before I got up the nerve to walk inside the gay bar. I'd used my phone to search for the biggest gay club in Cork and thought I'd just stop in for a drink and look around. Not... not to *do* anything with anyone. Just to watch.

I was desperate to discover if this attraction to Charlie was an isolated event or if I had somehow unlocked some latent, heretofore unknown queer side of myself I'd never noticed before. I mean, it was all just so strange.

Needless to say, by the time I entered the place, I was a bit blurry and shaking like a leaf.

There were just so many *men* in there.

"Hiya, sweet cheeks," a voice purred from behind me. I felt the barest brush of a hand on my ass through the thick fabric of my jeans. "Get you a drink?"

"Oh, no, thank you," I said as politely as I could. "I'm just here to look."

"Fuck," a familiar voice muttered. "You can't say shit like that, Hudson."

I glanced up and realized I'd had more to drink than I'd realized. I'd conjured up the man of my fantasies. Clearly he wasn't really there, so I attempted to ignore the specter and made my way toward the bar.

"Oh, so you're just going to pretend I'm not here?" he said, clearly miffed.

I swung my head around in surprise. "You're really here?"

His face was so fucking gorgeous, I almost whimpered. "You seriously still look like that even after midnight? Fuck, Charlie. It's not fair. I mean... good god."

I reached my hand out and caressed his angled cheek, running my thumb softly over a few freckles next to his nose. "Look at you, Charlie," I sighed. "So damned perfect."

Someone next to me let out a swoony sigh, but I only had eyes for the man in front of me.

His eyes softened, and the edges of his mouth turned up. "You're drunk."

"Can I tell you a secret?" I whispered, leaning in to brush his hair away so I could say it up close to his ear. I felt him shiver under my touch.

"Mm-hm," he drawled. "What is it?"

"I want to kiss you so badly, it aches. It hurts right here, Charlie," I said, grabbing his hand and pressing it against the middle of my chest. "Please come back to my hotel with me and let me kiss you a little bit."

"Oh fuck," he breathed, leaning into me. "Fuck, Hudson."

"Mmm, maybe," I said without thinking. "Dunno yet. Just know I need your lips on my lips and my hands all over that creamy skin. I want you naked underneath me in my bed."

I could feel Charlie trembling now, his entire body pressing closer to mine in the crush at the bar.

"Hudson," he said in a gravel-filled voice. "You don't know what you're saying right now."

"But I do. I *do*, Charlie. I've been dreaming about you all week." I dropped my voice even lower and pressed my lips to the shell of his ear. "Naughty dreams. Dreams where you bossed me around and touched me in places no one ever has before. Every morning I woke up hard for you, but you were gone with the ending of my dreams. Now you're here though. You're here, and I'm so fucking hard again."

Charlie was panting now, the fast, hot breaths puffing against the skin of my neck.

"This is such a bad idea," he said, lowering his chin to his chest. "What are you doing here, Hudson?"

I took a chance and slid my arms around him to hold him closer. "I want to feel what it's like. I want to know if it's just you who does this to me." Some deeper part of my brain realized how selfish that sounded. "I'm sorry, I know you don't want to be anyone's experiment..."

Charlie looked up at me, green eyes deepening with an open heat I hadn't seen in them before.

"Let's go."

THE TAXI to the hotel was a blur. The driver chatted Charlie up with an accent so thick, I couldn't pick out a single word. Charlie's voice, on the other hand, was tinged with an edge of nerves. I realized I'd already reached for his hand at some point, and our fingers toyed with each other softly on the seat between our thighs. With each brush of our skin, my stomach filled with more and more flipping fish until there was an ocean of excitement and nerves churning in my gut.

Every movement of Charlie's body alerted the hairs on my skin like tiny sensation receivers. His feet were crossed over one another in the footwell, and there was just a peek of ankle skin visible below the hem of his pants. I felt my breathing speed up as I glanced at him out of the corner of my eye. His gaze was focused straight ahead as he responded to something the driver had said, but his body moved slightly closer to me while he spoke. By the time I spotted the sign for my hotel, we were pressed together from knee to hip to shoulder.

It took all of my self-control not to pull him even closer. My heart hammered for his nearness. My skin begged for his touch. My lips tingled for his kiss. I looked away, wondering how this one man could have so quickly turned me into such a confused mess.

I watched misty rain coat the windows of the overheated car and sighed a breath of relief when it pulled up in front of my hotel. I didn't realize how tightly I'd ended up clasping Charlie's hand until I reached for my wallet and felt his own grip loosen.

After paying the driver with some of my last cash, I grabbed Charlie's hand again and led him into the cold night air and through the hotel lobby to the elevators, not even caring that people would see me touching him so intimately. My need grew and grew as we neared the bank of elevators until it just became too much to contain and I found myself suddenly pulling Charlie into an alcove. I turned him and used my larger body to back him up against the wall. He opened his mouth to say something, but I just couldn't wait another moment to kiss him, to touch him, to taste what that delectable mouth offered.

The second my lips landed on his, I was gone.

Gone.

They tasted so sweet... pure and plump and ripe for the taking. I wanted to keep my mouth on his for the rest of my damned life if this was how good his kiss felt.

My hands held each side of his face while I plundered his mouth, my tongue seeking more and more and more. I wanted to learn every last bit of what it felt like to kiss the beautiful man, and I wanted to drag my lips down across the inches of creamy skin to find the warm expanse of silk under his clothes.

I'm kissing a man.

That sentence ran through my mind on repeat several times before I recognized I was mentally squealing with glee rather than freaking out. The adrenaline rush seemed to sober me up in a blink.

I'm kissing Charlie.

And dear god, it was hot as hell. Hotter than the time my high school girlfriend went down on me in the limousine on prom night. Hotter than the time my old girlfriend Charlotte let me try anal sex with her. Hotter than the night Darci answered the door in nothing but thigh-highs and stiletto heels.

All this from just a kiss.

I couldn't stop from lifting my fingers to trace his plump lips. I marveled at how similar and yet so very different they were from any others I'd ever kissed before. My eyes connected with Charlie's as I caressed his mouth, and my breath caught in my lungs when he softly kissed the tip of one of my fingers. The move should have been nothing, but somehow it changed *everything* in the blink of an eye.

I couldn't even imagine how incredible it would feel to do more than kiss Charlie. Without even thinking about it, I knew I wanted to see his creamy skin. I knew I wanted to taste it. My hands were on the hem of his shirt before my next breath, and it took me a minute to slow down and remember there was another person's feelings to consider. I didn't want to attack the guy if he was an unwilling participant.

I pulled back, chest heaving with shaky breaths. We stared at each other for a beat. He didn't say anything, so I forged ahead.

"I should have asked first, but I'd really like to kiss you some more and maybe not just on your lips... if... if you're willing, that is."

It was only then that I realized we were still in public.

10

CHARLIE

Charlie's Words To Live By:

When all else fails, kiss the fucker's brains out.

If I was willing? *If I was willing?*

Jesus, what the hell was he thinking? Of course I was willing. Experimenting het guy or not, I'd never seen or felt a more beautiful set of lips on a man. The idea that I could taste them again made my heart practically skitter out of my chest.

Did I care that he was straight?

I looked into his half-lidded eyes again and was swallowed whole.

Hell no, I didn't care. But I did want to understand what was going through his head before I took advantage of him.

"I thought you were straight?" I asked, not surprised at all how husky my voice sounded suddenly.

His beautiful face was adorably berry colored. "I am. I mean I was. I mean, I *am*," he said before wincing. "I mean... clearly I don't know what the hell I am."

I raised an eyebrow. "First things first. Have you ever kissed another man?"

"No," he said, blowing out a big breath. "And I've never wanted to before now. I mean, before this week. Before..." Another deep breath. "Before meeting you."

"My sister told me you had a girlfriend," I said, hoping like hell Cait had got it wrong.

Hudson's eyes widened. "I don't! I don't, I swear. We broke up. We... I mean, she thought I proposed, but I didn't. I didn't propose. It was all a big misunderstanding, I promise. I wouldn't cheat. I'm not a cheater. And I hate it when others cheat. Fuck!"

I jumped a little at his outburst and had to bite back a laugh when he continued. His hands were raking through his hair, leaving it messy and every which way.

"How many times am I going to say the word 'cheat'? I'm sorry, Charlie. I do this sometimes."

"Do what? Proposition unsuspecting Irishmen in gay bars?" I teased.

"What? No." Hudson looked up and realized I was taking the piss. His face cracked into a relieved smile. "Oh. You were joking. No, it's just... when I get nervous I say stupid shit. Actually I don't. Not usually. But around you for some reason, I do. And I have no idea why. Maybe it's because if I just keep talking, I won't do something stupid. Like... like touch you. Or ask you a personal question or... Or touch you—"

I stepped forward and reached for Hudson's hand to pull him toward the elevator. His eyes were practically bugging out of his eye holes, and the entire terrified lamb-to-slaughter look shouldn't have been so damned alluring, but it was.

"What floor?" I asked.

We were in his room within moments, the door solidly closed and locked behind us.

Hudson's hand was large and warm in mine even though it was plenty clammy with nerves. I sat him down on the edge of the chair in the corner of the room and then straddled his lap with a knee resting on the cushion to either side of his hips. Hudson's breathing ramped up even further, and his pupils widened quickly as I settled my arse on his thighs.

I cupped his face, reveling in the feel of the soft scruff on his cheeks.

"Are you sure you want to do this, Hudson?" I asked in a soft voice. "I'm fine being your experiment, but I'm not fine being your regret. Think about this before you—"

"I have," he blurted. "You have no idea how much I've thought about you. I can't *stop* thinking about you. The way you smile... and laugh... and light up when someone you know comes into the pub. You're like sunshine, Charlie, and I want a taste. Besides, I already told you. The whole time you were gone, I..."

His words sent my heart rate running on rabbit feet. My cock was already standing and cheering me on from its spot mashed against the zip of my jeans. I wanted desperately to rub it against Hudson, but I assumed one feel of mancock would send the poor hetero screaming down the hall and out into the October night.

"Then kiss me," I whispered, bringing my lips close to him but leaving the final gap for him to cross. "Please."

I felt his warm hands land gently on the top of my thighs and slide up the denim of my jeans until he reached my hips. His movements were hesitant until something shifted in his gaze, and then his touch became more sure. His fingers snuck under the hem of my jumper until they reached the skin of my sides and caused me to suck in a breath. A little sound escaped my throat, and it seemed to urge him on.

"You're so fucking beautiful," Hudson murmured. "I could spend all night staring at you... or just tracing your smooth skin with the tips of my fingers... or trying to make you smile and laugh."

The heat in his eyes might as well have been his touch all over my body. I felt every single inch of my skin desperate for the touch he'd just promised.

"Please," I breathed. "Touch me."

His warm hands moved further underneath my shirt to my lower back and up my spine to my shoulder blades. Hudson's eyes remained locked on mine. His tongue came out to lick his lips as if preparing to devour me. Goose bumps prickled along my skin everywhere, and I couldn't stop from rocking slightly into him with my hips.

When my stiff cock brushed Hudson's stomach, he squeezed his eyes closed and groaned through a full-body shudder.

His palms moved up to hook around my shoulders, and he used them to bring me forward that last little bit. Before our lips touched, I realized I'd been more turned on in those few moments of touch and eye contact than I'd ever been in hours of foreplay with someone else. Every nerve in my body was vibrating with need, and every corner of my soul wanted to be pressed up against him. My nostrils flared at the masculine scent of him. The smell of a man at the end of the day had always turned me on, but with Hudson it was magnified.

My lips brushed his lightly at first. It was enough to pull a soft "*Oh god*" out of him, and I couldn't help but smile. When I did, my lips brushed his again. I repeated the gentle, closed-mouth kisses until I felt his hands pull out from underneath my shirt and move to cradle the back of my head.

After a mumbled "*More*," Hudson changed the pace from barely there smooches to full-on snogfest. His hands moved around to cup my neck, and his full lips devoured mine. The moans and whimpers were clearly coming out of me this time, and it was all I could do to follow his lead. He kissed me like he'd been waiting to do it his entire life, and part of me wondered if that was the case. Not *me* specifically, but a man.

"Charlie," he gasped before moving to suck a mark up on my neck. This aggression was so incongruent with the insecure man I'd met that first night in the pub that I almost wondered if he was on something stronger than alcohol. Before the thought could catch hold, Hudson's lips reached my collarbone and dropped little sucking nibbles along its length. The fucker had found my weakness.

"Hud, yes there. *There*," I begged as his lips remained on my neck and his hands snuck back under my shirt to begin exploring my stomach and chest. "Please don't stop."

He grunted what sounded like the word *never* before his fingers found my nipples and lightly tweaked them. I hissed in response and tilted my hips up to grind my pelvis against him as hard as I could. I was desperate and begging, and the man had done little more than kiss me.

I brought my hands up to thread into his thick hair and pull his head back. The eyes that met mine were wild and glassy. His face was flushed, and his lips were red and puffy. Fuck if he wasn't the hottest thing I'd ever seen.

"What does it feel like?" I asked with a panting smirk.

"Huh? What does what feel like?" His chest heaved with labored breaths.

"Kissing a man for the first time?" I emphasized my question with another tilt of my hard cock into his belly. If a nob was going to scare him off, better it happen sooner than later.

His debauched look turned wicked.

"It feels like I finally know what the hell my brothers are always going on about," he said with a grin. "And it feels like I might not be able to ever give up the incredible taste and feel of your skin against my lips."

I tried to ignore the way his words in the second part of that made me feel. Instead, I focused on the first part. "Your brothers have tried to convert you, yeah?" My tease brought out more pink along his already flushed skin.

"Let's just say they're free with their bragging," he said, leaning in for more kisses. "And I'm starting to think if they were right about this, maybe they were right about other things. Which might mean very good times for you later."

A teasing Hudson Wilde. Who knew such a thing was possible?

"What kind of good times, Hudson?" Before I finished saying his name, his hands were on the button of my fly. My eyes shot to his and found them molten blue-green with lust.

"Can I take your clothes off, Charlie?"

11

HUDSON

Hudson's Words To Live By:
When all else fails, get naked.

The heat in Charlie's eyes was unmistakable.

Definitely on board with the naked plan.

"Do you want to get on the bed, Hudson?"

The way he said my name made me shudder. My pants strangled my throbbing erection, and I knew "get on the bed" might mean I'd be able to take my pants off and finally get some relief.

"Yes. God, yes," I sighed. "Are you... I mean, is that okay with you? I don't want to make you do anyth—"

He shut me up with a quick kiss before pulling back with a grin. "You are sexy as hell and clearly enthusiastic. That is most definitely okay with me, Mr. Wilde."

After kicking off his shoes, Charlie led me toward the large bed in the middle of the room. How I made it across the small space without tripping remained a mystery since I couldn't take my eyes off the way Charlie's small tight bottom flexed and shifted in his jeans. All I could think about was how that ass had probably had some other man's hands on it at some point. The thought of someone else's touch on Charlie's naked ass made me fucking crazy. It was a bizarre combination of lust and extreme jealousy.

I didn't want anyone else's hands on him.

At the same time, it was hard to picture my own hands on his bare ass. And wasn't that just ridiculous?

"Hudson?"

I looked up to see him staring down at me from where he knelt on the edge of the bed. I was frozen at the edge of a cliff. This was really happening.

"Yeah, good," I said, clearing my throat and attempting to smile. Shit was getting real. "Lead the way. To the bed. Well, you're already on the bed. Which means all that's left is me... me getting on the... the, ah..."

I swallowed.

Charlie's face softened, and a teasing glint reached his eye. "The bed?"

Instead of being mortified by my stupid nerves, I was comforted by his sweetness.

"I'm sorry," I said with a sigh, stepping up the final two steps until we were nose to nose. I knelt onto the bed in front of him and then reached out my hands to pull his hips toward mine. Once our lower bodies were pressed together and he could feel my excitement against his belly, I told him the truth. "I'm not going to pretend I'm completely at ease here. I'm obviously not. This is new to me. But you're the sexiest human being I've ever met, and I want to get you naked more than just about anything I've ever wanted in my entire life."

I leaned in and pressed my lips to the edge of his mouth before moving to kiss him on the cheek and then below his ear and down his slender neck into his collar. While I slid my lips along his skin, I asked him to be patient with me and told him how much I wanted to touch him and kiss him.

By the time I pulled the loose neck of his sweater down to reach his collarbone again, he was panting.

"Christ," Charlie gasped.

Climbing onto the actual bed made what we were doing more real, but instead of flipping out, I was revved up and nervous all at once. My hands were shaking, and I worried about saying or doing something stupid.

"Get naked," I blurted.

Charlie snorted as his eyes crinkled. "You don't fuck around, do you?"

I shook my head. "I'm sorry... I didn't mean it like that. I want to see you... want to touch you."

"Are you sure about this?" His hands were clutching the bottom of his sweater, and I willed them to lift it up and off.

"Uh-huh. Very sure. Take that off."

Charlie's nostril's flared. "I think I like bossy Hudson. Didn't know he existed, but I have to say... it's working for me."

His grin was adorable and made his lips look even more like ripe cherries than they already did. Within seconds, his sweater was off, revealing a soft threadbare concert tee underneath.

"You like One Direction?" I said in surprise.

He lifted an eyebrow and crossed his arms in front of his chest to hide the faded band logo. "Shut up."

"For real? Or are you wearing that ironically?" I couldn't help but tease him. He was so fucking cute. "Wait... are you *gay*?" I gasped the last word and put my hand in front of my mouth in feigned shock.

"Just for that, I'm going to keep it on and make you look at it." He unfolded his arms and held them out to the sides in a Rose from *Titanic* move. His arms were pale and slender with small but noticeable muscles. I wondered if they were from lifting kegs and equipment for the breweries and pub.

I stepped closer to him. "What if I don't want to look at it?" My voice came out huskier than normal, and it seemed to make the green of his eyes deepen. Another move closer and I reached for the hem of his shirt and skimmed the back of my fingers along the bare skin of his abdomen underneath. Charlie's breath hitched, and his muscles shifted beneath warm skin.

"Then I guess you'd better take it off," he breathed.

I felt the warm air of his breath at the base of my throat and was reminded of our height difference. His thick red hair was a glorious, sexy mess from pulling his sweater off, and I wanted to mess it up even more.

Before lifting his T-shirt up, I leaned in for another kiss. Charlie let out a soft moan the minute our lips met. His were so soft and plump, I wanted to suck them into my mouth and toy with them for hours. I let go of his shirt and cupped his face, surprised by the feel of his evening scruff but not in a spooked way. Just... different.

He smelled different too. Not artificial or full of beauty products but earthy and... and somehow alluring in a way I couldn't put my finger on. Something that reminded me of home. I moved my lips down his jaw to his throat and inhaled the crook of his neck.

"Mm, that feels good, but I'm sure I still smell like a pub," he murmured, half kiss-drunk and practically humming with need. "I should shower again. Shave and... ahhh." When I took his earlobe between my teeth, Charlie melted against me with a whimper. "Fuck, right there. That's the spot, Hudson."

My hands had made their way under his shirt again to the warm, smooth skin of his back. I pulled him close to me until I could feel his erection against my inner thigh. Good god, I wanted him so badly—it scared me how much I wanted him. But I was terrified of rushing my one wild night—the single moment of crazy I'd planned on allowing myself.

What if I let it pass too quickly and then it was over forever? I couldn't even fathom how much regret I'd feel if I looked back at my night with Charlie and decided I took things too fast.

I moved my mouth back to his and was surprised when he took the lead as soon as our lips touched again. He must have thought I was moving too slow, and I was 100 percent on board with him setting the pace.

I moved my hands down to the waistband of his jeans and wanted to slide my fingers into the back of them to feel the cheeks of his ass, but I hesitated. What if instead of moving too slow, I was moving too fast? How fast did guys move? I wouldn't be that forward with a woman, so did that automatically mean I shouldn't be that forward with a man either?

Instead of grabbing his ass, I rested my hands on his waist as if we were slow dancing at prom. *Stupid.* My head began to spin with all kinds of random thoughts. The alcohol buzz had worn off, but the buzz of how-awkward-am-I-right-now remained strong.

Where the hell should I put my hands? God, his tongue feels amazing in my mouth. What if guys don't kiss this long and I look like an idiot for wanting to kiss him so much?

Charlie pulled back and gazed at me. He looked so incredibly hot and thoroughly kissed, my dick jerked hard at the sight of him.

"What's wrong?" I asked, sure that something in my stupid brain had been broadcast to him. "Is it the kissing? Too much kissing? Or my hands? Was that weird? That was weird." I clasped the offending objects together behind my back.

"You okay, Hudson?"

"Yeah, of course," I said, leaning back in to pick up where we left off. Charlie dodged me and moved back, pulling out of my reach. I knew I should have stuck my hands down his pants earlier. Then he wouldn't have been able to get away as easily.

"We should slow down," he said. His hands found his hair again and clutched thick hanks of it while he blew out a breath. My eyes went straight to the exposed strip of pale skin between the hem of his tee and the low waist of his jeans.

And then my eyes went even lower... to the prominent bulge fighting with faded denim. My heart banged like giant tribal drums in my chest.

"You're really hard," I said without thinking. Of course he was hard. And I already knew that from feeling it against my leg. Why was I stating the obvious?

Charlie barked out a laugh. "Ah, yeah. Yeah, Hudson, I'm hard as fucking nails. And you?"

I pulled at my own uncomfortable crotch. "Harder than I've ever been in my entire life," I admitted. "So why'd you stop?"

His entire face lightened with relief. "Thought maybe you needed a break."

I nodded. "Yeah. Okay." I looked around the room as if assessing its decor. My fingers clasped each other again hard enough to turn my knuckles white. "This is nice. I like the... ah... wall color in here."

My cool act needed a little work.

I looked back at those incredibly green eyes. "Break over," I declared in a rush. And then I tackled him onto the bed.

12

CHARLIE

Charlie's Lament:

Shoulda packed condoms. Size: big.

Hudson caught me off guard, but I was up for whatever he had in mind. If he wanted a male body to experiment on, I'd already decided I was all in. Something about the Yank both put me at ease and revved me up. The man was glorious to look at and even better to touch and taste.

His mouth was on mine before I had a chance to catch my breath. My hands went to the buttons on his shirt and began working them open as fast as possible.

"How many damned things are there?" I gasped between Hudson's nibbles to my lower lip. "Fuck, get it off already."

His grin was irresistible as he pulled back and yanked the entire thing over his head, revealing a muscled chest with the perfect amount of dark brown hair covering it.

"Nngh," I said. "Unghh."

"Acceptable?" he teased with a shy grin.

I ran my fingertips through the chest hair to feel the taut skin over his pecs. "Mm-hmm."

Hudson rucked up my T-shirt, exposing my lily-white ghost skin and the few ginger hairs sprinkled over my lame-ass bird chest. His eyes zeroed in on my nipples, and his tongue came out to wet his lips. Those hungry eyes made my stomach tighten in anticipation.

Whether he realized it or not, Hudson was dry-humping my leg with the thickest, hardest cock I'd felt in ages. I pushed up into it without thinking, drawing a deep moan from his throat before his lips landed on one of my nipples. He sucked it into his hot mouth, and my eyes rolled back in my head as I arched back into the mattress.

"Mm-hm," I repeated, burying my fingers in his thick hair to hold his head against my chest. The suction on the tender nub might as well have been on my dick for how much it was stealing my breath and making my cock leak. I wanted his mouth on me in other places, but I knew that was about as likely to happen with Mr. Wilde-But-Straight as getting first place in the international dog trials with a new pup.

Hudson moved his hands down to work the opening of my jeans. The minute I felt the back of his knuckles brush against the top of my pubic hair, I gritted my teeth against the impulse to come all over his damned hand.

"Fuck," I blurted. "Fuck, Hudson. You're killing me."

I quickly took over and worked the rest of my clothes off as fast as I could while he remained braced above me on the bed. My eyes zoomed in on the pulse point thrumming under the skin on the side of his throat. Once my clothes were off, I went to work on his until we were both blessedly naked on the bed together.

"Look at you," he murmured, shifting onto his side next to me so he could run a hand down my chest to my lower belly. My dick jumped as his hand got near it, and I squeezed my eyes closed to will his grip closer to where I so desperately needed it. I knew he needed time to get used to all of this dick business, but I wasn't sure how much patience I had for it.

Hudson trailed his fingertips through the trail of hair between my navel and the nest of curls at the base of my cock.

"Red," he murmured. "Red everywhere."

"You're killing me," I said under my breath. "Seriously. Just fucking kill me now and get it over with."

He grinned up at me like he'd discovered a new planet. "This is sexy as hell. A happy trail surrounded by so much smooth, pale skin." His eyebrows furrowed as he traced his fingertip over to my hip. "I can see your hip bones. Makes me want to feed you."

I rolled my eyes. "Yes, Hudson. I know I look twelve years old."

His eyes locked on mine, the blue-green shining with an emotion I couldn't name. "No. You're perfect, Charlie. I've never seen anyone as enticing as you."

Oh fuck this. No. No sweetness. No tenderness. It's one fucking night. His experiment. Don't fall prey to those meaningless words from his gorgeous lips.

"Suck my cock," I commanded in a gruff voice.

My tone startled him, and there was a part of me that felt like an arsehole. But if he truly wanted to experiment with a man, he needed to get over the dick-shame bullshit.

"Will you tell me if I do something wrong?" he asked in a soft voice. Wrinkles of concern marred his forehead.

His words were so earnest, so vulnerable, I wanted to take him in my arms and apologize before sucking his own dick to make up for my rudeness.

But I didn't.

"Haven't you ever gotten a blow job before?" I asked instead. "That should give you some do's and don'ts."

Hudson swallowed before glancing at my erection and slowly reaching out to brush his fingers over it. The feel of his touch on me was almost enough to make me blow. If I hadn't lost some of my excitement by being an arse, I probably would have come on his hand right then.

"Yes," I hissed. "Feels good when you touch me. Please."

His touch became surer as he wrapped his hand around my

length and tugged gently. His thumb came up to swipe across the slit where precum was making a sticky mess.

"I've never... seen someone uncut up close like this," he admitted. "Does it... I mean, do I need to do anything... special or...?"

The wrinkles were back on his forehead as he glanced up at me, and his look of insecurity hit me like a kick to the chest.

I reached out to brush my palm against his cheek. "Come up here," I whispered.

He stretched back up so we were face-to-face again. "Did I do something wrong? Is it all the questions? I can shut up. I'm not usually like this, I swear."

I pulled his face down for a kiss. It was tender and slow, and I tried to tell him with my lips that he was all I wanted and needed in that moment. "I like you like this," I whispered without thinking. "You didn't do anything wrong. Let me make you feel good, Hudson. I want to taste you, okay?"

"Are you sure? I can do it. I *want* to do it. I just don't really know how yet."

"Let me show you," I said with a grin, appreciating the way he used the word *yet*. "You can focus on what parts of it you like and make mental notes for things to try on me. How does that sound?"

"It sounds like more than I'd be mentally capable of with your tongue on my dick," he said with a straight face. "So it might take a few practice rounds before I get all the notes down."

I snorted and pushed him onto his back before crawling down his body. "I see. Then we should get started right away. This might take all night."

I dropped openmouthed kisses along his luscious chest hair down to the trail below his navel. My hair dragged along his skin, making his muscles twitch.

"Fuck that's sexy," I murmured before dragging the tip of my tongue down the arrow of dark hair to the wet tip of his cock.

"My thoughts exactly," Hudson said on a sharp inhale. His strong hands held my head, but I could feel him working hard to keep from moving my head where he wanted it. "Sexy. So sexy," he murmured.

I licked the fat drop of precum sliding down the dark pink head of his cut cock. He tasted of salt and promise. I wanted to suck more of it out of him, so I immediately licked his shaft and drew it deep into my mouth.

He was hard as fuck, and the sounds coming out of him made me just as hard.

"Oh shit. Oh god. Fuck, fuck," he chanted. Hudson's voice was husky and rough, and his fingers tightened in my hair. "Charlie. Charlie, *please*."

I had one hand on his shaft below my mouth, and the other cupped his balls and gently rolled them in my hand, sliding my thumb over the furry, wrinkled skin of the drawn-up sac. The feel, taste, and smell of him were going to make me shoot before he did. I sucked and tugged, losing myself in pleasing him until I heard him cry out.

"No!" he gasped. I pulled away quickly, assuming I'd done something to hurt him, when his spunk shot out and hit me full in the face. The warm fluid took me by surprise, but my shock was nothing compared to Hudson's horror. The look on his face was almost comical.

"Oh my god! Charlie, shit. I'm so sorry. I tried to warn you I was going to come, but the only word I could get out was 'no.' I can't believe I just did that. I can't believe—"

"It's okay," I said, trying to smile to reassure him. I kept one eye closed while I attempted to wipe the junk out of it with a knuckle. "I thought I hurt you or something."

He reached out his hands and began wiping the cum off my face with delicate swipes of his fingers and thumbs. The concern in his eyes was sweet as hell, and the creases in his forehead just confirmed how worried he was about it.

"I'm sorry," he said again. After a second, he held his messy hands up and grinned sheepishly. "What the hell do I do now?"

"If you were really gay, you'd lick them clean."

Hudson hesitated for a beat before he realized I was joking. "Maybe if it was *your* spunk, I would," he said, taking me by surprise.

"But I have no interest in tasting myself. Tried it once when I was a teen and decided it wasn't my thing."

I stood up to lead him to the en suite so he could wash his hands. My dick bitched and moaned the whole way, especially when I turned to see Hudson's naked body standing tall in the brighter light of the bathroom beside me. Fuck, he was something to look at. Muscled thighs atop long legs, capped with a meaty, squishable arse. I wanted to put my hands all over him.

Once his hands were clean, he turned to look down at my little problem.

"Get on the bed," he said with a low voice that made my stomach drop. He leaned in and kissed my lips softly, lingering along the bottom one before sucking it into his mouth and running the tip of his tongue along it. The move only made me harder. "We're nowhere close to done yet."

I was on my back in the center of the big bed in half a second, splayed out and desperate for more of Hudson's hands on me and his commanding voice in my ear.

13

HUDSON

Hudson's Words To Live By:

Oral sex is like Christmas. 'Tis better to give than to receive. Oh, who am I kidding? 'Tis better to do both.

Hudson's Words To Live By: (Take Two)

Oral sex is like voting. One should do it early and often.

Suddenly it was my turn to get Charlie off, and I felt like I was under the spotlight on center stage. There he was, laid out in all of his creamy-skinned glory, and I had a momentary panic of not knowing what to do with him.

The man must have read my mind.

"Come up here and kiss me, Hudson," he said softly. His voice was like a siren song, and I followed it to his mouth.

As soon as I went in for the kiss, I naturally slid on top of him and felt the expanse of his naked body against mine. It felt so damned good. Even though he was smaller than I was, he felt solid and warm, strong and firm. His dick poked up into my lower abdomen, and the feel of it only made me hotter for him. There was not one bit of strangeness about the fact he was a man instead of a woman. Nothing about that part of it made me feel wrong. What made me feel odd was the slight tremor of unease that this was only a onetime deal.

But it was. It was my one wild night, and I was going to make the most of it.

I moved my mouth down along the angle of his chin to the slender expanse of his neck. He smelled delicious and tasted both salty and sweet. My fingers found one of his nipples before I decided to move down and nibble on it. Charlie threw his head back with a hiss and wrapped his legs around my back. The move aligned his cock with my chest as he arched up into me.

"Yes, Hud," he breathed. "Feels good. Your mouth on me, your lips..."

I ran my fingertips down his breastbone to his belly button. His stomach muscles contracted and bunched as my hands roved lower.

"Please," he whimpered as his cock pushed into my chest again. "Please, Hudson."

He was hard as hell and dripping. The sticky fluid from his tip made a track up my torso and lit a fire in my groin. I tucked my chin to my chest so I could take a swipe at it with my tongue to see what it tasted like.

The sound that came out of Charlie when my tongue hit the skin of his cockhead made my balls tighten. He was sucking in air and whimpering with need. It made my desire to please him even greater than before.

I wanted to make it good for him. I wanted him to have the best orgasm of his life.

My brain frantically flipped through the Rolodex of every oral-sex tip I'd ever heard my brothers spout. I mouthed the tip and then sucked it onto my tongue and licked underneath.

Another hiss from Charlie. "Whatever you do, don't stop."

I wasn't planning on it.

My hand cupped his balls like he'd done to mine. I pulled more of his shaft into my mouth and tried not to gag when it went too far. As soon as I pulled off a bit, I was back at it, trying to suck it in as deep as I could stand since I knew that would feel good for him.

I gagged again and kept trying.

"'S'okay," Charlie slurred. His hands were gentle on the side of my face. "Slow down, baby, it's okay."

The endearment made my insides cramp. Tears were already dripping from the corners of my eyes from the gagging, but I wanted so much to please him.

I kept going, sucking and licking and jacking as best I could until he couldn't help but rock his cock in and out of my mouth with his hips.

"Gonna come," he gasped.

I pulled off and jacked him while tonguing his tight sac. Gagging and spitting out his come wouldn't have been very elegant, so I knew better than to try and swallow on my first attempt.

He came with a cry and a clutch of his fingers in my hair. White ribbons shot across his flawless skin, and I scrambled up to taste them. I wanted every single bit of him I could get.

"Jesus fuck, Hudson." His voice was gritty and hoarse. "What the hell?"

After one last pass of my tongue along his skin, I moved up next to him on the bed and collapsed.

"God, you're sexy when you come." I lay on my side and ran my hand down his chest until it rested on his opposite hip. "Will you let me do that again in a little while?"

He stared at me. "In what scenario would I say no to that question?"

I grinned and nestled closer to his side, inhaling the masculine scent from his armpit. "You smell delicious. Not like week-old cheese. And this red armpit hair is just about adorable."

"You just called my pit stink adorable."

"No. I called it delicious. I called the baby ginger fuzz adorable. Like a kitten."

He snorted and smacked my shoulder. "Fuck off."

I sniffed again. "Man stink. I think I like it. Is that weird? I liked how your balls smelled too. Am I a freak?"

Charlie rolled onto his side until he was facing me. He ran his hand up and down my arm. "No. That's all very common, I promise. I may have enjoyed getting a whiff or two of you as well. Surely, though, this isn't the first you've realized you like those things?"

I thought about it. "I keep racking my brain to come up with any signs I might have missed that I found another man attractive, but I just... I can't think of anything. And it makes absolutely no sense. My brothers are gay. Do you have any idea how many gay bars and clubs I've been to? I've dirty danced with men, had them hit on me and grind against me on the dance floor. I've seen my brothers' boyfriends shirtless on the tennis court and at the swimming pool. I've been in locker rooms with half-naked men. Not once did I feel that pull I feel with you. Not once."

"I still can't believe you have five gay brothers. You must be taking the piss."

"I'm not... taking the piss. Whatever that means. If you don't believe me, I'll get them on the phone right now," I said. "Make them... I don't know..."

"Pull out their gay licenses?" he teased. "Drop trou and wank each other?"

I pretended to gag. "Stop. Please. We're talking about my brothers."

His face creased with confusion. "All jokes aside. How the hell do you have five gay brothers? And if your brothers are all gay, how did you not know you were too?"

"I'm not gay," I said without thinking. It was a habit, I guessed, after years of people assuming I was gay because everyone else in my family seemed to be.

Big mistake.

Charlie's eyes lost their twinkle, and his mouth closed. He rolled back over until he was looking at the ceiling. "Right. Not gay. My mistake."

Fuck.

I laid my hand on his shoulder and tried to ignore his slight flinch. "No. That's not what I meant."

He turned his head back to lock eyes with me. "But it's true, Hudson. Both of us know this was just a onetime experiment for you. It's fine. It's honestly not really my business. You wanted to see what it was like with a man and you did. I was up for a nice orgasm. No harm done. One night is all we have anyway, yeah?"

I'd lost him. The easy intimacy we'd shared that evening evaporated the minute I reminded him I was straight. The loss of it gutted me more than I would have expected.

I moved my hand up to brush through his messy waves. "I'm sorry," I whispered before dropping a light kiss on his shoulder where my hand had been. "Please be patient with me. I didn't mean it like that. I'm trying to be honest with you, and until I met you, Charlie, I *wasn't* gay. And now... and now I don't know what I am other than very fucking happy to be naked in this bed with you right now."

He turned back toward me and leaned into my body, nestling his face in my neck and nipping at the skin there.

"I'm the one who's sorry, Hudson," he mumbled against my skin. "This must be very strange for you, yet here you are sucking cock like you've been doing it from birth. Well done, you."

I barked out a laugh and pinched his ass.

"Call me a cocksucker one time and I'll make that pinch hurt worse next time," I promised.

He leaned his head back to fake a look of innocence. "But technically you *are* one, right?"

I rolled him over and wriggled my fingertips between his ribs in retaliation. His screeching and laughing led us to wrestle around on the bed, tickling and humping each other until we found ourselves turned head to foot. By the time I realized I was in the middle of my first sixty-nine, I was basically fucking Charlie's face while gagging on his cock.

The Hudson Wilde who'd mastered vanilla-flavored missionary sex with a string of sweet girlfriends was long gone, and I didn't dare wonder who the hell this sex-crazed man was who'd taken his place.

Hudson's Words To Live By: (Take Three)

Oral sex is like competitive sports. Go big or go home.

14

CHARLIE

Charlie's Words To Live By:
Fuck Forever Man.

After the second pair of orgasms, it took us a while to catch our breath. Any trace of alcohol buzz had long since worn off, and I got up to fetch a bottle of water on the desk.

"Want some?" I asked, returning to the bed. The duvet was piled up in a messy heap at the bottom of the bed, and Hudson lay sprawled out under just a thin white sheet. His hair looked like he'd gone hillwalking in a stiff wind.

He sat up and leaned against the headboard before accepting the bottle. "Thanks."

"Feeling okay?" I asked. "No regrets?"

Hudson swallowed a few sips. When he handed back the bottle and looked up at me, his eyes were intense.

"I regret you're not in this bed with me right now."

Jesus, Mary, and Joseph.

I set down the water and climbed onto his lap, straddling him again the way I had in the chair earlier.

"Better?"

"Mm. Much." He kissed me softly and ran his fingers through my hair. "Your hair is the first thing I noticed about you. Did I tell you that already?"

"Not in so many words. With you it was those eyes. They kill me," I admitted. "They make me want to do things to you, Hudson."

"I give you permission to do things to me as soon as I recover from the last time," he said with an enthusiastic grin.

His hands kept playing with my hair, and it was putting me into a trance. "I take it you've never had the luxury of playing with a man's long hair before," I teased.

He chuckled softly. "A man's? Definitely not. I'll just add that to the list."

"What list?" My own fingers found the edges of his hair on the back of his neck and began returning the favor. I ran blunt nails lightly along his scalp until he hummed in pleasure.

"The list of things I thought I'd never do."

I rolled off him and lay on my side next to him. He slid down to mirror my position so we were facing each other, heads on separate pillows. I reached for one of his hands to thread my fingers through it. Part of me was laughing at myself for acting like he was my boyfriend instead of a hookup, but I wasn't experienced enough with casual sex to know how to behave with a one-off.

"What's something else you think you'll never do?" I asked.

Hudson thought for a minute. "I mean, besides the obvious ones like murder... I guess... I don't think I'd ever quit my job without having another one lined up. What else? Run away from my family. Deliberately let someone down. Those are probably the biggest ones. What about you?"

"Mmm, probably leave Ireland. Certainly I wouldn't turn my back on my family which means never leaving Fig and Bramble either. I'll protect our heritage with everything I have."

Hudson seemed to pale. "Wait, what? You're related to Devlin Murray?"

My stomach dropped as I realized I hadn't told him I was a Murray. Why had I thought that was a good idea?

I winced. "I'm his nephew. My dad and Dev own the company jointly. But my dad recently remarried and fucked off to Brazil, leaving Uncle Dev with power of attorney."

Hudson fell onto his back, pulling his hand out of mine and putting his arm over his face. "I didn't know." His voice sounded hollow. "So when you sounded so proud of the inn's history it was because..."

"It's my family legacy. My dad still owns the majority share, so when he passes, the business comes to me. I'm the heir for what that's worth."

He was quiet after that for a while. I wasn't sure if it had something to do with mixing business with pleasure or if he'd suddenly felt like he was sleeping with the boss or something, but there was a noticeable difference in his body language. There might as well have been a wall of ice bricks between us in the bed.

After a while, I couldn't stand the distance any longer.

I climbed on top of him and pressed my nose into his neck, opening my mouth and sucking some skin between my lips until I could nip it hard with my teeth. Hudson yelped and pulled away.

"Fuck, Charlie. Ow."

"You said I had permission to do things to you. I've come to collect," I promised with a thrust of my hardening cock into his belly. "Whatever got into your brain needs to get the fuck out. You're mine until the wee hours of the morning when you have to catch the airport shuttle, yeah?"

Hudson let out a defeated sigh and smiled that soft smile of his. "Yeah."

"Say it," I growled, thrusting again.

"You're awfully cute when you get mean," he said with a soft smile, pushing my hair behind an ear again and peppering soft kisses on my chin, my jaw, my cheeks, and eyelids. "Feisty redhead," he murmured, continuing the sweet and tender torture.

"Fuck that, Hudson Wilde. Say it," I gasped.

His lids dropped as his face flushed. "I'm yours, Charlie Murray. Yours."

This time around there was nothing sweet about what happened between us. I braced his hands above his head with a tight grip and attacked his mouth with mine. I ground my cock into his until he was gasping and begging, and then I refused to let him come. Over and over again.

When he tried to bring his hands down to touch himself or me, I barked at him to stop. When he was unable to stop arching up into me, I shoved him onto his belly and thrust my cock along his crease instead, my copious precum providing more than enough lube to slick the way. He begged for relief until his words no longer made sense. Until he was shaking and sobbing and I thought we both might break apart into a million pieces.

There was a tiny hidden part of me that was furious—angry beyond measure for him coming into my life just long enough to get me on the fucking hook before he took off again forever. That part of me wanted to punish him. Wanted to make him regret his little "experiment" and vow never to try it on with another man.

I licked and kissed and sucked down his back until I was tasting the sticky trail left by my own pulsing cock. Hudson's wrecked voice was muffled by the pillow, but I could make out whimpers of *need to come* and *Charlie* and *please, baby*.

My hands spread his cheeks with zero tenderness, and my tongue landed on his arsehole with even less. I ate him out like I was teaching him a fucking lesson, but god only knew what it was a lesson in.

My balls were crying out for relief. All I wanted was to kneel up and shove my dick so hard in that virgin arse, Hudson would walk funny for weeks. But I didn't. Of course I wouldn't.

Instead, I licked and sucked and pressed my tongue into him until he was just loose enough for me to slide a spit-slicked finger in and find the spot that would bring his big crazy experiment to an end.

Once he was almost passed out in a pool of his own cum and drool, I shot my load all over his beautiful muscled back and arse before washing up and tiptoeing out into the night.

If there was one thing I knew for sure, it was that one more look at his bedroom eyes would tumble me right over the cliff into a deep fucking vat of wanting what I couldn't have.

My sister had been right. Fuck Forever Man. From here on out it was One-Night Man or nothing. My heart couldn't take anything more than that.

15

HUDSON

Hudson's Words To Live By:

When you're overwhelmed and exhausted, ask for an extra pack of those cinnamon cookie things on the airplane. They won't fix anything, but they're very tasty.

The flight home was long as hell. I'd expected to see Charlie still there when my phone alarm went off, but he must have ducked out after I'd passed out. As much as it had stung, I couldn't blame him. If his preference was for a one-and-done, it made sense he didn't want an awkward run-in the next day.

But it still rankled. Maybe it hadn't been anything special to him, but it sure had been to *me*. Seeing the empty bed next to me put a painful lump in my throat that refused to go away.

My night with Charlie had changed things. Kissing him had gotten me harder than any encounter I'd ever had with a woman. Something about being with him had made me feel like I could be myself more than I'd been with a woman. Maybe I could be rougher or bossier, or maybe I could let go of worrying about being polite and gentle for a little while. When he'd taken control during our last encounter, I felt like I'd floated way past normal sex into some kind of upgraded sex stratosphere. Whatever it was, it had blown my fucking mind. And even more than the sex, I knew with Charlie I'd never felt quite so... *myself* before.

After realizing that, I began to second-guess every relationship I'd ever had. The guilt swamped me. Had I ever given any of my girlfriends my true self? Was it because I was supposed to be with men all along? Was I gay?

No. I didn't think so. I'd been plenty attracted to the women I'd dated. Granted, I'd never truly been in love before, but I'd honestly cared for and enjoyed the women I'd been with. Did that make me bisexual? I didn't like that term. It had always seemed... limiting. Like there were only two choices. What about nonbinary people or transgender people? Bisexual implied you liked both sexes, but what about gender? It was all so confusing to me. I tried to recall conversations with my siblings about sexuality.

Was I pansexual maybe? Would that be more accurate?

Did it matter? Did I have to choose a label because of this strange change in my circumstances?

No. This was ridiculous. I wasn't anything different than I'd been before. How could I suddenly not be straight after all these years? And if I wasn't straight, what would everyone say when they learned all the Wilde boys were gay or bi? It was too weird, too unbelievable. I couldn't stand being in the spotlight on a regular day, but being the punchline in a joke about the "last one finally succumbing" seemed like hell on earth to me.

I needed to shut my fucking brain down and put the crazy night behind me. I decided to relegate it to what it truly was: my one wild night. No one needed to know. My family *sure as hell* didn't need to know. They would ask me questions until the cows came home, until Grandpa's long-dead cattle came back from the dead and came home. That's how insane the inquisitions from my siblings would be if anyone found out I'd kissed a man. They'd label me and revisit my entire past. They'd force me to the clubs and set me up on dates "just to see" who I might be attracted to under this new reality. No, thanks.

So there it was. What happened in Ireland stayed in Ireland.

But I couldn't stop thinking about Charlie Murray. The Charlie I'd fallen so quickly for turned out to be one of the Murrays who'd be devastated to lose control of their family pub. And I was the one to make the recommendation to Bruce Ames about the acquisition. How would Charlie feel if he knew what I'd really been there to do? Would he hate me? Would he be happy? Did he know the business was in money trouble?

I didn't want to do anything to upset him, but at the same time, my promotion was riding on this project.

Thinking about it had exhausted me. I hadn't been able to sleep on the plane and when I'd attempted to work on my laptop, I hadn't been able to focus. Thoughts of Charlie had consumed me until I felt sick with worry. Why had he left that morning? Had I done something to upset him? Had I let him down somehow? My biggest fear was having done or said something that made him feel as though I was using him. Had he felt like I only wanted to experiment with a man, any man? Because that wasn't it. Did he know I couldn't possibly have felt this way for another man besides him?

What if his feelings were hurt? What if he tried to erase the memory of me by staying in Cork another night and going back to that bar to find someone else? I couldn't bear the thought of another man seeing what he looked like when he came, touching his smooth skin and hearing his sweet laughter. He was so kind... what if someone took advantage of him? What if he fell in with a new guy and got left again? It would break his heart.

By the time I landed in Dallas, I was confused and overwhelmed. Instead of driving home to my apartment in the city, I drove straight to Doc and Grandpa's ranch in Hobie.

As soon as my car came to a stop in front of the old farmhouse, the front door opened and a motley crew of three dogs came scrambling out. I reached down and threw my arms around the coonhound.

"Grumpy Gus," I murmured into his mottled brown fur. "Sweet boy."

Grandpa stood at the front door, illuminated by the porch light. He held a kitchen towel in his hands as if he'd been drying dishes when he heard the car, and I could see the confusion on his face at the sight of me. I hadn't called or texted to let him know I was coming and I had to look like death warmed over. I knew it didn't matter—they'd be happy to see me regardless.

After a quick pet on the head for the two smaller dogs, I brushed my hands together and stumbled up the steps and straight into Grandpa's arms. I was taller than he was now, but the broad shoulders of the lifelong rancher had always made me feel safe. His strong arms wrapped around me and held me tight. My eyes stayed dry, but it was a close thing.

"It's okay. You're home now," Grandpa said gruffly. "Whatever it is, it'll be fine, I'm sure. Come inside, son."

I followed him inside without meeting his eyes. My feet automatically led me toward the sitting-room side of the kitchen where Doc was dozing in a recliner with a worn afghan pulled over him.

"Liam, sweetheart, wake up," Grandpa said. "Hudson's here."

Doc's eyes were unfocused at first, but as he realized I was really there, a big smile overtook his face.

"Hey. I thought you were in Ireland on business?"

"I was. I just got in this evening." I took a seat and kicked off my shoes before putting my feet up on the coffee table and slouching down into the deep cushions of the sofa.

Grandpa sat next to me and squeezed my knee. "We're glad you're here. How did it go?"

"Fine." I shook my head. "I mean, the work was fine, but..."

I didn't even know how to begin. I had a moral dilemma, and I needed their guidance.

Doc and Grandpa projected their usual calm and soothing air. Doc was one of the most patient men I'd ever met, and Grandpa wasn't far off. The two of them were so easy to be with, I knew if I didn't speak up on my own, they'd simply leave me be. They'd never push or prod.

"I guess there's something I need your help figuring out," I began. "I was sent over there to assess a historic pub and brewery for majority-share acquisition. The assessment was straightforward, and it's definitely a good investment for Ames."

Grandpa sat back and crossed his arms in front of his chest. "So what's the problem?"

I picked at the worn edge of a sofa cushion near my thigh. "While I was there, I met a few members of the Murray family and learned all about the pub's history." I looked up at my grandfathers. "It's truly amazing. They've been there for hundreds of years, right at the Cliffs of Moher on the coast. It's gorgeous and... *special.* The property has been in the family for so long, I can't picture it being owned by an American, a stranger to the Murray family and someone who doesn't give a damn about all that history. It's... it's not right."

"Why are they selling the shares?" Doc asked. "I assume it's not something Ames is considering taking by force. If the family is selling and Ames is buying, that's really all there is to it."

"I don't think they want to sell. From what I could piece together, it's owned by two brothers, Sean and Devlin. Sean always managed the books, but about ten months ago he remarried and moved to Brazil. Since then, Devlin, who used to manage the brewery operations, has had to do his best with the finances on his own. I found evidence Devlin made some mistakes with the accounting and wound up trying to make up for it with his own money. It's all fine now, except I'm guessing Devlin is in personal financial trouble. If that's the case, maybe he's selling his shares because it's the only way he can recoup his personal investment. Once I got to thinking about it, I remembered something Bruce mentioned before I left on the trip. I think Devlin originally wanted to sell only a portion of his shares, but Bruce said he wouldn't consider it unless it was a majority share in the business."

"Hmm," Grandpa mused, rubbing the coonhound's big furry butt with his bare foot. "So maybe he doesn't need as much money as this transaction would bring him, but he doesn't feel like he has any other option."

I shrugged. "I mean… this is a ton of assumption and speculation. But that's what I think."

Doc shifted in his recliner to face me more fully. "So what if you could find an investment option with Devlin that would be just as exciting for Bruce but would save the pub from being majority owned by Ames?"

"That's what I've been wondering. I can't see how Bruce truly wants to own a historic pub in Ireland as an investment. Honestly, I think he took a trip over there, liked the feel of the place and the taste of their custom brews, and wanted a piece of it. It's more of a pet project than an actual serious addition to his portfolio. So how do I finagle it so he gets his pet project without messing with the ownership of this historic pub?"

Grandpa stood up and stretched. "Let me grab us some thinking juice," he said with a wink.

"Bailey's please," Doc called out with a grin. "On ice if it's not too much trouble, sweetheart."

"Anything for you, dearest," Grandpa teased. "Hudson?"

"Same. Thanks."

I turned to Doc. "What about beer distribution rights in North America?"

"Does the brewery have capacity for that?" he asked. "You'd have to research the profitability of it. Make sure it's as good of an investment if you're going to recommend it instead of the acquisition."

"Are you going back over there?" Grandpa asked.

"I don't think so. I have to give my report to Bruce on Monday and see what happens. On the one hand, if the acquisition happens, I might get to go back over there and it will go a long way toward helping me make VP at Ames. But if it doesn't, then the Murrays will get to retain more control over their family business which would make Ch… them happier. So… I kind of have to hope the acquisition falls through. But that will mean I don't get to go back to Ireland again." I shrugged. "At least that family will have retained ownership of their legacy. That's more important than me making vice president anyway.

"I wonder if I could come up with other ideas in case Bruce doesn't like the distribution one," I mused. "Something that would be a win-win for both Ames Investments and the Murray family."

Doc scrambled out of the recliner and came over to pull me into his arms. He smelled familiar, and his hug was comforting.

"You're a good man, Hudson Wilde," he murmured into my hair. "Not everything can be solved tonight. Now head to bed and get some sleep. You've got to be dead on your feet. No problems get solved on a low tank of fuel and sleep."

He was right. After wishing them both good night, I made my way to the guest room and fell into bed. I'd only have Sunday to get my brain together for work the following day, so I needed all the sleep I could get.

Despite my best intentions, I fell asleep to memories of my hands and lips skating across creamy skin sprinkled with freckles. The vision of Charlie's freckled face smiling at me from across the Fig and Bramble bar made me feel safe and comfortable. Happy.

While I slept, the four-leaf clover I'd found outside the pub sat on the bedside table safely ensconced in a tiny keepsake jar I'd found in the airport gift shop in Cork.

16

CHARLIE

Charlie's Words To Live By:
Never trust a bloody Yank.

"Fuck him! No seriously. *Fuck. Him*," I bit out. "I hate him. Just another corporate wanker who's out to make rich people richer on the backs of small business. I should have known."

Cait's eyes were wide as saucers as she joined me on my little sofa with two mugs of tea. We'd just retreated to my cottage after a horrific and enlightening meeting with Uncle Devlin in which we'd been told about some changes happening around here. I'd have been throwing back shots of something stronger if Cait hadn't announced her pregnancy a few days before. She'd made me promise not to tempt her with the good stuff.

"Shh, you're making my headache worse, and you're scaring Mama."

I reached my hand down to soothe my pup. "Sorry, sweetie," I cooed to my best girl. "Next time you see Uncle Dev, feel free to nip at his man candy to make up for ever giving Hudson Wilde the time of fucking day." I looked up at my sister with narrowed eyes. "And so help me, if I ever see that arsehole around here again, don't be surprised if you hear a scream come from over the edge of the cliffs."

I was desperate for this new anger to overtake the heartsick feeling that had been gnawing at me since I'd left Hudson in Cork the month before. Since I was a bloody idiot who couldn't help but fall for all the wrong people, I'd allowed the man to steal my heart and leave me gasping with loneliness since his absence. Finding out he was responsible for some American investor to cheapen my family's history by trying to franchise Fig and Bramble... well, that was just the icing on the bloody cake. Typical. Just my fucking luck.

My sister rolled her eyes. "Drama queen," she muttered. "It could be worse. Dev could have lost the whole damned business instead of just franchising it out. If Dad knew what a mess he'd made of the company since he left..."

I blinked at her. "It's practically the same thing," I insisted. "Some rich American wanting to copycat hundreds of years of authentic Irish history in Shithole, Texas, for fuck's sake? And you don't think that cheapens what our ancestors have spent centuries building here? Look around you, Cait. How the hell is some brand-new prefab building in goddamned small-town Texas going to come anywhere close to capturing the magic of what makes Fig and Bramble unique? It's impossible."

"What do we care? We're never going to see it. We can just take their money and pretend it doesn't exist."

"Wrong. So wrong. Uncle Dev promised that corporate fat cat he'd come oversee 'quality control' or some shit. They're making him bring the 'special Murray touch of authenticity to the tiny-town heart of Texas.' I'm pretty sure I threw up a little bit when I heard that bullshit," I griped, making generous use of finger quotes. "But I'll bet fifty quid he bails and sends you or me."

"Well, he can't send me now that I'm expecting. Donny would never let me go so far away." Cait's eyes lit up. "Oooh! You'll get to see Hudson again. Maybe you can convince him to go for round two."

Technically it would've been round four, but I wasn't about to tell my sister that. It was bad enough she'd weaseled the hookup out of me in the first place. "No, thanks. Plus, he lives in Dallas. This disaster project is happening in bumblefuck."

"Maybe you can go to Dallas at the weekend," she suggested with a saucy smirk. "Bring him over to the dark side again."

I ignored her. "Maybe I can use one of those hookup apps and find all the gay cowboys in Texas. Surely they'd love a round with a girly Irishman with an accent, yeah? Make it my fuck tour of America trip? I mean, if I have to fly over there anyway, might as well treat it like a gap year or something."

"Twenty-eight's a bit old for a gap year. Just saying," Cait muttered before taking another sip of tea. "Plus, you're not the fuck-around type. Remember?"

I winked at her. "I am now. I hardly knew what I was missing before. After my night with the American, I'm all for fucking around with one-offs. They're hot as shit. Who knew?"

I was a liar and we both knew it.

With a straight face, my sister looked up at me. "Everyone you've ever dated."

My jaw dropped before I tossed a cushion at her face. She got her hand up just in time to block it. "You are bloody awful! Besides, there's no chance Uncle Dev is stuffing me in a flying steel coffin. I'd rather quit the family business and panhandle my way to Waterford and throw myself at Pat's feet."

LUCKILY, by the time I had to board that plane, I'd been able to spend the holidays with my family and say my final goodbyes in case I died in a fiery crash into the Atlantic.

Ames's process of finalizing the business plan, finding the right retail space, getting the appropriate permits, and whatever the hell else was involved in starting a pub from scratch took a couple of months. It was long enough for me to wrap things up with my dog training clients and reach out to the Texas Sheepdog Association to find out about upcoming trials on the off chance I made it safely to Texas.

In the end, I was barely speaking to Uncle Devlin. The man had admitted to fucking up and finding himself desperate for cash. He'd been relieved when Bruce Ames had requested Texas franchise rights rather than acquiring shares of F&B. He'd made a botch-up of the whole thing, and my father wouldn't even entertain a discussion about it. As far as he was concerned, he was living la vida loca with his new love on the sunny shores of Rio and the rest of us could fuck the fuck off.

Needless to say, my resentment was as big as the same ocean that was going to swallow me whole any minute. I'd felt so betrayed by Hudson, but it had been made ten times worse by the fact the stupid man held my heart. I hadn't been able to stop thinking about him even after several months. The loss of him was crushing me. For some reason, I simply couldn't get over it. Cait had accused me of being moody, had even told me the regulars at the pub were avoiding me for being snappish.

And it was all bloody Hudson's fault.

"Ma'am, are you feeling okay?" the man sitting next to me asked.

I narrowed my eyes at him. I was in no mood to be misidentified for the millionth time. "Must be getting my period," I shot back in the deepest voice I could manage without sounding like a cartoon character.

The man's eyes widened when he realized his mistake. "Oh, uh, sorry, dude. All I saw was your long hair. But are you okay? You look a bit green."

I appreciated him not mentioning the hot-pink hoodie I wore. I hated the thing, but it was the closest I had to a good-luck charm, and I figured I needed all the help I could get.

"Never flown before. Pretty sure we're all going to die." The plane made a thunk sound somewhere below us and toward the back. I clutched the armrest between us. "That was clearly a bird strike."

The man leaned forward to look around me out the window. "You know we haven't taken off yet, right?"

I rolled my eyes until they were closed and my head was leaning back against the headrest. "Semantics," I muttered. "Most airplane accidents happen on the runway anyway. We're doomed either way."

"You sound pretty chill for someone who thinks we're going down," he said with a chuckle.

"I'm high. Really very high."

There was a beat of silence. "Well, this should be fun," the man said.

"Should be fine," I slurred. "I took two instead of halfsies, so I'm sure I'll drift off and sleep the whole way."

I did not drift off and sleep the whole way. I was awake enough to take two more pills midway through the flight, which only ratcheted up my chill factor to a most-excellent level.

When we landed in Dallas, I was half-surprised there weren't police officers waiting to board the plane in search of the passenger the flight attendants kept referring to as "the drunk woman in 34A who won't stop singing Irish pub songs." Or, as my seatmate called me, "the best thing since sliced bread." It could have been worse, I guess. He could have had to sit next to a toddler or newborn.

I was so grateful to be on the blessed earth again, I suddenly wanted everyone to know how much I loved them.

"Cheers, welcome to America," I said to the young mother behind me. "This your first time? You'll love it. Almost as much as I love all of you and the pilots for all this." I waved my arms around, unsure of what I was referring to.

"I'm from here," she said in a thick Texan accent. "Born and raised in the Lonestar State. Honey, I bleed red, white, and blue."

"Sounds messy," I admitted. "But maybe you're the right person to ask about this. Are gay cowboys easy to find? I heard there's some kind of hankie code, but I don't have a hankie and I think you need a hankie for the code. Think they use Grindr too just in case for people who don't have their own hankies? Hankie. Hankie... wait. How do you spell that? With a *y* or an *i-e*? Hankie. Hankie-pankie... oh! Do you think that's where the phrase came fr—"

The next thing I remembered was waking up in a luxuriously soft bed in a small dim room. I was toasty warm under a thick pile of blankets, but the comfortable feeling was ruined by the steel band cinched around the top of my head.

"Oh fuck," I breathed, nearly knocking myself out with morning breath. I moved slowly to sit up. The first thing I noticed was the simplicity of the room. It was furnished with only the double bed flanked by basic side tables and a high-backed wooden chair in one corner. Opposite the bed was a narrow door I hoped led to the toilet.

I gingerly made my way to the edge of the bed and noticed a half-full bottle of water on the bedside table next to a full bottle. I grabbed the full one and heaved a sigh of relief when I heard the telltale sound of a new seal breaking. I took a few sips carefully before realizing my stomach was fine. Apparently the headache was the only problem.

That and not having any idea where the fuck I was.

Oh, and only being in my underwear.

I wondered if this was normal for Texas... if this was, in fact, the actual origination story for the famous phrase "Houston, we have a problem."

17

HUDSON

Hudson's Luck:

Just when I think I've figured shit out, it all goes to hell in a handbasket.

Another of the endless calls Bruce Ames referred to as "quick check-ins" interrupted my early-morning breakfast with the family.

"Hudson Wilde," I answered, stepping away from the table where I'd been cutting up pancakes for my niece Pippa. She sat fat and happy in her big high chair off the end of the giant wooden kitchen table that separated the farmhouse kitchen from the attached family room area. My brother West caught my eye and nodded before moving seats to continue helping his daughter with her food.

"Good morning, Hudson," Bruce began in his booming voice. "Hope I'm not bothering you on a Sunday morning. Listen, I've had another idea for the pub..."

As he continued to spout off about yet another one of his ideas, I clenched my teeth in frustration. I hated every bit of this project. When I'd busted my ass at Texas A&M to get an MBA in finance, I'd pictured myself working my way up the corporate ladder as a financial analyst the way my father had—business suits and corner offices, spreadsheets and board meetings. I certainly had not pictured myself managing the grand opening of a small-town pub in a graphic T-shirt and blue jeans. My business education had been accounting heavy and marketing light. It had been all about high-level analysis and not at all about low-level daily business operations in the fickle restaurant business. My corporate experience was about the nuances of negotiating multimillion-dollar mergers. Now here I was trying to figure out which napkins to order and how many highball glasses were needed.

What the hell had I gotten myself into?

"Have you had a chance to meet with Ms. Murray yet?" Bruce asked, shaking me out of my distraction.

"Yes, about that. I thought we were expecting Devlin Murray himself to come help out?" I asked. It would be a big relief if Cait had come in his place. She and I got along well, and I knew the town would adore her.

"Something came up, I guess. The driver said it was a young woman he dropped off last night. She told Hank that Devlin was her uncle. You didn't meet her when she arrived?"

When I'd learned Devlin was coming over for a few months to help launch the pub, I'd arranged for him to stay in my grandfathers' bunkhouse to save the poor man from the excessive showy wealth of the Ames family manse. I hadn't gotten to know Devlin very well the week I'd spent there, but I'd learned enough to know he wouldn't fare well watching Veronica Ames and her lady friends order the housekeeper back into the house for another pitcher of Bellinis before their next tennis match. I assumed he'd be much happier cracking open a cold one on the ranch porch with Doc and Grandpa.

"The contractor needed to go over a few things, so I was at the building until late. By the time I got in, Grandpa and Doc had already taken care of everything. I guess she's not awake yet." I didn't dare mention overhearing Grandpa tell Doc their new guest had overindulged on the flight to Dallas. No need to start anyone off on the wrong foot with Bruce. There was a lot riding on the success of this launch. No reason for him to know Cait seemed to suffer from the same fear of planes Charlie did.

I cursed myself for letting the Irishman enter my thoughts for what had to be the millionth time since I'd left Ireland.

"Well, then I'll let you go greet her and make sure she has everything she needs," Bruce said. "We'll all meet up bright and early tomorrow morning to get started with the interior designer. See you then."

After hanging up and sliding my phone back in my pocket, I returned to the table to reach for my mug of coffee. I hadn't taken the second sip when my sister Sassy walked in.

Followed by Charlie Murray.

Not Cait.

Charlie. *My* Charlie. The Charlie who'd abandoned me without saying goodbye as if I was some cheap trick he'd picked up in a bar. Well... maybe I *had* been a cheap trick he'd picked up in a bar, but I'd still been stung by the rejection. And considering the sleepless nights his memories had caused for me the past few months, I resented the hell out of him and his perfect, sweet self. How in the world was I going to handle Charlie Murray here for the next few months? That was easy: I wasn't. It wouldn't work. No way.

I felt something land on my foot, and suddenly my leg was burning. "Shit!" I cried, jumping back out of the way of my fallen mug. Hot coffee had spattered all over the floor, barely missing the legs of the high chair. The thought of any coffee marring Pippa's perfect baby skin shot adrenaline through my veins in a rush. I snapped my head around to Charlie. Why was Charlie Murray in my grandparents' kitchen? Seeing him walk into a room filled with my family members had caused a near-horrific accident. This was all his fault. "I thought they were sending Cait. Why are you here?" I snapped across the room.

Everyone went completely silent and gaped at me. I kept my eyes on the intruder as I felt my heart hammer dangerously in my chest.

He was so damned beautiful I wanted to cry. But not nearly as much as I wanted to scream at him for showing up out of the blue without giving me time to prepare, to figure out how I felt about it.

Charlie's voice, when it came, washed over me like the familiar sea breeze that blew across the cliffs near his home. "I'm here to protect what's left of my family's reputation, you lying piece of..." He caught sight of Pippa and stopped before adding the curse word. "The question is, why are *you* here? I thought you lived in Dallas?"

My family watched the proceedings like a tennis match. I didn't care. As far as I was concerned, the only people in the room were me and the man who held my most terrifying secret. One of us needed to go, and it wasn't me.

"You should go," I ground out, pointing toward the door.

He crossed his arms in front of his chest, and I noticed for the first time he was wearing the same loose-necked fisherman's sweater he'd been wearing the first time I'd seen him. Only this time he had a T-shirt on under it, covering what I now knew to be the most delicious shoulders on earth.

I swallowed.

Charlie's nostrils flared. "I'm not leaving, but don't let me keep *you* here, Hudson. Feel free to go back to the city and your big corporate job of *stealing people's family businesses*." His voice lowered to an angry growl at the end, and I knew right away he blamed me for everything.

"I'm not stealing your business," I said. "And you're definitely leaving. If you think I'm spending the next few months working with *you*, you're mistaken. Go back home, Charlie." I turned around to find some napkins to begin wiping the coffee drips off my shoes.

"Why should *I* leave?" he asked, clearly exasperated with me.

I turned back around and let it fly before my brain could kick in and save me from making a huge mistake.

"Because leaving is your thing, isn't it? That's all you seem to do when I'm around anyway." My heart was already in a million pieces just seeing his face and hearing his voice, but when I let those angry words fly, I realized just how hurt I still was after waking up to an empty bed that morning in Cork. I'd thought we'd shared something special that night. Waking up alone had proven I'd been the only one who'd felt that way.

It was then that I noticed his eyes weren't sparkling with anger, they were sparkling with unshed tears. *Oh god.*

"Charlie," I breathed, taking a step toward him as he swiveled away from me and brushed past Sassy toward the door. I wanted to touch him, to hold him, to run up to him and throw myself at his damned feet to beg his forgiveness. But my entire family was watching. I cleared my throat. "Charlie, wait."

He turned to me, his gorgeous red hair following around in an arc. My fingers itched to touch it, to feel the familiar silky thickness against my skin.

Charlie's anger was gone, and he looked... lost.

"I won't..." He looked around, seeming to acknowledge the rest of my huge family for the first time before looking back at me with pleading eyes. "I'm sorry. You know I won't..." He sighed. "You're right. I'll go. It's best if I go. This clearly isn't going to work."

He turned back the way he came, Sassy running after him begging him to wait up for her.

I stood there in shock, lips numbing quickly and hands beginning to tremble. "I have to go," I whispered.

But before I could move toward the direction they'd gone, my brother West stopped me with hands on both my shoulders. "Woah. Dude, hang on. Let Sassy go after him. She's not going to let him go anywhere until he calms down anyway. Now sit down and tell us what the hell that was all about. You have never, in my entire lifetime, lost your shit at someone like that. Not even me."

I glanced toward the front door. "No, I need to go talk to him. I was just surprised, that's all."

"Who the hell is that guy?" Otto asked. "I thought he was a chick. One of Sassy's friends or something. He's fucking gorgeous. The kid looks like a model for Christ's sake."

His husband smacked his man in the stomach. "Ass," he muttered.

Otto looked at Walker with a sheepish smile. "Tell me you didn't think the same thing and I'll apologize."

"Shut up. That's beside the point," Walker grumbled, unable to meet Otto's eye. Otto laughed and kissed Walker's temple before putting his arm around the guy and pulling him in close.

My brother Saint adjusted the front of his sweats like a horny teenaged punk. "I wouldn't mind a few minutes alone with that gorgeous boy. Those lips. Did you see how full they—"

I wanted to punch the fucker, but instead, I cut in, trying not to flare my nostrils like an angry bull. "He's none of any of y'all's fucking business. Hands off. He's here to work, dammit. Not be... whatever you're thinking. And he's not a kid. He's twenty-eight."

"Oooh, you know Hudson's building up a head of steam when his Texas twang comes out in full force," Nico said with a laugh. "Y'all better watch out," he teased.

"Everyone shut the hell up," I barked. "Seriously. This is my job we're talking about. The success of this project is the difference between me handing out lollipops and dog bones in the drive-thru at the Hobie Credit Union and me making vice president at Ames International. Don't you see that? This is a big damned deal to me."

Saint's twin sister, MJ, stood up and walked behind me to rub my shoulders. "Dang, Hud. Now it all makes sense. You were acting like a freaker, and it turns out you're just scared for your job. That's something we can all understand. For a minute there, you were coming off as... I don't know. Weird. Like a lover's spat or something," she said with a laugh.

My siblings all cracked up at the idea of their one straight brother getting territorial over a man. My stomach clenched. That wasn't what had happened, was it? It had just surprised me was all. I'd been expecting Cait. Marketing guru Cait. Not Charlie. Sweet, funny, too-tempting Charlie.

I closed my eyes and pressed into them with my fists.

This was going to be a disaster. I had to find a way to send the beautiful man home.

18

CHARLIE

Charlie's Luck:

What happens in Cork never stays in Cork.

Before I realized where I was heading, I found myself aiming straight at the huge barn across the gravel parking area next to the house. Sassy had let me set Mama up in a stall that opened up to a fenced area. I'd intended to leave her there while I had breakfast in the main house, but I guessed now I had to gather her up and figure out where to go next. I wasn't about to subject her to another international flight again so soon. I wondered if there was a hotel nearby that allowed animals.

As I entered the darkened opening at the front of the barn, I noticed my pulse was still jackhammering from the confrontation with Hudson. I couldn't believe things had gone pear-shaped so quickly.

Despite knowing I was being put up at the Wilde Ranch, I'd truly not had any expectation of seeing Hudson. From what I'd learned online, Hobie was two hours away from Dallas by car. There was absolutely no reason Hudson would be at his family's ranch on a random January weekend.

But that was just my luck.

When I'd walked in and spotted him in track pants and a long-sleeved T-shirt, my heart had thunked almost loudly enough to be heard over the din. He'd looked so dear, still half-asleep and hair messed up. I'd felt my grin come on faster than I'd been able to stop it.

Until the moment he'd spotted me. And then it had all gone to shit.

Instead of grabbing Mama's things and heading right back out the door as I'd intended, I sank to the floor and threw my arms around my sweet collie to bury my face in her fur. Stupid fucking straight boys. Total jackasses when confronted with their little experiments. Was this a good time to give myself the old *I told you so*?

I gritted my teeth until they hurt. Of all people to reject me so soundly... Hudson had turned on me the same way everyone else seemed to. I wanted to laugh at myself for being such a dope. Why had I ever thought leaving after sex that night would somehow spare my heart from breaking? It had only prolonged his rejection until now.

I'd left him, but he still managed to pull the rug out from under me with one small sentence.

You should go.

Hadn't I sworn I wasn't going to let myself fall for someone like that again? How stupid could I have been coming here to Hudson's territory? Once I found out who he worked for and what their designs were on franchising F&B, I should have known I'd run into him at some point. And of course he was going to flip the fuck out. Seeing the only other person on earth who knew his dirty little secret was bound to throw him at sixes and sevens. And if he was predictable, he'd turn around and embrace his heterosexual proclivities with a newfound fervor. I wouldn't be surprised to see him parade a new girlfriend or string of various women around to prove to himself and others the man was straight as a rail.

Fucker.

A light knock made its way to my ears. Poor Sassy hadn't known what to do with me after the showdown in the farmhouse kitchen. Maybe I needed to reassure her I wasn't bothered by her brother's annoying outburst.

I looked up only to find a different Wilde standing there on the other side of the stall door. Hudson's hands were laced behind his neck, and he looked like he was about to carve permanent stress lines into his forehead with all that brow furrowing.

"Relax," I muttered, standing and gesturing for him to enter. "I'm not about to tell anyone what happened between us in Cork."

He hesitated before stepping into the stall and closing the door behind himself. I was sure he didn't want anyone to witness our little reunion scene.

"That's not... that wasn't..." He let out a sigh. "Look, I owe you an apology. I shouldn't have spoken to you that way, especially in front of my family. It was rude and unprofessional. I don't know what got into me."

"It's understandable, I guess. I surprised you. Clearly you didn't know I was coming."

He let out a derisive laugh. "No. Definitely not. I was expecting Devlin or Cait."

Right. Anyone but me, then.

"Sorry to disappoint," I said. "But I'm the Murray you got. Don't worry, I'll leave. And as far as I'm concerned, what happened in Cork stayed in Cork."

Hudson seemed to take a moment to process what I was saying. He had a funny expression on his face I couldn't quite assess. I was expecting relief, but it seemed a bit more like... disappointment.

Was he disappointed in me? What, had he expected me to apologize also? Pfft. As if that was going to happen. I'd done absolutely nothing wrong, either in Cork or in the farmhouse kitchen. If Hudson Wilde expected me to—

"Well hello there," he crooned, squatting down to pet my girl.

Dammit. I didn't want him to be sweet to my dog. That was a bridge too far.

I let out a sigh. The man was trying to be nice and all I wanted to do was fight. "That's Mama."

"We've met before. While you were in Waterford doing those deliveries she kept me company in the office. Hey, sweet girl," he cooed as he scratched her ears and then her flanks just the way she liked it. "Long flight, huh? Poor baby... what a good girl." He continued to murmur sweet nothings to her as if he was actually a thoughtful, kind man.

Selfish prick.

"I, ah, saw the horses out there," I said with a cough, nodding toward the other stalls. "Is one of those yours?"

He looked up and smiled like a damned rainbow after a storm. It was so unexpected, the warmth of it made me dizzy.

"Yeah, let me show you."

I followed him into the central corridor between the stalls and watched him transfer his animal love chatter from Mama to a large brown horse with lovely black eyelashes and ear tips.

"This is Kojack," he said with a shy smile. There was a hint of both pride and vulnerability in his smile, and for the first time, I saw a fragile part of him I'd only caught the barest glimpse of back home.

"He's very pretty," I said. "And big." Were there other ways of describing horses? I wasn't sure.

Hudson chuckled. "He is." After stroking along the horse's nose, he moved to the next stall and introduced a smaller horse named Bumble Bee. With every silky nose he stroked and made sweet eyes to, he seemed to come more alive. He snuck treats to them and talked to them as if they were each special in their own way, all the while telling me whose favorite each one was and what their temperament was like. By the time he introduced me to a barn's worth of animals, Hudson was relaxed and beaming.

"You're really good with them," I said softly. "I can tell you love it here at the ranch."

He glanced up at me through his lashes before looking away. "Maybe... maybe while you're here we can go riding sometime."

Even though I wanted to let the words wash over me and take away the rejection I'd felt from him earlier, I knew it was too dangerous. I truly needed to leave and put Hudson Wilde firmly behind me.

"That sounds nice, Hudson, but you were right earlier. I should go. I'll have Cait or Devlin take my place. It's not fair to—"

"No, I... I don't want you to go," he blurted. "I shouldn't have been so dismissive. I was... I was surprised, that's all. Surely we can get past this and work closely together just fine. If we can both agree to buckle down, maybe we can finish sooner than three months and get you back home. I can't imagine you're very happy being away from home that long anyway."

It took me a moment for some of his words to sink in.

"Pardon?" I asked. "You and me... us... working *closely* together? I don't understand. Devlin said I was to be the pub manager until things were running smoothly enough to replace me. What is your role in the project, exactly?"

I had a bad feeling about this.

Hudson fiddled with some leather straps hanging from a nearby hook, untangling them until they hung straight and tidy.

"You'll be the pub manager, but I'm acting as the business manager," he said. As if that made any fucking sense.

"What does that mean?"

"You'll be responsible for setting up and running the pub like the original Fig and Bramble, including adding those touches that make it look and feel authentic, while I will be managing the budget, the contractor, and the accounting."

"In other words, I play the part of the leprechaun while you hold the purse strings like Big Daddy," I clarified. This was so not going to work.

Hudson swallowed and looked away. The blush I'd loved so much a few months ago crept up the sides of his neck. It was impossible to remain angry at him when he was that delectable.

"I don't intend to be your Big Daddy," Hudson said before realizing how that would sound.

He snapped his head around and locked eyes with me before I coughed out a laugh and his cheeks stained ten shades of pomegranate.

"Y-you know what I mean," he stammered. "I'm not planning on riding you hard or anyth— *Oh dear god*, shut up, Hudson."

By this point, I couldn't hold back the laughter, and even Hudson's lips were twitching. I dropped down onto the edge of a nearby bench and pointed at him before managing to speak through the tears.

"Yes, but might you make me beg for it? I do like to beg, Hudson."

"Stop," he said with a snort. "I can't help it. My words don't come out right when I'm around you."

Our laughter died down as our eyes met again. He was so lovely then, face flushed and eyes sparkling, that I wanted to give him something.

"I know you're just doing your job here. My anger isn't personal against you. I'm pissed at my uncle, and I'm pissed at my dad. Not to mention Bruce Ames, the fucker. So... I just want you to know that. It's not like any of this was your idea. I get that."

Hudson seemed to startle a bit before nodding. "Thank you. For what it's worth... I'm sorry about all of this."

"Thank you. That means a lot. Now, about Mama," I said, deciding to put the shitty work stuff away for the moment. "I hope it's okay I brought her."

Hudson's face lit up. "Of course. But why is she out here in the barn?" he asked, reaching down to scratch her head. "I assumed you'd want her in the bunkhouse with you."

"That's the awkward bit," I admitted. "She went into heat, so Sassy helped me put her in an empty stall in the barn to keep the mess down. I hope your grandfathers don't mind. Sassy was going to tell them about it for me."

"I'm sure it's fine. Doc and Grandpa would want me to tell you to make yourself at home. They're two of the most gracious hosts you'll ever meet. Their motto is always the more the merrier, so I'm sure they'll be thrilled to have you here."

If his grandparents were anything like him, I knew they'd be genuine, polite, and sweet.

An awkward beat of silence passed. I could tell he was unsure of his continued welcome, and I was unsure of how to convince him to stay with me in the barn just a little longer.

"I thought you lived in Dallas?" I asked.

He looked down at his feet before clasping his hands together on his lap and releasing them again. After smoothing down his shirt front, he slid his hands under his thighs as if to keep them still.

"Yeah, I do. I mean, I did. Well, I do." He chuckled and rolled his eyes. "Whenever I sound like a babbling idiot, just remember it's your fault, okay?"

I smiled at him, wishing like hell he was actually flirting with me the way he had back home. I knew his discomfort this time was caused by his insecurity at my unexpected presence, but I still thanked god for that irresistible self-deprecating grin on his face.

"So... you do but you don't," I teased.

"No, I do. I had an apartment in Dallas, but I let it go when Bruce said he wanted me in Hobie full-time for this project. So I'm staying here. I'll have to find a new apartment in the city when the project is complete. My brother Saint and I might move in together since he's almost never home anyway."

"You're staying here? As in here on the ranch? Where? In the bunkhouse?" I asked in surprise and with a heavy dose of trepidation. How the hell would I keep my hands to myself if we were under the same roof?

Hudson looked surprised. "Oh, no. Sorry. I'm staying in a little cabin on the property. It was my cousin's, and then my brother stayed there. I guess at this point it's like a guesthouse or something. Anyway, it's just up a gravel drive. You can see it from here. If you need me for anything..." He let his words trail off, and things were uncomfortably silent again.

"Hudson," I began, feeling a need to get us out of the awkward turn the conversation had taken. "Do you think maybe your family would still feed me breakfast even though I've left them a bloody terrible first impression?"

His grin was as big as the Boeing 777 that had defied all logic and transported me safely to Dallas the day before. "Absolutely. Charlie, you're about to learn what it means when people call something Texas-sized. C'mon."

19

HUDSON

Hudson's Words To Live By:

Never let them see you sweat. Or pine. Or just whimper a little.

After I introduced him to my family and left him alone to be handed around like a new baby by all of my meddling siblings, I returned to my cabin to get control of myself.

Charlie Murray is here in Hobie.

I wasn't able to stop repeating that new fact in my head.

Charlie Murray is here in Hobie.

It just didn't compute. I couldn't even picture him here. It was almost like... the wild Irish coastline was such a part of the man, it was hard imagining him anywhere else.

Once back in my cabin, I took the opportunity to indulge my inner toddler for a minute since there wasn't anyone around to hear.

"He's so sweet and sexy. What the hell is wrong with me?" I whined out loud, thrusting my fingers into my hair and yanking. "Ugh, fuck! He's here to work, you asshole. *Work.* And so are you. Remember that."

I reminded myself what exactly that meant. *Work.* So I sat down and made a list of all the reasons why lusting after the Irishman would be a terrible idea.

Ultimately it came down to the most important one: I couldn't jeopardize a shot at making vice president for a fling. My mind automatically rejected the word "fling" to describe Charlie, but I didn't know how else to describe it. It honestly didn't matter whether it was a fling with a man or a woman because it would be a fling with a business partner critical to the success of this project. And to make matters worse, Bruce Ames was not a sensitive new-age guy who thought love was love. He was a stereotypical Texas good ole boy who thought gay was a four-letter word and holding another man's hand in public was akin to bitch-slapping Jesus. I was sure he'd be unhappy when he realized how femme and out Charlie was, but I was just as sure he'd be willing to put up with it for the sake of the success of his pet project. What he wouldn't accept was his future VP dating not only someone else right in front of him after said man accidentally *didn't* propose to his daughter, but also dating a guy who looked like a girl but was very much *not* one.

Sure enough, when Bruce showed up a few days later for the first meeting and clapped eyes on the beautiful petite Irishman in the skinny jeans, F&B-branded golf shirt, and high ponytail, he was visibly taken aback. For a split second, he'd smiled—the same smile I'd seen him give the attractive young woman who served beer out of a cart near the ninth hole of Bruce's country club in Dallas. But then he had the same ah-ha moment I'd had. The one in which your world flips over as you realize you're drooling over the most beautiful man you've ever seen. I had to hide my smile behind my hand.

It turned out, Bruce Ames was almost as much of a nervous babbler as I was when embarrassed. As he fumbled his way through introductions, Charlie snuck a wink at me that almost knocked me off my feet. It took everything I had not to bark out a laugh, but I managed to keep myself together in front of Bruce and pay attention in the morning meeting that followed.

Bruce had brought all the key players together for the first official management meeting. While Bruce himself wouldn't be on site unless needed, the contractor, chef, head bartender, and brewery manager were already in place at least on a part-time basis to begin training and participate in the setup of the pub and attached brewery.

Charlie's playful friendliness won everyone over right away. He had the energy of a new puppy and was damned near just as cute. Everyone he met loved the hell out of him, including my family. *Especially* my family.

And of course, I was no different. I hung on his every word and used any excuse to stay in the same room with him while we were working.

But if I thought having Charlie at the ranch was hard, it was nothing compared to working alongside him all day every day.

Two weeks into the project, I was exhausted from keeping my hands to myself. From keeping my lust to myself. From keeping my dick to myself. From jacking off several times a night thinking about the man down the hill in the bunkhouse.

"You're doing it again."

I turned around and found Charlie straightening up from where he'd been leaning over a folding table jotting notes on a legal pad.

"Doing what?" I asked.

"Staring off into space."

I was staring at the way your silky hair falls down around your face when you lean over. And how your front teeth sink into your bottom lip when you're concentrating.

I cleared my throat. "It's getting late. You want to go grab some dinner at the Pinecone? West and Nico texted to say they were headed over. I guess Goldie showed up to spend some time with Pippa and booted the two of them out."

By then, Charlie had been around the ranch enough to have become familiar with my family, at least the ones who lived full-time in Hobie. Since my brother West was my closest friend in the world and the local physician in our small town, Charlie had seen plenty of him and his family.

"Cheers. Let me make a few more notes first," he said before leaning over again. This time when the hair fell down in his way, he absently scooped it all up in a messy bun on the back of his head with an elastic band he kept around his wrist.

Had you asked me several months before how I felt about man buns, I would have laughed you out of the room.

But were you to ask me now?

I'd get a man bun boner before you even finished the question.

I looked away and took the opportunity to determine what lights I needed to turn off before locking up. By the time we exited the papered-over glass doors at the front of the pub, I was already thinking about the rum and Coke I was going to order as soon as I sat down to dinner. Lord knew how much I needed to chill the hell out about everything. The job, the delay on some of the millwork, and my attraction to Charlie.

The two of us had spent many meals together over the past couple of weeks. Quick working lunches on a folding table at work. Long, lazy takeout dinners in the bunkhouse discussing the budget for the interior design of the pub. And even a couple of chaotic family brunches at Doc and Grandpa's in which no work was discussed but Charlie was undoubtedly the center of everyone's attention. Within a span of a couple of weeks, Charlie had become almost an extension of me. Where I was, Charlie was too. Where Charlie went, there I followed.

And during all of it, we both acted the height of professionalism. It was as if I'd never seen him naked, never had his hard dick pushing into my mouth or his slender finger sneaking into unspeakable places. We were coworkers. And that was all.

When we got to the restaurant, West and Nico were already seated in a booth, talking quietly with their heads together. I stepped back to let Charlie slide in first before I took the seat next to him.

West pulled his focus away from his partner enough to greet us. "Hey, guys, dare I ask how the project is coming along when you both look like warmed-over shit?"

"Gee, thanks, brother," I mumbled. "Such a sweet-talker. Nico, you lucky bastard."

Nico's eyes crinkled as he laughed and bumped his shoulder into West. "While I wouldn't have said it in quite the same way, he's kind of right. Are you two getting any sleep?"

This time it was Charlie who answered. "I'm getting enough sleep but not nearly enough time outside with Mama. There's a sheep trial coming up down near Austin in a couple of weeks I was hoping to go to. If I can't get some training time with her, I'll have to scrap it."

A young woman introduced herself as our server and began taking our drink orders. When it came time for Charlie to give his, he looked up at her with his natural flirty nature. "What's good here, love?"

Nico snorted into his fist, and West grinned from ear to ear. The server, swear to god, almost wet her pants and fainted on the spot.

"Ohmygawd, your accent! Where y'all from?"

"Ireland. Have you ever been?"

Nico tilted his forehead against West's shoulder to bury his laughter in his husband's arm, while West reached up to run his fingers through Nico's dark hair.

"Ohmygawd, no! I've never been but that..." She swooned and sighed. "That's just awesome. Seriously awesome. Say something else. Say something to me in Irish."

"I don't speak Irish, sweetheart," he said, laying it on thick. "Just the Queen's English with an Irish accent the same way you speak it with a Texas twang."

The girl's face was flushed with flirty excitement as she called to another female server who walked by.

"Ashley, ohmygawd, c'mere. You hafta hear this guy talk."

I snorted and was quickly elbowed in the side for my insubordination.

"Calm down," Charlie scolded. "What's your problem?"

"I'm thirsty."

Ashley walked up and made fluttery eyes at Charlie. Who could blame her? With his delicate facial features, dark eyelashes, mesmerizing green eyes, and unique red hair pulled back, he seriously looked like he'd just walked off a runway in Milan.

"Say something. Anything," the first girl said with a look of eager anticipation on her face.

"Something," Charlie said with a grin. "Anything."

The young women both dissolved in a fit of giggles. I couldn't stand this. It was so stupid. And it had nothing to do with the fact they were eying Charlie like they were imagining what he would sound like in bed.

Nothing at all.

"Would you mind grabbing those drinks for us please?" I asked our server as politely as I could. "Thank you."

She narrowed her eyes at me before walking away with her friend.

West eyed me with a smirk. "Problem?"

Jackass brother.

"I'm thirsty," I repeated through clenched teeth. "Some of us were working hard on a construction site all day."

"Fuck you," Charlie said under his breath. "I know you didn't just imply I didn't do my fair share of—."

I looked at him out of the corner of my eye. "I didn't mean it like that."

"Then how exactly did you mean it?"

West and Nico looked back and forth between us.

"I meant that woman might not realize how in need of a drink I am. It has nothing to do with you."

West looked over at Charlie. "What did my brother do?"

Charlie squeezed my arm to stop me from answering. "Someone had to go sit in a cushy design studio half the day to make the final decisions about fabrics and shit. I told Hudson to go, but he insisted it had to be me since it was critical to the authentic look and feel of the place. Now he's complaining about having to work the site by himself." Charlie turned to look at me. "You know I would have rather stayed back and fixed the damned glass rack situation instead of trusting it to Mark."

"Dude," I said, still salty over my lack of beverage and the fawning women who were still shooting glances at Charlie from across the restaurant. "I didn't say a word about that or about you. Someone needed to go get their Rhonda on. Better you than me anyway. You know I'd do just about anything to get out of running into her."

Rhonda Dolas was an interior decorator who had tried on several occasions to get me to ask her out. We'd gone to high school together, and she'd been close friends with one of my high school girlfriends. It seemed like she'd accepted that as the reason nothing had ever happened between us back then. As soon as she found out I was working on the big pub project Bruce Ames had hired her to consult on, she'd renewed her mission to pin me down for that elusive date I "owed" her.

"Oh right, Rhonda," Charlie said, getting that mischievous twinkle in his eye I was beginning to know so well. He turned to face Nico and West. "She's got the hots for our Hudson here. Asks about him all the damned time. I would have been back to the pub much quicker if I hadn't been having to tell her everything I knew about him."

I gaped at him. "What? Are you kidding? What the hell did you tell—"

"Yes, Hudson. I'm kidding."

West and Nico chuckled. "I remember she used to bribe her older brother to let her borrow his car so she could go to all of Hudson's away football games. The car was a very unique shade of teal, and every time we saw it at one of Hudson's games, we'd laugh and say—"

I dropped my face into my hands, remembering. "'Surprise, it's Rhonda's Honda.' You guys weren't very creative."

Charlie snickered. "Figures you were a football player."

"What's that supposed to mean?" I asked.

"You're so... all-American. Tall, handsome, clean-cut. Small-town Texas boy who plays by the rules. You're like a walking cliché. I'll bet you were prom king or some shit too."

He thinks I'm handsome.

West's eyes lit up. "Tell him, Hudson."

"Fuck you," I said, craning my neck for that damned server. Was I ever going to get a drink?

West leaned across the table toward Charlie. "He was homecoming king, which is almost the same thing. Homecoming in Texas is a big deal."

Charlie turned to me. "See? Told you so. Now tell me something about you I'd never be able to guess. Something not cliché."

It was clear he didn't think I'd be able to come up with anything. And as long as those clover-green eyes were sparkling at me, it was true. I couldn't even think when those eyes were on me. But Nico spoke up instead.

"He left boxes of fresh vegetables on the porches of the poor families in town every year at harvest time."

I stared at him in surprise, and West turned to do the same. Nico ignored us and continued to talk with a soft smile on his face.

"I'm sure he thought no one ever knew who'd done it, but I saw him once. It was the middle of the night, and I was outside sneaking a cigarette. We had a gravel drive, so my mom, my sister, and I had never been able to figure out how they left the box without us hearing footsteps. That night I learned his secret. He parked his pickup at the street and walked all the way down to our front porch in the weeds so not even his shoes would crunch on the gravel. He set the box down and snuck back up to his truck. I know for a fact he left those boxes in front of at least fifteen houses around Hobie. I used to hear my mom talk about it with some of the other ladies."

I didn't want to hear this. It was never meant to be a thing people knew about. If my father had found out, he would have accused me of stealing from Grandpa and Doc. "No, I didn't—"

West turned to me with a look on his face that made it seem as if he'd never known me before.

"You did. You totally did. You and Grandpa spent so much time planting a kitchen garden, yet we never seemed to eat much of the food you grew. Why didn't you tell me? I would have helped. Hell, we all would have helped."

I craned my neck again in desperate hopes of spotting *anyone* who worked at the Pinecone and had access to alcohol. "Can we not—"

"What made you start?" This time it was Charlie who spoke. I glanced at him and saw genuine interest. But I still felt uncomfortable talking about it.

"Is it just me, or do we still not have our drinks?" I asked, raising my hand for attention from any server even if it appeared rude. "You know what? I'm going to go find her."

I stepped out of the booth and went to look for our wayward server.

20

CHARLIE

Charlie's Revelation:

You truly can't judge a book by its cover.

The rest of the dinner was straightforward. West and Nico were good company, and when we finally got some alcohol into Hudson's belly, the four of us ended up having a great evening. We laughed and talked and teased until it was late enough to remind West and Nico they had a little girl.

"We have to go relieve Goldie," Nico said out front of the restaurant. "But I meant what I said about us taking you to Dallas one of these weekends to check out the clubs. Otto and Walker will go with us too. Otto's always trying to give Seth a taste of the big-city gay scene for some reason."

"I'd love that. There are only two gay bars in Cork, and neither would hardly be considered a club. I was hoping to be able to hit a big one while I'm here. I could go for some dirty dancing," I admitted with a wink. Was there a part of me trying to bait Hudson? Maybe. I wondered if he even noticed or cared. How would he feel if I found someone at the club to snog?

Oh, who was I kidding? If Hudson was there, I wouldn't be able to even think about kissing someone else. I was sick with wanting him. Only him. I needed to get past it. I'd already been there weeks with no hint of him wanting to renew anything physical with me. I could tell he still wanted me. I'd catch him looking at me with a heated gaze or hear him suck in a breath if I got a bit too close to him at work. But he never made a move, never even left an opening to imply he'd be open to *me* making the move.

West put his arm around Nico. "I'll text them and see when they have the same weekend night free and we'll make a plan. Sometimes Hudson's even willing to go with, though he doesn't appreciate it like we do."

I glanced at my supposedly straight coworker. His blush was on in full force, and he was studying the pavement as if it had the cure for cancer written on it in pebble script. I wondered what would happen if his brother and brother-in-law knew Hudson wasn't quite as straight as everyone thought. But apparently that subject was verboten. God forbid anyone think Hudson Wilde liked men.

"That's so generous of him," I said. "To be willing to give up an entire night of tits and arse just for us."

He didn't raise his head, but I saw Hudson's nostrils flare.

Suddenly he raised his face to me in challenge. "There are plenty of straight women in those clubs. Don't you worry about me."

Good, now we were both annoyed. Perfect.

We said our farewells to the two of them before making our way back to the pub car park to retrieve Hudson's truck.

We didn't speak during the ride back to the ranch, which was unusual. I'd gotten into the habit of riding to and from work every day with him rather than drive the fancy SUV Bruce Ames had loaned me. The thing was huge, and I was convinced that driving a barn would be easier than driving that monstrosity.

"I had a nice time tonight," I began in an effort to cut the silence on the final stretch of the long ranch driveway. "I really like West and Nico. I can see why you and your brother are so close."

After a brief hesitation, he sighed. "Yeah. I'm thankful he moved back home to take over Doc's practice. I was half-afraid he'd wind up across the country or something."

"I didn't realize Nico was from here too. He seems... I don't know. He doesn't seem like a small-town Texas boy, I guess."

Hudson rubbed his thumb lightly over the center of his chest. It was a little subconscious gesture he did sometimes. I'd begun to notice he primarily did it when talking about his family. "He lived in San Francisco for many years before moving back. He owned a tattoo shop there. But his sister died and left him Pippa. When he moved back, he and West got together."

I was sure there was more to the story, but I was also sure it would be better to ask Nico or West to tell it.

"Since the two of you are so close, was it hard for you when the two of them started dating?"

He pursed his lips in thought for a few beats. "I was happy for him. I mean, I still am. Nico's a stand-up guy, and of course, he brought us Pippa."

I lay back against the seat of the car and stretched my legs. "I remember when Cait and Donny got together. I was a pain in the arse. Resentful, jealous... annoyed. It took me a while to let go of always being her number one person, yeah?"

Hudson nodded. He seemed distracted somehow, and I wondered if the subject of his relationship with West was making him uncomfortable for some reason. "Yeah. There was a little of that. But I feel like I kind of abandoned him first when I decided to settle in Dallas instead of Hobie."

"Why did you choose the city?"

When he didn't answer me, I thought maybe I'd stumbled onto another forbidden topic. I was about to apologize when he suddenly whispered, "I can't..." After pulling to a stop by the bunkhouse, he turned to face me in the dim cab of the truck. "I can't just pretend that

I don't want to kiss you all the fucking time. It's killing me, and I just wanted to tell you I'm sorry."

I stared at him.

"Why are you sorry for wanting to kiss me?"

He rubbed his hands over his face. "Because it's selfish and stupid. And we work together. It's inappropriate, and—"

I didn't let him get any further. I lurched toward him and slammed my lips into his before he could get another word out. The kiss was hard and unforgiving, almost punishing in its ferocity. Our teeth clacked and I almost gelded him with my knee while straddling his lap.

His cold hands hit the warm skin of my lower back under my shirt, and I bit back a squeak of surprise, arching into him to get away from the icicles. Hudson's body was warmer than his hands, so I pushed closer to him while our mouths continued to compete for dominance. His teeth bit lightly on my lower lip before his hands clasped the sides of my face and turned it so he could move down to nip at the skin of my neck.

"Fucking creamy skin drives me batshit," he murmured between nibbles.

I reached between us to feel the hardness straining against his zipper and couldn't help but push hard against it with a groan. Fuck, I wanted to see that beast again.

"Please," I whimpered like a horny kid. "Let me suck you off."

Hudson's teeth grazed my collarbone, causing a bit of damp in my shorts that was only going to get worse if he continued along in that manner. His cold hands had warmed up against my skin and found their way into the back of my jeans. I wiggled off his lap and reached for his fly, but his large hands clamped around my wrists to stop me.

I looked up in surprise. His face was flushed, eyes bright with huge pupils, and lips wet from our kisses. He wanted me, wanted this. So why was he stopping me?

"Wait," he said between heavy breaths. "We should talk about this. What if... I mean, I'm not... I can't give you what you need, what you deserve. It's not fair. And we work together. And I..."

My sex-addled brain could not make heads or tails of what he was trying to say, but I damned sure knew the bit he *hadn't* said there at the end was about him being straight.

His rejection might as well have come in the form of a bucket of ice water.

"Right. Silly me. Fucking with the resident heterosexual. Off I go, then. Good night, Hudson."

Before he had a chance to respond, I was out of the truck and hauling arse toward the bunkhouse. I heard the slam of the driver door but didn't look back to see if he was following me. I made my way quickly into my bedroom and locked the door behind me, slipping my earbuds on as fast as I could and jacking the music up loud enough to allow me to pretend he hadn't followed me and banged on the door, begging me to come back to him.

21

HUDSON

Hudson's Luck:

You always want what you can't have.

I chased after him and pounded my fist against the door to his room, but he ignored me. He thought I'd rejected him because I was straight. Clearly I wasn't straight, and I damned sure hadn't rejected him. I'd just wanted to slow down enough to be clear about what was happening between us. That hooking up couldn't lead to anything more than casual sex. We each had families we weren't willing to leave. He lived in Ireland for god's sake, and I lived in Texas.

And his sister had been right: Charlie was looking for his Forever Man. There was no way I could be that guy for him. Besides the problem of geography, there was also the issue of my sexuality. Didn't Charlie deserve to be with someone who knew what the hell he was doing? Someone who had a clearer sense of himself than I did?

But he hadn't even let me explain.

I made my way back to the little cabin for the night and

succumbed to an angry session of stroking myself off to images of Charlie's lean body and soft smile despite my better judgment.

It made seeing him awkward, which left me grateful for the weekend when I could avoid him like the plague. The only problem was my meddling family. Grandpa and Doc wanted to know why I didn't join them for Saturday breakfast, and my sister Sassy called me out on being a grump when I finally turned up at the barn for a trail ride late in the morning. If I'd waited to show my face on my own family's damned ranch until a certain Irishman's vehicle had left the premises, it was nobody's business but mine.

"What the fuck is your problem?" she asked from the other side of the pony she was saddling. Our niece Tisha was coming to ride with us, and if memory served, she'd expect her new pony to be the first one ready to mount when she arrived with Seth and Otto.

"Are you talking to me or Peanut?" I asked, even though I knew she wasn't talking to the pony.

"Is it Darci? I heard something happened to her last night and she ended up at the hospital."

I snapped my head up. "What? What happened? Is she okay?"

Sassy met my eyes and shrugged. "I figured you might know. Stevie told me he saw her there when he was working the coffee cart overnight."

I handed her Patty Cake's bridle and asked her to take over for me so I could call Darci and make sure she was all right. Even though we weren't together anymore, I still cared about her a great deal.

When she picked up on the third ring, I almost didn't recognize her voice. She sounded tiny and exhausted. "Hudson?"

"Hey, yeah, it's me. I heard you were at the hospital and wanted to check you were okay."

"Not really," she said, sniffling. "Can you… I hate to ask you this Hudson, but can you come get me?"

My heart clenched. She sounded plain worn-out and not at all her usual perky self. "Yeah, of course. You still there at the hospital?"

"Yeah. I'm done, but I don't want to go home right now."

Since Darci worked at the regional hospital outside of Hobie, she had an apartment on the outskirts of town. She refused to live at her parents' hobby farm in Hobie because she took great pride in supporting herself. If she didn't want to go home to her apartment, I wondered why she didn't just stay at her parents' place.

"I'll be there as soon as I can," I told her. "Leaving the ranch now."

I apologized to my sister for ditching the trail ride and told her to give my apologies to Tisha. By the time I pulled my truck into the hospital parking lot, I'd come up with any number of possibilities about why Darci had asked me to come get her instead of a friend or her family members. Maybe I was wrong and her parents were in the city. Maybe her closest friends at the hospital were on shift and couldn't leave to run her home. I also couldn't help but wonder what she was doing there in the first place. Had she been mugged? Or worse?

I quickened my pace as I made my way into the emergency room and saw her huddled in a corner with her face buried in her hands. Her blonde hair was halfway out of some kind of up-do, and she wore a pair of royal blue scrubs that seemed to want to swallow her whole.

"Hey," I said quietly so as not to startle her. "I'm here."

She lifted her face up, and it took all I had not to gasp at the black eyes and large bruise on one side of her chin.

"What the hell happened?" I asked, reaching out to cradle her chin so I could get a better look at it. I realized she didn't have black eyes but a big mess of dark runny makeup from crying.

She burst into tears and reached up to hug me, wrapping her arms tightly around my neck and burying the good side of her face in my collar. I held her and let her cry but noticed she smelled like the perfume she saved for special occasions. There was a white plastic bag on the seat next to hers, and I caught a glimpse of a black sequined number inside. Ah, that would explain why she was wearing strappy high-heels with her scrubs.

"C'mon, let's get you out of here," I said, pulling her off me as gently as I could. That was her workplace and I knew she wouldn't want her co-workers to see her so out of sorts.

I led her out of there with an arm wrapped around her shoulder and her slim frame tucked into my side. Her sniffles tapered off as I sat her in the cab of the truck and made sure she was belted in. Over the hood of the truck I locked eyes with a male nurse everyone called Norm who was known for being the biggest gossip in the place. I saw the minute he realized who I was and what I was doing. So much for privacy. This part of small-town Texas wasn't known for its discretion.

Once I pulled out of the lot, Darci turned to me. "Do you think I could stay with you at the ranch for a little while?"

I wondered what the hell had happened to make her not want to go home.

"You know you can, but are you going to tell me what's going on?"

She sighed and looked out the opposite window. "I got mugged and some jerk stole my purse. Can I get some sleep before I tell you the rest? I'm running on fumes here, Hudson."

I nodded and stayed quiet after that, letting her drift off in her head the way she clearly wanted to. When we got to the cabin, I helped her into bed and brought some toast and juice for her to have before going to sleep. Once she drifted off in the middle of my big bed, I closed the bedroom door and made my way to the small table in the kitchen to do some work on my laptop. It was a beautiful sunny day for January, and I longed to be outside, either riding horses with my siblings or prepping the kitchen garden for spring planting. I'd had to sacrifice those things to live in Dallas, and since moving back to Hobie for the pub project, I'd realized what a loss that had been.

A couple of hours later, there was a knock on my door. West and Nico stood on the front porch to ask if I wanted to come to Dallas with them for the night.

"We're taking Charlie clubbing and then staying over at Saint's place. He's in town if you can believe it," West said.

"Who's watching Pippa?" I asked, stalling for time. I wanted to say yes. I wanted to tag along and find an excuse to dance with Charlie. The idea of him on the prowl in one of the big clubs in the city without me set my teeth on edge. But I couldn't leave Darci, and honestly, I had no business going to a dance club in the city just to sit and stew over someone who wasn't mine.

"We just dropped her off with Doc and Grandpa for a sleepover. They've been begging to keep her, so it worked out. Saint's stoked about seeing Charlie again," Nico added with a grin. "He might have mentioned how freaking pretty the guy is. I can't help but want to ink all that virgin skin."

The Irishman was going to be the cause of my broken molars one day soon.

"You're not inking him," I ground out. Nico's eyes widened in surprise, so I tried to soften my tone. "He doesn't have any tattoos, so clearly that's not his thing."

It didn't occur to me until later that I couldn't possibly know how virgin his skin was unless I'd seen him in something more revealing than the long sleeves and long pants he wore to work every day. I hoped like hell neither Nico nor my brother had caught the slip.

"Anyway, I can't go. Darci's..." I realized I couldn't tell them what had happened since I didn't know myself. "Staying here," I finished lamely.

"Oh," West said, reaching for Nico's hand. "We'll leave you alone, then. Sorry."

I wanted to correct their obvious assumption that she was there for some kind of romantic reunion, but I owed it to her to keep the real reason for her presence at my place private. If she wanted to lie low for a few days, it wouldn't be fair to feed the rumor mill about her injuries.

"Have fun, and be safe on the road," I called out to them. At the last minute I couldn't help but add, "Take care of my coworker. Don't let him out of your sight; we've got a busy week ahead at the pub."

Was I petty? Maybe.

I heard a chuckle and turned to see Charlie wandering up behind West and Nico with an overnight bag in his hand.

"Don't worry about me, Hudson. I'm still in my twenties, remember? I can handle a night out and still make it to work on Monday unlike you old fellas."

"Hey," I said stupidly.

"You coming with us?" Charlie asked. Was that insecurity I saw in his eyes before he plastered on the smile?

"I can't. I..." I took a breath, trying to figure out how to say I wanted to come but had to help a friend instead.

Just then Darci came shuffling out of my bedroom half-asleep and took the turn into the bathroom, calling out to ask if I had any clean towels for her shower. None of the men could see her from where they were standing, but it didn't matter, because there was no mistaking the unintentional insinuation. I felt my stomach drop out when I was sure I saw what looked like flash of pain in Charlie's eyes.

"Oh," Charlie said, dropping the smile. "Sorry. You're busy. We'll leave you alone then."

Before he could turn to leave, I blurted, "Wait!"

He turned back to face me. This time the hurt and disappointment were clear as day. My heart squeezed tightly in my chest while West, Nico, and Charlie all waited for me to explain myself.

"I'm... I'm sorry. I just..." I took a deep breath and locked eyes with Charlie, trying desperately to send him an unspoken message of some kind. I wasn't even sure what. "Have fun, okay? Be safe. Those places are breeding grounds for—"

"West has hand sanitizer and condoms, don't worry," Nico teased. "Let's go."

As the three of them made their way back toward where West's SUV was parked, I heard West mutter, "I don't carry hand sanitizer and you and I don't use condoms."

Nico laughed and threw an arm around his husband. "Shhh, you'll worry your brother. Let him think we've got all the bases covered. I'm sure Charlie has condoms."

I turned back inside before I could hear if Charlie answered. I didn't want to think of him needing condoms at the club in Dallas. The very idea of it made me want to beat the shit out of something.

When Darci finished showering and made her way out to the main room of the cabin, I shook myself out of the mental pity party and got up to help her settle on the sofa under a patchwork quilt that lived in a basket by the TV.

"Want some tea or coffee?" I asked. "I can make your favorite cheesy pasta if you want."

She looked up at me with a grateful smile, and I was reminded of the sweet woman I'd initially been attracted to the year before.

"That would be perfect, thanks. But just some ice water with it. I'm probably going to go back to sleep before long if I can."

Once I got everything fixed and set on a tray, I brought it to her so she didn't have to get up. I took my own bowl of pasta and a beer and made myself comfortable in the armchair next to the sofa.

"Are you going to tell me what happened?"

She glanced up at me through her bangs. She'd brushed her hair at some point and pulled it back into a loose ponytail, and her face was devoid of the traces of makeup that had been on it at the hospital.

"I was out on a date," she said hesitantly, as if worried I'd be upset at the news.

I nodded as encouragingly as I could. "It's okay. Go on. I heard you were seeing a pharma rep at work. I assume it was with him?"

"Yeah, his name is Greg. Anyway, we got into a big fight after being out late at a fundraiser. We ended up calling things off, which is how I wound up coming home in the middle of the night."

I opened my mouth to interrupt her to ask if he'd hurt her, but she stopped me with a hand up.

"I know what you're thinking, and the answer is no. He didn't touch me."

I let out a breath. Thank goodness. If he'd laid a hand on her, I was going to have to kill the man. "Go on. Tell me exactly what happened," I said.

22

CHARLIE

Charlie's Words To Live By:

Gay men are the same all over the world. Horny and handsy. God love 'em.

When I'd heard the woman call out to Hudson from what I could only figure had been the bedroom, I was gutted. It was a complete shock, but more than that, it was a visceral reminder the man was attracted to women. Nico was the one who'd mentioned on the way to the car that the woman was Darci, and I'd remembered seeing a picture of her on Bruce's phone when he'd shown me some photographs of reclaimed wood he'd thought would look good in the pub. The blond woman was lovely, and I could picture her and Hudson together like some kind of perfect couple on the cover of a magazine. Whether they were together or not, I had to admit it was yet another sign things with Hudson weren't progressing the way I'd hoped for.

He'd never been for me. What had I been thinking dreaming of such a thing with Hudson Wilde?

The drive to the city was long enough for me to talk myself into the right frame of mind though, and by the time we arrived at Saint's apartment downtown, I was ready to get some drink in my belly and some man hands on my bum. Anything to wipe the memory of Hudson's mouth on mine and his hands on my bare skin.

"Let's go," I said after we'd had beer and pizza at the apartment. "I'm ready to shake my arse." I stood up and shimmied a little to prove it.

West laughed. "Dude, it's eight o'clock. No one's there yet. Have another beer."

"I'll dance with you," Saint suggested with a teasing twinkle in his eyes. "Better yet, let me keep watching *you* dance."

I had an internal debate on whether or not to encourage Saint's attention. He'd definitely raised an interested eyebrow when we'd greeted each other a couple of hours earlier, but it was hard to tell if he was planning on acting on that interest. Did I want him to? If I hooked up with one of Hudson's brothers, wouldn't that be crossing some kind of line?

But I'd come on to Hudson in his truck the other night, and he'd stopped me. If Mr. Plays-by-the-Rules didn't want me, maybe that freed me up to kiss and sleep with whoever the hell I wanted to. And I really fucking wanted to. It had been a dry three months since I'd last come with someone else in the room, and that had been with Hudson in Cork. At the very least, I could use a blow job in a dark corner to let out a little tension.

But it didn't happen. As soon as I drank enough to loosen up on the dance floor later that night, men had their hands all over me. I loved the attention and took every opportunity to grind and dance my little heart out. But when the first guy asked me for more, I got a sick twist in my gut and convinced myself it was a fear of strangers in a strange land that was holding me back.

By the time we returned to Saint's apartment, I was half-langered, full horny, and overwhelmingly angry.

"Your brother is an arsehole," I grumbled in the direction of my three companions when we collapsed in the sitting room of Saint's apartment.

"Not gonna argue with you there," Saint said with a chuckle. "But which one are we talking about?"

"Why do you say that?" Nico asked, eyeing me like I was a mystery waiting to be solved.

I was just drunk enough, I'd decided, that I was going to tell them all about it.

"He," I began, leaning forward and poking my finger in the air in preparation for making all my points.

"Woah, I'm gonna stop you right there," West said with a penetrating stare. "I think it's time for us to get some sleep before any of us say something we'll regret."

Fuck that. "But I—"

"Bup-bup," Nico said with his own pointed look at me. "Honeybear is right. Let's table this discussion for breakfast. If you still want to pontificate on Hudson's shortcomings at that time, I'm sure his brothers will commiserate with you."

"Honeybear?" West asked his husband as he pulled him up and led him toward the guest room. "Seriously? What about Thor or Adonis? Maybe..." His voice trailed off as they closed the door behind them.

Saint looked at me with a grin. "Ahh, now that it's just us mice, can I get you a drink?"

I noticed how easy and open his face was. For all his big muscles, the man had a bit of a baby face. It was hard to take him seriously as the Navy SEAL-turned-bodyguard Hudson had told me he was. He was pretty easygoing and fun-loving as far as I could tell. Quite different from his oldest brother, the guy who panicked when the salt shaker was separated from the pepper.

I thought about how amazing a tumble with that big easy man would be. I could get him naked and explore miles of smooth muscle before sucking him off or demanding he suck me off.

But despite the vast difference in their looks, I could not get Hudson's image out of my mind. I knew I'd superimpose it over

Saint's face the entire time. I'd compare one brother's attributes to the other's and one, namely Saint, would come up seriously lacking every time.

"No, thanks. It's best if I call it a night," I said with a regretful smile. "Big workweek ahead. We're hiring all the kitchen and waitstaff. That means long nights, and I can't stand it when Hudson has more stamina than I do."

Saint's eyes widened slightly, and I bit back a wince at my words. I actually would love it if Hudson had more stamina than I did in some ways. But not when it came to playing a game of "how late can we work" chicken. Or, at least, that's what Sassy had called it one night when she brought us dinner after nine at night.

Saint stood up and then did something unexpected. He smoothed my hair down before leaning over to drop a kiss on the top of my head. "I'm assuming an offer to share my bed wouldn't be welcome?"

I kept my eyes down and shook my head.

"You're a good man, Charlie," he said. "I'm sorry you've set your eyes on the straight one. I know how hard that is, man. I'll grab you a pillow and blanket."

And then he disappeared into the back of the apartment while I closed my eyes and let out a massive sigh of self-pity. He was right. It was hard as fuck in more ways than one.

I fell asleep wondering if there was a gay man on earth who hadn't felt this shitty feeling of hopelessness. Who hadn't in the dark of night admitted he'd fallen for the unattainable straight man. The man who, but for one pesky exception, seemed his perfect match.

It wasn't until the ride home the following day that West brought up the subject of Darci again.

"Why was Darci at Hudson's cabin?" Nico asked his husband.

My ears perked up. I knew Darci was the woman Hudson had dated before accidentally proposing to her with some doohickey that wasn't really a ring. Even if Cait hadn't told me about it back home, I would have overheard enough bits and pieces of local gossip in Hobie to piece it together.

"I don't know," West said. "Sassy mentioned Hudson going to pick her up from somewhere, but didn't give me any details. I'm sorry."

"Are they back together?" Nico asked.

My stomach dropped so quickly at the idea I thought I might be sick. I'd assumed they were back together, but hearing West and Nico speculate about it made it more real.

"I don't know," West said, flicking his eyes up to me in the rearview mirror before answering Nico. "You have as much information as I do."

I looked out the window, pretending to be too bored to listen to their conversation. In reality, I hung on every word as if I were a spy overhearing secret plans for a nuclear strike.

Nico continued. "I really like her, but I'm not so sure about the two of them together long-term."

"Agreed," West said. "She's a wonderful nurse. The patients love her. But I always thought she was a little too sweet for Hudson. Doc said they reminded him of that couple from *Pride and Prejudice*. The sister and the friend."

"Hm," Nico said with a chuckle. "Can't remember their names, but the ones so nice their servants will steal from them. Doc's right. Anyway, I think your brother is a closet sub. He needs someone who can boss him around and get firm with him."

I almost choked on my saliva while West's deep laugh cut through the SUV.

"Can you imagine Hudson with a collar? We should tell him about that club King mentioned. What's it called?"

"The Sanctuary?" Nico's laugh had turned into a giggle. "The germs alone would keep him out of the place."

"We could get him a little leather holster for his hand sanitizer," West added.

I tried to bite back a smirk because they were so right. Hudson was a freak about germs, and he was way too clean-cut and prim to be caught dead in a BDSM club.

But the conversation had put images in my head that certainly made the rest of the ride home more pleasant. Thinking of Hudson kneeling at my feet, of his bare arse on the receiving end of a paddle, of his deadly gorgeous eyes pleading me for mercy… well, let's just say I could get on board with some more intense fantasies than I'd ever want to actually pursue in real life. Imagining taking out my Darci jealousy on the man's virgin arse was pretty damned satisfying if I did say so myself.

Since those thoughts were immeasurably more satisfying than the speculation of Hudson reuniting with his girlfriend, I enjoyed the filthy mental stimulation until we pulled into the ranch's gravel drive and I heard the high-pitched screech of what had to be a banshee.

23

HUDSON

Hudson's Note to Self:

Dogs can be ~~deflowered~~ impregnated up three weeks after onset of their heat.

I was relieved to learn Darci's bruise hadn't been caused by the man she'd been seeing, but I was furious to learn there was still an asshole responsible.

When Darci had entered her apartment building that night, some punk had come racing out of the apartment below hers and knocked her down onto the bottom of the staircase. She'd banged her chin and bitten her tongue, but before she'd had a chance to get up, the guy had stolen her purse and raced off. Since that was the apartment that always had suspicious comings and goings, she'd reported the incident to the cops. Shayna Diller had been the responding deputy and had urged Darci to go to the hospital since there was so much blood coming from her chin and mouth. She also happened to let slip Darci's neighbor was a suspected drug dealer.

Understandably, Darci didn't want to go back to the apartment.

I'd offered for her to stay at the cabin of course, but I wasn't about to share the single bedroom with her. I debated whether or not to move into the bunkhouse. Would I be able to keep myself from barging into Charlie's room and making inappropriate advances? Ah, *no*. Definitely not.

For now, I'd sleep on the sofa in the cabin just to be on the safe side.

When I stepped out of the cabin to take out the trash late on Sunday afternoon, I thought I heard a shrill scream from the direction of the farmhouse. It was nearing dinnertime, and I wondered if maybe one of the animals was in trouble. After the little cabin I was staying in had been set on fire the previous summer, all of us were a bit more paranoid about intruders on the ranch than we'd been before.

I took off in the direction of Doc and Grandpa's house and came upon a scene out of a telenovela. Doc was trying to calm Grandpa down. Two other people were arguing on the porch, and as I got closer, I could tell from the familiar body language and long red hair that one of the men screaming was Charlie.

"What's going on?" I called out. Doc and Grandpa's two little dogs were yapping up a storm, and I wondered where Grump was.

Charlie turned to me with a look of such anger on his face I nearly stumbled. "Ask this rawny fucker. So, Doc and Grandpa decided he could be trusted with Mama, but he made right bags of it."

If I hadn't known how important his dog was to him, I might have laughed at how Irish he sounded. "What happened?"

Stevie Devore, the colorful character who helped out at Nico's bakery, was there and was clearly the source of the screeching noise. I thought if he didn't get control of himself soon, he'd pass out.

"It's all my fault! Mama got sullied on my watch. Oh my god, *oh my god*." It was enough to make our ears bleed.

The young man was dressed in a lavender polar fleece pullover with a pair of darker purple leggings tucked into white knee-high fur-lined boots. He waved his arms around so wildly, Doc had to duck periodically to avoid getting coldcocked by accident.

"Everyone calm down," Grandpa commanded.

I looked around at the assembled group. Grandpa, Doc, and I were calm. Charlie was steaming mad but silent, and Stevie was hyperventilating loudly.

"Oh gawwwwd! It's all my fault she's been ruined!" he wailed. "I didn't know she was having *her female times*, and I let her in the house with Grump."

Charlie snapped, brows furrowed and cheeks flushed in anger. No man should look that sexy while angry. "I don't even know who the hell you are. What the hell were you doing with my bitch?"

Stevie's tear-streaked face turned feral. "Don't you dare call her that! She's a good girl," he snarled.

Charlie lunged toward the man, and I was struck by how for once he wasn't the smallest guy in the group. For a split second, I feared for Stevie's safety. I knew the muscles Charlie hid under his clothes. They were small, but enough to take out young Stevie.

I reached my arms around Charlie to hold him back, but he pulled away with a jerk. Doc looked up at me with a guilty expression in his eyes. "Grump got to her. We had no idea she was still fertile. We had Stevie bring her in the house with us after he fed the animals."

"Shit," I muttered. Mama was a prize-winning trial champion with bloodlines more impressive than Queen Elizabeth. Grump was a junkyard coonhound who was as old as dirt and about as energetic as the same.

"Yeah, *oh shit*," Charlie spat. "Do you have any idea what this means?"

Grandpa picked the wrong time to get clever. "Collie hound pups about as cute as baby bunnies and confused about whether to herd or nap?"

Stevie wailed again. "Don't mention baby bunnies. I'm already upset enough as it is. Oh sweet baby Jesus on the cross."

"Grandpa," I warned, shooting him a look. "This is a big fucking deal. Mama is a purebred champion trial dog. Her pups go for thousands."

Charlie made a whimpering sound in the back of his throat, and my dick misunderstood its meaning. I looked around and noticed the two fuzzy lovebirds were conspicuously absent.

"Where are Grump and Mama?"

Charlie's lips pressed together in a thin line. "Knotting happily in the family room. I thought maybe I'd go out for a pack of smokes in case they decide to finish one of these days."

Clearly, the man was pissed.

"I thought she was in heat two weeks ago?" I asked.

Charlie's eyes widened. "Are all of you thick as planks? You live on a fucking ranch. Is a woman fertile during her period?"

Stevie shot him daggers with his big wet eyes. "How the hell are we supposed to know anything about women's fertility, you dumbass? Everyone here is jee-ay-why, *gay*. Suuuuper gay. Like, really very—"

"We get it," I said.

Charlie lunged at Stevie again, and I reached out to grab him around the waist.

"Easy, killer. Punching the little dude isn't going to solve anything," I warned in a low voice.

"Wait," Grandpa said, getting serious finally. "Isn't there a shot we can get for her to cancel any pregnancy?"

Charlie sighed. "I won't do that. It causes metabolic stress and doesn't always work right. I've seen firsthand bitches who've had to have C-sections with singletons after the mismate jab," he muttered. "And I'm not quite sure how I feel about subjecting her to any of it when this wasn't her fault."

I let go of his waist but reached out to rub the tension from his shoulders without thinking. He flinched and pulled away, spearing me with narrowed eyes. I held my hands up in a placating gesture. "I'm sorry. It's not your fault. It doesn't need to be anyone's fault."

"Of course it's not my fault. It's *his*," he growled, pointing a finger at Stevie. "Bloody wanker."

Stevie started crying again, and Doc pulled him in for a hug.

Grandpa looked guilty. "Charlie, we're so sorry. We should have used our heads. We hired Stevie to do some chores around here and didn't think to tell him about the dogs. And there's no excuse for Grump not being fixed in the first place. We rescued him when he was around six years old and just never got around to it since all he did was sleep all day. The other two are fixed."

Charlie turned to look up at me. The warm light from the setting sun illuminated two bright spots of pink on his high cheekbones. "I… I was kind of looking forward to showing everyone what she can do in that competition near Austin.." Charlie actually looked at *me* when he said the word *everyone*, and my heart jumped in my chest.

"It was stupid," he continued, letting out another sigh. "She'll be fine. She's a good mum. Whelps easy and all that… Plus, Grandpa's half-right. The pups will either be cute as hell or ugly as the devil."

Something warmed inside of me when I heard him refer to Grandpa the way the rest of us did instead of by his first name. Most people in town called him Weston, but all of the kids in my generation and younger called him Grandpa even if he wasn't their own grandfather. I knew how much it meant to Grandpa since he wasn't blood relations with anyone in Hobie, and it meant even more to Doc that everyone treated him as if he were.

"Maybe when I move back to the city, I'll have to find a place with a yard," I teased, trying to lighten the mood. "Since I'm sure you're going to force one of those ugly-ass collie-coons on me."

Charlie took a swipe at me with the back of his hand, catching me in the gut. "You'll take more than one, Hudson Wilde. If it's a big litter, you're taking as many as I say."

Seeing the partial smile on his face helped me let go of the stress of the situation. I grinned back at him and gave him a salute. "Yes, sir. As you wish."

I caught Grandpa's eye over Charlie's head and noticed him wink at me. I wondered if he was able to see past my lame attempt at casual friendliness and see just how much my heart was beating out of my chest for the man beside me. If anyone knew how torn up inside I was about him, there would be no end to the ribbing I'd get from my siblings. I couldn't even imagine what it would be like if my family discovered I wasn't straight after all. The questions, the intrusion into my privacy... all of it would make me the center of attention in a way that horrified me to think of.

I cleared my throat. "Stevie, you need a ride back to town?"

He shook his head and gestured vaguely toward the barn. "Thanks, sugar, but I drove. I'll be going." He sniffed and looked forlornly at Charlie. "I'm really sorry. I didn't mean to deflower your sweet Mama."

Charlie met Stevie's eyes for a beat before blowing out a breath and yanking the younger guy into an embrace. "Oh for fuck's sake. It was an accident," he muttered. "Sorry I gave you the what for."

Of course that set Stevie off again, only this time he wailed happy tears. "Oh my god you're the sweetest thing ever. You think maybe we could get a coffee together sometime? You're kind of disgustingly beautiful, and the two of us together might blind people. Hobie could stand a good old-fashioned blinding."

Charlie laughed, and I turned around quickly to keep from doing something stupid like grabbing the beautiful Irishman and running for the hills to keep him all to myself. I couldn't remember a time I'd ever felt so possessive of anyone in my entire life. Not even Darci.

I couldn't deny my feelings for the man weren't going away anytime soon. It was harder and harder to convince myself not to act on my attraction.

Instead of standing around watching Stevie flirt with the Irishman, I mumbled a good night before turning and making my way back to the cabin. I'd left Darci fixing us something for dinner in the small cabin kitchen.

When I returned, she was serving up a couple of giant plates of salad. It looked like she'd used every vegetable in my fridge and even found some fish filets in the freezer to go on top of it. I opened up a bottle of wine and filled our glasses before digging in.

"Thanks for making this. You didn't have to," I said before taking another bite. "But it's really good."

She smiled. "You're the only man I know who'll accept a salad as a main course."

I shrugged. "That's what you get with a couple of doctors in the family, but we both know if you weren't here, I'd be having a bowl of cereal with a cookie chaser," I said with a wink in her direction.

She sighed and put down her fork. "Do you think you could ever give me another chance, Hudson?"

My own fork clattered against my plate before I almost flipped my wineglass onto the floor. By the time I made sure nothing was going to topple over, Darci's eyes were as big as Frisbees.

I coughed. "I… I mean… I didn't expect you to say that. It kinda caught me off guard."

"I miss being with you. You're a good man, Hudson. I should have realized it at the time." Her eyes went down to gaze into her glass of wine. "I feel like an idiot. Just because you weren't ready to get married doesn't mean I should have broken up with you like that."

My heart hammered in my chest, and I wondered at it. Was her plea something I wanted?

No. The spiked heart rate was a bit more like panic. "I… I understood though. You know?" I babbled. "It made sense since I made a mess of the whole thing and in front of your parents no less. And it's not like I don't want to get married. *Some*day. But not now. I mean, not anytime soon. What I mean to say is—"

Darci's hand came out and squeezed mine gently. "Stop. It's okay. Let's just put this conversation away for another time, all right? Maybe you can think about what I said. I didn't expect an answer right away, and I didn't mean to spoil our dinner either."

I swallowed and dove back into my salad, thinking of it as The Greatest Salad That Ever Saved A Man From A Serious Conversation. When we finished up, I cleared our dishes and made quick work of them in the sink before refilling Darci's wine and moving us both to the sofa.

"You know you're welcome to stay here, but why don't you want to tell your family?" I asked gently.

Her answer shocked me.

"My mom will only say 'I told you so' since she'd warned me it was a crappy apartment complex, and Dad has too much else on his plate right now with selling the company and everything."

It took me a minute to process what she'd said, and then my first reaction was to bark out a laugh. "Your dad would never sell his company. That's ridiculous. What made you think he was selling?"

But then I saw her eyes. "He didn't tell you? Damn, I shouldn't have said anything. He wants to retire."

I scrambled to picture busy, successful Bruce Ames kicking back on the golf course during the week, but it was difficult. The man was a workaholic, and he loved his job. "He asked me to come to Dallas for a meeting this coming week but didn't say what it was about. I assumed it was simply a routine thing or a new opportunity to assess."

"I'll let him tell you then. Please don't let on that I mentioned it."

Even though I was sure she knew what she was talking about, I still couldn't picture Bruce selling Ames. It was impossible.

"Wow. I don't know what to say," I told her. "I'm shocked, but I guess I understand. He's over sixty now and has plenty of money. Your mom's always mentioned wanting to travel more."

Darci nodded. "Now do you see why I don't want to bother them with this? They'll flip out. The timing is terrible. I'm afraid if my dad found out what that guy in the apartment building did, he'd go after him with a gun."

She wasn't wrong. Bruce Ames was a Texas good old boy deep in his heart. The man wouldn't stand for some asshole to lay a hand on his baby girl.

Darci grabbed my arm. "Now can you see why I just want to lie low?"

"Of course. You can stay here as long as you want," I promised.

She nodded and leaned her head against my shoulder before letting out a shuddering breath. The poor thing was exhausted, and I'd have to pour her into my bed before long to get some more sleep.

Our conversation had brought up several issues, but I couldn't help but focus on the one that had the potential to change everything. If Ames International transferred ownership, I wasn't the only one whose future would be affected. In addition to Ames's employees, the Fig and Bramble business could wind up a casualty depending on how the new owners felt about Bruce's side project. What if they decided to sell off the pub to a big restaurant holding company?

If something like that happened, Charlie would never forgive me for bringing his family business into this mess.

24

CHARLIE

Charlie's Words To Live By:

Don't fuck with the Irish. They're a mad lot.

That week at work, Hudson was different. Distracted maybe, and more serious than usual. I assumed it had something to do with his getting back together with Darci, which only caused me to be even pissier at him than I'd been before.

My anger was irrational. I knew that. But it didn't mean I was able to hide it any better. Late on Tuesday, it came to a head.

"Fer fuck's sake," I hissed. "Can't you leave me to do anything myself? Back the fuck up."

I hadn't meant to snipe at Hudson, but it was like everywhere I went in the pub and everything I tried to do, he was in my blind spot waiting for me to make a deadly mess of it.

Hudson jerked back and began apologizing, which only made me feel more of an arse.

I turned to him with a scowl. "Look, I get that you don't trust me to know what the hell I'm doing here, but consider for a second I actually do. I've been pulling pints and sweeping up after my auld man for twenty years in one of the oldest pubs in Ireland. This shit is in my blood. I was born to do this, yeah?"

As I bitched, Hudson's eyes grew wider until I thought they might bug right out of his head.

"Charlie," he began, his voice low and calm as usual. "I only wanted to offer to hold the railing while you screwed in the bracket. I thought it would make it easier with two pairs of hands."

I glanced at the long brass bar I'd been struggling with and let out a sigh. He was right. It would take me half as long to mount it if someone held the other end while I used the screwdriver.

"Fine. Hold it there," I muttered.

While I concentrated on getting the bracket mounted, I sensed Hudson sneaking glances at me. Finally he caved.

"Are you mad at me?"

"No."

I made sure the bracket was the straightest fastener that had ever been fastened.

"Because you've either iced me out or bitched at me for the past two days. I want to know why. Did I do something?"

Yes. You kissed me and then walked away. You reunited with a woman, which proves what happened between us was truly just an experiment.

You rejected me like everyone else I've ever been with has done.

"No."

He sighed and stopped asking. The tension between us was hideous and only served to make my muscles tense up to the point of pain.

Hudson couldn't handle the silence. "For god's sake, Charlie. Will you at least talk to me?"

"After you called me a bitch?" I snapped. "No, thanks."

He threw his free hand up in the air. "Are you kidding? I didn't call you a bitch. I said you were bitching at me. That's not the same thing. Clearly I've done something to upset you, and if you won't tell me what it is, I can't fix it."

I finished the bracket and moved to the next one down the rail.

Hudson shuffled down a bit too, but we ended up closer than before. The crisp fabric of his pressed denim shirt brushed against the bare skin of my upper arm below the short sleeve of my T-shirt. I'd pulled off my hoodie after helping carry in loads of tables and chairs earlier when I'd gotten overheated, but now I was chilled again in the underheated space of the half-finished pub. I felt the warmth coming off Hudson's larger body in comforting waves. I wanted to lean over and soak it in.

"It's not you," I lied. "I'm in a funk since the weekend. Ignore me."

I could tell he was trying to puzzle it out, and the moment he thought he'd come to a conclusion, his eyes widened again.

"The club. In Dallas. What happened?"

I looked over at him in confusion. His eyes were narrowed and his lips pressed angrily together. The storm was clearly brewing in his expression.

"Charlie, did something happen? Did you... meet someone? Did it... go badly?"

He tripped over the words he wasn't used to using. Clearly he meant to ask if I'd hooked up with someone and he wanted to know if they'd fucked me over somehow.

Hudson's hand suddenly gripped my arm, and he pulled me around to face him. "Charlie, what happened this weekend? Why weren't West and Nico there? And Saint?" At the mention of Saint's name, Hudson's face fell. "Did Saint... did you and Saint... did...?"

I rushed to correct him. "No. Nothing happened with me and Saint. There is no me and Saint."

The relief on his face spun my heart around in circles until I didn't know which end was up.

"Then what happened? Please talk to me. I know it can't be easy being so far from home and from Cait."

He was so thoughtful, I wanted to confide in him. If only my problem hadn't been *him*, I might have.

I suddenly thought of an out. "I'm still upset about Mama. I know I shouldn't be, but I feel guilty for leaving her with your grandfathers because now they feel responsible. And poor Stevie. I thought the bloke was going to pass out in the garden. I'm going to have to work hard to make it up to him," I said with what I hoped was a chuckle.

"Oh, right. Will she be okay, do you think?"

I nodded. "Yes, as long as you all help me find good homes for the pups. Usually I don't breed her until I already have her pups spoken for by farmers or trialers. I never want to be the cause of an unwanted pup."

Hudson's smile lit up the dim pub like a ray of Texas sunshine. "We'll all help. And if we can't find homes elsewhere, I know a couple of guys who have a ranch with plenty of space and love for extra dogs."

I leaned my shoulder into his for the briefest moment. "Thanks. I'll try to relax about it, then."

We continued working together in companionable silence. I tried to put away my bratty attitude about his reconciliation with Darci because it was stupid and immature. If he was attracted to women, and if he was in love with this woman in particular, my silly crush on him needed to die a swift death.

I thought about the date I owed Stevie. The man wasn't really my type, but I assumed he'd be a good person to know in case he wanted to go clubbing together. I couldn't very well ask West and Nico to leave their daughter every weekend, and I wasn't quite so desperate to drive all the way to Dallas by myself.

When it was time to break for lunch, I walked out of the pub into the early-February sunshine and made the call. Stevie answered with the same dramatic enthusiasm he'd showed on Sunday.

"Hello, gorgeous! I hope like hell you're calling to ask me out because, honey, I have plans for you."

I couldn't hold back a laugh. "I am calling to ask you out. I owe you an apology and would love to meet under less-upsetting circumstances."

"Praise Jesus and pass the potatoes. Just tell me when and where, Sugar Britches."

"Did you just call me Sugar Britches?" I asked with a laugh. Stevie's Texas was showing, and I loved it.

His warm laughter tinkled through the phone. "No, but I may do so in the future. That's the name of the shop, silly. I was greeting a customer. Haven't you come in for coffee yet?"

I remembered everyone mentioning Nico's bakery and coffee shop in town, but I hadn't been there yet.

"No. Hudson always picks up the coffees after he drops me off at the pub. I'll have to come in and try your muffins."

Stevie's gasp didn't surprise me. "Well, aren't you a fresh one? You might need to try some of my other things too if you catch my drift. So, when are we doing this, sweetheart?"

A night out with this character was going to be great fun. I decided to give as good as I got. "You free tonight, cutie pie?"

25

HUDSON

Hudson's Words To Live By:

Never assume. It makes an ass *out of* u *and* me.

Of course I overheard the end of Charlie's phone call that afternoon where he was Flirty McFlirtson with whoever was on the other end of the phone. I assumed it was Stevie, who was known as the flirtiest gay man in Hobie. And considering how many gay men lived in Hobie these days, that was saying a lot.

I tried to put the image of the two of them together out of my head. If Charlie wanted to screw around with someone else, that was his decision. It wasn't like I'd offered him an easy alternative, and Charlie wasn't looking to screw around really. He was looking for a relationship, in which case maybe I should warn him about Stevie's reputation for being big on the casual hookup.

No. It was none of my business. Plus, I had bigger things to worry about. I couldn't very well sleep on the sofa forever, which meant I needed to help Darci find a new place to live.

She kept herself busy Monday and Tuesday with shifts at the

hospital and came home each night to the cabin where we shared meals, researched apartments, or did our own thing. Wednesday night took me completely by surprise, however. I should have known with both of them living on the ranch, Darci and Charlie would eventually meet, but I didn't spare a moment to consider what that would actually look like.

Doc texted to let me know he was making gumbo and cornbread for whoever wanted to show up. Bruce had put off our meeting in Dallas until later the following day, so I asked Darci if she wanted to join me over there for dinner. She happily agreed and raced off to touch up her makeup so she didn't have to answer any questions about the bruise on her chin. I knew she'd appreciate a chance to see Doc and Grandpa, but it didn't even register with me that Charlie might be there as well.

When we entered the kitchen, Charlie was singing a bawdy pub song at full volume into a wooden-spoon microphone and shaking his little round ass as much as he could in the tight red jeans he was wearing. The same tight red jeans I'd been trying my hardest to ignore all day at work.

The lyrics to the song didn't help my libido stand down at all.

"As I went home on Sunday night as drunk as drunk could be, I saw a thing in her thing where my old thing should be, well, I called me wife and I said to her: Will you kindly tell to me, who owns that thing in your thing where my old thing should be!"

I froze on the spot and felt my face heat up right about the time I realized what the "thing" was.

Darci, on the other hand, joined in.

"I know this one! It's called Seven Drunken Nights," she exclaimed with a smile, joining Charlie when he got to the chorus of "*You're drunk, you're drunk, you silly old fool.*"

I thought I might die of mortification when Darci's higher voice alerted Charlie to our presence. He whipped around, hair following in a silky arc over his shoulders. He wore only a tight white undershirt that barely reached the low waistband of his jeans, and I caught a flash of pale bare skin over one of his hips as he turned. He had old battered sheepskin slippers on his feet, and part of me melted at the realization he felt completely at home in my grandparents' kitchen.

Charlie took in Darci's tall frame. She was dressed in jeans and a long-sleeved T-shirt but had grabbed one of my new fleece hoodies for the walk from the cabin to the farmhouse. Charlie's eyes took in the familiar Fig and Bramble logo and widened a bit before shifting to me. I thought I detected disappointment or hurt in his gaze, but I wondered if that was some kind of sick wishful thinking on my part. And if so, what kind of selfish idiot wished jealousy on someone? I was an ass.

"Uh, hi," I said, as if we hadn't spent ten hours together already that day.

"Cheers," he muttered before putting the spoon down on the counter and wiping his hands on his thighs. He reached out a hand to Darci and flashed the fakest smile I'd ever seen. "Charlie Murray, pleased to meet you."

Darci was all smiles and charm as usual. "Darci Ames. I've heard so much about you."

Charlie's quick glance at me betrayed his confusion.

I cleared my throat. "I told her what a great job you've been doing at the pub."

He pursed his lips together and nodded. "Yes. The pub. Hopefully *your* father will be happy," he said to her.

His emphasis on the term "your" brought my head up. Was his own father aware of what was happening with Fig and Bramble's franchise agreement with Ames? Was he upset about it? And why hadn't I thought to ask Charlie about it before now?

Because you avoid personal conversations with him like the plague.

Darci continued to gush about how exciting it was to have an Irish pub opening in Hobie. I knew she was trying to be her usual friendly self, but I also knew her chipper chattiness was the last thing Charlie wanted to listen to right now.

"Would you like a drink?" I asked her.

"Sure. Wine if there's some open." She smiled at me before moving over to give Grandpa and Doc hugs hello.

I made my way to the fridge, not realizing until I got there I hadn't offered Charlie anything. I turned back to him. "Sorry, would you like something?"

"Yep, but I'm quite sure you don't have it to give," he said softly with a wink before turning back around and busying himself with Doc's little dog Sweets.

As his words sunk in, my heart dropped. He'd said it with a teasing voice, but the lightness hadn't reached his eyes. He was clearly disappointed in me, and who could blame him? I was acting like the freaked-out straight guy he'd probably pegged me as.

I poured a glass of white wine before grabbing a beer for myself. After handing over the wine to Darci, I took a seat around the large wooden table in the center of the large kitchen and living room area. Darci propped her hip on the table next to me but angled herself toward Charlie, who stood at the kitchen counter picking his way through a bowl of mixed nuts.

"So, Charlie, my dad has told me how charming your family holdings are in Ireland. What was it like growing up in a historic pub?"

I closed my eyes for a second, knowing how he'd take her inquiry.

He scraped his lip with his teeth before answering. "Well, I didn't know any different, did I? It was good and bad, I suppose. Boring for a little tyke living on the cliffs, but more exciting when I was old enough to nick a pint behind my dad's back."

Darci smiled. I knew she was genuinely interested in him and his family's business, but I also knew her Southern manners would come off as condescending to someone like Charlie.

"Are your parents missing you? You have a sister too, I believe."

Charlie's eyes flicked to mine before looking back at Darci with the same fake smile from before. "My parents aren't there. My mom took off when I was younger to pursue her career in the city. My dad recently met someone and moved with her to Brazil. That left my uncle in charge. My sister, Cait, and I help out where we can."

Darci opened her mouth to ask more questions, but I cut her off in a desperate attempt to save her from igniting the Irish temper in the room.

"How did your date with Stevie go?" I blurted.

You could have heard a pin drop. My grandfathers gawped at me, Darci turned to me with a questioning eyebrow, and Charlie's eyes widened.

"Sorry, I didn't mean to—" I stammered.

"No, it's fine. We had a nice time. I took him to the Italian place out past the hospital. What's the name of it?"

Darci clapped her hands in excitement. "Nonna's. We get takeout from there all the time at work. Ooh, how romantic."

"What did he wear?" Doc asked with a devilish grin.

Charlie snorted. "Yellow trousers, purple button-up, and navy jumper. I believe his shoes were silver glitter trainers."

Grandpa wandered over to stir the giant pot of gumbo on the stove. "Navy sweater, huh? Seems he toned it down a bit for you."

Darci glanced at me. "I love how confident he is to be himself. That can't be easy in a town like Hobie."

"No, certainly not," I agreed.

I caught Charlie sneaking a glance at me. "It's not easy in many places. I'd imagine anywhere other than the biggest cities."

I wondered not for the first time what it was like growing up gay in the isolated coastal area of Ireland where he lived. I was surprised he was as out and proud as he was. Maybe Ireland was more accepting than Texas was.

"Was it hard for your siblings, growing up gay here?" Charlie asked before realizing Doc and Grandpa might be better ones to ask. He glanced at both of them. "Or what about you two? I can't imagine being out here a few decades ago."

Doc and Grandpa shared a look before Grandpa answered. "It took us a while before we were brave enough to come out. For a long time, we let people believe I was simply the foreman on his daddy's ranch. Liam was a physician in town, so everyone understood the ranch needed someone else looking after it once Mr. Wilde passed. Then people began to suspect we'd become close friends. It wasn't until the kids were old enough to refer to me as Pop that people realized we were more than friends. Soon after that, we began to suspect our daughter Gina was gay. We realized we had to set an example and show her how to live out and proud. I won't say it's been easy, but it surely gets easier every day."

He shot a warm glance at his husband. Doc looked at Charlie with a mischievous glint in his eyes. "It helps if you recruit all your grandchildren to the dark side and populate the town with your own little mini-gays. We're still working on poor Hudson here, but so far the gay hasn't stuck."

Grandpa gasped and smacked Doc's ass. "Hush. People will talk."

Doc snickered. "They already think we turned them all gay, babe. Might as well have fun with it."

My stomach lurched, and I couldn't help but glance at Charlie.

This. This was exactly why I was scared to tell my family what I'd been going through with my attraction to Charlie. The speculation between nature and nurture, the idea some people had in town that my gay siblings had been influenced by my grandfathers. They joked about it, but I knew there was some part of them that worried about what people thought. And how in the world could I come out as questioning at the age of thirty-five without starting up all that chatter and speculation again?

Charlie didn't look over at me, and I closed my eyes in relief. I wasn't sure I could handle making eye contact with the only person in the room who knew how I might be feeling about this right now.

The rest of the evening progressed with an uneasy balance of Darci trying her hardest to be friendly to Charlie and Charlie trying his hardest to resist. It was a losing battle. Darci Ames was the kind of woman who'd become a nurse to help people feel better. She had one of the biggest hearts I knew, and her greatest wish was for people to be happy and healthy. Resisting her charms was almost impossible, and sure enough, by the end of the evening, Charlie was agreeing to Darci's suggestion to visit an Irish pub she knew of in Dallas.

"You'll love it, I promise," Darci gushed. "They have excellent meat pies and a woman who plays a gorgeous fiddle on the weekends. I'll finally have someone who can sing with me. Hudson refuses to sing even though he has a lovely voice."

"You had me at 'meat pies,' woman," Charlie said with a soft smile. "Let me know when you want to go, and maybe we can impose upon Hudson's brother for an overnight at his flat. He said I was welcome to come back and stay anytime."

I felt the familiar jangle of jealousy at the idea of him being cozy with my brother Saint, but I knew it was stupid. Even this night, Charlie had implied his interest still lay with me. And if that was the case, I needed to decide what, if anything, I wanted to do about it. It was time for me to stop acting like a bear with a thorn in its paw and *do* something.

26

CHARLIE

Charlie's Revelation (and Lament):

Of course Darci is a good person. Why else would Hudson have chosen her?

Meeting Darci had been a shock, but I had to admit the woman was a sweetheart. Of course she was; it would be way too easy if she was a villain I could love to hate.

But she wasn't. And after a miserable Thursday at work with no Hudson to sneak glances at, I had the opportunity to spend more time with her. As soon as I finished running Mama through some exercises in one of the fields behind the barn, I made my way into the stalls to visit Kojack. It was silly, and I wouldn't dare admit it out loud to anyone, but part of me felt like being close to that dumb horse was a bit like being close to his owner.

"Your man's in the city tonight, big guy. Ask me how I know. Spent the whole day feeling sorry for myself," I murmured into his neck. "No pretty eyes to gaze at. No cute bum to admire. Poor me."

I whispered more silly words to him and stroked his nose for a bit before hearing a sound from the direction of the barn door. Hoping it was Hudson, himself, I was utterly disappointed to see it was Darci instead.

"Oh, hiya," I said, willing my fair skin to keep its blush to itself.

She jumped in surprise when she saw me but then smiled. Her smile was genuine and friendly which galled me. I didn't want her to be nice.

"Hi Charlie."

She was dressed in pink patterned nursing scrubs and I was struck by how tall and beautiful she was. Despite her lovely looks, however, her eyes shone with the same natural openness that made me feel as though I could tell her anything. I could definitely see why Hudson had been attracted to her and why she most likely made a good nurse.

"Sorry about Mama," I added, gesturing to the gray ball of fluff whimpering at her feet. "She's a bit affectionate."

"What a sweet girl you are," Darci cooed at her, crouching down to scratch under her chin. "Are you daddy's girl, hmm? Such a good girl."

And she's nice to dogs. Fuck me.

"Do you ride?" I asked, nodding my head toward the curious equine faces peering out of the stalls around us.

"A little. I took lessons as a child, but I never seem to find the time these days." As she spoke, she straightened back up until the light from a nearby fixture illuminated traces of a yellowing bruise on her chin I hadn't noticed the night before. I couldn't help but gasp.

"What happened?"

She reached for her chin and touched it gently, wincing a bit. "Oh crap, can you see it?"

I wasn't quite sure whether or not I should lie. "Um..."

"My makeup must have rubbed off. It was one of those days at work," she said with a soft chuckle. "Hudson didn't tell you about what happened to me?"

I thought of the cold shoulder I'd been giving him at work until that afternoon. "No. We haven't talked much lately about personal stuff."

"He's kind of shy and quiet anyway," she said.

I thought about the man who'd babbled all night across the bar the first time we'd met and wondered if we were talking about the same man.

Darci continued. "I had this terrible date with a guy I'd been seeing. After we broke things off, I trudged my sorry ass home to my apartment, only to be laid flat by some jerk running out of the downstairs apartment."

"You're kidding? You poor thing," I said. I wondered if I was more surprised she'd been dating someone or more upset she was no longer seeing him? Either way, I was a selfish prick.

"Yeah, I kind of landed on my face. Anyway, I filed a report with the sheriff's deputy and found out the people who live there are drug dealers. After that, I was kind of scared to go home, you know? Hudson came and got me and let me stay at his place. He's an angel."

The fact he'd rushed in to rescue her didn't surprise me at all. Hudson Wilde was that sort of man. The good sort.

"Christ, Darci. I'm so sorry. Are you okay?"

She smiled and nodded. "It could have been worse, I guess. But I have to admit to feeling better being here at the ranch than living above people who might be up to no good. Plus, with Hudson around all the time, I feel safe. Well, all of you, really."

"For what it's worth, I'm not sure I could stand up against someone like that in a stiff wind, but I could at least tell Mama to bite the man's arse," I admitted.

Darci chuckled. "Hudson told me you have a sister. I'm sure you're protective of her the way Hudson is with his siblings, right?"

I thought of how in a scuffle, Cait was more likely to have to protect me than the other way round. I let out a laugh but then realized something. "Hudson told you about Cait?"

She nodded. "He talks about you all the time; I feel like I know you. He told me about your dog training, about where you grew up in

Ireland, and how everyone in Hobie swoons over your accent. I can see why. It's lovely."

I felt the heat rise on my skin, but it was quashed with a rush of guilt. I had no business being flattered by the man she might still have some kind of relationship with or feelings for.

"You're lucky to have Hudson in your life," I said, clearing my throat and pretending to fuss with Mama's collar. "He's a good man."

"He is. One of the best. I hope he still feels the same way about me. It was a mistake for me to ever let him go."

The tone in her voice sounded the way I felt, lovesick and wanting. It was clear she had plans to get him back. Hell, for all I knew, they were on their way to reconciliation already. I reached out to squeeze her shoulder and mumbled something about letting me know if she ever needed anything. Before she finished thanking me, I was whistling for Mama to follow me back to the bunkhouse so I could try to escape my head in sleep.

On Friday, while Hudson was still in Dallas, I lost track of Mama. Ever since the Grump incident, I'd been bringing her to work at the pub where I could keep a closer eye on her. Now that she wasn't fertile any longer and she'd gotten to know several Hobie residents fairly well, I left her to her own devices most of the day.

Round about lunchtime I realized I hadn't seen her for a while and raced around like a spinning top trying to track her down. I searched everywhere in the pub, out back in the patio garden area, and out front in the village green. No sign of her. By the time I began checking other shops nearby, I'd gathered quite a team of helpers.

"Mama's been snatched!" Stevie's screech notified half the town who came to assist in the search. I tried to remain calm, but the more places we searched with no success, the more I worried.

Finally, someone called out from the direction of the dusty old antiques store a couple of doors down from the pub. "She's here. Awww, look at that. How sweet."

The crowd bustled over, and I spotted her, curled up in the display window on an oriental rug. Nestled into her belly like the little spoon in a snuggle was a spotted calico kitten.

"That's Milo," someone behind me said. "The new shop owner's cat."

Someone else jumped in to correct them. "Nah, Milo's the man. Augie is the cat."

"Augie is the man. It's short for August. Milo is definitely the cat," someone else said.

I didn't particularly care one way or the other but I needed to extract my dog back.

"Excuse me," I muttered, making my way to the front of the pack to open the shop door. Inside I found an attractive man about my size fussing with a large wooden crate.

"I'm sorry to bother you, but I'm afraid my dog has trespassed on your hospitality," I said, nodding my head toward the window display. "I hope she didn't cause any damage."

He turned toward me with a little jump of surprise. "What? No, of course not."

I nodded, stepping closer and holding out my hand. "I'm Charlie Murray. I work at the pub opening up down the way."

"Oh, sorry," he said, wiping his hands on an actual linen handkerchief pulled from a back pocket. "I'm August, but my friends call me Augie. You have a nice dog. She's well trained. All I have to do is give her a look and she seems to know what I mean."

I let out a chuckle. "That's Mama. Some say she's smarter than I am. I, myself, am sure of it."

"She's welcome here anytime... as are you," he said, blushing at his own words and glancing down at his feet. "I mean, it's no bother."

He was kind and attractive, yet I felt nothing. No desire to flirt with him. No need to ask him out in order to get to know him better. No mental undressing of his button-up shirt and tweed trousers. Hell. Maybe I was broken. Hudson had ruined me and now I would never find anyone else.

No wonder Cait accuses you of being dramatic.

I smiled at Augie. “Same goes for you at the pub. Come see us anytime.”

After exchanging a few more friendly words, I extracted my wandering canine and made my way back to the pub. That afternoon, Mama made four more trips to the antique shop. Four more times I found her curled up in the window with Milo. By the time I found her that fourth time, Augie simply laughed and told me to leave her there.

Within the span of one day, she’d become a kitten whore and the centerpiece of the town’s entertainment. I left work to collect her for the ride back to the ranch and saw the most recent display in the window. Mama was dead asleep on her back, and Milo was stretched out on top of her from her neck to her belly like a calico necktie. At least twenty people stood out front of the antique shop smiling and pointing at the merry image in the window. When they saw me coming, several people called me by name and pulled me in to see the charming sight.

I couldn’t help but smile and feel a part of the magic of this small Texas town.

Just another Friday night in Hobie.

27

HUDSON

Hudson's Words To Live By:
Be careful what you wish for.

Thursday and Friday were spent in a kind of haze. Darci had been correct: Bruce Ames was retiring and selling the company. He'd been approached with an offer from a larger international investment firm and wanted my help in the negotiations.

"Hudson, I'd like to move forward with your promotion so that you transition to the new company as vice president," he explained in one of our first meetings on the topic. "I'll put in a stipulation guaranteeing you at least a couple of years with them at that level. That should give you time to prove yourself to them and continue to succeed with them or to find a new position with a different company if that's the direction you choose."

I couldn't believe the opportunity he was offering me. I'd left my previous firm less than a year ago as a senior analyst with a reputation as a successful negotiator, and now I was going to be a VP for a giant firm with experience negotiating the sale of a billion-dollar portfolio. It was my dream come true.

So why wasn't I more excited? Why wasn't I bouncing off the walls, waiting to get out of there so I could text my father the good news?

"I can't thank you enough, Bruce," I said with as much enthusiasm as I could. "I appreciate the opportunity working with Ames has given me. I'm prepared to work hard to make sure you get the best deal possible."

The large man leaned back in his chair and smiled. "I know you are. You've always been a hard worker, Hudson. Bill and Shelby must be very proud of you. I know I certainly am."

My heart squeezed a bit. It was kind of him to say and almost as nice as hearing it from my own parents. It also illustrated he held no ill-will toward me for the break-up with Darci. I wondered what had caused the change of heart. Maybe he thought she was still happy with Greg?

I sat up straighter in my chair and began taking notes on my laptop. "I'll start by pulling together everything I can get my hands on about their other acquisitions," I said, referring to the company making the offer for Ames. "We should be able to get an idea of their negotiating techniques that way."

We continued to work together for the rest of Thursday and all day Friday. Bruce treated me like an equal and over the course of our time together I realized how much he trusted me. Before I left the office Friday afternoon to return to Hobie, he pulled me aside.

"Listen. Even though I'm counting on you to help handle the negotiations, I don't want to pull you completely off of the Fig and Bramble project. I know things are going well there and I'd hate to fumble it on the one-yard line. I need you back in the office on Tuesday for a meeting, but otherwise I'd like you in Hobie working on the pub. Any work I have for you on the acquisition can probably be done in the evenings. After the pub's up and running, we'll get you back here and on track to move forward with the transition."

I should have felt elation at being brought back into the corporate fold, at being given higher-level responsibilities again. But the idea of leaving Fig and Bramble after all of the work I'd put into it was bittersweet.

And the thought of no longer working with Charlie was damned near impossible.

~

On Saturday morning, I found out about Charlie's next trip to the dance club by accident. He'd been acting cold toward me for several days so I shouldn't have been surprised he hadn't wanted to include me.

I'd agreed to help Sassy move some furniture around in her apartment. When I asked why West and Nico weren't helping us since the apartment was above West's medical practice, she looked at me funny.

"They're taking Charlie to the city. I assumed he'd told you. They've been planning it for days."

My heart sunk like a brick. "No. No one told me."

She wrinkled her forehead. "I would have thought they'd drag you along with them. It's not like you ever complain about going to a gay bar with everyone."

I felt stung. It would be one thing if West and Nico were going on their own, but to take Charlie without even asking if I wanted to join them? I was their connection to him. I was the one who'd introduced them. I guess I shouldn't have been surprised they hadn't included me after I'd declined to join them the previous weekend. Charlie had clearly decided I wasn't into him like that anymore. I assumed he was still pissed about our aborted attempt to hook up in my truck the week before Darci's accident, but since I hadn't gotten up the nerve to talk to him about it, the awkwardness between us remained.

After Sassy and I finished moving the furniture, I kissed my sister on the cheek and headed back out to my truck. I couldn't help but text my asshole brother.

Hudson: *Thanks for including me, jackass.*

West: *What, Dallas? I didn't think you'd be interested in dancing with a dick in your ass.*

I felt my face heat up at the idea of a dick in my ass. My own dick expressed interest in the concept, especially if the dick in question was attached to a certain long-haired beauty with an Irish temper.

Hudson: *When have I ever complained about going out with you guys?*

West: *We haven't left yet. But if you want to come, pack a bag. We're staying at Saint's.*

I thought about it. Did I really want to go and be tempted by Charlie's tight ass and sinewy body? I couldn't imagine the agony of watching him dance with other men, and after last week's episode, he sure as hell wasn't going to want to dance with me. Clearly the idea of me going was a terrible one. Darci was working overnight shifts at the hospital, which would mean I could finally get some good nights' sleep in my own bed.

Hudson: *No, I guess I'd better stay here. Been a long week.*

West: *That's what Charlie said. He told us you wouldn't be able to go.*

Well, well, well. Now it made more sense. They hadn't included me because *Charlie* had suggested I wouldn't want to go. Did that mean he didn't want me to join them? And if so, why? Because he thought he knew what was best for me? Or maybe he thought he knew what I wanted? Or wanted to be able to hook up with random strangers without me watching over him?

Fuck that.

Hudson: *Changed my mind. I ain't an old man just yet.*

West: *If you say so. Pick you up in an hour at the bunkhouse.*

By the time I walked over to the bunkhouse with a duffel slung over my shoulder, I was spoiling for a fight. Only I'd decided the best way to fight fire was with fire. If Charlie wanted to pin me as a straight arrow who couldn't handle being at a gay bar, he was going to be in for a rude awakening. I may not have wanted to fuck around with his feelings by leading him on, but I certainly wasn't above flirting with other guys to show him just how comfortable I was going out dancing with my brothers.

I should have known by the way I couldn't fucking stop thinking about him that things with Charlie would soon come to a head.

And by the time I got into West's SUV, I hoped to hell they came to a head while Charlie Murray and I were both naked.

28

CHARLIE

Charlie's Luck:

Just my luck when I'm at my absolute horniest, Hudson tags along.

When Hudson turned up for our second trip to Dallas, I let out a decidedly unmanly squeak. Nico shot me a smirk from the front seat, but I did my best to brush it off.

"Sorry, just pinched myself with the seat belt," I muttered.

"Sure you did," he replied, deadpan. The man was clearly onto me.

Hudson slid into the big SUV next to me, and I couldn't help but catch a whiff of his scent. It was the same unique smell I always noticed first thing in the morning when we rode together to work in the cab of his truck: a combination of whatever laundry soap he used and the sharp, sporty scent of his deodorant. When we'd gotten together back in Ireland, I'd made a point of inhaling the delicious smell from his pits like some kind of psychopath. The minute I caught a whiff of that familiar smell in the narrow confines of the vehicle's back seat, I felt my dick perk up and act like a bloody nuisance.

"Hey," he said before clearing his throat. "Hope you don't mind me tagging along."

"Mm, the more the merrier," I said with a decided effort to project an *I don't give a shit* attitude.

"How's Darci?" West asked as he began to pull down the long gravel lane to the road. "She still staying up at the cabin with you?"

I noticed Nico's eyes flick back toward me, confirming he knew I gave a shit. And he was right. I gave plenty of shits. It was fine for Nico to think I had a little crush on his brother-in-law as long as he didn't discover I knew what the man looked like naked.

When Hudson responded, he acted like I wasn't even there.

"Yeah. She's still there. She's staying with me until she finds a new apartment."

I couldn't help but butt in. "She doesn't mind you're going out with us?"

Hudson's brows furrowed. "No, why would she mind?"

I shrugged. "Some girlfriends don't like when their man goes clubbing without them, I guess."

My nonchalance act was for shit. I'd never been any good at fishing.

Hudson's eyebrow lifted, and the side of his mouth curved up. "Who said she was my girlfriend?"

I felt my cheeks fire up. No telling how red my pale skin was turning. I leaned forward to let my hair fall over my cheeks. If that hid my blushing, it was a pleasant side effect of my studying the very interesting interior fittings of West's vehicle.

"She's not?" I asked. "It seemed like she was hoping otherwise."

Blasé. I am all ease and detachment. Watch me not care about your answer. La-la-la.

"No, definitely not," Hudson said

Thank bloody Christ.

"Oh. Shame. She's a nice woman."

I looked out the window at the farmland rushing past before

closing my eyes and taking a deep breath. Suddenly, it was a bit hard to swallow, and I was sure it was from the dry air of the vehicle's heating vents.

Irritating dry air.

"What about you?" Hudson asked. "You didn't want to invite Stevie to join us tonight?"

"Stevie?" I asked, turning to him in confusion. "Oh, right. Stevie."

Play it cool. You have options. All sorts of men want to be with you. No need to look desperate for him.

"I asked him this morning at breakfast, but he said he had to work," I replied. If he assumed breakfast was a Morning After thing as opposed to a stop in at Sugar Britches for coffee and a croissant, then who was I to correct him?

"Oh."

He was jealous of Stevie. Well, what do you know?

My heart beat triple time.

Nico turned to West in the front seat. "Why is Stevie working so much these days? I give him as many hours as I can at the shop, but I know he's working the hospital coffee cart and feeding animals for Doc and Grandpa for extra money. Stevie feeding animals in a barn is a cry for help, don't you think? Could he be in some kind of trouble?"

West shrugged. "Maybe you should talk to him. Ask him about it. I thought you guys were close."

"We are, that's just it. If he's not talking to me about it, it must be really personal."

They continued discussing it while I tried my hardest not to sniff Hudson.

It was a long couple of hours.

MAYBE I'D MADE a mistake when I'd declined Hudson's offer to dance with him, but I was still annoyed at him for being so hot and cold around me. Keeping my distance was probably the right plan.

However, watching Hudson grind against strangers made me want to simultaneously vomit and beat some fuckers to death.

I wondered if my teeth might crack from how tightly clamped my jaw was.

"You're going to break that glass if you don't ease up," Nico yelled over the house music. He gently unclenched my fingers from the glass I held and moved it to the center of the table. "What's wrong? Guys have been trying to pick you up all night, and you've only danced a couple of times."

How could I explain to the tattooed man that his brother-in-law was all I could see? That every man who'd come up to me that night looked like the arse end of a wheelie bin compared to Hudson Wilde?

I caught the subject of my peevish thoughts glancing across the table at me as he returned to take his seat, so I made a big production out of throwing back the rest of my drink and standing up. Many of the men in the club had their shirts off, so I peeled mine off and tossed it to Nico. His eyes widened and his grin flashed.

"Now that's what I'm talking about," he whooped. West leaned over and covered Nico's eyes, shooting me a wink.

I ran my hands down my chest to my stomach and then shifted my cock as if no one was watching.

Everyone was watching.

I flicked my hair back over my shoulder and sauntered into the center of the dancing mob. Within moments, I was surrounded by men reaching out to touch me and pull me against them, using the deep beat of the bass as an excuse to grope and feel.

Despite having partied plenty at college, it was nothing like this. I'd never actually been pawed by several men at once, and it began to scare me a little. I wasn't a big guy. I was femme and skinny and likely unable to defend myself if a big man truly wanted to have his way with me, but I was in the middle of a crowded dance floor, so how dangerous could it be?

I closed my eyes and tried to enjoy the attention, tried to experience what it was like to play with the big dogs in a big American gay dance club where the music was hot and the men were hotter.

Someone's hands tweaked my nipples, and someone else's grabbed my ass. I took a deep breath, reminding myself to relax and just give myself over to the new experience.

I felt coarse beard scruff on my shoulder and then the sharp pain of a bite to my skin. I yelped and jumped, turning to glare at the man grinning behind me. Before I had a chance to tell him where to shove his fucking vampire teeth, he was gone.

They were all gone.

And in their place was Hudson. His arms were wrapped tightly around me, and his face was feral. He eyeballed anyone and everyone who even considered getting near me. At one point, he even growled when someone reached out to grab my hips from behind. By the time he was done marking his territory, I was wrapped up in his arms and legs so tightly, I felt like he was wearing me like a vest.

His lips grazed my ear, causing me to shudder violently.

"Please," he said into my ear with a hoarse voice. "Please stop. Please don't let them touch you anymore. *Please.*"

I felt my eyes smart. The desperation in his voice and his protective physical shell around me nearly brought me to my knees. Who the fuck was this guy who ran so hot and cold with me? One minute he was confessing to wanting to kiss me, the next he was pushing me away. And now here he was begging me not to be with anyone else. I didn't understand.

"Why?" I asked before tucking my face into his chest and inhaling the smell as comforting as home.

It took him a minute to respond, and I thought maybe he hadn't heard me over the music. And then it came.

"I told you the reason the first night we met."

I thought back to what we'd talked about as he sat in the bar that first night. There wasn't anything about relationships or... *wait.*

That was the night Hudson had looked at me and said *mine.*

I pulled back enough to look up at him in confusion. "But, you—"

His lips met mine before I could finish. The kiss wasn't aggressive and possessive the way his reaction to my dance partners had been. It was tender and slow, the way my dreams of him were. He sipped from my lips as we swayed together to a slower beat than the actual music surrounding us. I lost myself in him for a minute until I remembered his brother and brother-in-law sitting only several yards away.

"Shit," I yelped, jumping back. My vision darted to the table where West and Nico had been sitting, but I didn't see them there. "Where's your brother?"

Hudson seemed to shake himself awake and look around. "There. At the bar. Why?"

I stared at him. "They could have seen us."

The wheels began turning in his head, and I could tell he was surprised to have acted without thinking first. Knowing Hudson the little I already did, it wasn't a usual state of affairs for him. He seemed the premeditated sort, the bloke who calculated best practices and chose the most appropriate path. Hudson Wilde wasn't the man who kissed someone without thinking about it first.

"I'm sorry," he said without making eye contact. "I shouldn't have kissed you here."

I grabbed the front of his shirt in my fist and twisted the fabric to pull him closer with a hard yank until our noses were an inch apart. I'd caught him off guard. "Don't," I seethed. "Don't fucking run me round like that. Make up your damned mind. I don't deserve to be played with."

I pushed away from him and made for the bar, finding my way toward West and Nico's spot in the queue for another drink. As soon as they saw me approach, they smiled and welcomed me in a way that made it clear they'd not seen the stolen kisses on the dance floor.

I wasn't quite sure if I was relieved or disappointed, but I knew thinking about it overmuch would have me fair pissed by last call.

And so it did.

I switched from pints to shots. Hudson made several attempts to get me alone for a conversation, even trying to drag me to the jacks at one point. I laughed and made a scene about what usually went on in the toilet of a place like that and how I wasn't sure Hudson was looking for that sort of action from me. Nico and West had laughed well enough at the joke, but I could tell Hudson was losing his composure the more I drank and the louder I became. Somehow I got it into my fool head to find someone and snog the hell out of them in front of him.

"'At's the one," I slurred, catching eyes with a right bear of a man a few tables over. I tossed my hair over my shoulder and bit my lower lip at him. "Downright climbable."

Hudson muttered a curse word into his beer.

"'Scuse me fellas," I proclaimed. "Don't wait up."

I stood up and took one step toward the bear before being yanked down into Hudson's lap.

"What?" I asked into the front of the most delicious-smelling shirt on earth.

"Time to go," he snapped over my head to his brother. "Someone has passed the point of legal consent."

I looked up at him. "'At means I don't consent to leave with you."

The look on his face changed from stern and angry to soft and sweet in the span of a heartbeat as he met my eyes. "If you think I'm leaving you here to get mauled by some stranger, you don't know me very well." He ran long fingers through my hair, leaving the lightest caress on my cheek as he did so. My stomach dissolved into an army of heart-eyed minions, every last one of them swooning and dizzy. "Let me put you to bed, Irish."

He said "Irish" with the soft affection with which he'd have said "sweetheart" or "love," and I drank it up like sweet summer wine.

"Hudson," I breathed, locking eyes with him. Those fucking eyes, what they did to me. I would follow those fuckers off a cliff if he looked at me that way and asked politely.

A drunken patron stumbled nearby, bumping into us and shattering the moment. Hudson's arms tightened around me protectively the same way he'd done on the dance floor. Within moments, he was leading me out of there tucked into his side to prevent any more jostling from strangers.

I didn't remember much after that, only the warmth of a body next to mine in a vehicle, the indecipherable murmurs of conversation around me as we made our way into Saint's apartment, and the bone-deep sense of relief when Hudson chose to share the guest bed with me rather than sleep on the sofa. I fell asleep curled up against his great furnace of a body and slept in the security of his embrace the whole night through.

When I awoke the following morning, I knew reality was going to rear its ugly little head and we were going to go back to being platonic friends at best and professional coworkers at worst.

So I took advantage of him while he slept and ran my hands over every bit of him.

29

HUDSON

Hudson's Luck:

When I finally get Charlie into bed, my brother is in the next room.

I felt like a complete ass. The way I'd behaved in the club had been subhuman. I'd never understood the caveman-type guy who felt like he needed to bang fists to chest and roar at anyone coming near his woman. But there I'd been in the club ready to take anyone down who dared mess with Charlie.

To make matters worse, I'd tried to imply a claim on him where there was none. And he'd given me plenty of opportunities to have that claim.

So not only was I the idiot caveman, but I also pulled the immature "I don't want you, but I don't want anyone else to have you either" bullshit. I was mortified by my behavior. And to top it all off, I'd shown physical affection to him in front of my family.

And the looks I'd gotten... I wasn't sure if West's face had held more confusion or hurt. He'd tried to ask me about it in the car on the way back to Saint's apartment, but I'd begged him to leave it alone for the time being. Thankfully, Nico had reached over to squeeze West's hand in silent warning to respect my wishes.

I lay there with Charlie's slender form curled against me and struggled with what I wanted to say to him. It needed to start with an apology at the very least, but I also realized with absolute certainty I wanted to ask him to give me another chance. A chance at… *something* with him.

Because, who was I to decide what was right for him? If he wanted a casual hookup with me while he was in Hobie on this project, maybe that was perfect for both of us. Maybe that was exactly what we both wanted and needed.

Of course, I was fooling myself. There was nothing casual about my feelings for Charlie. A casual hookup would leave me completely gutted when he left to return to Ireland. But was it worth it to have him in the short term?

My eyes were still closed in thought when I felt him shift against me. Just the feel of his warm body against mine already had my dick raging for attention. I'd gotten up half an hour before to sneak to the bathroom for a pee and toothbrushing in an effort not to bowl him over with ineffective morning wood and foul morning breath.

After I'd returned to the bed and slid my arm back underneath his body, one of his hands had found its way onto my skin and moved south to rest on my inner thigh. I'd almost swallowed my tongue. I shifted a little to press my hard-on against his hand instead. *Fuck* I wanted him to touch me.

We'd both slept in underwear and T-shirts which, for me, meant an undershirt and boxer briefs, but for him meant a tight designer tee and a tiny pair of black briefs that made me want to strip them off with my teeth.

It had been too dark to see much of them the night before, but when I'd returned from the morning bathroom visit, I'd made sure to take a very good look under the sheets.

The man was just as gorgeous as I'd remembered. Creamy skin and slim, shapely muscles. Tiny spatters of freckles in places that begged attention from my tongue. Dark auburn eyelashes, thick and shiny just like his hair. Every single thing about him made me insane with desire.

I turned and wrapped my other arm around him, pulling us closer together face-to-face. He arched his own morning wood into my belly.

"Wake up and play with me," I whispered into his ear.

Charlie's eyes opened in surprise. He looked noticeably awake for having been dead asleep a moment before, *the little faker*.

"But," he said in a hoarse morning voice, "you didn't want..."

"I was an idiot, and I owe you an apology," I admitted. "I shouldn't have acted like a possessive boyfriend when I have no claim on you."

"No, you shouldn't have," he agreed. His neck began to turn pink. "But I have to admit I kind of loved it. I only wish it had been real. And you were right to get me out of there when I was too drunk to make good decisions. That was my own stupidity. You did what any good friend would have done."

There were sleep creases on his cheek and little lines of worry across his forehead. I reached a thumb out to smooth them over.

"I'd like it to be real..." I pulled back enough to look him in the eyes. "At least... as real as it can be considering our temporary circumstances."

"What exactly are you saying here?" he asked. "Because I've got to point out you're a bit up and down about this."

"I know. And that's not fair to you. But I really want you, Charlie. I want to... be with you. Like this. I mean, in bed."

Could I sound more idiotic?

I groaned and rolled onto my back. Charlie grinned and rested his chin on his hands over my chest. "That was clear as mud. Try again."

I let out a soft growl of frustration. "You're going to make me spell this out?"

He nodded enthusiastically. "Yeah. That. What you said. Go on."

"Fuck. I want to touch you. To kiss you... I want to sleep naked with you and suck you off and explore your body and make you smile and hear your laugh and—"

"And not fight?" he interjected.

"And not fight."

"And what about your family? Are you going to be out to them about this?"

I froze. It was a fair question.

"There will be so many questions. So much teasing." I groaned. "Is it a deal breaker?"

Charlie seemed to consider it. "No. Not really. I mean, I'm not staying in Texas forever, so it's not like we're going to be *dating*."

Something about the way he said that rubbed me the wrong way. I pressed the center of my chest with my thumb where the tightness was.

He continued. "But I think if your family found out you were questioning things or trying stuff on, they'd support you. You have an amazing family, Hudson."

I nodded. "I know. I'm lucky."

"Damned right you're lucky. You're the only person I know who's actually come to Ireland and found a four-leaf clover," he said with a smirk.

I snorted. "Shut up. I was tongue-tied around you that night. I couldn't help it."

"I liked it," he said. "It was cute as hell."

I thought of something. "If we... if we spend personal time together, we can't let Bruce Ames find out about us."

Charlie's smile faded. "Yeah, okay."

I could tell I'd hurt his feelings and soured the mood. "No, it's not... *fuck*. It's my job, Charlie. I'm getting a big promotion, and if he finds out I'm sleeping with a coworker, he'll lose respect for me. It's one of the reasons I tried to stay away from you. It's inappropriate and unprofessional. And... and there's more going on there than you know. I just... need to keep things on the up-and-up."

His eyes narrowed and he pulled away from me to sit up. Before he could build up a solid head of steam, I reached out and cupped his cheek. "Stop. Please don't get mad at me. I've worked a long time for this promotion, and I don't want to do anything to fuck it up. I swear this has nothing to do with me not wanting people to know about you. It's one thing for my family to find out. It's another for my boss to find out. Plus, what if he yanked me off the project? Then I'd have to go back to Dallas sooner rather than later."

As soon as I said it, I felt that same tug in my chest. The one that made my life itch and feel off somehow. I'd never regretted settling in Dallas before, but knowing Charlie was in Hobie made me sure I wanted to stick around a while longer, at least while he was in town.

Charlie's face softened. "Okay. I get it. You're right. All either of us needs is judgment from the resident homophobe anyway."

I combed my fingers through his hair to brush it away from his face. "Can we close out the negotiation portion of this deal and get to the good stuff?"

His grin was back and he had a wicked twinkle in his eye as his lithe body slithered fully onto mine. Just as he was opening his lips to suck one of my nipples into his hot mouth, the door opened.

Before West peeked around the open door, Charlie hit the floor on the other side of the bed with a loud thunk.

I was fairly sure I hadn't chucked him off me, but I was equally unsure of how he'd come to hit the ground.

"Uh, is everything okay in here?" West asked, craning his neck to see over the mattress.

I sat up and hugged my knees in hopes of disguising the quickly deflating tent in my shorts.

Charlie popped up from the floor with a grin. "Yep! You just startled me, that's all. Sorry."

My brother's eyes took in the slim beauty before us. Charlie's black briefs rode low and his tight tee had risen up to expose his flat belly and delectable happy trail. The shapely muscles of his pale thighs stood out against the dark fabric of his briefs, and I thought West might actually pull out his phone and take a photo.

"Do you mind?" I growled at my brother. "Charlie, put some pants on before West winds up divorced."

West's eyes snapped to me, and he shook himself. "Just appreciating a fine example of healthy quads and abs, brother. Clearly the man takes care of himself. It's my duty as a physician to assess—"

I stood up and slammed the door in his face, punching the button lock on the handle and turning to scowl at Charlie.

"Was that necessary?"

"What?"

"The preening. You might as well have stripped for him."

Charlie's questioning glance turned devious, and his hands moved to the hem of his tee. As he worked the tight fabric higher over his chest, he made a show of running his palms against smooth skin and long fingers across dusky nipples.

"Motherfucker," I breathed.

"Mm," he teased, pulling the shirt the rest of the way off and running his fingers through his long hair. "Like that?"

I crawled across the mattress until my face was in front of his stomach. I dropped openmouthed kisses along the trail of ginger hair leading from his navel to his low briefs. His cock hardened behind the dark fabric, and I mouthed that as well, dampening the cotton and inhaling the scent of him.

Charlie's fingers dropped into my hair as he let out a shaky breath. "We don't have time. Your brother's waiting for us."

I shook my head and reached up to peel his tiny briefs down his legs. His dick jutted out as soon as it was free from its confines, and I immediately grasped it in one hand so I could taste it.

Charlie's hand tightened in my hair, and his other hand landed on my shoulder as if to keep his balance.

"Fuck, Hudson. Feels good," he murmured.

I looked up at him through my lashes and saw the red blotches of heat on his chest and neck. His bottom lip was caught in his top teeth, and his eyes were closed, thick lashes spilling across freckled skin.

I pulled off his cock long enough to tell him how beautiful he was.

Charlie's eyes opened halfway, and his hands cupped the sides of my face. I continued to lick and suck and pull while our eyes locked together. We'd done this before, back in Cork in my hotel room, only this time things between us were very different.

We'd known each other for months instead of days. We'd worked side by side for weeks. I'd seen him naked and soaked up the feel of his bare skin against mine halfway around the world. I knew more of his hopes and fears now than I had then and held them in my heart in a way I hadn't before.

This time might have included the same sex act, but it was eons away from a quick one-nighter. It meant something... at least, to *me* it meant something. I had no way of knowing what our coming together meant to Charlie, but I could at least tell by the way he stared at me, it wasn't completely casual or transactional.

I ran a free hand up his flat abdomen to his chest, feeling the bumps of muscle beneath his skin. The salt of his precum gave me a taste of things to come, and I redoubled my efforts to please him. I pulled against his hard length with my tongue on the upstroke and sucked in my cheeks on the downstroke. I felt the heaving breaths under my palm on his chest and heard his attempts to stifle his gasps and moans. As he neared his climax, his fist shot up to his mouth to muffle the cry as he shot long and hot into my throat.

Watching Charlie Murray lose himself to an orgasm was glorious. His entire face bloomed pink, his eyes squeezed closed, and his chest heaved even more with stuttered breaths. I smoothed my hands over his hips and around to cup his lovely ass cheeks as I gently licked up any trace of his ejaculate left behind.

After he'd caught his breath, he looked down at me in wonder.

"I wasn't expecting that, to be honest."

I couldn't hold back the grin. "What do you know? It's your lucky day. Mine too, come to think of it."

"Mm, a little luck o' the Irish in ya, is that right?" Charlie's eyes sparkled with teasing.

"I guess so, although I wouldn't mind having a *bigger* luck of the Irish in me later," I said brazenly, glancing back down at his spent cock.

Charlie looked shocked. "Surely you jest."

I felt my own face heat up and tried to ignore my still-pounding dick. "I've been thinking about it. Don't know if I could take you, but I'd like to try sometime." I couldn't quite meet his eyes as I said it. "Or not. I don't know what you prefer."

Charlie reached down and tilted my chin up until I was forced to meet his eyes. They were almost full black with just the slightest mossy-green ring around the pupils.

"Oh, I'd prefer it all right. My cock in your virgin arse? Christ, Hudson. Just the thought of it is getting me hard again already."

His voice was a sexy low rumble that went straight to my own seriously pissed-off erection. My ass clenched at the thought of him breaching me, and I felt the sudden nerves I might somehow disappoint him.

"Can I spend the night with you in the bunkhouse tonight?" I asked, trying desperately not to get my hopes up.

"Unless you want to explain to Darci why there is a naked Irishman in your cabin, I think that would be a good idea."

I mentally thanked my four-leaf clover for the incredible luck of meeting Charlie Murray.

30

CHARLIE

Charlie's Words To Live By:

There's nothing better than casual sex.

Watching Hudson stammer and stutter around his brother was the highlight of my morning.

"Why are your ears so red?" Nico asked him.

"What? They're not red. I'm hot. They're red because it's hot in here. What does Saint keep the heat set to? Where is Saint? Is he out of town? Still on that same job? What does—"

I reached a hand over and squeezed his thigh underneath the kitchen table. "Maybe it's the coffee. Why don't you wait a bit and let it cool?"

Hudson flashed me a look that was half-panic, half-relief. There was no way we were making it back to Hobie without beans being spilled.

I tried to take the focus off him. "Nico, I was thinking about getting some ink. Do you think you can fit me in sometime this—"

Hudson cut in. "What? Why? What kind of tattoo? I thought you didn't want any ink?"

Nico and West exchanged a look while I turned to glare at my idiotic… what? Friend? Lover? Coworker? None of those felt right. But I cared about him enough to try and get him out of this mess.

"Hudson, I don't tell you everything, all right? We work together —why would I tell you about getting a tattoo?"

Another look exchanged between West and Nico, only this time I felt noticeable hurt coming off the gorgeous man to my right. Jesus. I couldn't win.

Nico cleared his throat. "Sure, man. Just stop by anytime and we can talk about what you want. Is it something small or a bigger piece?"

I didn't want to go into detail in mixed company, so I just replied, "Small and simple. No worries."

The next few minutes were so awkward I wanted to scream. Apparently I wasn't the only person who felt the same way.

"Jesusfuckingchrist, are you going to make me ask?" West blurted after serving four plates of eggs and toast. "Is something going on between you two?"

Hudson gagged on his eggs, and I tried my best not to roll my eyes at the dramatics. But I faithfully kept my mouth shut and let him handle it.

When he finally got a hold of himself, Hudson glared at his brother. "Two men can share a bed without sleeping together. I mean, they'd be sleeping together technically, but they wouldn't be having sex. Necessarily. What I mean is—"

Nico sighed and turned to West. "See? I told you. When have you ever seen him like this? It's adorable."

"Oh dear god," Hudson muttered, dropping his face into his hands.

"Your brother and I only shared a bed last night, if that's what you're wondering. We were dressed the entire time," I said, carefully sidestepping the complete truth.

"Then why does he get so weird around you?" West asked.

"Fuck," Hudson groaned.

"Because I make him uncomfortable," I replied, flying by the seat of my pants. "He thought I was a woman when he first saw me, and I think he's so worried about offending me, he—"

"Stop," Hudson said with a chuckle. "I can't listen to you make shit up. It's ridiculous."

"It's all true! Tell me one thing I said that wasn't true."

He gazed at me with hearts in his eyes that made me want to crawl into his lap and beg. Hudson's hand came out to brush my hair back behind one ear before smoothing a thumb over my cheek. "Thank you. You're very sweet to try and protect me."

West and Nico were staring at Hudson's caress of my face. Clearly it wasn't platonic between the two of us. They must have seen the same gesture last night at the club.

Hudson faced his brother again, reaching over and holding my hand under the table. "I'm stupidly attracted to Charlie. We hooked up in Ireland."

West and Nico's jaws both dropped for a split second before they turned to each other and started arguing loudly. Apparently Nico had called it, but West had stubbornly denied Hudson had a gay bone in his body.

"The man's so straight he refused to drink out of a bendy straw when we were little," he said. "Hudson used to have Drew Gasticki sleep over at our house, *in our room*, and not get a boner. The rest of us were hard as fucking nails all night long whenever that kid stayed over. You don't get it. My brother's never once been attracted to a guy." He stopped and turned to Hudson. "Have you?"

Hudson's smile looked like it held a measurable amount of relief. "No, West is right. I've never been attracted to guys before. Charlie is an anomaly."

I wasn't sure how I felt about that.

Both West and Nico turned to study me, as if by staring they'd be able to puzzle it all out.

"Huh. I mean, you're pretty and all... but you're still a guy," West said.

"Last I checked," I muttered.

"He is," Hudson declared proudly. "I checked too."

I didn't know whether to laugh or cry. "Really, lad?"

His ears turned red again, and he tucked his face into my neck to drop a quick kiss on my skin. "Sorry," he whispered.

I couldn't believe he had the guts to kiss me in front of his family members.

"It's okay," I murmured before kissing him on the ear. "Big day, huh?"

"Guess so."

"What does this mean?" West asked. "Are you bi? Are you two together? What's... what's happening here?"

Hudson pulled his face out of my neck and sat up, his hand still holding mine tightly. "I don't know, West. That's why I didn't tell you guys. I just know I want to spend time with Charlie while he's here. After that, I have no idea. Will I want to go back to dating women? Who knows? Will I ever find myself attracted to another man? Stranger things have happened."

I tried my best to ignore the angry minions in my gut. The ones who didn't like hearing about who he may or may not date when he was done with me. It wasn't like I could blame him for feeling that way. It was clear I was only there temporarily, and he certainly wasn't going to move to Ireland to live out his days in a crumbly cottage by the sea. I swallowed down my nerves.

"Are you going to tell everyone else?" West asked. Clearly, by "everyone else" he meant the family.

"I didn't particularly want to answer all of their nosy questions," Hudson said pointedly.

Nico nudged his husband with an elbow. "He means *your* nosy questions," he said helpfully.

"So you'd rather us keep it quiet, then?" West asked.

Hudson looked at me, and I squeezed his hand in support. I understood why he wanted to keep things from becoming a big deal.

"Yeah," Hudson admitted. "I mean, I don't expect you to lie for me, but I'd prefer keeping our business to ourselves. You know how everyone is. Hallie alone will tell the entire state of Texas."

Nico nodded emphatically. "He's right. And sometimes Doc is even worse."

"I don't think he even knows when he's spilling people's secrets," Hudson said with a chuckle. "How the hell did he manage as a doctor?"

"He practiced before the days of HIPAA," West said with a wink. "Thank god."

Nico elbowed West. "Surely he never broke any patient confidentiality?"

"No," West said, grabbing the offending elbow and using it to yank Nico onto his lap. "He just likes to gossip about regular stuff. He gets to talking with Goldie, and the two of them together are a force to be reckoned with. When Pippa first said 'Gamp,' the entire town had heard about it before sundown. I'm still convinced she was talking to the dog, but if it makes him feel better to think she was saying some form of Great-Grandpa, so be it."

He leaned over and kissed his husband, paying special attention to one of the lip rings Nico sported. It was funny watching the clean-cut doctor and the pierced tattoo artist together. They were the perfect study in opposites, but they obviously loved each other fiercely. I noticed Hudson's hand grip mine a bit tighter.

"Is it okay if we head back? I'd like to spend some time in the field with Mama this afternoon since the weather is supposed to be nice," I said.

"Sure thing," West agreed. "Let's pack up and go."

The drive back to Hobie was much more pleasant than the ride to Dallas had been. West went out of his way to tease Hudson in front of me by telling stories from when they were little and calling him out for his idiosyncrasies. Hudson's self-conscious laughter was sweet, and at some point I must have felt comfortable enough to lie down on his lap and doze. I'd had way too much to drink the night before and had been guzzling water as much as possible to make up for it.

By the time we pulled down the bumpy drive to the ranch, I was ready to be done with the vehicle for the day.

We gave West and Nico our thanks before Hudson headed to the bunkhouse with our bags, and I made my way to the farmhouse to collect Mama.

After thanking Doc for taking care of her, I met Hudson out by the barn and led him to the large open field I'd used for training since I'd been staying at the ranch. It was a shame I didn't have any sheep on hand to truly show off what she could do, but he could at least see how responsive she was to commands and how her body went low and fluid when she hit top speed.

As I ran her through a list of whistled and called commands, I let the afternoon sun warm my skin through my shirt. It was warmer than usual, according to Hudson, and it almost felt like a summer day in Ireland.

Hudson was suitably impressed with Mama's tricks and seemed to relax even more than I did in the winter sunshine. We wound up taking a long walk around the ranch. Hudson pointed out places he'd played as a child and the direction of the home he grew up in. He told me about the house burning down the previous year and how his brother Otto had come to be with the town sheriff. At one point he reached for my hand and threaded his fingers through mine as we walked. I thought about how similar our childhoods were but how different they were at the same time.

We ended up by a shady creek and sat down on a large rock by the water. "This is my thinking spot," he said softly.

"Mm. You love it here," I said. "On the ranch I mean. You talk about it like it's your favorite place in the world, and I've seen you take a horse out after work the few times we've gotten home before sunset."

"Yeah, I guess. I used to daydream about taking over for Grandpa when I got old enough," he admitted. "I always wanted to be a rancher when I was little."

"We both dreamed of working outside," I said. "I used to pretend I was a sheep farmer. Before I learned to work with dogs specifically, I still knew I wanted to work with animals in some capacity. Why didn't you grow up to become a rancher?"

He shrugged. "My dad was a financial analyst. He always made it seem like an intelligent man's pursuit. He wanted me to go to college and get a master's degree in business so I could join the finance world like he did."

"Is that something you wanted?" I asked. "We talked about this a bit before, but..."

He opened his mouth to respond but then stopped and sighed. "You know what? Not really. I wanted to make him proud of me more than anything. I followed in his footsteps because it seemed to be what was expected of me. I wanted him to be happy. I think part of me wanted to prove to him I could look after our family if anything ever happened to him."

I chuckled softly. "The dutiful oldest child. A role I know quite well."

Hudson smiled and glanced at me. I stood up and pulled him close with a hand on the front of his shirt.

"Kiss me," I murmured. "I see your lips sometimes and it's all I can think about."

Those full lips landed on mine before I took my next breath. They were soft but firmly pressed into mine. He tasted like the peppermints West had offered us on the drive home.

"You taste so good, Irish," he whispered into my mouth. "I could kiss you forever."

I wrapped my arms around his neck and tried to stand on tiptoes to keep kissing him. When my legs tired out, I climbed him until he got the message and held me under the arse. With my arms and legs wrapped around him and the late-afternoon sun on my back, I thought maybe I'd reached one of those golden moments in my life—the kind that imprint and burrow forever inside the heart.

His beard scruff scraped at my chin as he moved to suck marks into my neck. His hands palmed my arse cheeks hard enough to separate them while pulling me tightly into the stiffness behind his jeans.

"Want you so much," Hudson breathed. "Never stopped thinking about being with you. Not once since then."

My heart flew higher and higher at his confession. I knew I could easily say the same to him, but I held back. In some strange way, I knew I had more to lose than he did. As if he could go back to his "normal" life after this temporary coupling while I would be left at least half-broken on the wreckage of stupid dashed hopes.

"Can we go somewhere?" I asked, temporarily forgetting the name of the building where my room was.

"You don't want to take me here in the pasture?" he teased before nipping at my collar bone. "Get a little dirty?"

"I'm on board with getting dirty, Hudson Wilde, but I'd prefer it not to be the literal kind."

When we got through the doors of the bunkhouse, I was half-naked and fully hard. Hudson's hands were everywhere, and I wasn't quite sure what had happened to my shirt.

My head was on the fritz, and my pulse pounded behind my zip. "I want to fuck you," I admitted with a gasp as his hand tweaked a nipple. "But I'm too wound up to do it right."

"Don't do it right," he suggested. He turned me around and walked me toward my bedroom. His lips brushed behind my ear. "Do it wrong. It'll still be perfect."

"No, don't want to hurt you. Want you to feel good."

His large hands lifted up my hair so he could move his kisses to the back of my neck. "What if I'm okay being hurt?"

My hands ripped at the opening of my jeans. If I didn't get my cock out before it broke in half, we weren't going to be able to do any of it.

"What kind of hurt?" I asked, hoping he wasn't truly into pain.

I wiggled out of my jeans and briefs until I was standing naked as the day I was born in front of a fully dressed Hudson.

His blue-green eyes bore into me.

"The kind where you hold me down and fuck me without giving a shit about being gentle."

Had Hudson's hand been on my cock when he said those words, I would have shot off right there and then.

31

HUDSON

Hudson's Revelation:

I like being the boss, but I also like being bossed around. Rawr.

I couldn't believe I'd said that out loud. I'd never in my life asked for anything sexual from another person. I'd considered anything my girlfriends wanted to do in bed or in the back seat of the car plenty exciting. Did I have fantasies that went beyond vanilla sex? Hell yes. Did I need to play out those fantasies in order to be happy in my relationship? I'd never thought so.

Until I met Charlie.

Once I'd had Charlie in bed back in Cork growling out the demand for me to suck his cock, I hadn't been able to get the aggression out of my head. The command had been so raw and honest, one man claiming exactly what he wanted in the moment. No politeness or forced niceties. No gentle sweetness. Not that I didn't love the act of making love when it was slow and gentle, because I did.

But there were times when you were just so fucking starved for it that you wanted to take, to give, to be pushed and to push back. To fuck and be fucked without any manners or euphemisms. Once I began thinking along those lines, I imagined hot nights in bed with Charlie in which he shoved my face into the mattress and took what he wanted. Random moments where he pushed my face down into his crotch and repeated the gruff phrase he'd said in Cork.

Suck my cock.

I'd balked back then. But not because I hadn't wanted to do it. I most certainly had, but I'd been so afraid of screwing up. This time I wasn't even going to wait for his command. I wanted his cock. In my hand, in my mouth, in my ass, anywhere he wanted to put it to receive pleasure from my body.

"Take off your clothes, Hudson."

This smaller, slighter man had such a way of saying things that made me want to give control over to him. It surprised me how even just the tone of his voice made me shudder with the need to please him.

I stripped down as quickly as I could before dropping to my knees in front of him.

"Please may I suck your cock again?" I asked softly, meeting his eyes.

Charlie reached a hand out and brushed his fingers through my hair. "Is that what you'd like?"

I closed my eyes and took a breath before answering. "So much. So, so much."

"Hmm." He reached for his cock and brushed the tip across my mouth. The sticky wetness from the tip smeared against my lips. I stuck my tongue out to swipe at it.

"Please," I breathed. "Please let me taste you, Irish."

He used the hand in my hair to pull my head closer and fed me his dick slowly. "Open up those sexy lips," he murmured. "That's it. Just like that. Use your tongue. Mm-hm. *Fuck*, Hudson. Yes. So good. Such a sweet mouth. You like sucking me, don't you? Like taking my cock deep in your mouth. That's right. God, you're making my balls tight. Want to come down your throat or deep in your arse. Would you like that?"

He kept encouraging me with soft words, half-dirty but somehow half-tender too. No matter what came out of his mouth, though, it was spoken with full control. There was no doubt in my mind who was in charge here, and it wasn't me.

Thank god.

I bobbed up and down, trying to make it good for him, using one hand to caress his sac while the other remained wrapped around his stiff length to keep me from gagging too much. My eyes stayed locked on his until I caught sight of his ab muscles bunching in anticipation of his release.

"Take it all," he said through gritted teeth. "You can do it."

He held my head tight and forced himself into my throat with one last push as his release hit. I gagged violently against the invasion and felt tears pour out of my eyes.

But I forced myself to calm down and swallowed every single drop.

As soon as I was done, Charlie dropped to his knees in front of me and launched himself into my arms.

"Bloody hell," he said against the side of my neck. "Fucking Christ, Hudson."

The amazement and gratitude in his voice coupled with the intense trembling of his entire body was praise enough. He was surprised I'd been able to handle it. I'd pleased him. It was then that I realized I'd held power the entire time also. The power to make him come so hard he lost control, the power to bring him to his knees with gratitude. The power to make him want to tackle me to the ground and pay me back in spades.

I lay beneath him on the braided area rug of the bunkhouse bedroom and felt the hot, wet suction of his gratitude. I wondered if I'd ever gotten a blow job on the floor before.

No.

I wondered if I'd ever had someone shove their finger into my mouth for me to suck on before sticking it into my ass.

Most definitely *no*.

I wondered if I'd ever been naked with someone, feeling on the verge of orgasm and wondering what it would feel like to come with another man's dick pounding into me from behind.

"Holy fuck," I gasped as I shot long and deep into Charlie's throat.

It took me a while to catch my breath. When I finally came down from the clouds, I noticed Charlie's head on my shoulder and his long index finger making circles in my chest hair.

"Just so you know," he said in a light, playful voice, "that was what we Irish call *foreplay*."

Luck of the Irish, indeed.

I finally had the foresight to move us up to the more comfortable bed from the hard floor. We settled in together under the blankets and naturally resumed the same position with Charlie's head on my shoulder and my arm around him. Our legs were tangled together, and Charlie's knee dragged softly up and down my thigh.

"Did you sleep with Stevie?" I asked. I'd been trying my best not to think about it, but after he mentioned having breakfast with the guy the morning after their date, how could I not assume they'd slept together? The thought of Charlie's naked body in bed with Stevie Devore made my stomach knot.

He chuckled and lifted his head up to meet my eyes. "No. Sorry I implied I did. I was bothered about you and Darci. Immature, yeah?"

I ran my fingers through his tangled locks. "Maybe. But even back in Ireland, I was peeved hearing about your ex Pat in Waterford."

Charlie sat up and faced me. "Pat? Who told you about... oh, Cait. What did she say?"

I reached for his hand, unwilling to stop touching him while we spoke. "She told me he'd fucked you over, disrespected you and your relationship, then toyed with you after that. Sounds like a douche."

Charlie's lips turned up in a grin. "That word sounds weird coming out of your mouth."

I pulled his hand up and kissed his knuckles, tasting the barest hint of hand soap with the tip of my tongue. "It's not a word I normally use, but this is an extreme circumstance, wouldn't you agree?"

"Yes. And I almost slept with the fucker when I did that delivery. I was so keyed up for a straight guy back at the inn, I was desperate to get off any which way I could."

I growled and snapped my teeth at him. "I would have had to steal a car and drive there just to cut a bitch in order to defend your honor. Since I'm absolute shit at driving on the wrong side of the road, that would have been a disaster."

Charlie's laugh was easy and bright. I reveled in it.

"Glad I resisted, then. Wouldn't want you to come to harm on the N24."

I reached for the back of his neck and pulled him in for a kiss simply because I could. His mouth was soft and easy, his tongue searching for mine and his body warm and relaxed as he fell back on top of me. We kissed for a while before things heated up again, hands smoothing over skin and taking the measure of each other.

While we'd kissed, he'd moved farther up my body until my shaft was now pressed up behind his balls and sliding into his crease. The subtle thrusts of his hips against my stomach caused my dick to slide along his warm skin in a way that felt surreal. I wondered what it would be like to change the angle just enough to pierce his entrance and push inside of him.

Charlie's lips grazed my ear. "Do you want to fuck me?"

I shuddered at my thoughts being put into words. "Yes."

He moved away from me, and for a split second I wondered if I'd said the wrong thing. I knew I'd implied I'd wanted it to be the other way around, but with his tight ass rubbing along my hard cock, I couldn't help but want to be inside him.

But he came back quickly with a bottle of lube and a condom in his hands.

"You sure? I don't want you to do anything you don't want to do," he said gently. "I'm versatile. Honestly happy either way. And we don't have to do any of it if you—"

I reached for the condom and ripped it open. Hopefully that was answer enough because my heart was hammering too fast for me to speak coherently.

While I rolled it on, Charlie smiled briefly and opened the lube, pouring some onto his fingers and reaching around behind himself.

"Turn around," I said, voice cracking from ramped-up excitement. "I want to watch."

Without seeming to think about it, he reversed positions. His tongue swiped along my dick before suddenly his ass was in my face. I reached out to spread his cheeks apart so I could watch him prep himself.

His puckered entrance was already slick with a swipe of lube, and I reached out with a finger to see what it felt like. As soon as I touched the darkened skin of his hole, it squeezed closed in response.

"Fuck," I breathed. "So sexy. What does this feel like?"

I ran my fingertip around the circle before pushing inside just a bit. The tight, hot channel contracted around my finger, wringing a moan out of me. I felt Charlie's hand squeeze around my thigh in response, but his mouth was busy exploring my inner thigh.

"Charlie," I breathed. "Where's the lube?"

I wanted more. More touching, more exploring. More of any part of him he was willing to share with me.

After he handed me the bottle and I slathered some on my fingers, I rubbed and massaged him until I was able to press two fingers inside him easily. His mumbled encouragement was unnecessary. I was like a kid in a candy store.

Charlie grabbed the lube from me and took care of slicking up my cock before he yanked my hand away and flipped back around.

His face was flushed and gorgeous. His hair was a knotted mess half in his eyes and pushed over one shoulder.

"You're so fucking beautiful," I told him, reaching out with my other hand to push the hair from his face. "Thank you for putting up with my fumbling."

His grin lit up his face. "Your fumbling felt just the thing, to be honest. Must remember to beg for your fumbling in the future. Now grab your cock and hold it for me."

I did as he said and watched as he raised up and then lowered himself onto me. The tight cuff of his body took my breath away, and everything inside of me begged to shove up into that welcoming heat.

"Oh god," I gasped. "Fuck, Charlie. You feel so fucking good."

His hands rested on my shoulder and chest, holding himself still while his body adjusted to the intrusion. Tension bracketed his face for a moment until it eased away, and he slid farther onto me.

I closed my eyes and willed my stamina to man up.

You will not come. Not yet. Not until you feel him all around you.

He groaned and began to slide up and down, dragging his tight channel along my hard dick in the most amazing squeeze and suction I'd ever felt. The only other time I'd even attempted anal sex, I'd been too terrified of hurting the woman to keep a full erection.

But this? This was the opposite of that. I was so jacked up and hot for him, my cock pulsed inside of him as hard as it'd ever been. I knew it wouldn't last. I knew I was going to blow shockingly quickly.

"Stroke off," I said, gritting my teeth against the telltale tightening of my balls. "Can't last."

His hand wrapped around his own cock and began pumping in time with his bounces on top of me.

"Charlie, fuck. Gonna come," I warned. I felt like my sac had never been so heavy and tight. My brain flashed an image of coming deep inside Charlie's body, and that's all it took for me to blow. "*Holy fuck, shit. Oh god.*"

Charlie's body squeezed me even harder, and I lost my breath. My chest felt like it had turned inside out as I pushed up into him one last time and came. Wet heat splashed into my abdomen as Charlie's shouted curse rang throughout the small room a moment later. He collapsed down on my chest soon after. His hair trailed over my shoulders, and my fingers automatically found a thick strand to toy with.

When my breathing steadied, I felt compelled to say something. "That was pretty... amazing."

Charlie snorted and lifted his head to look at me. "Amazing, huh? Glad you liked it. Were you in any doubt you would?"

I rolled my eyes. "No. And amazing isn't the right word. I just can't think of another right now. It was hot as hell and felt like nothing I've ever experienced before." I rubbed my hands up and down his slender back to the swell of his ass. "Thank you."

His face turned serious. "You okay after that? You can be honest with me."

I smiled to reassure him. "I'm so much better than okay. I'm bloody fantastic," I said, trying to fake an Irish accent.

Judging from his snort, I must have failed. But it hardly mattered when there was absolutely nothing that could bring down my good mood after sex with Charlie Murray.

32

CHARLIE

Charlie's Words To Live By:

There's nothing worse than casual sex.

Hudson and I spent the rest of Sunday night alternating between dozing and enjoying each other's bodies in some way. By the time we finally fell asleep for the last time after midnight, I felt beyond sated and borderline dehydrated. But nothing in the world would have pulled me away from curling up next to Hudson's warm body in my bed.

I slept like the dead until I heard a door open. I looked up to see Hudson disappearing into the small bathroom opposite the bed in my room. His bare arse was pale in the dim morning light, but I could make out the twin divots above it on his lower back.

I rolled over and smiled into the pillow. The memory of riding Hudson the night before played back through my mind. His face had been so reverent and his reactions so intense. The man was a careful lover, always minding my own pleasure and comfort before his own.

But I could tell there was a part of him just begging to let go. To take as freely as he gave.

After the sound of the toilet flushing and the tap running for a moment, he came walking back into the room. The effect of his full-frontal nudity hit me in the balls in the very best way.

"Come here," I said. "Gimme."

His eyebrows furrowed in concern. "Are you sore?"

"In the very best way. Now come here." I reached out a hand to him and pulled him close when he took it. He climbed on top of me and settled between my legs. His hands were cold from washing, and his breath was suspiciously fresh.

"Cheater," I accused. "Your punishment is having to kiss moldy cheese mouth here."

I forced the kiss on him, although he didn't put up a fight. His tongue came happily into my mouth and shared the sweet minty flavor with me.

"Didn't I ever tell you I like moldy cheese?" he teased between kisses.

"What time is it? Do we have to get ready for work yet?" I ran a hand down his back to cup his full arse. He had the best bum of anyone I'd met so far in Texas. The man's arse was perfection. Every time I caught sight of him at work from behind, I imagined walking over to him and squeezing it with my hands. I was downright giddy that I could do so now.

He thrust his cock into my stomach. "I forgot to tell you. I have a meeting in Dallas early tomorrow morning."

I stopped feeling him up and stared at him.

"Again? Why?"

His eyes skittered away, and immediately I knew something was off.

"Hudson, what's going on? Is it a problem with the project? Do I need to come with you?"

He looked back at me. "No. No problem with the pub. I promise it has nothing to do with Fig and Bramble."

I was reassured, but I still wondered what he wasn't telling me. "Is everything okay with your job? The situation with Darci hasn't put your position in any jeopardy, has it?"

Hudson's hand reached out to brush hair away from my forehead. He loved doing that, and I loved it even more.

"No. Quite the opposite. Things are going well. I'm just disappointed I'm not going to get to sleep with you tonight," he said softly. "It's my new favorite thing."

His weirdness had been because of me. My heart squeezed tight with the sentiment, but I didn't trust myself to respond without hearing my voice rise up several octaves. So I kissed him thoroughly before going down on him.

By the time we drove into work, I was officially dehydrated but overwhelmingly relaxed and happy. I spent the entire day flirting with Hudson and counting how many times I could make him blush. When a carpet installer came by to fix a spot in the office, I asked him how to treat rug burn. I thought Hudson was going to faint right then and there, but he surprised me.

"Babe, I told you. My hands and knees feel fine. Stop bothering the nice man."

And when Stevie stopped by to get us to try his new nut bar, Hudson beat me to the punch.

"I've got all the nuts I can handle from this guy already, Stevie. But thanks." Hudson took a swat at my bum as I walked past him.

"What the hell has gotten into you, freshie?" I asked with a laugh.

"I'm happy. You make me happy."

Stevie froze for a beat before squealing. "Oh mah gawd, what is happening right now? Do my eyes deceive me?" Stevie's melodrama was back, and it reminded us we'd just inadvertently revealed Hobie's biggest secret to Hobie's worst secret-keeper. "Did someone finally turn him? Did anyone else see what I just saw? Is this for realsies?" He looked around comically only to discover we were the only three people in the building.

"You didn't see anything," I said.

Hudson walked right over and took my face between his hands, kissing me full on the lips until I was dizzy. When he pulled away, Stevie had a boner.

And he wasn't the only one.

"You can't tell anyone," Hudson said with a straight face.

Stevie was practically hyperventilating. "I can't... I can't... *what*?"

"My family doesn't know. You have to give me time to tell them without everyone in Hobie finding out. Promise me, Stevie."

Stevie's eyes fluttered from Hudson to me and back again. "Maybe you're not gay. Maybe you should kiss me like you did Charlie as some kind of test just to be sure."

Hudson chuckled, stepping forward as if to do as Stevie had suggested. I grabbed the back of his belt and hauled him against my front.

"Easy fella," I growled against his ear. "Back over here. No need for tests. And if there were, *I* do the tests. *He* doesn't do the tests."

Stevie's face softened into mush. "Aw, that is the sweetest thing ever. You two are totes adorbs. Can I take your picture with my phone? I won't show anyone, I promise."

Hudson shot me a look that clearly called Stevie a liar.

"Not today, Stevie. We need to get back to work," I said with a laugh before walking the man out of the pub. Once I was out front, I saw a few people in front of Augie's shop clearly admiring the display in the window. Needless to say, I hadn't seen my collie in a while.

I wandered over to Augie's shop to retrieve her before leading her back to the pub.

"Where'd you go?" Hudson asked before catching sight of Mama and leaning down to croon at her. "Oh, never mind. That cat has you wrapped around his little finger, huh? I know how you feel. Just want to spend the whole day wrapped up in him with nothing else to worry about, don't you?"

As he continued to murmur sweet words to my girl, I fell even harder for him.

33

HUDSON

Hudson's Revelation:

When being with someone feels this right, there's no need to second-guess showing affection.

That day at the pub was the most fun I'd ever had during a workday. I reveled in the freedom to flirt with Charlie on and off all day as we worked together. Every time I looked over at him and saw his sweet smile or heard his laughter across the room, I felt lighter and freer than I'd ever felt before. He was so easy to be around. I didn't feel like I needed to be anyone other than myself when I was with him, and that was a gift I hadn't realized I'd needed.

By the time our workday came to an end, I'd realized in all our time together, we hadn't actually been on a real date.

"Will you go to dinner with me?" I blurted.

Charlie had stepped closer to the carved wooden door of the pub, and the warm glow of sunset caught him through the small window panes in the top half of it. His hair lit up like luminous flames, and the green of his eyes struck me dumb for the hundredth time. My heart skipped as I waited for him to say yes.

"Don't you have to head to the city?"

"I'll get up early and drive in. What do you say?"

"Sure. Chinese takeaway or something different?" he asked as he gathered up a few empty boxes to take to the dumpster on our way out.

"No, I mean… I want to take you out. Like *out*." The words weren't coming right, but he seemed to understand what I was trying to say.

"You want to… take me out on a date? Here in town?"

I nodded like an eager child. "Yes. That. I want to take you out on an official date. Where would you like to go?"

His smile was worth the bumbling, and it took all my self-control to keep from leaping at his lips with my own.

"Well, if you're buying… can we go back to the Pinecone? I know we've been there quite often, but I'm craving their filet and those little roasted potatoes with the bacon in them."

I stepped closer to him and took the empty boxes, placing them back on the floor so I could wrap my arms around him. "You and your potatoes," I murmured, leaning in to taste his lips because I simply couldn't wait another minute to be close to him that way. We kissed for several minutes until someone cleared their throat behind us.

"Sorry to interrupt," a man said. We turned to see someone I didn't recognize, a petite quiet-looking man matching the description of the antique-shop owner Charlie had told me about. "But I'm closing to head out of town to an estate auction and needed to bring Mama back."

Mama wiggled her way over to us before sitting politely at Charlie's feet.

"Thanks, Augie," Charlie said. "Have you met Hudson Wilde? Hudson, this is August Stiel, the owner of the shop down the way."

I reached out to shake his hand. "Nice to meet you. Thank you for looking after Mama. I've heard she's made herself at home in your store."

Augie looked at his feet, his hands, the interior of the pub, anything to avoid making eye contact. It appeared the poor man was incredibly shy. "Yes, well, she's a sweetheart. Keeps my Milo company while I'm busy working."

Charlie stepped forward to touch Augie's shoulder, causing the man to startle. Charlie glanced up at me with concern before looking back at the other man. "Do you need us to look after Milo while you're gone?"

Augie's face softened. "Oh, would you? I was going to leave food and water out for him, but I'd feel much better if someone could look in on him every once in a while. I'll only be gone a couple of days."

Charlie's smile seemed to put Augie more at ease. "It's no trouble. Plus, this way Mama won't cry in her tea over missing Milo."

We followed Augie over to his shop to get instructions and a spare key before making our way to the Pinecone. When we were seated, Charlie glanced at me with mischief clear in his expression.

"What? You look like an evil mastermind," I said with a chuckle, glancing at a menu I already knew by heart.

"We should set Augie up with someone."

I rolled my eyes. "You're crazy. Any of the gay men we know would eat that poor little man for breakfast."

"I'd bet ten quid Augie would enjoy being devoured," Charlie murmured before smiling at our approaching server and setting down the drinks menu he'd been perusing.

My snort turned into a full laugh when Charlie sweetly ordered a Hanky Panky "with extra Panky please."

The server was the same young woman who'd swooned over his accent once upon a time. She'd never stopped flirting with him in all the times we'd been there. "Charlie, I should have known you'd order one of those. Are you sure you wouldn't rather have a Sassy Lassie? I think it would suit you."

He clutched his chest. "Och, Tiffani with an *i* might be right," he teased, glancing at me. "Sweetheart, would you like a Sassy Lassie or some Hanky Panky? We could get both and share. You already know I don't mind swapping spit with you, and I adore sharing hanky panky with y—"

I clapped a hand over his mouth before the poor woman's eyeballs turned inside out. "Tiffani, how about one of each please? At the rate this one's going, he'll enjoy both. Thank you."

After she left, Charlie's tongue came out and slid deliciously over my palm, stirring up regret at being in public.

"Stop," I said under my breath. "You're making me hard."

"I like making you hard."

I glanced at him with a wink. "That's all well and good, but you wanted steak. Which means you need to leave the other meat alone until we get home."

"Oh my word, Hudson Wilde, is that you?" I jumped at the sound of the older woman's voice over my shoulder. When I turned to look, I recognized my old elementary school teacher Mrs. Buck. I stood up to give her a hug, grateful my cock had turned to jelly at the sound of her voice.

"Yes, ma'am. It's good to see you. West told me you'd retired."

"I certainly did. Two years ago now. Howie and I are busy as bees managing a few lake rental properties we've invested in. I'm sure your family has told you how much Hobie's lake tourism business has boomed in recent years."

I noticed her glance at my dinner companion, and I realized I'd neglected to introduce them. "I'm sorry. Mrs. Buck, this is my date, Charlie Murray. Charlie, Mrs. Buck was my teacher when I was about nine or ten."

Charlie's eyes widened briefly at the word "date" but he quickly stood up to shake the older woman's hand. "Nice to meet you. You must be good at your job Mrs. Buck, if Hudson is an example of the young minds you helped mold. He's a hard worker and brilliant financial analyst. I've been lucky to work on a project with him recently, and I've seen it firsthand."

The words warmed something inside of me, the little boy's heart that still yearned-for approval maybe.

Mrs. Buck looked at me with the same maternal affection she

showed all of her students. "He's always been a good egg. So responsible and organized. Hudson was the kind of student I could put in charge of the class if I needed to step out. It's nice to know he's fulfilled his potential. Well, I'll let you two get back to your dinner. I just wanted to pop over and say hi."

After she left, I must have been looking at Charlie with hearts in my eyes.

"You look like I just handed you a winning lottery ticket," he said.

"You did. Thank you for saying all of that."

He lifted a shoulder as if it hadn't mattered. As if it hadn't been everything I'd ever wanted to hear from someone I cared about. "I didn't say anything that wasn't true."

I reached across the table and took his hand. "You impress me too, Irish. I couldn't be more amazed at how you've managed to come work on this project without losing your damned mind at the injustice of it all."

"Injustice?"

"I... I know how hard it is for you to see Fig and Bramble being franchised like this. Yet you've handled it with grace. I'm not sure I could have done the same. And more than that... I'm sorry I had anything to do with getting you mixed up in the middle of this."

He squeezed my hand and flashed a soft smile. "I know you're the one who saved the pub from being bought out full stop. Devlin told me before I arrived here. At first I was still mad at you for being the cause of any of it, but now I see what a difficult position you were in. You did the best you could, and I'm grateful. I'd even go so far as to admit I'm happy with the result. I think we've done a bang-up job of it, honestly. But don't go spreading that around."

I lifted his hand to my lips and kissed each knuckle in turn. "Do you think you'd be willing to offer Tiffani your body in exchange for getting our food out quicker? I'd really like to get you home and naked as soon as possible."

His laugh was one of my favorite sounds. "No need to give her this scrawny body. I'll just belt out an Irish ballad for the young lady or recite some Yeats, yeah?"

When Tiffani came by to deliver our drinks, Charlie couldn't resist.

"Had I the heavens' embroidered cloths," he began.

Tiffani's eyes spouted cartoon hearts.

"It's a Yeats poem," I muttered as Charlie continued reciting with dramatic flair. "He's not making it up on the fly."

"Ashley!" she yelled across the restaurant. "Get over here! He's reciting poetry for god's sake."

As several people gathered around to watch my beautiful date recite Irish poetry, all I could do was sit back and take pleasure in the fact he was coming home with me.

THE FOLLOWING DAY I awoke painfully early and extracted myself from the warm sleeping Irishman who'd been wrapped around me like an octopus. I hated to leave him for the day but was grateful I'd stayed the night.

My morning meeting with Bruce found us both working hard to hammer out the best severance package offering we could. Bruce was generous with his budget allotment and had some great contacts in the Dallas recruiting community to help us create a list of resources to make available to all Ames employees. I was pleasantly surprised as Bruce illustrated his dedication to his employees in his actions.

Before breaking for lunch, I got up the nerve to ask him about Fig and Bramble.

"I noticed the pub isn't listed in the assets transferring ownership," I began. "Do you have plans to retain it as a personal investment?"

Bruce looked up from his laptop. "I'm not sure, to be honest. OQI would probably turn around and sell it to a big chain, and I'd hate to see what they'd do to it. At the same time, I never intended to run a pub myself."

"If someone in Hobie could gather the necessary capital, would you be interested in selling it to a local?"

What was I even saying? It wasn't like I had that kind of money, and I sure as hell didn't have a desire to run a pub for a living.

"I've thought about talking to a few local investors, yes. But I don't have the time to tackle that until the bigger deal is completed. You might ask your grandfathers if they know anyone who'd be interested. They own quite a bit of Hobie commercial real estate in the square. It's a large investment. Not many people in Hobie have that kind of capital."

He was right. Even if I used every dollar of savings I had and asked my grandfathers for help, I still wasn't sure I could invest enough in it to make it worth Bruce letting it go. The man wasn't stupid; he was a professional business investor. He'd insist on getting out way more than he'd put into it even if he sold it to a friend.

I nodded and thanked him before heading out to pick up a sandwich. As I made my way down the street toward the deli, I pulled the phone out of my pocket out of habit. Instead of thumbing through my email or news apps, I pressed the button to call Charlie.

"Hiya, handsome," he answered with a smile to his voice. "Miss me already?"

More than you know. The stress from my conversation with Bruce evaporated with the familiar sound of Charlie's voice.

"I might be heading home earlier than I expected and wanted to find out if you were going to be around tonight."

"Hmm," he teased. "What's in it for me if I make myself available to you?"

My voice came out deeper and hungrier than I'd intended. "Very, very good things, I assure you."

"Fuck," he muttered. "Hoist on my own petard."

I barked out a laugh. "I'd rather you be hoist on *my* petard if it's all the same."

"I think I could manage that. What time shall I expect you to come a calling, kind sir?"

I felt a bubbly lightness in my chest that could only come from flirting with someone new and exciting.

"I'll call you when I leave Dallas?"

"That works." I heard him mumble something to someone else in the background.

"I didn't mean to interrupt you," I said, not really wanting to let him go but knowing he had a busy day at work.

"It's fine. They're hanging all the framed photos. It looks good. You'll like it."

I hesitated to ask, but I did it anyway. "Do you like it?"

Silence for a beat. Then, "Yeah. Yeah, I do. Reminds me of home."

I closed my eyes for a moment to savor the gift he'd given me. It was a benediction of sorts, an acceptance of what my visit to his family's pub had set in motion.

"Hudson," he said in a much quieter voice. There was less background noise too, and I wondered if he'd escaped into the small office in the back of the pub. "Is everything okay?"

For a moment it felt like he was my partner, the one person I could come home to at the end of the day and confide in. But he wasn't. He was as likely to be screwed over in this company transaction as many of the other Ames employees. How in the world could I tell him?

"Yeah. It's fine. I'm just looking forward to coming home soon, that's all," I said.

It wasn't until long after we'd ended the call that I realized I'd referred to Hobie as home. Or had I been referring to *him* as home? Either way, it was the first time in many years Dallas hadn't felt like home to me anymore.

34

CHARLIE

Charlie's Luck:

I finally get the man into bed and he leaves town quick as that.

With Hudson off to Dallas, I spent the entire day at work with half my brain on work and the other half back in my bed at the ranch with a naked Hudson Wilde beneath me. It wasn't until midafternoon when I headed into Sugar Britches for a coffee break that I realized I had a major problem.

"Well hello, you beautiful thing," Stevie called out from behind the counter. Once he noticed my face, he frowned. "What's wrong, sweetie?"

I shrugged. "Just tired from the weekend. How are you?"

His eyes narrowed at me while he reached for the largest paper cup they had. He knew what I wanted to drink without asking.

"Lying McLyerson. Tell pookie-bear what's wrong."

"Do you have something chocolate?"

He tilted his chin down and looked up at me like I was insane.

"No, cutie pie. We don't serve sweet things at Sugar Britches. This here's a bakery."

I let out a pathetic whine. "Gimme chocolate and a hug dammit. I'm having a day."

Stevie's smile was full of commiseration. He came out from behind the counter and pulled me into his arms. I couldn't help but compare his petite hug to Hudson's big strong one. Stevie smelled like blueberry muffins and caramel while Hudson smelled like sporty deodorant and, more recently, sex.

"Seriously though," Stevie said quietly, even though we were the only ones in the shop at the moment. "What's wrong?"

"I have a crush on the wrong guy," I admitted.

Stevie put a hand on either side of my head and tilted it down so he could kiss my forehead. "Well, bless your heart. Join the damned club."

"You too?" I asked, hoping like hell it wasn't me. I didn't think it was. Despite his flirty nature, I'd gotten the distinct impression on our date he'd been just as happy as I was to end the night with a hug.

He shrugged and smiled. "Oh yeah. This one's a doozie. Been crushing on the wrong guy for quite a while."

"Is he straight?"

"No," he said, moving back around the counter to finish my order. "I'm pretty sure he's bi, but he's way out of my league. Treats me like a kid."

"You ever had it bad for a straight guy?"

"Haven't we all?" he asked before using a thin pair of tongs to select a powdered sugar brownie from a tray in the display case. "I had a particularly strong crush on one of my friends' dads once. He was divorced and lived in a house with a pool. Whenever my friend had us over to swim, I had to hide my stiffy in swim trunks. That man was like a Greek god."

"Have you ever gotten one to let you kiss them?"

"Honey, if I could have convinced him to kiss me, I would have let him *kiss* me as much as he wanted for as long as he wanted. I would have taken anything that man was willing to give me."

He handed over the drink and held onto it until I met his eye. "And if Hudson Wilde ever kissed me, I'd grab onto him with both claws, and if anyone tried to wrench him away from me, I'd cut a bitch."

When I left the bakery with my drink and treat in hand, I'd decided I quite agreed with Stevie about the situation. If I was going to be possessive and upset over Hudson once our time together was over, I might as well push that time off until the far future and enjoy him while I could.

After all, I'd told my sister I was the king of casual sex.

There was no reason for her to know that deep inside my heart, Hudson was mine and I was his. Even if that only lasted a few more months and only truly existed in my mind.

Luckily, the rest of the workday went by quickly, and I was able to head home to the ranch shortly after six. I still hadn't heard from Hudson, so I turned up at the farmhouse to see if Doc and Grandpa had anything on for supper.

As had become my habit over the previous weeks, I knocked and pushed the door open, calling out "hullo" through the house to make sure I wasn't interrupting anything.

Mama came careening round the corner from the kitchen and wiggled herself into a frenzy of greeting. I'd had to leave her behind today because of some wet paint at the pub.

"'At's my girl," I murmured, scratching her under the chin and on the chest. "Good girl."

"There he is. Come on in. We're making curry chicken and rice." Doc's arms were outstretched, and I walked right into them. My dad was a hugger, so Cait and I had grown up as huggers too. I'd felt so comfortable with the senior Wildes from the outset, by now it was easy to take the comfort Doc offered. I hugged him tightly before letting go and following him into the kitchen.

Grandpa was checking something in the oven but waved a free hand in welcome.

"Glad you're here, Charlie. I made enough to feed an army. I figured if no one showed up, it would make good leftovers for Liam and me this week. But of course, it's better to have your company than a fridge full of Tupperware. Come in and grab a beer."

I helped myself to a bottle of Smithwicks I found. I'd noticed they'd stocked an assortment of Irish beer since my arrival, and it was one of the many little gestures that had made me feel quite welcome during my stay.

"Where's your sidekick?" Doc asked, taking a seat on one of the stools at the large breakfast bar.

"He went to Dallas for the day to work in the office. Said he's headed back tonight, but I'm not sure he's left yet."

"Well, we can save some for him in case he turns up hungry. Now, tell us how the pub is coming along," Grandpa said.

I told them about how well the framed photos had turned out. Cait had managed to scan and send historic photos from home, and we'd taken them to the framing gallery on the square in town. After inviting them to stop by and see the place soon, I told them about Rhonda's visit to the pub earlier that day.

"That woman thinks your grandson is a tasty treat," I said with a laugh. "She's coming back tomorrow just so she can ask his opinion on the design work she did in person. In fact, you might want to time your visit with hers tomorrow just so you can watch her in action. Poor Hudson."

Grandpa's eyes glanced behind me a split second before I felt strong arms wrap around my waist. I froze in shock. According to my Hudson radar, which was finely tuned, the man hugging me intimately in front of his grandfathers was none other than my straight lover.

A cold nose pressed against my neck. "Why 'poor Hudson'?"

I gritted my teeth against a full-body shiver at the sound of his voice. Instead, I kicked it up a good twelve octaves and squeaked out my surprise.

"What are you doing back? I thought you were planning on calling first."

As I spoke, I tried desperately to wiggle away from his embrace. Couldn't he see his grandfathers' jaws on the ground?

Hudson's hand threaded through my hair as he turned me to face him. "I decided to surprise you instead."

And then he fucking kissed me full on the goddamned lips.

I should have jumped back and made a joke. I should have laughed it off as funny Hudson pulling a prank on his grandfathers. But I didn't. Instead I let myself melt against him and surrender.

Kissing Hudson was like shooting heroin. Or, at least, what I'd imagine shooting heroin would feel like. Warmth ran through my veins and left a euphoria behind. All I could do was ride the wave of pleasure, not giving one whit about any other thing in the world.

I lost myself in him. His lips were firm and attentive, even though the kiss itself was fairly chaste. His strong arms wrapped around my waist and held me close, ensuring I didn't actually melt to the ground in an undignified puddle. I didn't even realize he'd stopped kissing me until his words made it through my stupor.

"...late. I meant to get here by six, but I had to change a flat. How long's it been since any of us had to change a tire on the side of the road?"

The deep rumble of his voice vibrated against my cheek, and I realized I was leaning my face against his chest and hugging him tight. His lightly stubbled chin rubbed across the side of my hair, and his hands roamed up and down my back in a reassuring caress. It felt so damned good being held like that, I wanted to stay in his arms forever.

But I didn't.

I cleared my throat and stepped away. "Did you run over a nail?"

"Um, can we talk about the gay elephant in the room?" Doc asked slowly, continuing to stare at his grandson.

Hudson's ears turned pink, but he managed to keep his composure. "It might be more of a bi elephant or a pansexual elephant. Or it might be one of those stubborn elephants who refuses to be labeled but doesn't mind wearing rainbow colors. Like Elmer from that book you have in Pippa's room. You know the one."

His voice was rock steady, and his index finger had snuck out to wrap around my pinky finger while he spoke. I squeezed it encouragingly. The man was braver than brave.

"Point taken," Grandpa said with a straight face. "But I'm afraid we're going to have to throw you a big Welcome to the Gay party. You know that, right?"

Doc pointed his thumb at his husband. "He's right. And Stevie will insist on being the emcee. We'll serve *cock*tails and mini wieners. Nico will make us all eat bananas in slow motion. I'll have to pick up more mixed nuts. It's going to be a thing."

Hudson groaned and threw a dish towel at Doc. "Don't make me regret being open with you."

Grandpa came around the counter and took Hudson into his arms. "I'm so fucking proud of you, Hudson Wilde. I don't say it enough, but you are an incredible man."

I could hear the emotion in his voice and glanced at Doc. His eyes were suspiciously damp also. I turned away and tried to blink back my own tears. This family and their love. It was unbelievable.

Hudson pulled away from Grandpa with a cough. "Enough. It's no big deal. What's for dinner? It smells amazing."

Grandpa and Doc let Hudson change the subject, but I noticed them continue to sneak assessing glances of him throughout the evening, as if looking at him through a new lens. I couldn't imagine what they were thinking right now, but I also knew they'd do anything to keep Hudson from being self-conscious about it. They had to know how very unlike him it was to share such personal information about himself before he was quite sure.

We spent the evening in good company. Grandpa told us about how old he'd felt that day chaperoning Pippa's class trip to a nearby petting zoo, and Doc showed us a baby announcement he received in the mail from one of his old patients. "Can you believe I delivered this baby's *grandfather*? Talk about something making you feel old."

When it was time to go, Hudson glanced at me. "I'm going to go check on the horses. Don't set the dogs on me when I come into the bunkhouse, all right?"

"I'll try to refrain from settin' the dawgs on ya," I said in my best efforts at his Texas drawl.

Hudson Wilde winked at me and damned near caused me to trip over my own feet. Grandpa must have noticed my reaction, because he let out a wolf whistle. "Kiss the man before you leave him, son. What the hell's the matter with you?" he teased.

Hudson strode back from the direction of the door and planted one right on me, leaning me back until I had to throw my arms around his neck to keep from falling to the floor. The kiss left no doubt as to the way things were between us.

Hot. They were hot.

A woman's voice called out from behind us. "Hudson?"

Jesus, Mary, and Joseph. It was Darci. All the blood had drained from her face, and she looked like she was reframing her entire life instead of one man's sexual identity.

Hudson's eyes closed for the briefest of moments before he smiled down at me. I tried not to interpret his affectionate look for something more than it was.

"I'm going to go talk to her," he said softly, standing me back on my feet. "I'll meet you back in the bunkhouse." He leaned forward and kissed my forehead before walking toward Darci. As the two of them left the house together, my heart went out to her. I couldn't imagine what it would be like to catch Hudson kissing someone else instead of me.

Once the two of them were gone, I turned back to give my own thanks to Doc and Grandpa but found them staring at me intently.

"That was awkward," I said nervously. If there was ever a reason for them to reject me, it would be this. I hadn't intended to come into the Wilde family and fuck everything up.

Doc walked forward and gave me another one of his big hugs. I wanted to sob with relief, but I squeezed my eyes closed to keep the emotion from coming to the surface.

"She wasn't the right one for him, Charlie," he said. "It's fairly obvious now, isn't it?"

Grandpa snorted.

"Is this where you question my intentions?" I asked with a sniffle. "You both look like you have a million questions."

"It goes without saying you'd better not hurt him," Grandpa began with a smile.

"What *are* your intentions?" Doc asked.

I intend to shag him to sleep tonight and start all over again at daybreak.

I swallowed. "I've been assuming I'm some kind of experiment for him. Honestly, I'm a bit more concerned with *his* intentions than my own."

"He's a fairly careful person. Not really the type to try something on if he hasn't thought long and hard about it first," Grandpa mused.

"It would seem that way. But the fact remains he wants the American Dream. The pretty wife, the well-behaved children, the picket fence," I said. "He can't have those things with me."

Doc's eyes lit up. "Sure he can, only instead of a pretty wife it would be a pretty husband. Don't forget who helped raise him, son."

I shook my head. "He's a bit too traditional for that, I'm afraid. He's had this picture in his head his whole life. I think he emulates his father. He mentioned that was who advised him about going into finance. Did you know he wanted to be a rancher like you?" I looked at Hudson's grandpa. "But he thought his father expected him to be some kind of junior version of himself. Finance, responsibility, looking after the family. I wonder if he's ever done anything spontaneous or just for him."

Grandpa and Doc exchanged a look. "You've known him for five minutes and you've seen something pretty major in him we never noticed before," Grandpa said. "I have to admit how upsetting that is."

I looked down at my feet. "I'm sorry. I didn't mean to imply—"

Grandpa reached out a hand to squeeze my own. "No, Charlie. That's not what I meant. I'm grateful to you for caring enough about him to notice. It's not that we didn't notice the direction he'd chosen, it's more we didn't realize it wasn't what he wanted. I wonder how we might be able to encourage him to follow his own path now instead of Bill's."

I'd been considering that very thing.

"I don't know how to ride horses. Would one of you mind teaching me enough so I might be able to go with him on some trail rides? The more we can get him outside and on a horse, the more he might reconnect with that part of him. At the very least, he'll enjoy the outdoors and fresh air. He works too much. Saint told me Hudson's never available to go out in Dallas because he's always working late, and one of the sisters heard the same thing from Hudson's assistant. Even if he stays in his current career, he can't have his life be all about work."

"Are you taking him to that dog trial with you near Austin?"

I shrugged. "Originally I wanted to take him so he could see Mama work, but now I've decided to leave Mama here, I'm not sure if he'd still want to come."

Doc laughed. "Don't be an idiot. If you're going, he's going to want to go."

My phone buzzed on the kitchen counter where I'd set it down earlier. I checked the screen and saw a text from the man of the hour.

FYI: I am naked in your bed.

"Sorry, gotta go," I blurted to the gents. "Thanks again for dinner!"

Pretty sure my feet didn't touch the ground until I was standing over a naked Hudson with the door to my room locked behind us.

35

HUDSON

Hudson's Words To Live By:

If someone offers to put their finger in your ass, politely accept.

I'd been so distracted on the drive home by the idea of sex with Charlie, I hadn't noticed a huge piece of scrap metal in the middle of the road. After my tire blew, I lectured myself for the stupid lapse in attention the rest of the way home. I'd been so damned giddy to see him and touch him, I'd known I couldn't keep my attraction secret from my grandparents all through dinner.

I had to touch him.

And, of course, I'd known Doc and Grandpa would understand. I didn't like the idea of keeping secrets from them anyway. Even after Charlie was long gone back to Ireland, the subject of sexuality would come up among my family, and I wouldn't want to feel like my time with a man was some kind of dirty little secret.

Charlie was the furthest thing possible from a dirty little secret. He was life and light, energy and personality and fun. Being around him made me feel at once freer and more grounded. There was something about his spirit that seemed to tap into something in me and let it out for the first time in my life. It wasn't just my sexuality but my willingness to see things in a different way.

Touching him, looking at him, laughing with him, were all ways of tapping into that feeling. As soon as I'd seen him standing in the farmhouse kitchen, I'd wanted my arms around him and my mouth on his sweet skin.

And now he was here.

"What took you so long?" I asked from my naked sprawl on his bed.

He looked nervous. "How did it go with Darci?"

I'd been so anxious to get back to him, I'd forgotten he'd be worried about how she'd taken seeing us together.

"Come sit down," I said, sitting up and moving over to make room for him.

Charlie scrambled up beside me. "Is she upset? Did she cry? Do you need to stay in the cabin ton—"

I reached for his face and pulled him in for a kiss before he could go into a full tizzy. "Baby, it's okay," I murmured after a nice long tease of his lips. "She was surprised more than anything. Asked me lots of questions about whether I'd known all along and if that was the real reason I hadn't wanted to get married."

"What did you tell her?"

"That I didn't have many answers other than the fact you and I are together and I am happy. Once she calmed down, she actually seemed to understand that was all that truly mattered. She's a smart woman."

He stared at me with those clover eyes. "Really?"

I ran a thumb across his lower lip. "She graduated top of her class from nursing school," I told him, even though I knew that wasn't what he'd meant.

"No. I mean, you're really happy? With me?"

I wanted to tell him what a lame word *happy* was, how it didn't come close to touching on how I felt when I was with him. But I couldn't go there. I wasn't ready to open up the floodgates of my true feelings.

"I mean... I'd be a lot happier if you were naked..." I smirked at him. "Just saying."

Charlie leapt off the bed and began stripping. His hands worked the buttons of his shirt and jeans faster than the eye could see.

"What about you?" I asked. "What took you so long to get back here?"

"Was getting raked over the coals by the patriarchs," he said with a sheepish grin.

I propped myself up on my elbows. "Seriously?"

Charlie nodded. "Yep. They wanted to make sure I knew Grandpa had a shotgun always loaded and ready."

"Shut up," I said. "They did not."

The last of his clothes came off, and he scrambled on top of me until we were chest to chest, his legs between mine and his lips brushing my jaw.

"Hi," he whispered before moving up to kiss my lips. "I missed you today."

"You have no idea," I said. "I couldn't bear the thought of sleeping by myself in a hotel room."

"Did you get all your work done in the office?"

I felt a little shimmer of guilt for not being honest with him about why I'd gone to Dallas, but I couldn't imagine breaking Bruce's confidence.

"Yeah," I said. "I was happy to finish today and come home early."

And that was the truth anyway.

Charlie's lips were still making a tour of my neck and chest. His hands found mine and brought them up above our heads while his hips made tempting little thrusts that pressed his excitement into my belly.

"Want you," I said, trying to pull my hands out of his grasp so I could run my fingers through his hair. He held strong.

"I want you too. But I want you to do as I say, Hudson."

My balls pulled up at the commanding tone of his voice.

"If you insist."

"I do."

His green eyes met mine and showed little mercy. It was obvious he had plans for me, and I was very much on board for whatever those plans involved.

"I want you to stay still," he said. "Do not move unless I tell you to. Do you think you can do that?"

My entire lower belly tightened with interest.

"Yes," I whispered. I hoped he hadn't expected me to call him Sir, because that was a little past my comfort zone at this point.

"Good. Keep your hands up here," Charlie said before letting go of them and moving down to lick a path over one of my nipples.

I swallowed back a gasp, not knowing if it would count as moving without permission.

His teeth clamped down gently on my nipple and tugged. He might as well have been tugging on my sac.

"Oh god," I whimpered.

His hands smoothed along my sides before moving down to my hips. He tongued a path down the center of my chest until he got to my belly button. Bright eyes glanced up between long lashes. He was so fucking beautiful. His golden-red hair was spread out along my skin, and his pale face was beautifully marked with pink patches of arousal on his cheeks. I wanted to stare at him and touch him and kiss all over that creamy perfection all at once.

"Charlie," I breathed.

Without taking his eyes off me, he ran his tongue down the trail of hair to the tip of my begging cock and then along its length. I squeezed my eyes closed, but he stopped until I opened them again.

"I want you to watch me swallow your cock," he murmured.

Oh fuck.

He did it quickly, before I had a chance to remember not to move. My entire body bowed up with a cry of pleasure at the sucking wet heat around me. Within seconds, he released me with a wet *pop* and moved down to nuzzle my balls, licking and mouthing before moving his fingers in to caress the skin below.

Charlie continued to shuffle his way down the mattress until he could press up on the back of my thighs to push them toward my chest.

Suddenly, I was laid bare to him in a way I wasn't used to. He could see *everything*, and it was right there in his face.

I wanted to bring my hands down to grab on to him, pull him back up to the social area where we could kiss and pretend none of that other stuff was happening. But I quickly realized that wasn't what I really wanted. It was what I thought I was *supposed* to want.

What I really wanted was for him to touch me there.

"Please," I begged. "Please, Irish."

Instead of a hesitant press of a finger, I felt a warm tongue lap firmly across my hole as if it were an ice cream cone that needed punishing.

"Holy fuck!" I cried, tensing up every single muscle in my body and damned near jackknifing on the bed.

"I told you not to move, Hudson," he reminded me. "If I want to rim you, you'll bloody well sit still for it."

Something in the back of my head pinged with the knowledge he was making these demands as a way of giving me permission to accept the pleasure. If he demanded me to stay still while he pleasured me, I'd be doing it for *him*. It was his way of making me feel less indulgent, less selfish. His aggression in bed was his way of forcing me to let go and feel.

So I did.

I closed my eyes and concentrated on relaxing and enjoying the feel of his hands and mouth on me. Charlie sucked and licked and nibbled on my ass until I was one giant ball of ass nerves clenching and begging for release.

"Please," I gasped over and over until the only thing I knew was stimulation and need. "*Please.*"

Charlie didn't say a word, just kept torturing me with his tongue and lips until he added a slick finger to the mix. The plaintive wail in the room came from me. I was so desperate, I was on the verge of sobbing, and when Charlie added a second finger inside of me and pulled them both against my gland while simultaneously sucking my dick again, I finally couldn't hold it any longer.

I came with a sudden cry of relief. My body clamped down on his fingers as cum shot into the tight warmth of his throat.

"Fucking hell, Charlie," I choked out.

He lurched up and kissed me deeply, and I finally took the risk of moving my hands down to hold him tightly against me. We kissed for several moments until I pulled away from his lips to tuck my face into his neck and catch my breath.

If that was how it felt to be fingered with multiple digits, how the hell would it feel to take his cock?

Amazing, that's how. Thirty minutes later Charlie rocked my fucking world.

36

CHARLIE

Charlie's Words To Live By:

If you ever have the chance to fuck Hudson Wilde, don't pass it up. Wait, scratch that. Stay the hell away from him. He's terrible in bed.

He was so damned beautiful when he let go. Those bedroom eyes watched me with reverence bordering on awe. After bringing him off the first time, he was anxious to return the favor.

"No. Stop," I told him. "Lie still."

"But you—"

"I'm not coming until I'm deep inside you, Hudson. Please stop arguing with me."

His mouth rounded into an O, and his eyebrows lifted into his hairline. "You're still going to fuck me?"

"Do you have an objection to that?"

"Oh hell no. But I want to do something that feels good to you too," he said in earnest.

I broke down laughing, and he looked wounded. When I finally caught my breath, I leaned up to kiss him softly. "Dear one, I promise your body wrapped around my cock will feel fairly good to me."

He seemed to realize what he'd said and blushed accordingly. "That's not what I meant and you know it."

I settled on his shoulder and ran a hand along his side. "Yes, I do. And I will let you do all sorts of things to me another time. But tonight I'd like you to stay relaxed and happy because that will also feel good to me. For now, just recover."

We lay in comfortable silence for a few minutes, our legs intertwined in the jumble of the sheets and our hands smoothing along each other's skin like Roombas left to roam on their own forever. I felt the warmth of Hudson's breath in my hair and had almost dozed off when he spoke up.

"How was work today? Did Max finalize the menu so we can finally have it printed?"

"I don't want to talk about it," I said with a grumble. The chef they'd hired wasn't exactly my favorite person in the world.

"What'd he do?" Hudson asked.

"If you must know, he added a patty melt to the menu as well as something called fried cheese." I said that last bit with disdain.

Hudson snorted. "Those are fairly popular bar-and-grill menu items around here."

"Mm," I sniffed.

Hudson flipped me onto my back and loomed above me with a grin. "Is the American cuisine offending your Irish sensibilities?"

"Is it an American pub or an Irish one, hm?"

"Did he take any of the Murray recipes off?"

I ran my fingers through the longer hair on top of his head that was usually styled but was currently flopping over every which way. "Yes. He removed the boxty. Needless to say, we had words."

"Did he say why? I like your dad's boxty."

The fact Hudson knew that it was my dad's recipe hit me right in the gut. I cleared my throat. "Said we already had too many potatoes on the menu. As if there's such a thing as too many potatoes coming out of an Irish kitchen."

"Did he leave on the bangers and mash, the fish and chips, the colcannon?" he asked, naming only a fraction of the dishes with potatoes in them. "I'm just teasing. I'll talk to him." His smile was still wide and indulgent. He wanted me to be best pleased with the way the pub was run.

"Thank you," I said. "Man's a bloody nuisance, you ask me. Too bad for everyone you can't have my auld man back there."

Before he met the Brazilian and went half-mad, my father was the best chef around. Took great pleasure in putting out the family recipes the best he could. The place wouldn't be half the legacy it was without his touch on the offerings.

"Do you miss him?" Hudson asked, sliding over next to me and running a hand along my collarbone. The light touch brought up goose bumps along my skin.

"I miss the man I thought he was."

"What do you mean?"

I sighed. "When he decided to leave, I was so disappointed in him. I always thought our family's history meant everything to him. That he'd stay and protect it at all cost. He'd raised me to be the same. That's why I didn't stay away after college. So when he up and left after meeting Daniela, I was gutted."

"You said you didn't care for her. His new wife, I mean."

I shook my head. "She's just too young to know jack all about the world and about life. Came to the pub with her parents for fuck's sake. She's younger than Cait."

"Why didn't she move to Ireland?"

"No sun. No beach. None of her family nearby. I think the idea of having a young one and living in Rio appealed to my Dad after years of working hard, yeah? Can't rightly blame the man. I miss him though."

"When was the last time—"

I cut him off. "Can we change the subject? I had plans for you tonight, and mention of my dad is throwing a spanner in the works."

Hudson leaned in and kissed me lightly. "Sorry, I didn't mean to push. Just know you can talk to me about it if you want. My parents moved to Singapore several years ago, remember? So it's something we have in common."

I kissed him some more, letting myself enjoy the feel of his mouth on mine and his tongue playing against my own. It didn't take long for my cock to decide it was time for some more fun with Hudson's willing body.

"I want to be inside you," I said into his mouth. "Tell me how you want it, gorgeous man. What's your fantasy?"

A groan pushed out of him, and his hard length jumped against my leg.

"Tell me," I repeated softly. "You want me to push into you slow and sweet, or do you want me to hold you down and fuck you?"

His jumping cock answered my question without him having to say the words. He wanted to be held down.

"However you want," he said hesitantly.

"Hands and knees, Hudson."

I climbed off the bed to find lube and condoms. Something about Hudson's shyness told me he'd appreciate a moment to get his head in the right place without me staring at him. But I had no doubt he wanted this. So many signals he'd sent me told me he wanted to be on the receiving end, and he wasn't the only one who wanted things that way between us. Whenever I took myself in hand with the thought of coming deep inside him, I almost shot my load on the very first stroke.

After gathering what I needed, I turned back to the bed. Hudson's round, muscular arse was raised in the air, and his face was buried in the pillow. The tops of his ears were so red, I thought he must be dying of mortification.

I crawled onto the bed next to him and leaned down to whisper in his ear.

"I've never been with anyone who turned me on as much as you do. I've never seen a body I wanted to own as much as yours. When I think about coming together with you like this, it makes me feel like I can't possibly be so lucky. Do you have any idea how much your trust means to me?"

He turned his head toward me and took my mouth in his.

"How did you know I needed to hear that?" he whispered.

"Because I see you. And I hear you, sweet man. You know I would be happy simply lying here in your arms, yeah? We don't have to do anything you don't want to do."

"I know. Now shut the hell up and bugger me."

I couldn't help but laugh at his word choice. After kissing him one last time, I moved around behind him and kissed his big muscular arse cheek before nipping it to leave a mark.

Charlie Murray was here.

I returned to the site of our earlier pleasure and rimmed him again with just as much enthusiasm. I snuck lube onto my fingers and stretched him while reaching around with my other hand to tug at his cock. By the time he finally relaxed around my fingers again, an assortment of lovely noises was coming out of him.

Please, Charlie, more.

"Shh," I murmured. "Let me take care of you."

Please, Charlie, now.

He was so much taller than I was, I had to stand behind him and crouch down to maintain control. I held on to his hip with one hand while pushing the blunt head of my cock against his hole with the other.

His body tensed for the briefest moment before remembering to relax. I murmured encouragement and took it slowly, allowing his body to adjust to the invasion. As soon as I felt the tight clench of his muscles, I knew I'd made a terrible mistake.

Why hadn't I let him make me come before now? It would have given me half a chance at lasting longer than two or three strokes.

I pulled out enough to squeeze the base of my cock and take a deep breath.

Think of auld Mrs. MacMahon who wore the same dress to Sunday mass every week. Think of Mr. Foley and his wretched poodle who wanted to eat Mama as a snack. Think of—

"*Jesus, Mary, and Joseph,*" I gasped as Hudson pushed back onto my cock, swallowing it inside his channel in one slick stroke.

"Did you fall asleep back there?" Hudson growled. "I thought you were fucking me?"

Oh, so it's like that, is it?

I pulled back and shoved in, making him cry out. It most definitely did not sound like a cry of pain. I pressed a hand around the back of his neck to keep him still.

"Fuck," I gritted out, repeating the motion. He felt so damned good, I thought I might cry.

"Yes, please," he added through sucking breaths. His fists were balled in the sheets, and his thighs trembled. I reached around to feel his hard cock and confirm he was doing just fine.

With one hand on his neck and one on the bed beside him, I went for it. I leaned into his back and pistoned myself in and out of his channel. The squeeze of his muscles made me lose all ability to think.

"Stroke off," I managed to say between grunts. I felt him shift his weight to free a hand for his cock.

After that it was straight-up animal fucking. I pushed his face into the mattress and thrust into him, rocking my hips in and out without fully pounding him. It was his first time, and somewhere in the back of my mind I remembered that. But it was a close thing.

"Gonna come," I choked. My balls pulled in and let loose in a crash of cymbals inside my brain. The orgasm traveled up and down my spine to my balls and arse, clenching everything in pleasurable pulses made even better by the noises and movements of the man beneath me.

"Oh shit, oh fuck," he groaned.

Suddenly his body's tight squeeze announced his own release, and he whimpered and shook after crying out my name.

I was brain-dead and sated, tingling and happy.

Confused and goddamned half in love.

I was in trouble.

37

HUDSON

Hudson's Revelation:
I'm not straight.

After Charlie pulled out of me and made his way into the bathroom to clean up, I lay there feeling numb. The sex I'd had with Charlie made all the other sex I'd had in my life seem like practice rounds or the warm-up before the big game.

And sex with Charlie was the championship.

It wasn't like I hadn't loved having sex with the girlfriends I'd slept with in the past. I had. I'd been turned on and into it just as much as they had been. But there was something about sex with Charlie that was on a completely different level. Was it because he was a man? Would I feel this way if I had sex with a different man besides him?

Or was it because it was Charlie himself, and maybe I'd feel this way if I'd found exactly the right woman for me?

Was it because it was sex with a man or because it was sex with *this* man?

My brain went round and round until I felt like I might be sick. Part of me wanted to immediately attach all kinds of feelings to whatever this was between us. I wanted to love him. I wanted to call this thing between us the beginning of something real.

But that was just my tendency to go from relationship to relationship, right? It was my way of avoiding the concept of casual sex—by imagining feelings where there weren't any. How could I be falling for him? I couldn't. He was sweet and funny and beautiful. But I wasn't his Forever Man. I couldn't ask him to leave his family behind and I wasn't sure I was willing to do the same either.

When Charlie returned to bed, I did something I'd never done before. I faked sleep.

Because if I didn't, I would say a whole bunch of stuff to him that would mortify both of us. I would tell him I didn't want him to leave. I would ask him to give me a real chance. I would confess how amazing I thought he was and how alive he made me feel.

So I closed my eyes and forced myself into the rhythmic breathing of postsex sleep. Only I didn't sleep. I stayed awake for hours drinking in the feel of Charlie's smaller body pressed up against mine. Of his slender hand resting over my heart and his bony knee sandwiched between my thighs. I listened to the slowing of his own breaths and concentrated on the little places our bodies touched.

I felt the tickle of his pubic hair against my ass, the warm, humid puffs of breath between my shoulder blades, the soft brush of his long hair against one of my shoulders.

How could I not fall for him? He was both soft and hard, funny and serious, loyal and defiant. He was fun and irreverent, brave and insecure. The man was a study in contradictions, but it worked to create the most interesting person I'd ever met.

When he left for home, how was I ever going to survive letting go of him? How was anyone I might find after Charlie going to compare?

It was simply impossible, and it scared me to death.

~

THE NEXT DAY at work was a comedy show. For some reason, half the town turned up to see the pub since it was almost finished. Opening night was scheduled for Valentine's Day, which was only a week away, and I could have used a productive day without everyone and his uncle showing up to get in our business.

"Well, if it isn't the man I've been looking for," Rhonda Dolas called out as she sashayed her way into the pub. Charlie and I were standing behind the bar double-checking our final drink order against our existing inventory. I looked up and bit back a sigh at the interruption.

"Hi, Rhonda," Charlie replied, happy as could be. I glanced at him. Something was going on. "I'm over here."

Rhonda's forehead furrowed in confusion. "I was looking for Hudson, silly."

It was a good thing she was still too far away to hear Charlie's soft snort and *no shit*. I elbowed him.

"What can I do for you today? The booths look great by the way," I said.

She flapped her manicured hand. "Oh, you. Such a sweet-talker, aren't you? You haven't changed a bit since high school."

Charlie opened his mouth to contradict her, but I shot him a look. He bit his lip to hold back a snicker, and I quickly looked away from the spot where his teeth pressed into that tender flesh.

I cleared my throat. "Charlie said you had something else to drop off today?"

There was a rustling sound behind her. "Helloooo," Stevie sang. "Special order for Charlie Murray. Is there a Charlie Murray in the house? Darling, where you at?"

Charlie snorted again. "Don't growl," he said under his breath. "It does things to me."

"Why is he here?" I hissed.

"Over here," Charlie said, waving his arm.

Stevie ducked around Rhonda and shimmied up to the bar, taking a seat on one of the stools. "One half-caff, no whip, caramel macchiato for the pretty boy, and one Maxwell House for the vanilla bean," he said, handing Charlie a giant paper cup and handing me a smaller one.

"Vanilla bean?" I asked.

Stevie rolled his eyes. "What else do you call a guy who only ever wants the plain house roast? There's cream and sugar in the bag if you want to go crazy."

He was right. I was a straight-up black coffee kind of guy. Did that make me boring?

"Simmer down, white bread," Stevie teased. "I also brought you a bear claw. Nico told me they're your favorite, but don't eat the other pastry in there. I wanted Charlie to try my cream horn."

Seriously?

"I'll bet you did," I mumbled, reaching for the bag.

As I reached in for my bear claw, I felt the edge of Charlie's shoe drag lightly up the back of my calf. I smiled without glancing over at him, remembering I was exactly where I wanted to be.

"So," Rhonda said, leaning over the counter to best display her assets to me. "Charlie said I might be able to sneak you out of here for a private lunch date."

I glanced at the Irishman next to me and shot him big eyes.

"I did not say that. Had she asked, I would have told her you had that conference call with Devlin during lunch. Isn't that right?"

I nodded and looked back at Rhonda. "Oh man, I forgot. But he's right. Can't put off a call to Ireland. If we push it any later, I'll be smack-dab in the middle of their dinner rush with the time difference."

"Oh sugar, you're gonna break my heart," she whined. "How about tomorrow? Just you and me?"

I was saved by the fuzz.

"Are we having a party in here?" The voice that carried across the space was the voice of the law around these parts. But he was also my brother-in-law.

Seth and Otto wandered into the pub. Otto held my niece Tisha on his back like a turtle shell.

"Hey, y'all," I called out. "Come join us. Tish, you might need to help me eat this bear claw. Look how big it is."

As soon as Otto and Seth moved out of the doorway, I saw they'd brought with them the tall, dark, and intimidating fire chief, Evan Paige.

One minute Stevie had been chatting across the bar with Charlie and the next he was crouched in a ball behind the bar next to Charlie's feet.

"I'm not here," he squeaked.

Augie entered the pub next, informing us Mama was safely ensconced in the antique shop with her paramour. Well, *one* of her paramours anyway.

"And I've noticed she looks a little... pregnant," Augie said. "It's not possible Milo..."

I leaned over and mumbled to Charlie. "Isn't Milo a cat?"

Charlie's smile was devious. "Should I pull a Stevie and screech to the heavens about someone deflowering my special girl?" he asked.

"Not fair." Stevie pouted from down by our feet. "I was beside myself with guilt. I'm going to be the father of a passel of ugly-ass bastards. *Me.* I'm too young and pretty to be a baby daddy."

Chief Paige's head snapped up at the sound of Stevie's voice. "Is that Stevie? Sweetheart, get out here, we need to talk."

Life in Hobie was never boring.

38

CHARLIE

Charlie's Luck:

When I finally get a chance to show off my trialing skills, Mama can't work.

That week was heaven. During the day we flirted quietly when no one was looking, and at night we took turns fucking each other until we were too spent to stay awake a minute longer. I could tell something was on Hudson's mind, but I was fairly sure it wasn't anything to do with me. I thought maybe he was still worried about Darci, who hadn't yet moved out of his cabin.

"Do you need to... I don't know, go stay with her or something?" I asked one night when we were taking a shower together after work. "I feel bad. I'm monopolizing your..." I couldn't take my eyes off his flaccid cock. We'd gotten off on a mutual handie when we'd first gotten in the shower, but now I wanted to make him hard again. "Time."

"Nah. She's actually staying with Sassy tonight. They're going to a painting thing."

"What kind of painting thing?" I asked, not really giving a shit. I soaped up his crotch, paying special attention to every single twig and berry.

"The kind where you drink wine more than *ah-ha-haaa*. What are you doing down there?"

"None of your business. What are we doing for dinner?"

Hudson's groan was deep and long, and he turned around to face the molded plastic wall before sticking his bum out at me. I dropped to my knees and tasted his clean skin. When I was done with him and our second helpings of ejaculate had splattered the cramped shower stall, I asked again.

"Dinner?"

"Oh, right. Doc and Grandpa went out, but Grandpa said there's stuff to make pizza if we want. Or there's still leftovers from the other night. What do you want to do?"

"Pizza's good as long as you know how to make it. I'll burn the place down, and we need another visit from the fire chief like a hole in the head."

Hudson handed me a soft blue towel from the rack behind the toilet. "Yeah, what was that about? Did you see Stevie cringe the other day when Chief Paige walked in?"

"Cringe? The man leapt the bar in a single hop."

"Evan called him sweetheart," he pointed out. "Are they together? He's twice Stevie's age."

We speculated about the two of them while we dressed in comfortable clothes and made our way over to the farmhouse. Mama showed as much enthusiasm for Grump in the evenings as she did for Milo during the day. I was beginning to wonder if my girl was a two-timer.

After we fixed the pizzas and slid them into the oven, Hudson grabbed us both a beer and gestured to the big sofa on the far side of the kitchen table.

"Sit. I need to talk to you about something," he said. There was a tone in his voice that worried me.

"What is it?" I wondered if he was going to tell me he couldn't come to the dog trial that weekend after all.

"There's something going on at work you need to know," he began. "I didn't want to tell you this because I don't want you to worry, but I was wrong to keep it from you. I trust you. And... well, it affects you too in a roundabout way."

I was torn between being worried and being touched he trusted me enough to confide in me.

"Go on."

"It has to do with work. With Ames itself, and the franchise."

I winced at the eff-word. I hated that word used in relation to my family's hundred-year-old business. It made it sound cheap and duplicable.

Hudson reached for my hand. "I'm sorry. That's partly why I was worried about telling you. This is important to you, and I'm afraid what I have to tell you is going to upset you."

I crawled over and straddled his lap before leaning in to kiss him on the lips. "Thank you for caring. Now tell me before I beat you to death with my beer bottle."

"Bruce is selling Ames."

It took me a minute to parse what he was saying. I slid off his lap but stayed snug up against his side. "Truly?"

"I'm not sure he planned it this way, but a very large firm has made an acquisition offer," he explained. "And since Bruce is over sixty now, he's decided to retire."

"What does that mean for Ames? For all the people there?"

"That's the million-dollar question. The investment assets will go to the new company, but many Ames employees will lose their position," he said. "Since I'm helping with the negotiations, I feel a responsibility to make sure they're covered somehow. I've been working with Bruce to make sure Ames puts together a strong severance package."

I was shocked. Companies were acquired all the time, but I'd never thought about what would happen if Ames was acquired once they had a share in the Fig and Bramble brand.

"What does that mean for the pub?" I asked.

I could tell by Hudson's face he'd been dreading the question.

"I don't know yet."

I reached up and caressed his cheek, feeling the late stubble on his handsome face. His eyes seemed to carry the weight of the world. "You're upset about this, aren't you? You feel responsible for everyone."

Hudson pulled me back onto his lap and leaned his forehead against my shoulder. I wrapped my arms around his head and ran fingers through his hair.

"Yes, but I also feel guilty because Bruce is looking out for me. He's promoted me to vice president and is making my continued employment a condition of the agreement."

Instead of resentment of any kind, I felt relief. I knew how much Hudson's self-worth was based on his career success. "That's a good thing, yeah? It's what you've always wanted. He must think very highly of you." Along with the relief came a sharp sliver of disappointment. Hudson's promotion meant even less chance of him miraculously leaving everything behind and following an Irish barman to an old rural pub in County Clare.

"I don't want things to change," Hudson admitted in a rough voice. "I want them to stay exactly as they are now."

The lump in my throat took me by surprise when it really shouldn't have. I hugged him closer and lowered my lips to his ear. "If things never changed, we'd never have met. And I can't wish for that."

I kissed along his jaw to his mouth and lost myself in deep pulls of his lips. We could have stayed like that the rest of the night if the pizza timer hadn't buzzed after a while. We shook off the melancholy and enjoyed the meal together gossiping about Hobie residents and speculating about how the pub's launch would do.

We finished eating and got up to clean up our mess. I thought about what it would mean for my family if the Hobie Fig and Bramble wound up owned by some large restaurant holding. Did it matter? We didn't own it, even though after all the work I'd put into it a part of me wanted to. Should we still care about what happened to it after we earned the bulk of the fees and I returned home?

I could tell Hudson was still upset about the idea of people losing their jobs after the acquisition. As we cleaned up the kitchen, I stayed quiet, assuming he was running around in mental circles attempting to solve the problem.

When we left the house to return to the bunkhouse, he finally started verbalizing his thoughts. "I wish there was a way of guaranteeing everyone a new placement before their severance package runs out."

I made sure Mama followed us across the gravel drive. "Hudson, a strong severance package is more than most people get when they're made redundant."

"I know, but—"

"You can't fix this for everyone," I said. "You're not Father Christmas. The economy is plenty strong in a city as big as Dallas right now for these people to find other work. It's not like an automobile plant laying off thousands of specially trained machinists. Ames employees are standard office workers and analysts. There are plenty of finance jobs in Dallas."

He shook his head before reaching out to hold the door open for me. "But what if there's a solution to this I just haven't thought of yet?"

We walked across the open recreation room to my bedroom door. It both broke and warmed my heart at the same time how responsible this man felt for others. "Can we set Ames aside for the rest of the night?" I asked. "We can brainstorm ideas on our road trip to the trial this weekend. Meanwhile, I can think of several more pleasant topics we could discuss."

Hudson's forehead smoothed. "Yeah? Like what?" He reached for me and began pulling off my clothes.

"Why you're ticklish behind your right knee but not your left. Why you don't like my tongue in your ear. Why you—"

The rest of my list was cut off with a kiss.

It turned out all of the talking could wait. The night was for touching and kissing and loving. And that was a language all of its own.

39

HUDSON

Hudson's Words To Live By:

There's nothing more breathtaking than watching someone you care about pursue their dreams.

When we arrived in Junction, Texas, Friday night, we discovered a large group of people from the dog trialing community on an outdoor patio at a restaurant called Lum's. The food was good, but the company was outstanding. Everyone Charlie introduced me to seemed to either know him or have heard of him. We spent several hours drinking and laughing with all of the people we'd see in the fields the following day.

Before we left the restaurant, someone talked Charlie into handling their dog during one of the events the following day. To hear the woman tell it, Charlie Murray was the best damned dog handler in the history of sheepherding.

"I once saw him tell Mama to pack his suitcase, and she had him all done up with shirts pressed and everything before it was time to check out of the hotel," a man named Glen said. Everyone around him laughed, and I saw a rare instance of Charlie blushing.

"I believe it," I said. "The other night I was fixing pizza in the kitchen and asked myself where I'd put my beer. And damned if that dog didn't walk over to the counter and point her nose at it. Oh—" I turned to Charlie. "—remember the other morning when I couldn't find my shoe and she found it behind your dresser?" I looked at him, remembering Charlie's naked ass in the air helping me search under the bed. I'd done way more looking at that than searching for the shoe.

One of the ladies winked at me. "And why was your shoe behind Charlie's dresser?" she asked with a knowing smirk.

I felt a full-body blush at my slip. I wasn't used to the casual outings that my siblings experienced all the time. What did Charlie think about his friends hearing we were most likely sleeping together? Had I been wrong to imply it? Did he live out and proud among these folks, or did he choose to keep things quiet around certain groups? Suddenly, I felt like a bull in a china shop.

I glanced over at him, worried I'd see his discomfort. But of course, all he cared about was me and my own feelings.

"Because he threw it at me when I overslept for a meeting," he said quickly. "I was late and didn't answer my door. He barged in and chucked his shoe at me to get me up."

I rolled my eyes, deciding to trust my gut read on the crowd. "That's only partially true. I did throw my shoe at him once, but it was an accident that happened when I was rushing to get naked."

The crowd burst into laughter with hoots and hollers. The only person who looked uncomfortable was one of the servers collecting dirty plates from the table. The man looked like any number of Texas guys I knew who didn't cotton to same-sex sinning. But the dog trainers around the table were kind and accepting. And they clearly thought the world of Charlie.

Charlie tucked his face against my shoulder to hide his blush, but I knew he was smiling. I wrapped my arm around him and pulled him closer, dropping a kiss on his wind-blown mane.

"You okay?" I asked softly.

"So very okay, Hudson. Thank you."

"For what?"

"For coming with me. I didn't realize how much I wanted you to see this."

I shifted far enough away to look me in the eyes. "We haven't even seen the dogs work yet."

He shrugged. "That's not all there is. It's the community, the people. The shared love of a hobby."

I could see how happy he was, and that made me feel euphoric. That feeling lasted the entire weekend. The following day I watched Charlie own the sheep. With clipped whistle commands I'd seen him demonstrate back at the ranch, he had a dog named Maya working like a dream. She took to him as easy as could be and would have followed him to the ends of the earth.

When she got up to top speed out in the far end of the course, her body took on the low, sleek form of some kind of water creature. It was the same fluid grace Mama had when running for a tennis ball sent deep into the fields behind the barn.

Every time Charlie commanded "Come bye" or "Away to me" to the dog in his Irish accent, I felt a little tingle of sexual awareness. It was embarrassing to be turned on by herding commands. But I couldn't ignore the tightness in my jeans as I thought about how this slender man with his hair pulled back in a messy bun and brows furrowed in concentration commanded me in the dark of night the same way he controlled these dogs in the light of day.

Effortlessly, decisively, firmly.

"Dammit," I muttered, shifting in my seat.

"Man knows what he's doing, yeah?" Glen said from the spot next to me.

"Sure seems that way," I agreed. "I've never seen him do this before. I mean, I've seen him go through commands with Mama, but it's not as impressive with no stock to herd."

Glen nodded. "You two going to the Houston stock show next month?"

"We were planning on it. It's in March, right?"

"March fourteenth, thereabouts," Glen said.

I wondered if we could make it work considering the pub would be newly open and we'd be preparing for St. Paddy's Day events. Correction: *Charlie* would be preparing. I, on the other hand, might be back to working long hours in Dallas.

Even if I could get time off for the Houston stock show, it was a reminder St. Paddy's marked the end of Charlie's required stay in Hobie. The plan had been for someone from Fig and Bramble to give us a couple of months to make sure the pub was set up right and launched successfully. Once we'd been open a full month, there'd be no need for him to stay.

My heart fell into my stomach.

"We'll see what happens," I mumbled.

Indeed.

"YOU COMING to Valentine's Day at the pub?" Charlie asked Saint over wings at a sports bar. We'd stopped overnight in Dallas on the way back to Hobie from Junction.

"Pfft. I don't like that romantic bullshit. Never did buy into Hallmark holidays," Saint said. "But if there are going to be hot guys there, I'm in."

"Spoken like a man without a current lover. You know... there are going to be hot guys there," Charlie said pointing a thumb over his shoulder at me. "Case in point."

Saint narrowed his eyes at me. "Ew. Don't make me hork up potato skins right here."

"Stevie will be there," I offered.

Saint seemed to consider it. "Hm. The guy's cute enough. I wonder if—"

"No," Charlie interrupted. "He's taken."

I turned to him. "We don't know that for sure."

"Taken?" Saint laughed. "From everything I've ever heard, the man's as available as watermelon on the side of the highway in summer."

"I don't know what that means," Charlie said. "But he's clearly pining for a certain someone we all know and think is hot as fuck."

"Speak for yourself," I grumbled.

"Oh please. Don't tell me if you were on fire you wouldn't let him douse you with his hose," Charlie teased.

"Stop," I groaned, dropping my face into my hands.

"What's happening here?" Saint asked.

Charlie turned to him. "We think Stevie has the hots for the fire chief."

"Stevie has the hots for anything with a nut sack," Saint said. "Count me in for Valentine's."

When it came time to decide where everyone was sleeping that night, we were saved by Saint's work calling.

"Dammit. I have to fly out. The prima donna pop star I'm protecting has decided to lunch in Paris tomorrow. Which means wheels up tonight. Sorry," Saint said after disconnecting the call. "Duty calls."

Once my brother took off for the airport, Charlie pounced. "He's gone. Can it be naked time now?"

The warmth in my chest bloomed hot and fast down to my groin. I pulled his hips closer to mine so he could feel my interest.

"Meh, I guess so. If you insist," I said. "But we should probably sleep if we want to get back to Hobie in the morning."

"Fuck that," he growled. "Sleep is for the weak."

Charlie led me back to the guest bedroom and threw me down on the mattress. "Strip."

He rifled through his bag and came out with the lube and a condom. I wondered who was going to wear it. I wondered if we needed to buy more condoms. I wondered if I should wash my hands first. I wondered—

"Stop," he said. "Your brain is spinning round so hard you might hurt yourself."

I'm falling for you.

The realization wasn't a surprise, but my brain finally putting it into words devastated me. It meant this wasn't what I'd set out to do. This wasn't going to be easy to extract myself from when Charlie left. This wasn't going to end smoothly or without a shit ton of pain.

You're going to leave me.

I pulled my clothes off without looking at him.

You're going to break my heart.

I climbed onto the bed to await his instructions.

What if you're the one?

Charlie climbed on top of me and began dropping sweet kisses all over my face. I swallowed past the lump in my throat and begged my eyes to stay dry.

What if I can't live without you?

I forced myself to let go and just feel.

40

CHARLIE

Charlie's Luck:

Just when I prepare to confront the old man, a different one turns up and confronts me instead.

Thursday evening Hudson and I were wrapping up final details with the contractor before a last-minute dinner meeting with Bruce when I heard a familiar voice bellow across the pub.

"What the fuck is all this?"

My phone flew out of my hands and crashed into the floorboards, bouncing against the brass foot rail before settling under a stool.

"Bloody hell," I gasped. "Dad?"

Hudson's mouth opened in surprise, but it was nothing compared to the shock I felt at seeing my father for the first time in almost a year.

"Charles Murray, get your arse over here." He sounded angry, but I knew it wasn't directed at me. It couldn't be. I'd been following Uncle Dev's instruction like a good soldier.

"Dad?" I repeated, shaking off my surprise enough to rush toward him. He was big like my uncle Dev, tall and broad-shouldered like a bloody Viking. Christ knew where my scrawny self came from.

I flew into his arms and squeezed him tight. How in the hell did he still smell like SPAR shaving foam after all this time in Brazil? I held him firm and tried hard not to lose my composure.

"What the fuck are you doing here?" I managed to ask.

"Came to see what's what. Seems Devlin has sold us out now, hasn't he?"

He looked angry as a hornet. I didn't fancy being in Dev's shoes when Dad got hold of him.

"Well, it's a franchise location in the middle of nowhere. Hardly selling his share of the original," I said. The irony of my defending the decision was not lost on me. Nor on Hudson from the look of it. He'd gathered the look of the smug about him.

"Dad, this is Hudson Wilde. Hudson, this is Sean Murray, my auld man."

Dad's eyes turned stormy as he focused on Hudson. I opened my mouth to stop him from whatever he was going to say, but I didn't get it out in time.

"You. This is all your fault," he boomed. His deep voice was loud enough to startle both Hudson and me.

"Dad," I gasped.

"How dare you come into my house and convince my brother to—"

"Dad! That's not what happened at all. Please stop. You don't know the story." It took a moment for my brain to catch up, but when it did, *I* was the angry one. "And who the hell are you coming in after the fact to give a shit? You left! You left us. You *left*."

My chest heaved in and out, and I was surprised to find I could hardly draw breath. The pressure from the pub opening, the emotion of knowing my time with Hudson was running out, and the sudden arrival of my auld man crashed together like waves on a rocky shore, crushing the air from my lungs.

I can't breathe.

The panic of thinking something was wrong with me made it

even harder to suck in air. I looked wildly to Hudson for help, but he was already rushing forward to pull me into his chest.

"Shh, it's okay. Just slow down." His whispered voice was like sweet honey in my ear, and I clung to it. "Shh, deep breath, sweetheart. That's it."

I shuddered and felt tears smart. I pushed my face into the warm skin inside his collar and clenched my fists in his shirtfront.

"Hudson," I breathed.

"I'm here. Your dad's here. You're fine." His hands made soothing runs up and down my back. "Irish tempers all up in this place, huh? Feel like you need to christen the place with spilled Murray blood instead of whiskey or Auld Best stout?"

I felt the giant familiar hand of my father on the back of my head. "I'm sorry, Charlie," he said in a gruff voice. "I didn't mean to upset you. Maybe we could go somewhere to talk about things?"

I forced my fists to release the front of Hudson's work shirt before quickly swiping fingers under my eyes. After taking a shaky breath, I leaned in to kiss Hudson lightly on the lips. The contractor had already seen Hudson comfort me and heard him call me sweetheart, so the cat was out of the bag. "Thank you," I said softly.

"Hello? Anyone here?"

We turned around to find Darci standing in the doorway to the pub on the arm of her father. If my auld man realized who he was before I had a chance to speak to him, all hell would break loose. My eyes shot to Hudson in panic.

"It's going to be alright, Irish." He dropped a kiss on the top of my head before meeting my eyes again with a twinkle and speaking soft enough for only me to hear. "But I have to say... my life was fairly dull before I met you, you know?"

I bit back a laugh. "And how was that working for you Mr. Wilde? Or should I say Mr. Vanilla Bean?"

He squeezed my hand before letting go. "Don't worry about dinner. I'll explain to Bruce. Get your dad settled at the ranch. See you later?"

I nodded.

Wild horses couldn't keep me away.

AFTER BEGGING a ride to the ranch from Stevie, my dad and I made our way into the bunkhouse and sat on the old plaid sofa in the main common room.

"So," he began with a gentle throat-clearing. "You and the Yank."

I nodded.

"Is it serious?"

"No," I said, breaking my own fucking heart. "He's mostly straight."

"The fuck?" Dad's temper returned to his ruddy face.

"It's a long story. What happened with Daniela? Where is she?"

Dad's face fell. "I found her in bed with another man."

I winced, mentally adding her name to the list of cheaters. "I'm sorry, Dad."

"Me too. But not more sorry than she was when she found out we weren't really married and she wasn't getting any money from me."

I blinked at him. "What? What the hell do you mean?"

"Long story," he said, parroting me.

"Try again," I snapped.

He sighed. "I didn't realize we needed to get married before entering Brazil. So I went on a tourist visa, thinking we'd get married with her friends and family in Rio. And we did. We had a religious ceremony. But I never did the courthouse part because it was going to be a big mess with the visa situation."

"How were you there for an entire year on a tourist visa?" I asked.

"They didn't realize I'd outstayed my welcome until I was leaving. And by then I was leaving, so what did it matter?"

I leaned back into the sofa and put my feet up on the coffee table. "Are you going to be all right?"

He nodded. "Course I am. I'm going back home to kick Dev's arse first, but then I'll sort myself out, don't you worry."

I closed my eyes and took a deep breath. "Think you can stay here until after St. Paddy's?"

"If need be."

"The chef here sucks. We need you."

"That's music to my ears, Charlie boy," he said with a laugh. "Maybe he needs to learn a thing or two from auld Sean Murray."

I smiled and nodded. "I think you're right."

I told him a bit more about the pub, both the one back home and the one here in Hobie. I told him that after meeting the people in town, I'd come around to accepting the little franchise location. We spoke about Dev's poor decision-making that had led to the financial predicament in the first place, and Dad apologized again for fucking off to Brazil and leaving us all screwed arseways on a Sunday. But I realized something I hadn't thought about before.

If he hadn't left for Brazil, I wouldn't have met Hudson. And I couldn't wish that away, even if it meant keeping the pub to ourselves.

"Where's the girl?" he asked, referring to Mama.

"Oh." I sat up and pulled my legs off the table. "She's in the farmhouse flirting with a coonhound. Let's go collect her. I'd like to introduce you to Hudson's grandfathers. If we're in luck, we can beg supper off them while we're at it."

My father got along well with Doc and Grandpa the way I knew he would. Sean Murray hadn't spent his life as a publican without being a charmer around other people after all. While they swapped stories with each other, I wondered how Hudson's dinner with Bruce was going. I checked my phone too often and even finally sent a text against my better judgment.

All is well here. You okay?

No answer. And when the answer finally came, it was Darci sneaking into my room in the middle of the night, not Hudson.

41

HUDSON

Hudson's Luck:

When I'm happier than I've ever been, Bruce drops a bomb on me. So much for my cheap-ass piece-of-shit four-leaf clover.

At dinner, Bruce informed me he'd been unable to get Ames's buyer to agree to keep me in Dallas. They wanted me in their Chicago headquarters for at least a couple of years to prepare me to take over one of the smaller satellite offices. While the opportunity for so much responsibility was incredible, the knowledge it meant leaving Texas knocked the breath out of me like the time I'd accidentally gotten crushed against a fence by Otto's horse, Gulliver.

The rest of the dinner was a blur. I couldn't eat anything on my plate and spent much of the time mentally chastising myself for wishing for the impossible. I'd already made two different attempts to reach my career goals without leaving Dallas, and they'd failed. If I wanted the next level, I needed to suck it up. It was only two years. After that, I could look for a position back here with another company even if my current company wouldn't relocate me to Texas.

Why was this such a big deal? People moved for their jobs all the time.

When we pulled up to the ranch, I told Darci I was going to check on the horses before heading to the bunkhouse. I was fairly sure she knew the truth, that I was conflicted and half heart-broken at the idea of leaving Texas.

Of leaving Charlie.

She gave me a hug and made me promise to text her when I was done in the barn. I watched her walk up the path to the cabin, until she was safely inside.

I turned to the barn and saw West walking out, peeling off exam gloves and dropping them in a nearby can. "Hey. Doc asked me to take a look at Bumble Bee. She has a cut on her flank that's not healing properly. I don't know why he didn't trust his own assessment, but it looks..." He trailed off when he got close enough to see my face. "What's wrong?"

West had been my best friend for thirty-four years. There was no one who knew me better. The affectionate concern in his face made me want to tell him everything, but if I told him about Chicago, it would crush him.

"Nothing. I'm fine," I said. I wandered toward the barn door, but West stopped me with a hand to my arm.

"Bullshit. Talk to me, brother. I know you're not fine. You've been walking around with leprechaun rainbows arching over your head, but now you look like someone shat in your pot of gold."

I scoffed. "There was never a pot of gold at the end of this rainbow."

"Sit down," he said, gesturing to the bench beside the door. The night air was bracing but felt good after the stressful dinner at the Pinecone. Once we were seated, he squeezed my shoulder. "Tell me."

I let out a breath. "I had dinner with Bruce. He's selling the company."

"Shit, Hudson. Are you losing your job?"

"No. I'll enter the new company as a vice president. The only catch is... they need me to move to Chicago for a couple of years."

West didn't say anything, but I could see the slight slump in his shoulders.

"I've always wanted this kind of opportunity," I added. "It's a dream come true."

My brother's soft smile surprised me. "Then why aren't you happier about it?"

"I... I've worked my whole life for this. I should be ecstatic. But I want the job *and* my family." I almost said *and Charlie*, but I wasn't quite willing to put those words out there into the world. It might crush my heart into a thousand pieces since it wasn't something I could have. I couldn't have it all. "Why am I so selfish? Why can't I just be happy for the opportunity? Why do I feel like leaving Texas is the absolute worst thing ever?"

"Family is important to you, Hudson. It's one of the things we all love about you," he said. "But you've always chosen family over your own goals, over your own happiness. Maybe it's time for you to be selfish for once. You deserve to fight for what you want. And if what you want is in Chicago, you should go to Chicago."

What I want isn't in Chicago.

I didn't say anything, just wallowed in my misery. West shifted on the bench before asking quietly, "Are you sure this job is what you want? What about Charlie?"

My heart was going to squeeze until it broke. I couldn't take it.

"I... um... he's... he lives in Ireland." Well, that was pathetic.

West's expression was full of sympathy. He saw right through me as always. "You should talk to him about it, Hudson. Ask for his input. At the very least tell him you're upset so he can be there for you. Otherwise you're bound to retreat into your head and he'll be stuck guessing." His smile was kind, but he spoke the truth. When I got upset, I tended to bottle things up. "Treat him like a partner, Hudson."

"Thanks," I said, pulling him into a quick hug. "For everything."

"Call me if you need to talk, okay?"

I nodded and watched him climb into his SUV before I turned to enter the barn. Kojack poked his head out of the stall as if he'd already heard and recognized my voice from outside. I slipped into the stall and murmured a greeting to him, handing him a tiny apple from a pail hanging from a hook nearby. The warm smell of horse and hay was comforting and familiar. After he finished crunching the apple, I slipped a bridle on him and led him into the center of the barn to saddle him.

We took off toward the creek, the moon enough of a light to guide us as long as I kept Kojack to a walk on the familiar trails. His large body shifted beneath my weight, and I leaned forward over the pommel to pat his neck. The last time I'd had a chance to ride him had been the night before when Charlie had surprised me by asking me for a ride. We'd set out together, and I'd shown him all my favorite places on the ranch. It felt like a million years ago instead of twenty-four hours.

It was clear I was at a crossroads. I was back to being in the position of needing to choose between my family and my career. Only now I felt like I also needed to choose between Charlie and my career. The lovesick puppy in me wanted to follow him back to Ireland. But what in the world would I do there? It wasn't like nearby Doolin had a position open for a financial analyst. I'd have to think of something new.

I wasn't very good at trying new things.

Except with Charlie. Somehow he made trying new things safe. Like I knew that even if I failed, it wouldn't change the way Charlie saw me.

As Kojack made his way toward the creek, I considered my options. I'd never before imagined I wouldn't grow up to be a financial analyst like my father. I'd never thought of building a life in which my career wasn't the number one priority. But this was my chance to change things, to determine where I wanted to live and what I wanted to spend my days doing. Not only did I have savings from working a good job for over a decade, but I'd also invested them well. I'd used my knowledge and experience to grow my money. For all those nights I worked instead of bar-hopping with friends, I'd saved money. For all the years I was too busy with my job to take a fancy vacation, I'd saved money.

The question was, what was I going to do with it? Continue to work hard and save or use that money to start something new? What if I could sell the patent for the tap nozzle ring I'd invented to make enough money to buy the pub off Bruce Ames? Would Charlie even be interested in that? Could he see himself living in a tiny town in Texas instead of on the windy cliffs of County Clare?

When Kojack lowered his head to the water, I realized we'd arrived. I slid down to the ground and dropped the reins, knowing the well-trained gelding wouldn't wander off. I was grateful to Doc for making sure to keep up with the animal's training in my absence. Seeing Kojack this obedient made me wish I was the one who got to work with him and the other ranch horses every day. I wondered if any of Charlie's dog training methods crossed over to horses.

I moved along the creek bank to a grassy spot under a tree. The moon shone through the bare branches above when I lay back on the cold grass. I watched a few thin clouds float across the bright light.

Even though Charlie wouldn't expect me back yet, I realized I should let him know where I was. I reached for my pocket and remembered I'd plugged my phone into the charger in the truck and hadn't grabbed it after I parked.

Dammit.

I closed my eyes and took a deep breath. Charlie's dad was here, and he wasn't happy. How had everything gone from a euphoria of being in a happy bubble with Charlie to this clusterfuck of Ames's acquisition, upset parents, and so many sudden changes I didn't even know what city I lived in anymore?

After Fig and Bramble's opening tomorrow, I was technically off the project and back to working in Dallas. Once I was off the project, I would no longer be working with Charlie.

My heart began to hammer harder in my chest, and I rubbed at it with my thumb.

Charlie.

It was time for me to show him how much he meant to me, but first, I needed to come up with a new strategy to see if my idea would actually work. I didn't want to get his hopes up before I even knew what was possible. Even if I was willing to make a leap of faith and try something new, I needed to have a plan in place first.

42

CHARLIE

Charlie's Revelation:

I love the vanilla bean.

When Darci snuck into my room, I damned near gave her a show.

"Christ Jaysus, whassat?" I gasped as the cold hand landed on my shoulder. I'd been in a dead sleep and almost jumped out of bed naked as the day I was born.

"It's me," Darci said. "Wake up. I can't find Hudson."

My heart almost leapt out of my throat. "How'd you lose him? You've only had him a few hours."

"He went for a ride and was supposed to text me when he got back. He never did, and if he's not here with you, that means maybe something happened."

"What?" I asked, sitting up and rubbing my eyes with the heels of my hands. I shot Mama a look for not protecting my life from sneaky ex-girlfriends. "What kind of ride?" The minute the words were out of my mouth I realized she meant a horse ride. "What? Now? In the middle of the night?"

"Charlie, it's ten o'clock. Get dressed. I'll wait for you out there," she said, gesturing to the main room.

I stumbled out of bed and found my jeans, a T-shirt, and one of Hudson's big hoodies. After slipping on my trainers and running fingers through my hair, I wondered if I should wake up my dad.

Better not.

If I found Hudson... *when* I found Hudson, I wasn't sure I should subject him to the full Murray straight off.

"I'm here," I mumbled when Mama and I joined her. "Let's go."

When we exited the bunkhouse, she began talking a mile a minute. "I don't even know where to start. Where would he go? The ranch is huge. He could be anywhere."

I glanced at her. "No. I'm sure he's at the creek."

"How do you know that? What creek?"

I knew better than to try and saddle a horse myself, but I also knew Mama could help me find my way to the creek on foot.

I turned back to face Darci. "If you haven't heard from me in twenty minutes, wake up the gents and tell them to come to the creek, yeah?"

She nodded and headed back toward the warmth of the little cabin. I whistled to Mama and took off in the direction of Hudson's thinking spot.

It took me the full twenty minutes to find my way in the dark, but I could tell from the large horse-shaped shadow I'd found the right place.

"Psst." I didn't want to startle the man into an early grave. "Hudson."

No answer. I wandered closer and pressed a palm over Kojack's long nose. "You keeping him safe?" I whispered to the big animal, catching sight of Hudson's form lying in the grass. For a split second I wondered if something was wrong with him, but then I noticed him shift and his sleep-hoarse voice drifted through the night.

"Irish? That you?"

After commanding Mama to lie down, I made my way over and dropped down next to him, leaning over to take his face in my hands.

"You scared me," I whispered. "I can't decide whether to beat you or kiss you."

He yanked me down into a kiss that stole the breath from my lungs. Without taking my lips off his, I climbed on top of his warm body. He felt like home. Kissing him in the middle of the night on the ground in small-town Texas was quite bizarrely exactly where I was meant to be.

"Mpfh," I grunted when he flipped me over onto my back. After pressing another hard kiss to my mouth, he pulled away and looked down at me.

"What are you doing out here?"

"Came to find you. Darci was worried. Said you've been out here a couple of hours."

"What? Shit. Really? Do you have a phone with you?"

I pulled it out and handed it to him. After a quick text to her number, he handed it back.

"I'm so sorry," he said. "How's things with your dad? He in the bunkhouse?"

I rubbed my hands up and down the back of his canvas jacket. "No, we had dinner at the farmhouse, and the gents insisted he stay in a proper guest room."

"Oh good. Is he still mad?"

"No. Not at all. Though he's single now. Long story."

Hudson dropped down next to me and laid his head on my shoulder as if we were in bed. "Bruce said they were relocating me after the acquisition."

My heart dropped to the floor. "Oh, Hudson. I'm so sorry." I couldn't imagine how disappointed he must be. I knew how much he loved being close to his family. "Where?"

Please say Dublin. Or London... hell, I'll take Paris, Frankfurt, or even New York...

"Chicago."

Fuck.

I moved my hands under his coat to the warmer surface of his button-up shirt and continued stroking the long muscles of his back.

"I'm sorry," he whispered. Heartache was plain as day in his eyes. "I—"

I put my fingers on his lips, and tried to hide how much he'd just gutted me. "Shh. I know. It's not your fault. We knew this was temporary, yeah? I'll be heading back home too. It wasn't like..."

I couldn't bring myself to finish the sentence. Instead, I leaned in and kissed him, pouring my broken heart into him and trying my best to take his as well. I didn't want to waste some of our last days together with heavy emotion.

"No, Charlie, you don't understand. I don't want to go. I want to find a way to—"

I interrupted him again. "I know, love. But we're not going to solve it tonight. The pub opens tomorrow and we're going to go back to the bunkhouse, make love, and then sleep. Yeah?"

My lips found his again for a good healthy snog.

When we finally pulled away to catch our breaths, Hudson's hand smoothed down the jumper I wore. "You're wearing my hoodie."

"Yes. It's cold as balls, Hudson. I was half-asleep when your girlfriend turned up in my bedroom." I was taking the piss, but he didn't realize it.

"I like it on you. And she's not my girlfriend. You are. I mean... you know what I mean."

Only the darkness around us could see what had to be a maniacal grin on my face. "No. Why don't you tell me what you mean?"

"You're not a woman," he said stubbornly.

"I realize that, thank you," I said. I almost couldn't hold back my laughter at hearing him so out of sorts.

"But you're my... my... I mean, you're the guy who... you and I..."

His stammering brought to mind how utterly adorable he was when we first met.

"Jesusfuckingchrist, Charlie. You're my person."

I closed my eyes to savor it. Even though I'd sworn off the heavy emotion, I couldn't deny the euphoria his words caused. My laugh broke the quiet night and startled Mama out of her balled-up sleeping position.

My lips pressed against the skin of Hudson's forehead because that was the only skin I could reach.

"How red is your face right now?" I asked through my laughter.

"I hate you."

"You don't. You really don't."

He leaned up and looked me square in the eyes. There was just enough ambient light to make out his serious expression. It was enough to make my throat close up.

"No, I don't," he whispered. "I actually think I might lo—"

I lurched forward and crushed my mouth to his before he could say the words. I wasn't ready. Neither of us was ready. There was too much going on in our lives to make the kind of declaration that would make this whole situation even harder.

The pub was set to open the following day regardless of what happened with Ames's future, and my father and I had decided to go into work early to prepare Max for Dad's interference in the kitchen. I had much more confidence in the success of opening night with Dad in the kitchen alongside Max. With all of those things on my mind, I couldn't give Hudson and our relationship, if that's what it was turning out to be, my full attention.

He was leaving, anyway. His future was in Chicago. He had more exciting things to focus on than whatever this was between us.

And I could hardly blame him. What future was there for a Texas boy and an Irish bloke? We didn't belong together long-term. There was too much against us.

Hudson pulled back from the kiss. "Charlie, I—"

"No, please," I whispered. "Can we go back and get in bed? I'm cold." It was a lie. We both knew it was a lie.

"Of course. Here, sweetheart, take my coat."

I loved him. Oh fuck, *fuck*. He was such a good man. I loved him so much. So very much, I ached with it.

The minute he'd almost said the words, I'd known for certain. I didn't *think* I loved him. I knew it. With everything I had and my whole heart. I was a bloody idiot. Why did I always fall for the wrong man? Even if he'd have me, I couldn't do that to him. I couldn't be the one to make him give up the pretty picture he'd always dreamed of, the wife and kids, the perfect family. The life someone like sweet Darci fit in a thousand times better than I did.

I couldn't speak to refuse the coat, so I allowed him to put it around my shoulders. He lifted me into the saddle and hopped up behind me. The ride back was quick, but every step felt like it was toward a hangman's noose. There was nothing for it but to rip the bloody bandage off and fly home with my father. Back to the original Fig and Bramble, to my family and my history, back to the land of green pastures full of sheep waiting to be bossed around, back to my bratty sister and the niece or nephew she carried in her belly. I would be all right. When I pictured myself back home, it was exactly what was always meant to be for my life. And when I pictured Hudson and a nameless, faceless woman standing in front of a lovely home with a couple of lovely children, I knew it was exactly what was always meant to be for his life.

When we returned to the barn, I helped Hudson put away the saddle and blanket while he gave Kojack a quick brushing. Neither of us spoke as we went through the motions of filling water pails, closing stall doors, and making our way back to the bunkhouse.

He reached for my hand and pulled me into the tiny bathroom, pulling off each stitch of my clothing while the water in the shower warmed up. Once we were both naked, he nudged me ahead of him into the stall and closed the door, wrapping his arms around me from behind and simply standing with me under the warm spray.

After a minute, I realized he was whispering into my ear so low I almost missed it in the noise of the water.

"I know you're not ready. Maybe you're scared, and I get it. But please don't give up on me. Please give us more time before you decide I'm not the right one for you. I'm going to fix this. I'm going to find a way for us to be together."

I felt the sting in my eyes and the lump in my throat grow stronger. I turned around in his arms and buried my nose in his neck before the tears came against my will. Thank god for the shower water and the noise.

His arms held me tight, and I wound up lifting my legs to wrap around him.

"Baby, it's okay," he said in a hoarse voice. "You don't have to say anything. I just want you to know... I can't... Charlie, honey, I can't not tell you that I love you. I love you so much I feel like my heart is going to break."

"I love you too," I breathed into his skin, letting go of my stupid urge to protect myself. What the hell did it matter? It wasn't like keeping the truth from him was going to keep me from getting hurt when it ended.

I could tell by the way his arms pulled tighter that he'd heard me. "But Hudson..."

"No. No buts. No buts tonight. Just you and me and this right here. *Please*."

We shared tender, wet kisses with our naked bodies pressed so tightly together not even the shower water could get between us. I finally pulled away and sniffled.

His beautiful blue-green eyes held everything I'd ever wanted from a lover, and seeing them locked on me right then pushed me over into stupid love territory. I had to scramble back to lighten the mood.

"Can there be some butts? The good kind of butts?" I asked with a smile. "I don't mind which. Your butt or my butt. Any butt will do."

Hudson set me down and swatted my arse. "First butt in the bed gets to choose."

For once, being smaller and faster had its benefits.

43

HUDSON

Hudson's Revelation:

Making love is a completely different thing than having sex.

Even though our words were playful, the touches we shared when we came together in bed were tender and loving. The words were still there between us, wrapping us in that warm, fragile feeling of new love.

I may have been unsure about how our future would look, but I wasn't confused one bit about the man himself. He was mine and I was his.

I rubbed my hands up and down his back and down to his little rounded ass. I'd never known what an ass man I was until seeing and feeling Charlie's. Maybe it was because I'd never felt the freedom to maul my lover's cheeks with firm squeezes and periodic smacks, but I thought it was more probably the knowledge he would welcome me into that tight heat anytime I wanted it.

Tonight I wanted it. I needed to as close to him as possible.

"Please," I hissed as he continued to writhe above me, rubbing our naked erections together and driving me insane. "Want to be inside you. Need you."

His green eyes were half-lidded, lips cherry red and slick from our kisses. His fiery hair trailed down onto my chest and cheeks. Charlie was the very picture of sex, and the image burned into my memory like a brand.

He reached for the supplies, and I had a thought of what it might be like one day when we were able to move past using condoms. To feel his bare skin inside me. To feel his naked channel around my own cock with no barrier between us. I wanted that with him.

His lips grazed the spot behind my ear that made my balls heavy and my stomach tight. He moved wet lips down my neck to my collarbone where he sucked up what would surely be a bruise tomorrow. I ran fingers through his hair to hold it back from his face. I wanted to see.

I love you.

He was so beautiful. I still saw the creamy skin with youthful freckles, the thick hair with a slight wave to it. But now I also saw the man inside. The beautiful, flawed human whose heart was made of the thinnest of spun glass. I wanted to hold it steady, keep it safe, make sure no one ever had a chance to crush it.

Please don't leave.

I wondered if I had the guts to follow him. What was I saying? Of course I'd follow him. It wasn't an issue of guts; it was unthinkable to let him go so far away from me forever. So much for bravery; it would be cowardice that led me there... fear of being apart from him for the rest of my life.

When his mouth landed on my hip bone and sucked slowly on a patch of skin there, I looked down at him and knew that I would follow the man wherever he led.

You are mine and I am yours. Forever.

And when I flipped him over and finally pushed into his body, stroking slowly in and out of his tight heat and kissing his lips with sweet softness, I was torn between sobbing in relief and shouting with joy. So this is what it felt like to give oneself completely over to another.

It felt like home.

~

When my body roused from sleep several hours later, it was still dark outside. The clock indicated it was shortly past six, so I decided to get up and embrace the day. I looked over at Charlie.

He was small and slender and feminine, skin so pale he almost looked fragile and with a sprinkling of freckles that made him look even younger than he was. But I couldn't think of anyone I'd rather have beside me when I was at my most vulnerable. He was strong and brave and loyal. Charlie was feisty and passionate and so very dedicated to righting a wrong.

I wanted the world for him. But I had no idea how to go about it.

My plan was to go into town early and triple check everything was ready for our grand opening. I could stop at Sugar Britches and have Charlie's favorite coffee ready for him the minute he arrived.

I slipped out of bed with a soft kiss on Charlie's cheek, just below the dark eyelashes closed gently in sleep. "I love you," I whispered to his sleeping form before making my way into the shower.

The note I left on top of his wallet explained my plan to meet him at the pub. I climbed into the truck and drove to the square, deciding to walk to Sugar Britches first thing.

Before I got out of my truck, I made a phone call. Bruce answered on the second ring. "You're up and at 'em early today, Hudson. I can't say I'm surprised."

I'd known he was an early riser too. "Yes, sir. Exciting day ahead. But that's not what I'm calling about. I was hoping you could help me with something else."

"Sure, what's on your mind?"

Bruce had been colder than normal toward me after catching me kissing Charlie, but during dinner he'd seemed to thaw. Maybe during the course of the meal he somehow realized I was still the same man he'd always known despite the change in who I was dating. I hoped my asking for his help would appeal to the part of him that couldn't resist new business opportunities.

"I wonder if you might be able to help me find a buyer for my tap nozzle invention," I said, trying desperately to keep my insecurity at bay. It was highly possible no one would want it. Just because one Irish bartender saw value in it, didn't mean anyone else would be willing to lay down an investment on it.

"Considering I'm in the business of investing, I'm sure I can find an investor interested in it. Let me make a few calls and see what I can set up."

"Thank you, Bruce. I appreciate it."

I entered the bakery with a noticeably lighter spring in my step, and I wasn't the only one. Stevie was chipper this morning.

"It's the vanilla bean! Maxwell House, coming right up." He turned to start my plain house roast, but I stopped him.

"Actually, I'll have a mocha latte," I said, reaching into my pocket for my wallet. "And a blueberry muffin. And whatever Charlie likes."

"Well, butter my butt and call me a biscuit. Hudson Wilde has gone round the bend," Stevie teased. "Fancy hot cocoa and a Charlie special coming right up. How's your boo?"

I felt my cheeks tighten with a big grin. "Gorgeous. Sexy. Mine."

Stevie's eyes widened. "Good for you, McSassafras. 'Bout time you claimed him for real. That man's a snack."

Instead of growling at him, I grinned even more. "A serious snack. Tasty and sweet and sometimes even deliciously salty."

I wasn't sure Stevie had ever been so shocked. He turned around to finish making the drinks and mumbled something to himself about wonders never ceasing.

After gathering my treats, I left the bakery and made my way over to the pub. When I entered, I saw a beautiful vision behind the bar. Only I knew this time it wasn't a woman. It was most definitely a man. Under those clothes were muscles and body hair, strength and steel, and a gorgeous uncut cock I knew almost better than my own.

I blinked.

That gorgeous man was mine. He was mine, and I was going to find a way to be with him when everything was said and done.

"Charlie Murray, get your arse in here," a voice boomed from the direction of the kitchen. "The man has no boxty on the menu! *Christ Jaysus.*"

Charlie turned around to answer but saw me first. His frustrated expression turned to happiness in a split second.

"Hiya, handsome," he said. "I missed you this morning."

I walked up and took him in my arms, not giving a shit who saw us or what they thought. The only inappropriate part was the coworking nature of our situation, and that was as good as over.

"I had to take care of some things. Is that your dad in the kitchen?"

"Mm, yeah. I expected Max to rage quit, but I think he's actually too intimidated by the auld man to leave," he said with a chuckle. "My dad can have that effect on people."

I kissed him quickly before taking a deep breath. "Think maybe I should meet him properly?"

"You look flustered. You all right?"

I kissed him again. "Way, way better than all right, Irish."

His eyes sparkled and his face flushed. "Well then, let's see what we can do to bring you down a peg or two, shall we? Dad!" he yelled in the direction of the war zone. "Hudson's here."

The big man came rushing out of the kitchen, a black apron tied smartly over a pub golf shirt he'd acquired somehow.

"There's the man," he said with a big welcoming grin. It was very different from the greeting the day before. "Come give me some love."

My eyes must have given away my shock because both Murrays started laughing at me. Sean gave me a giant bear hug and then held me out from him with big hands on my shoulders.

"Lemme get a look at ya. Charlie says you're a good one, yeah? Gonna treat my boy right?"

"Dad, fuck," Charlie muttered, flushing even deeper pink.

"If he'll let me. Yes, sir. He's the good one, not me."

Sean looked at his son. "I reckon he'll do." And then he turned and went back in the kitchen yelling for Max to get his hands out of the stew.

I turned back to Charlie. "Big day. I'm here. Put me to work."

The day went fast after that. We mostly went over everything and taste tested Max's efforts at compliance with Sean's stricter standards. When five o'clock rolled around, I was stuffed and Charlie was borderline manic with nerves.

"Baby, relax," I murmured into his ear after taking him into a hug for the millionth time today. I'd used any excuse all day to touch him. "It's going to be perfect. You've done an amazing job."

"*We*'ve done an amazing job," he corrected.

Bruce walked in the door, calling out a greeting and walking up to congratulate us on the arrival of the big day.

"Hudson, after we got off the phone this morning, I booked a big meeting for you on Monday in Chicago. I hope you don't mind me tagging along to help smooth the introduction. We fly out Sunday night. I think this is going to make for an exciting future for you, Hudson. There are several investors up there excited to meet you."

My heart skipped a beat. This could really be happening.

"Of course not. Thank you, Bruce. I can't thank you enough for arranging that opportunity for me."

Sometimes in life you don't realize when you've uttered words that have the power to fuck everything up. This was one of those times.

I didn't realize how the conversation had sounded to Charlie.

And by the time I figured it out, he was gone.

Hudson's Lament:

Old habits die hard.

44

CHARLIE

Charlie's Luck:

There's no such thing as Forever Man.

The grand opening was a smash hit. Everyone loved the pub, and Dad and I identified several regulars right out of the gate, men we knew would be parking their bums on the same stool most nights for the foreseeable future. We worked hard to make the night a success, and judging by the standing-room only and the hours-long wait for a table, it succeeded.

I worked my arse off for the sake of my family's reputation. I couldn't help but want anything with the Fig and Bramble name to be good and right, even if the entire enterprise could be handed over to someone else in the near future.

Hudson had left to take my father home shortly after midnight. It was after two in the morning when I finally made it back to the bunkhouse and slipped into bed with him. I vaguely remembered thrusting my hips into his hot mouth and releasing down his throat, but then I was out like a light.

We were run off our feet the rest of the weekend, and when I woke up Monday morning, it was to the reminder Hudson had left the night before. The two of us had never had the chance to discuss his job options, and now he was in Chicago presumably meeting his new bosses.

The usual familiar faces were present for breakfast in the farmhouse kitchen when I walked in.

"Morning," I mumbled, focused on making my way to the coffeepot.

"You look rough," Doc said with a smirk. "And here I thought Irishmen could handle long nights at the pub."

Dad barked out a laugh as I pretended to elbow Doc and swallowed the first sip of the good stuff. "Funny. Full of craic this morning, yeah?"

"Something like that."

Darci looked like I felt. Depressed as hell. "Hudson's off to Chicago today."

I shuffled over to her stool and wrapped my arm around her from behind, kissing her on the head. "I know, love. It'll just be us chickens. Think we can keep each other company?"

"Will you teach me how to pour a pint if I come by the pub later?"

"Of course I will. Be sure and bring your friends for a few rounds of darts. I'll see if I can find a photo of Hudson and run copies to put on the dart boards. Serves him right for leaving us."

That got a smile out of her.

We got on with our breakfast routine as usual, and when it came time for me to head to the pub, I remembered my goodbye with Hudson the previous night.

"You'll let me know when you arrive? Eat a hotdog for me? Let me know if it's truly windy there? And phone sex me tonight?" I'd asked, batting my eyelashes.

He'd smiled. "Slipped that one in there, huh?"

"It had to be said."

We'd kissed for a long time before I'd finally pulled away. I'd gazed at his lovely face. "Don't fuck anyone else in the city," I warned.

"Damn. And I had such big plans too. You think if I did, I might get to see that Irish temper again?"

"You haven't seen Irish temper yet, Hudson Wilde. If you're lucky, I'll show you this weekend when you get home."

I arrived at work with a big smile on my face and the memory of his twinkling eyes. Anyone could make it a handful of days before seeing their love, right?

But it turned out to be a full week. Because his first meeting turned into more meetings. I could hear the excitement in his voice and began to realize he was happy there. Which, of course, gave me mixed feelings. I was thrilled he would be going to a good situation, but I was selfishly disappointed he was so happy there.

We called and texted plenty. Several times a day, every day. But it was damned near impossible to feel close to someone that way. It reminded me of how useless any of this was. When I went home to Ireland, we'd never be able to keep it up anyway.

When he cancelled his flight home Thursday night and swore, yet again he only needed *one more day*, I realized I needed to end things. Make a clean break and let him go to Chicago without the drag of a boyfriend holding him back.

"What's got you in a funk?" Doc asked Friday morning when we were sitting on the porch swing sipping coffee.

"I miss him," I said.

"Oh, honey," he said, moving over closer so he could put his arm around my shoulders and squeeze me into a side hug. "He'll be home tonight."

"I know, but this isn't going to work, and right now it doesn't even seem like I can get enough time with him to tell him that."

Doc kissed me on the head.

"He does this, Charlie. Throws himself into his job. Talk to him. Make him to listen."

I shrugged. "I don't want to force him to take me into consideration when evaluating his career options. And I sure as hell don't want to force him to give up work that's important to him to spend time faffing about with me. But he told me he has to fly back for another meeting in a few weeks. He'll miss the stock show in Houston. The thing is, he was really looking forward to it. It wasn't just me. I've been to a million of them. But he has a childhood memory of going to the Houston show with Grandpa and seeing the dogs, and he said going back with me was on his bucket list. And now it'll be over for another year. At this rate, I won't be here another year. If nothing changes, I'm only here for another month or so."

I felt like a whiner. This man didn't want to hear someone disparage his grandson. And, honestly, I didn't want to be someone who disparaged him either.

"You're right," I admitted before he could say anything. "I just need to talk to him."

After showering and dressing for work, I called him.

"Hey, gorgeous," he said when he answered. The deep comfort of his voice calmed me.

"Hiya, stranger. Look, I know you're probably busy, but I was hoping to schedule a time for us to catch up. When do you fly back?"

"I land in Dallas tomorrow night late. I thought I might stay over at Saint's and drive to Hobie first thing Saturday morning. I'll call you when I get settled at Saint's though, if that's alright? Around nine thirty?"

My heart sank. I'd hoped he'd drive to Hobie directly from the airport regardless of the hour.

"Okay. Everything going well in Chicago?" I asked.

"Yes. Exciting things going on here. I can't wait to tell you all about it."

"You sound happy," I said, picturing the smile on his face I could hear in his voice.

"I am. Very happy. But I'd be happier if I was with you."

After we ended the call, I felt even worse. I'd hoped he'd ask how I was. I guess I'd hoped for anything other than to talk about his job, the job I was fairly certain would kill him softly.

But I decided to give him the benefit of the doubt. I couldn't very well expect him to talk about our relationship while he was in some corporate office building in Chicago. I'd be patient and wait until our nine-thirty call.

Only, when nine thirty came, the phone never rang.

45

HUDSON

Hudson's Revelation:

You snooze, you lose.

My flight was canceled, and I wound up rebooked on another airline. When we finally approached DFW, we circled in the air for three more hours. I understood the weather delay, but every moment we remained up in the air, my stomach clenched harder with nerves over telling Charlie about the tap ring deal.

I didn't want him to feel pressure from me. Plus, what if all of this was too much too soon? What if I was reading more into his feelings for me than there was? And what if he had no interest in moving to Hobie and running the pub?

We landed after midnight. I knew Charlie had to have been exhausted from working late the night before, so I assume he'd long since fallen asleep.

Should I wake him?

I wondered if I could make the trip to Hobie this late at night without falling asleep. Maybe I could slide into bed next to his warm body and hold him until morning.

Otto's stories of responding to motor vehicle accidents popped into my head. He'd lectured me time and again about how dangerous the roads were late at night. Better not chance it.

My phone's text alert chimed when I turned off Airplane Mode. *Bing, bing, bing, bing.*

Shit.

I hit the button to call him, but it went straight to voicemail.

I took a breath and checked the texts to see how much trouble I was in. They started out timid, asking where I was and if the flight was delayed. Then they became more worried until finally there was a thread of frantic scrambling in his tone.

If you've died in a crash, I'm never forgiving you!

The internet said your plane never left. Please tell me you're asleep in a hotel bed in Chicago and just didn't care about me enough to let me know you weren't coming home or had changed your flight.

It's storming here, I'm pretty sure you crashed. Asshole.

Oh hell.

Finally, the last one was the worst.

I can't handle this. I'm turning off my phone. If you're miraculously alive tomorrow, lose my fucking number. I love you and I hope you're okay.

It was enough to wake me fully for the long drive to Hobie, but I couldn't let my panic force me into an irresponsible decision. I texted him.

I'm safely in Dallas. It's too late to drive up there, but I will leave first thing in the morning. I love you and I'm sorry.

I expected Saint to be asleep or out of town, but he was sitting on the sofa when I entered the apartment. He looked as tired as I felt.

"Hey," I said, dropping my bag by the door.

"You're back late. Was it the storm?"

"I guess." I dropped into the sofa next to him. "I hope it's okay if I stay tonight. It's too late to make that drive."

"Fuck that. If I had a man that pretty waiting for me in my bed, I'd be hotfooting it home right now."

"Do you know how many fatal accidents happen on highways in the middle of the night? It's not safe."

Saint blinked at me. "I'm worried about you, Hudson."

"Why?" I asked, even though I knew.

"Doc and Grandpa called. They said Charlie's a mess."

My heart leapt into my throat. I was such an ass. "He thinks I died in a plane crash. He hates flying."

"He booked his flights home. He decided to leave before it's too late to travel with Mama."

"What? When? Are you kidding?"

I wondered if I might throw up. He was giving up on me because I'd never told him what I was working on. Because I was too scared to run off half-cocked without a plan to present to him.

"I fucked up," I whispered. "What do I do?"

He shrugged. "What would you want him to do if the situation was reversed?"

I'd want him to come racing home to me the minute he got off the plane.

I took a breath. "I have to go."

He lifted an eyebrow. "You sure you want to take that risk? Might get in a car crash."

I felt my nostrils flare. He was right to call me out on my bullshit.

"It's okay. I have a lucky four-leaf clover I never leave home without. It will bring me luck."

It didn't.

When I arrived in Hobie, Charlie was already gone. His room was completely empty, and there was no sign of him anywhere in the bunkhouse. It was as if he'd never been there.

I flew toward the farmhouse and let myself in with the spare key. Without even knocking, I barged into Doc and Grandpa's room. It had to be four in the morning by then.

"Where is he?" I cried. "Where'd he go? A hotel? Where?" My heart was thundering and I was frantic.

They both sat up groggily, rubbing their eyes. The sound of dogs snuffling came from a giant round dog bed in the corner of the room.

When Mama extracted herself from the pile to wiggle over to me, I heaved a sigh of relief. He wouldn't have left her.

"He went back to Ireland, honey," Doc mumbled.

My heart stopped. "No."

Grandpa reached for his glasses and slid them on. "He and Sean left before midnight. His sister called to say their uncle had been rushed to the hospital. They didn't give us any details."

I processed the words but still came up with the same result. Charlie wasn't there.

Could I follow him to Ireland?

No, don't be ridiculous. You have responsibilities here. At the office, or maybe at the pub if Charlie isn't around... People don't just up and fly across the ocean on the spur of the moment. That's like a scene out of a cheesy movie. Regular people don't do that. What would everyone think if I dropped everything and chased after a man? Plus, I hate to travel almost as much as Charlie. And I just got off the flight from hell.

I let out a breath. There was no question. I would follow him anywhere.

"Can one of you make some calls while I grab my clothes?"

My grandfathers' grins could be seen in the dark room. "Atta boy. Go get him."

46

CHARLIE

Charlie's Lament:

I never had a chance to kiss him goodbye.

When I left Hobie, I was so angry at Hudson for being dead in a plane crash, I tried not to spare him a second thought. My rational brain was nowhere to be found.

Devlin made it through surgery, but it was going to be a long recovery from the stroke. Poor Liv had found him on the floor of the kitchen in the morning and thought it was a heart attack. After he'd gone into the operating theatre, Liv had called me and told us to come home. We'd spent the entire flight assuming the worse.

The whole thing had rocked me to my core. It happened so fast, so unexpectedly. The man was only fifty-three. Granted he was an unhealthy one, several stone overweight and still a smoker, but he'd seemed so big and strong. Seeing him frail and unconscious in the hospital bed had been a shock. We'd gone straight to see him in Galway, and Liv told us we'd just missed Cait and Donny who'd gone back to the pub for a rest.

When we finally walked into the pub, I got a good look at my sister's growing baby bump. "You nick a mini keg?"

She threw her arms around me and cried. "I can't believe you're here. I can't believe he's made it through. Did you see him? Doesn't he look awful? I'm going to kill him for this. How dare he almost leave us too."

"C'mere, love," Dad said from behind me. Cait screeched so loudly I though my ear'd fallen off.

"Dad! Oh Dad, you're here thank—"

"Hush, child. Now, let me look at you. Who's the man what done this to my girl?"

He shot a glare at Donny before clapping him on the back and flashing a grin. "Good to see you, son. Thanks for taking care of these ones."

Soon the pub filled with neighbors and friends turning up to share a pint and toast Devlin's quick recovery.

It was all so surreal. I'd come so close to thinking we'd lost him, and it had finally struck me that he'd been the one who stayed when both my parents left. Uncle Dev was a moody git, but he'd always tried hard to keep the place together. Thank fuck he was going to be okay.

Late that night, I was attempting not to fall asleep on Davie Turner's shoulder when I heard a commotion by the door. Suddenly Mama was wiggling all over me, licking and whining like she hadn't seen me twenty-four hours before. I hugged her neck before looking up and finding the most beautiful man in the world standing there.

My man.

"You shouldn't have brought her," I said. "I didn't want her in the cargo like that."

Hudson squatted down in front of me and reached for my hands, pulling them each against his lips in a kiss. "She didn't fly in cargo. She flew in a private jet. I didn't want to stress her out, but I knew you probably needed her."

The tears pricked and then began falling in earnest. "I did. I did need her. But I needed you more."

I lurched into his arms, damned near bowling him over. He held me tight and stood up, whispering words of love and reassurance in my ears that only made me cry more.

"Shut up, you'll make my eyes puffy," I said.

"No amount of crying will make you less beautiful, sweetheart," he murmured. "I'm sorry about Devlin. So sorry. And I'm sorry I wasn't there for you."

"You're not dead in a crash?" I asked, a poor attempt to lighten the mood.

He shook his head. "Not for lack of trying. I hope you don't want to go home anytime soon, because I'm not sure I can handle getting back on a plane right now."

Home.

The way my heart lurched, I knew his words were spot-on. Hobie was my home now, and I hoped like hell it was his too.

"Home?" I asked.

"How's Devlin?" He was nervous as if preparing for the worst.

"He's going to be okay," I assured him. "But why... Hudson, why are you really here? You came all this way. I still can't believe you're here."

His eyes blinked frantically as the babbling began in earnest. "I... I wanted to have everything planned before I told you... and... and I wanted to have the money in place to give you everything... the pub, the... the tap ring... it's yours, and I know this is a bad time to talk about it but I quit my job, but that doesn't mean you have to be okay with everything. I mean, I need you to know it's fine if you don't want to do it. Better than fine, honestly. I'll come here... well, I'll move here is what I meant to say, with you, and—" He stopped long enough to take a breath.

As for me, the air had left my lungs right around the part where he'd said he'd quit his job.

Hudson glanced around at the crowd of people staring at him before turning back with a nervous grimace. His ears were so red they were purple, and I thought he'd never looked more perfect.

"Let me try again," he said, taking a breath. "I turned down the offer at the firm in Chicago. I quit my job at Ames. I… I left my family. Someone has offered an obscene amount of money for the tap ring I invented. We have options. We can buy the pub in Hobie. We can start a ranch with sheep for Mama. Or we can move here and build our life on the beautiful cliffs at the edge of the sea. I don't care. No matter what, I plan to follow you around until you get sick of me. And even then, don't be surprised if I keep turning up like a bad penny. All I care about is being with you."

They were words I'd waited my whole life to hear, and hearing them from the man who wore commitment like a sacred commandment made me feel fairly certain they'd stick.

"I love you, Hudson. And I want to move to Hobie with you. I really like it there, and the pub needs us."

Hudson's face relaxed like he'd been afraid of rejection. If only he knew I'd never reject him again for the rest of his life.

He held my hands tightly and met my eyes. "Irish… I'm sorry I didn't tell you sooner. I should have. The fear of not having all the details worked out ahead of time kept me from treating you like an equal partner, and I'm so sorry."

He leaned in and kissed me gently on the lips, whispering, "I love you."

Cait sniffed from behind him like a truffle pig. He turned in surprise.

"Oh, hi, Cait. I brought you something," he said, clearing his throat.

"Looks like you brought Charlie a little something too," she said with a wink. "I'm happy to see it."

Hudson reached into his pocket and pulled out something too small for me to see.

"It's a four-leaf clover. I just found it outside before I walked in. I thought it would be good for the baby."

"Aw, how sweet, but don't you want to keep it for luck?" Cait asked.

Hudson reached for my hand and pulled me against his side to wrap his arm around me.

"I've got all the luck I need, right here."

EPILOGUE

HUDSON - SIX MONTHS LATER

Hudson's Luck:

I'm lucky enough to get a bit of Irish in me.

"Stop scratching your arse. People are going to think you have the clap."

I glared at Charlie. "I don't think the clap makes your ass cheek itch. And anyway, this is your fault."

He dropped his jaw. "My fault? I wouldn't be caught dead with a tattoo on my arse, not to mention a tattoo of a fecking four-leaf clover. How cliché can you get?"

"Forgive me for wanting to commemorate the moment I met the love of my life," I muttered, trying to scratch it without attracting his attention again. It was impossible.

"Do we need to go in the lavatory so I can put some cream on it, Love?"

I twisted around to see if there was a line by the lavatories. "Forget the cream. Can we do other things in there?" For once, it didn't even occur to me to consider the germs in the place. If Charlie was game for mile-high sexcapades, it would be worth the hazmat-level decontamination required afterward.

"And risk throwing the entire plane off balance? I don't think so. Sit there and be still. Say your final prayers or whatever you need to do to make things right with your god before this all goes pear-shaped. Plus, I threw away your last bottle of hand sanitizer."

Lucky for me, I'd hidden an extra one in—

"And the one I found in your sunglasses case. It's like you think I don't know you at all."

"Did you take your pill?" I asked.

"Yeah. A couple of times. Just to be sure."

Umm...

"Say again?" I asked.

"It's fine. West told me I can take a handful."

"Babe, West said you can take a pill before you get on the plane with *a handful* of water from the bathroom sink. We were talking about not being able to take a drink through security."

"Oh."

"You're going to make a scene, aren't you?"

"No, I promised you after last time. Besides, I'm fine with flying now," Charlie said. I detected a slight slurry softness to his voice already.

"You need to get used to it if we're going to keep going back and forth like this."

"'Snot my fault the baby got his first tooth." He closed his eyes and slid his head onto my shoulder. Long ginger hair fell across my white shirt, and my fingers immediately went for it. I loved playing with his hair. Sometimes in front of the TV he'd let me brush it and braid it. I wondered if we'd ever have a little girl with long red hair like his. Charlie wanted kids as much as I did, but we were both keen to wait until we'd been together longer and had our home life in Hobie a bit more settled first.

"I'm not sure your sister was thrilled with us popping in to see Mackie's new tooth. She looked put out."

"Only because the flat's so small. They need to move back to the pub with Dad."

"Donny said he's trying to start something with a couple of mates so he can work from Doolin. I think Cait has designs on your cottage," I said. His hand had fallen on my leg and was sneaking its way higher and more inward. My dick was acutely aware of the sensual invasion. "Stop," I warned, but there was no heat in the word.

"Make me," he mumbled.

I laughed at the idea he'd be awake long enough to cause trouble. During the last flight we'd taken, he'd tried to suck me off under the blanket. Unfortunately he'd banged his elbow on something sharp and screamed bloody murder, which had essentially ratted us out to everyone around us.

He shifted until his lips were against the bare skin at my throat. "Did you hear back from Bruce about the thing?"

"Yes. I already told you this. You forgot because you're high."

"Tell me again."

"You're finally the official owner of Fig and Bramble US. Congratulations on your lifelong commitment to getting people drunk."

"Shut it. I'm a publican," he slurred. "It's what we do."

"That word has never sounded right to me. I keep thinking you're saying *pelican*."

"And we're going to build a ranch," he added.

"We're going to build a *house* on the existing ranch," I corrected. I slid down a little in my seat, pulling him with me and getting more comfortable.

"And now that you got the brewery stuff up and running, you're going to think about what you want to do next, but not in Dallas. And not with long hours. Farming probably."

I refrained from reminding him of the differences between farming and ranching. Farmers planted crops, ranchers raised livestock. I was beginning to think he mixed up the two terms on purpose just to fuck with me.

We'd spent many hours researching Delaine Merino sheep for their hardiness in warmer climates. I'd decided to start with a specialty sheep herd so Charlie and Mama would have something to play with. He was also determined to make a sheepherding dog out of our new puppy, the coon-collie, or *coolie* as Doc called it, that we hadn't been able to part with from Mama's litter.

I glanced across the aisle and noticed a familiar tabloid headline on a magazine cover someone was reading.

One Wilde Night: Gemma's Bodyguard Puts Pop Star In Her Place!

Poor Saint. He'd really fucked things up for himself this time. Maybe I should have found him a four-leaf clover on my last trip to Ireland. Sounded like he could use it right about now. I shook my head before leaning it back against the silky red hair on my shoulder and nuzzling my favorite Irishman.

"We're gonna plant sheep, right?" Charlie murmured, snuggling closer to me. "Good, 'cause I think he's gonna be a keen one."

"Who's gonna be a keen one?" I asked, knowing full well he meant the puppy.

"Lucky."

I smile and lay back, thinking of the little metal ring I had in a small box in my bag. The one-year anniversary of when we met was coming up, and I was ready.

My luck had finally changed for the better.

~

Keep turning the page for deleted scenes!

DELETED SCENE - BEST WESTERN

CHARLIE

We left the following day after work and drove south to a little town called Junction. The swankiest hotel in the entire town was a Best Western, which Hudson promised me would be an experience. I tried to explain that I'd once stayed in a guesthouse named the Spread Eagle. If I could spend the night at the Spread, I could survive a couple of nights at Junction's fanciest motel.

The older lady behind the desk was not impressed with my homosexual ways.

"Two rooms you say?" she asked, eyeing me as if I was on the verge of stealing the silver.

Fairly sure there was no silver.

"No, just one room. King bed please," Hudson said as if he'd been fucking other blokes his whole life. Did the man not have a survivalist bone in his body?

"You sure you don't want *queens*?" she sniffed, hitting the word *queens* like she'd accidentally seen *Priscilla* once on the telly and it had ruined her life and the lives of everyone in Texas.

"Honey, if you saw this man naked," I drawled, "you'd know he meant *king*."

I felt Hudson stiffen beside me before his head swiveled toward me in slow motion. "You did not."

"I did. Now grab the feckin' key and let's go."

DELETED SCENE - LOVE POSSE

WILDE FAMILY

Overheard at the Wilde ranch in Hobie, Texas:

In which Hudson's siblings and grandfathers talk about the poor man behind his back.

"Hudson needs a love posse," West said, looking around at all of the other Wildes assembled in the family room attached to Doc and Grandpa's kitchen. "He hasn't been himself since the split with Darci, and I'm starting to freak out."

Hallie took a sip of her cocktail and sniffed. "You know he's not coming tonight, right? He got called away on business."

Winnie grabbed the glass out of her twin's hand and took a large swig before speaking. "To Ireland. That fucking piece of shit boss of his sent him away."

West whipped his head around. "Darci's dad? Why?"

Winnie nodded. "Yeah. Apparently Bruce is testing him. Said if Hudson can successfully navigate their acquisition of some beer company in Ireland, he'll make VP."

"Finally," Hallie muttered.

"Never gonna happen," Saint interjected. "That guy's an ass."

"No he isn't," said Doc. "He's simply upset about his daughter's broken heart."

"Fuck," Otto said, leaning forward to rub Walker's shoulders where the sexy sheriff sat against Otto's legs in front of the sofa. Walker groaned in appreciation. "Does Hudson realize what a mistake he made going to work for his girlfriend's dad?"

"He does now," Hallie said. "But you know Hudson. His main goal in life is to be the perfect worker and make everyone around him happy. He'll still do his best to impress Bruce."

"Quintessential over-achiever," West added.

"Pot," Nico coughed. "This is Kettle, you're black."

West pulled Nico into a headlock to knuckle the top of his head. "Not anymore, asshole. Now I'm penis-whipped and come home on time every day."

West pulled out of his husband's hold and pulled his head down for a kiss. "And Pippa and I love you for it."

MJ had been sitting quietly, seemingly ignorant of the conversation around her, when she suddenly sat up and snapped her fingers. "I have an idea."

Everyone stared at her.

"And?" Sassy prompted from her spot on the floor.

"We need to force him to take some time off."

Otto chuckled. "Good luck with that, sister. Never gonna happen."

MJ shook her head. "Hear me out. What if we somehow extend his stay without giving him any advanced notice? And then we pile on a bunch of 'errands' he needs to do for us while he's over there. You know, shit that gets him out of the hotel room and out into the countryside. Something that makes him take a damned break for once and get some fresh air."

Everyone seemed to take a minute to process what she said.

"I like it," Doc said. "What kind of errands and how do we extend his stay when the travel is booked through the firm?"

MJ was quick to answer part of it. "I'm friends with his assistant, Nadine, remember?"

"As for errands," Nico pulled up his shirt and twisted around to show some of the ink on his back. "Somewhere on here is an illustration of Ross Castle in Killarney. I've always wanted to see it in person. I could ask him to go and take pictures for me."

West ran a gentle hand along the varied ink on Nico's back. "Why didn't you ever say anything? I'd love to take you there."

"That's a good idea," Hallie said. "Not you taking him there, I mean. But asking Hud to go. What else?"

Walker lifted his head from the relaxation coma he'd been in. "Jolie has always wanted something from the Waterford crystal factory over there." Otto stiffened behind him, causing Walker to turn and put a hand on his leg. "Simmer down, hot stuff. Daevon asked me for ideas for her birthday. I told him I couldn't think of anything, but this would work."

Sassy stood up from the floor with a squeal of excitement. "The Cliffs of Moher!"

Several sets of eyes blinked at her.

"Remember when I was little and watched The Princess Bride ten thousand times?"

"Yes," West said. "Of course we do. You made Hudson pretend to be Fezzik and carry you up the cliffs as Buttercup, but then as soon as you got to the top you wanted to be Inigo Montoya so you could sword fight."

"Good memory," Nico said with an affectionate squeeze of West's hand.

MJ rolled her eyes. "Who do you think insisted on being *West*ley?"

West preened while his sisters groaned and Grandpa and Doc laughed.

"Anyway," Sassy continued. "The real-life Cliffs of Insanity are the Cliffs of Moher which are in County Clare."

It was Grandpa's turn to speak. "You all know he'd never say no to Sassy if she asked him to go there."

"Ok," Hallie said, looking up from where she was making notes in her phone. "So far we have three side trips. The tattoo thing in Killarney, the crystal in Waterford, and the cliffs in County Clare. Let's think of at least one more. Something he really, really wouldn't be able to refuse."

There was silence for a few minutes while everyone tried to think. Doc kept sneaking meaningful glances at Grandpa until Grandpa couldn't take it anymore.

"Okay fine. I have one," Grandpa muttered.

Doc let out a breath. "You sure, sweetheart? You don't have to."

"Liam, love." Grandpa reached for his husband's hand and held it tight. "You know Hudson won't be able to say no. I can ask him to take a picture of their graves."

"Whose graves?" Winnie asked.

"My grandparents," Grandpa said softly. "My mother was Irish. Her parents are buried in County Clare."

A hush fell over the room again before West spoke up. "But you don't ever talk about your parents. We don't even know who they were or where you're from exactly. I guess I just assumed you didn't know them."

"He knows," Doc said, pulling Grandpa closer against him to wrap an arm around the old rancher's shoulders. "He just doesn't like to talk about them. It's painful for him. They kicked him out when he was still young."

"Who were they?" Sassy asked, coming over to sit on the floor by Grandpa's feet.

"My maternal grandparents were Moira and Seamus Dugan. I don't know the name of the cemetery, but I know the name of the village where they lived."

"You were Weston Dugan?" Sassy asked. "No, wait. That was your mom's family. What was your dad's family name?"

Grandpa blew out a breath. "Marian."

~

LETTER FROM LUCY

Dear Reader,

Thank you so much for reading *Hudson's Luck*, the fourth book in the Forever Wilde series!

There will be more Wilde tales to come, so please stay tuned. Up next will be Saint's story as he finds himself pulled off protection detail for a famous pop star in order to teach a shy bookworm self-defense.

Be sure to follow me on Amazon to be notified of new releases, and look for me on Facebook for sneak peeks of upcoming stories.

Please take a moment to write a review of *Hudson's Luck* on Amazon and Goodreads. Reviews can make all the difference in helping a book show up in Amazon searches.

Feel free to sign up for my newsletter, stop by www.LucyLennox.com or visit me on social media to stay in touch. We have a super fun reader group on Facebook that can be found here:

https://www.facebook.com/groups/lucyslair/

To see fun inspiration photos for all of my novels, visit my Pinterest boards.

Finally, all Lucy Lennox titles are available on audio within a month of release and are narrated by the fabulous Michael Pauley.

Happy reading!

Lucy

ABOUT THE AUTHOR

Lucy Lennox is the creator of the bestselling Made Marian series, the Forever Wilde series, and co-creator of the Twist of Fate Series as well as the maker of three sarcastic kids. Born and raised in the southeast, she is finally putting good use to that English Lit degree.

Lucy enjoys naps, pizza, and procrastinating. She is married to someone who is better at math than romance but who makes her laugh every single day and is the best dancer in the history of ever.

She stays up way too late each night reading M/M romance because that stuff is impossible to put down.

For more information and to stay updated about future releases, please sign up for Lucy's author newsletter on her website.

Connect with Lucy on social media:

www.LucyLennox.com

Lucy@LucyLennox.com

ALSO BY LUCY LENNOX

Made Marian Series:

Borrowing Blue

Taming Teddy

Jumping Jude

Grounding Griffin

Moving Maverick

Delivering Dante

A Very Marian Christmas

Made Marian Shorts - Coming Soon!

Free Short Stories (available at www.LucyLennox.com)

Forever Wilde Series:

Facing West

Felix and the Prince

Wilde Fire

Hudson's Luck

Twist of Fate Series (with Sloane Kennedy):

Lost and Found

Safe and Sound

Body and Soul

Also be sure to check out audio versions here.

audible
an amazon company

25831289R00207

Made in the USA
Columbia, SC
04 September 2018